All author proceeds from *Blue Colla*  *of Work* will go directly to fund the fi publishing programs offered by 826n.

Since the birth of 826 National in 2002, our goal has been to assist students ages six through eighteen with their writing skills while helping teachers get their classes passionate about writing. We do this with a vast team of volunteers who donate their time so we can give as much one-on-one attention as possible to the students whose writing needs it. Our mission is based on the understanding that great leaps in learning can happen with one-on-one attention, and that strong writing skills are fundamental to future success.

Through volunteer support, each of the eight 826 chapters—in San Francisco, New York, Los Angeles, Ann Arbor, Chicago, Seattle, Boston, and Washington, D.C.—provides after-school tutoring, class field trips, writing workshops, and in-school programs, all completely free of charge. 826 centers are especially committed to supporting teachers, offering services and resources for English language learners, and publishing student work. Each of the 826 chapters works to produce professional-quality publications written entirely by young people, to forge relationships with teachers in order to create innovative workshops and lesson plans, to inspire students to write and appreciate the written word, and to rally thousands of enthusiastic volunteers to make it all happen. All of our programs are challenging and fun, and ultimately strengthen each student's power to express ideas effectively, creatively, confidently, and in his or her own individual voice. By offering all of our programming for free, we aim to serve families who cannot afford to pay for the level of personalized instruction their children receive through 826 chapters.

At 826michigan, our tutors work one-on-one with more than 2,000 young people each year. Projects range from a hardcover bound-and-illustrated book of bedtime stories by Ypsilanti second through fifth grade students (*Don't Stay Up So Late*) to college essay writing boot camp for high schoolers to the publication of dozens of poems on placards inside Ann Arbor Transit Authority buses, all written by 11- to 15-year-olds. Donations—large and small—comprise most all of our funding. 826michigan also operates Liberty Street Robot Supply & Repair, whose proceeds cover many of our organization's basic costs.

TO LEARN MORE OR GET INVOLVED,
PLEASE VISIT WWW.826MICHIGAN.ORG.

BLUE COLLAR, WHITE COLLAR, NO COLLAR

BLUE COLLAR,

WHITE COLLAR,

NO COLLAR

Stories of Work

EDITED BY RICHARD FORD

HARPER  PERENNIAL

NEW YORK • LONDON • TORONTO • SYDNEY • NEW DELHI • AUCKLAND

For Ray Carver, in memory with love

HARPER PERENNIAL

An extension of this copyright page appears on pages 603–607.

BLUE COLLAR, WHITE COLLAR, NO COLLAR. Copyright © 2011 by 826Michigan, Inc. Introduction copyright © 2011 by Richard Ford. All rights reserved. Printed in the United States of America. No part of this book may be used or reproduced in any manner whatsoever without written permission except in the case of brief quotations embodied in critical articles and reviews. For information, address HarperCollins Publishers, 10 East 53rd Street, New York, NY 10022.

HarperCollins books may be purchased for educational, business, or sales promotional use. For information, please write: Special Markets Department, HarperCollins Publishers, 10 East 53rd Street, New York, NY 10022.

FIRST EDITION

Designed by Michael P. Correy

Library of Congress Cataloging-in-Publication Data is available upon request.

ISBN 978-0-06-202041-3

13   14   15   /RRD   10   9   8   7   6   5   4   3   2

CONTENTS

Richard Ford

INTRODUCTION

When I was growing up in Mississippi, in the 1940s and '50s, my father worked as a traveling salesman. And you might say we—my family—lived in a world dominated by work. My father had gained his job during the heart of the Depression, in 1935, and kept it until his dying day, in 1960. It was a source of considerable pride to him—not to mention relief, and the sponsor of most of our family's material well-being—that he had one job through the Depression, the World War, and all of the 1950s. His job meant viability to him—and to us as well. It meant self-esteem. It meant he was a producer. It suggested important self-knowledge and self-mastery. It implied some hold on good character. It solidified him as a family man. Work—having a job, being employed, making a living—became virtually synonymous with its gifts, and as such became a virtue in itself. Yes, the days were long, lone-liness palpable and oppressive; the pay wasn't very good. There were no benefits. The work was sedentary and repetitive and humdrum. But those things didn't matter when stacked up against the alternatives: no job, low self-esteem, fragile viability, no pay, no nothing. His job, in other words, defined part of his moral world view.

In this environment it always mattered (and was inevitably pronounced) what a man did for a living. Ed Manny worked for Nabisco. Lew Herring sold furniture. Ish Smith was a manufacturer's rep. Rex Best traveled for General Foods. Barney Rozier worked in the oil patch and wore a silver hard hat. What you "did" might not have meant who you were. But what you did sure made who you were more plausible. And not having work made the whole contraption of human character fairly unsteady on its pins—more unsteady than usual.

This institution of my early life—the transcendent significance of work—eventually and not surprisingly became a factor in my later life and vocation: writing novels and stories. Of course, there was the standard dilemma (Thoreau suffered it, too) of writing not being considered as actual work by the world around me—a view I secretly shared but didn't admit I shared, and in fact worked hard at disproving. In the late seventies, when I was thirty-five, and after writing two novels, each of which brought some credit to me, I was offered a fairly low-level, no-future teaching job by Princeton—a fact that wasn't so impressive to me but caused my mother virtually to swoon. "Oh, Richard," she rhapsodized, "I'm so glad you're finally getting started." Not that I hadn't had jobs before then. I'd had plenty—being a locomotive switchman on the Missouri Pacific Railroad at age seventeen, being a house detective in a bilgy old drummer's hotel in Little Rock. And that wasn't all. But as a "working writer," I thought—very much like the young novelist in Nicholas Delbanco's story "The Writers' Trade"—that I'd already made a start, had even made some substantial strides. Except to my mother, a young wife of the Depression, work ("getting started") meant something else: it meant all those things I've been talking about, and that came with a steady paycheck and a future you could see playing out in front of you. I lacked the paycheck and the future, and possibly I was shaky on the other parts, as well. My mother loved me and told me so often—but I was never quite plausible to her after that, never totally solid, love aside.

The other significance that work's validating force imposed on me was that in the process of writing made-up characters in novels—my type of work—I discovered that unless I could say (usually right in the story) what an important character did for a living, then that character didn't achieve the kind of persuasiveness I needed, the kind to make "him" or "her" "real" to me so that the character could carry moral weight, create consequence, transport the reader, be "round," as Forster said good characters should be.

Even for the fictional characters I was merely reading—those flimsy fascicles of somebody else's words and imputations that try to register as people on my mind's screen—work packed a big wallop, carried a payload of artful plausibility, was (still is) a need-to-know ingredient in making characters take hold. Surely it's one of the great pleasures and impacters in Elizabeth Strout's majestic story "Pharmacy" that the principal character is a small-town druggist, patiently seeking a prescription for complex life—his own, and others' as well. Likewise in Charles D'Ambrosio's subtle and nuanced "Drummond & Son"—wherein a loving typewriter repairer unsuccessfully seeks to shelter his grown-up, schizophrenic son in a halfway house—the story's almost prayerful, physical environment plays out in the language of . . . well, typewriters: Platens. The resistance of querulous keys. A type bar falling back "with an exhausted plop before it reached the paper."

Yes, I'm completely confident there are plenty of stories and novels wherein we never learn how the main character earns his or her keep. But at the moment I can't think of one. The elegant, harrowing James Salter story in this volume is much about people who *seem* not to have jobs, or who lose them; but that's merely the other, possibly direr side of the same moral coin.

To engage the issue of work, then, as all these luminous stories variously do—some concentratedly, some symbolically, some peripherally, some only as a small, bright detail by which to flesh a character up out of dim abstraction—is to put into imaginative play all of those provident concerns my father (and his son) drew strength from or suffered in his lived life. These are stories that in one way or other seek to imagine how human viability is found and held onto; how self-mastery comes about or doesn't; how moral good is identified and corroborated, loneliness combated or succumbed to; or—in the case of the classic Donald Barthelme story "Me and Miss Mandible" (in which an insurance investigator takes the client's part and is sent back to the sixth grade)—what it means to be a producer.

Fiction, indeed, has plenty to tell us about work and its stamp on us. For one thing, fiction performs for the institution of work (labor, job, paycheck, vocation, career) exactly what it performs for all of its considered subjects: it elevates what we might've thought we already knew, or what we'd overlooked or consigned to the oubliette of conventional wisdom, and focuses a new gaze upon the matter. In some instances it re-dignifies its subject, or in others reappraises it, or attaches different consequences to it from the ones we'd previously entertained or presumed or just ignored. In other words, literature that engages the subject of work thereby reproclaims work to be a proper subject of our notice—ultimately a moral transaction.

F. R. Leavis, in an essay about D. H. Lawrence, helpfully points out that one of literature's chief jobs is to provide us readers with a "new awareness" about our lives. The stories in this collection manage in every instance to make us newly aware of many important things— one being our work: our starkly ambiguous feelings about it (which reveal us); work's centrality (. . . or absurdity) as a component in our private and national characters; about work's basic intransigence as a preoccupation we struggle with and seek to understand along the way to understanding ourselves. And more. God knows, there are plenty of sociological and philosophical treatises on work ("Miss Arendt, it's time for your close-up"). But Umberto Eco is surely correct when he said in his recent *Paris Review* interview that what we can't theorize about, we must narrate. Work—always present somehow, always close to our thinking lives—is itself near enough to us that theorizing can miss the grainy, interesting, unexpected bits and take us only part way round to the truth. We make up a story, then, to get in as much as can be told, and in so doing manage to create the whole truth we seek.

A couple of years ago, at one of those early-evening cocktail-parties-on-the-white-banistered-porch-with-a-bay-view that take place up and down the American seaboard (this one was in Maine), I found myself talking to "our host," an extremely affable, quick-witted seafaring type of about my age—expensive, sockless deck shoes, white duck trousers, blue linen blazer sans coat of arms, a nice haircut and tan. After a certain period spent coddling iceless drinks and chatting about who-knows-who, the Democrats' then burgeoning hopes, my personal aversion to sailing and his belief that this was easily curable, I began to notice this man hadn't once mentioned work—unusual and notable in Americans; probably unusual and notable everywhere. It was all the more conspicuous to me because this fellow wasn't retirement age and seemed to be completely loaded with dough (I now realize how naïve I truly am). I was raised, as I've already said, with a heightened awareness of what everyone did, and its importance in the grand scheme of things; but also—since a man's occupation was central to who he was and what he was morally worth—with a near obsessive drive never to inquire about such sensitive things, even in the most casual and harmless of ways. Far too impolite. Too aggressive. Too coarse and obvious. It was as if in doing such a garish thing one would basically be saying, "Well, now, Locklear, what makes *you* so goddamn sure you're solid on the earth?"

However, after a third trip to the drinks table, during which time it was revealed that I wrote books and that my host happened to have at least one of them open on his bedside table at that moment, I felt freed up enough to say—in a mock-accusatorial, Humphrey-Bogartish, noir kind of way—"So. Okay. Spill the beans, P. J. What do you do for a living?" Whereupon P. J. grinned at me, widened his blameless blue eyes, cast a glance to the darkening heavens, put a heavy, confessional hand on my shoulder, drew me to him so that our collar points conspiratorially touched, and in a mock whisper said . . . "Richard, old son, *I don't work*. I don't work a lick. And what's more, I intend for things to stay that way. There's no future in work. Hah! You're a writer. You know that as well as I do."

My embedded point in telling this story (which you might think I just made up, but I promise you I didn't) is that my sense of this perfectly decent man was forever cemented in a way that probably wouldn't have been true if he'd confessed to me he'd gone outside his marriage with a flight attendant, or that his daughter had Asperger's, or that his father'd just died as the oldest Medal of Honor Winner in Rhode Island, or that he'd just the day before decided to dedicate his life to the Lord Jesus Christ and was becoming a Dominican and moving to Flagstaff. How I might narrate and imagine how I came to feel what I came to feel about P. J. would certainly require a svelte little short story to work out—and I don't have time for that now. But it certainly would involve mingling my nascent respect and probably my envy of my host, along with my own attitudes toward work (bred-in by my parents), plus my previously mentioned naïveté about sizing up others and how poorly that augurs for me ever to be a good writer. Fiction can bring together a mighty lot of life's frail filaments and produce surprising results.

To my mind, it was the significant subject of work which hit me amidships: its effect on me as a pure attention grabber, as a moral direction pointer, and as an ignition mechanism for illuminating and identifying something important and up-to-now unknown about humankind.

To get swiftly, then, to the end so the stories can have their way: It's at the heart of this book's conception that stories of work—offered at this particular moment in our nation's history (a time of shortage), and on behalf of 826michigan, an organization deep in the thick of life here in our American state most closely identified with the working woman and man—that this was a proper alignment of needs and supplies, demands and enthusiasm. We imagined the book from the start as a suite of stories expressly collected for Michiganians. Yet we soon realized that it was a book for anyone who feels the urge to apply the consolations of literature to the complex, often perplexing matters of earning a paycheck, showing up on time, getting the job done, taking the job home, getting hired, laid off, promoted, demoted, reclassified, sent home, or of just plain being fed up and ready to take a hike. Work, as you will see, is imagined broadly in these stories—as labor, as chores, as business, as duty, as habit, as memory, as art, and as a priestly vocation. The idea here is that, within the wide array of everything work may be said to encompass, one finds a vital connective tissue to be the thriving human spirit. V. S. Pritchett once wrote, "I have wished I had spent my life in industry. The sight and sound of traditional expertness is irresistible to me." The great story-writer, of course, may have been slyly conceding my mother's argument from years ago—and that in her mind, I always lost: that writing is not really work; it's at best a figment we writers hold out as true, much as we do our own stories. But what was irresistible to VSP is irresistible to me: that work, however we do it or define it, is near the heart of human things; and as with all we know of the heart, its truth is most tellingly found in the acts of our imagination.

Max Apple

BUSINESS TALK

James and I have been worrying about things. I'm bored, restless, and in late afternoon always depressed. He tries to be helpful. The children are not too bad. My education is more than adequate. I understand what's happening as it happens. Still, I'm powerless. At four I get morose, by five I am tearful. When James comes home I look as if I've been pinched by devils all day long.

"Every day is driving me crazy," I say. "I don't want to fall victim to the malaise of the times."

"You need to get out. You need to do something. A job," he says.

"What about a business?" I say. "Something small enough to afford, big enough to make me proud of my achievement and aware of my responsibility."

James is a solid man. Around him I shouldn't be so sad. "I'm open for anything," he says. "Give it a try. But first let's get down to brass tacks." We discuss insecurity, the care of the children, guilt, the dinner hour, vacations, the minimum wage, tax brackets, the effects of the climate on perishables, growing old, profits, and free time.

"What the hell," James says, "small business made this country. I'm with you one hundred percent."

I call my friend Jeannie, who wants to be my partner. She has no children but is going crazy anyway. In Peru, where she grew up, there was always a clutch of servants to iron her pure cotton clothes. Here, she has no help and can't get used to permanent press. Everything she wears is heavily starched. You can hear her fabrics moving down the hall.

"I'll be a partner to anything," she says. "My father grew up on the pampas of Argentina. He skinned cattle and walked among bulls. I can't go two blocks from my apartment without worrying about some black man cutting my throat. Also, being out in the world will improve my English. We have two thousand dollars saved for a Christmas trip to Peru. I'll risk it."

"What about Bill?" I ask.

"He doesn't want to go anyway. He is just going along to please me. He would rather go to a convention in Las Vegas. I'll save him two hundred dollars."

I talk about renting a space in the Gypsy Market, and then just before the health inspector comes I dream that I find the rotting carcass of a dog underneath the sink. I know even in the dream that it is the same dog I have been seeing for weeks at the corner of University and Greenbriar when I jog past every morning right after carpool. I've called the city four times but nobody picks up the body. So now that dog enters my dreams and makes me apprehensive about going into business.

James laughs it off. I remind him about Caesar's wife. "Literary references," he says, "belong in the classroom, not the real world. Anyway, Caesar's dream was life and death. Yours is just about a health certificate. If necessary you can bribe the inspector."

"I'd never do that," I say.

"In business sometimes you have to resort to the underhanded. Wait. You'll see."

Jeannie calls and is nervous. I will go it alone if necessary. She is strengthened by my resolve. We decide to gather as much information as possible and talk to a lawyer before we sign a lease. Jeannie wants us to be a corporation with stationery and a logo. I spend the early morning calling long distance until I find out that there is a distributor right here in Houston. I leave my name.

At ten, Norman the food distributor answers my message. "You can still jump in early," he says. "Frozen yogurt is going to vanquish ice cream. It's got the texture of Dairy Queen, the taste of Baskin-Robbins, and is loaded with vitamins and beneficent bacteria. There's also low start-up costs and a product that has a fifteen-day fresh life. That's a hell of an advantage in the food business. Ice cream loses flavor after a week no matter what the temperature. And Dairy Queen never has any taste to begin with. You ought to be able to clear a hundred a day just about anywhere."

He makes an appointment to come over in an hour.

Jeannie is too nervous to meet him. "Take notes," she tells me. She has always done badly at job interviews and doesn't want to jinx our business. She thinks it's because her English turned bad in Peru. "You be the public relations person," she says. "I'll do a traffic survey of the location."

Norman brings me a sample, strawberry, in a little carton. It has melted. I put it in my freezer. We await its return to form.

"I didn't know you were this young and attractive," Norman says. "Most of the housewives who want to go into the restaurant business are old ladies hoarding some secret recipes that they think will make them rich. It's nice to see young mothers getting into the business world. Who will take care of your kids?"

"You too?" I say.

"Wait a minute, don't get me wrong." He runs to his station wagon, returns with a paperback copy of *Playing Around: Women and Extramarital Sex*. He touches my breasts and tries to move me toward the couch. "It gives people confidence to know they are desired," he says. "It's good business psychology."

I go to the freezer for my product. It's not bad. "A little too sugary," I tell him.

"We've got to sugar it. Bacteria is bitter. The health nuts and anti-sugar people are only a tiny fraction of the market. Believe me, we've got the data. Only fifteen percent of the population has tasted yogurt. But in this new shape it will hit everyone. This will do to ice cream what television did to radio."

Norman is about forty. He talks quickly. I know that he would scare Jeannie.

James calls to tell me that he is deeply involved with the Saudi Arabians and may have to go to Antarctica. "It sounds crazy but they want to move an iceberg to the Middle East. They can't drink oil, and they think this may be cheaper than desalinization. Who knows? Anyway, they want us to do a feasibility study. I'll be in charge. It's a twelve-million-dollar contract but I'll have to spend two months in Antarctica.

"Don't change your plans," he says, "everything will work out." He has to take the Saudi Arabians to lunch. "They love the topless places but in the long run it saves money. A few years ago you would have had to take them to whorehouses in bad neighborhoods."

"I'm going to the Statue of Liberty Bank at one thirty," I tell him, "to inquire about a loan. I hear that they're receptive to female entrepreneurs."

"I'll be at the Boobie Rock just across the street," he says. "Peek your head in if you have a chance."

Norman offers to accompany me to the bank. "I'll help you sell them on the idea of frozen yogurt as the backbone of a little natural-food dessert shop. You've got everything going for you. They'd be nuts to turn you down for a small loan." While I drive, Norman tries to rub my leg. "I have to spend most of my days with men," he says. "Getting women into the business world is the best thing that could happen. After all day in the office I'm too tired for my wife. If she could just be there at noon dressed as a waitress, our marriage would be much better." He wants me to tell him everything about James. He is even envious of Antarctica. "Food is OK," Norman says, "but the real money is in heavy things. If you need cranes and a lot of equipment, then it's easy to hide costs. I'm hoping for a job as a steel salesman; that's where the money is. When you sell tons rather than cases, you're in the big time. Jesus, you've got wonderful legs. I love to watch your muscle when you hit the brake."

At the Statue of Liberty Bank, Mrs. Fern Crawford, V.P., talks turkey to the ladies.

"Face it, sister," she says, "you're talking about a one- or two-woman operation. A three-thousand-dollar machine and a kinky product. On the next block are thirty-one flavors, the Colonel, and

Roy Rogers, with Jack-in-the-Box and Burger King within walking distance. Who's going to blow a buck twenty-nine on frozen yogurt with wheat germ and sesame toppings, followed by herbal tea and a fortune cookie?"

"Everybody," Norman answers. "We're already in malls and supermarkets from coast to coast. We're moving in institutions and package sales as well."

Fern Crawford taps her heel with her pen. "Still, it's a fad."

"So was lipstick," Norman reminds her, "and the Frisbee."

"Frankly, we're looking for women who want to go into previously all-male areas like auto parts. Just this morning I approved a woman for tool rental, and a former elementary school music teacher for an electroplating shop. Fast food has had its day." Still, she says that tomorrow they'll loan me $3,000 using my IBM stock as collateral.

When we leave I walk across the street to see if James is in the Boobie Rock. I see absolutely naked girls carrying trays. The three Arabs are in traditional dress. James isn't there.

"These expense account guys have it made," Norman says. "When I take someone to lunch it's at Taco King, and that bitch tells you fast food is dead. God, how'd you like to eat here every day, with all that stuff watching you? Still, I like you lots better. I prefer serious people."

Jeannie has been talking to David Simmons, our prospective landlord. He remodeled an old house in barn wood and has turned it into a tiny mall and restaurant. His wife left him last month. He lives in the attic and eats his meals in the restaurant. We think we could get his restaurant customers to buy our frozen yogurt for dessert.

David wrings his hands. He is always worried. Two gay cooks and a waiter run his restaurant. They are constantly arguing. They buy their ingredients fresh every day. David drives across town to the Farmers' Market for the vegetables. He has already had three minor accidents on the freeway. When he returns they stop arguing and cook whatever he buys. The staff all hate David for his inefficiency. His wife hates him because he is not successful. In the attic he caught gonorrhea from a waitress who was converting to Judaism.

"You can have a room for a hundred and twenty-five dollars a month, one-year lease, first and last month in advance, and you're responsible for all improvements." Jeannie writes down the terms. She thinks her ties to the Spanish community will also bring in a little business. David Simmons thinks we would be smarter to open a gem and mineral business. "I know an absolute dummy who made fifty thousand his first year in a store as big as a shoebox. But he didn't pay any taxes and they took it all away." David's wife is suing him for everything. "She'll probably evict me from the attic," he says.

There are already two potters named Bob, a leather worker, and a Scandinavian importer in the Gypsy Market. David himself sweeps the floors and does the general maintenance. He wants to put an art gallery in the dark hallway. People complain that there is only one restroom and everyone has to stand in line during the noon rush.

"I don't like it," Jeannie says. She thinks we would do better to pay more rent for a better spot. Bill thinks so too.

James comes home with the three Arabs. For the children they bring a two-foot wooden figure of King Faisal. For me a digital watch with an Islamic face. The children run wild, break the figurine, eat, take a bath, and are in bed by seven thirty. Alma goes home at seven twenty. She waits for her bus in the rain. The Arabs want James to leave for Antarctica next week. They have plane tickets hidden in their loose robes. James tells them about my plans for a small tearoom featuring frozen yogurt. The idea of freezing anything makes them talk more about Antarctica.

When they leave in a yellow cab I tell James all about Norman and the business possibilities.

"Men are like that," he says. "They aren't prepared to treat you as an equal in business. It will take another generation. You are in the forefront."

I tell him that Norman has been fondling me.

"Typical salesman," he says. The Arabs have been driving him crazy buying souvenirs of Texas. He will have to buy a winter wardrobe tomorrow. He doesn't even know where in Houston to look for arctic gear. He will call Neiman-Marcus in the morning.

I shower, shave my legs, and begin to read the book Norman gave me. Jeannie calls to say that maybe we should take the Gypsy Market location after all. Not doing anything for all these months has probably warped her judgment, she thinks. Bill suggests that we both take a course in real estate.

In the morning after Jessica goes to school and Alma takes the baby for a walk, I sit down to think things over. I think about how I sat through all those awful hours of school and college, how I fell in love with James and several others, and how quickly the children are growing. I wonder if a business will make me a more responsible person. I check my navel to see if that dark line down my middle that appeared after Sam was born has become any fainter. James calls it the equator. Dr. Thompson says it is perfectly normal but I don't think I'll ever wear a bikini again.

Jeannie has a friend who is a lawyer. He specializes in charity work and will check our lease for $125. She and Bill now think that even if the business doesn't earn any profit, it will be a good experience for both of them. I wear my new Italian T-shirt and soft flannel slacks. When I get to the Gypsy Market the cooks are already unpacking the vegetables from David's car. Jeannie and David are talking about the lease. At ten thirty Norman arrives looking for me. "I can't stand it," he says. "All I did last night was think of you. My wife thinks I'm coming down with a cold. I had to take a sleeping pill." He and David talk about the restaurant business and retailing in general. Jeannie's friend, the lawyer, meets us for lunch and looks over the standard contract. "Are you making any money here, Simmons?" he asks David.

"I'm making money, but what good is it?" David says. He wrings his hands. "I haven't seen my kids in three weeks."

"I'm going before the parole board this afternoon on behalf of a man who hasn't seen his kids in eleven years," the lawyer says. We all have spinach salad and eggplant Parmesan. David doesn't offer to treat as a gesture of goodwill. Norman suggests it. Jeannie and I sign the lease, then David tells the waitress to give him the check. Jeannie gives the lawyer a $125 personal check. Norman orders a bottle of champagne. We go into the room that will be ours. As a surprise Norman has already put the frozen yogurt machine on the counter. It is about twice the size of a microwave oven and is shiny as a mirror. Jeannie is so excited that she kisses the bright surface and says "I love you" in Spanish to the machine. We all drink a toast.

"To a new life and a new business," Norman says.

"Actually," the lawyer says, "a corporation is a legal individual. You really should be a corporation."

I call James at the office. He is already wearing a sealskin coat over a down jacket just to see how it feels He congratulates me and sounds excited for us.

Norman wants to come home with me. For the time being I put him off. Jeannie is already planning the decoration of the room.

At night when the children are asleep and James has put away his atlas, when I've washed my face with Clinique and he has clipped his fingernails and we estimate if we have any energy for each other after all the activity of the day, I ask him if he ever thought that I had any talent for business and whether he considered me a frivolous person who is just going from one thing to the next in constant search of release from the boredom of daily life, which shouldn't be so boring, should it?

He is thumbing through my book, reading courtesy of Norman about the extramarital adventures of twenty-six New York women over a fifteen-year period.

He looks up from extramarital adventure. The frozen tundra is on his mind. He scratches his chin. I wrap my arms around my knees. Next month he'll be at the bottom of the earth and I will be an entrepreneur, making change.

"You want a business," he says. "I want a yacht and sunshiny carefree days. Jeannie wants good diction. The Arabs want topless girls and an iceberg. Everyone wants somebody else's husband and wife and all their possessions. And the kids are the worst cannibals of all."

"It's true," I say, thinking already of gingham tablecloths and big stacks of dollar bills stuffed into the blue sacks that the bank gives to business people. "I'm excited," I say, "but apprehensive about every-thing. I could lose the money or run off with Norman, or begin to bicker with Jeannie, or neglect the children. And you might get the comforts you want in Teheran or Riyadh and send me a meager ali-mony. Lots might happen when I leave the house."

"Business is business," he says. We sigh like cats.

I get the lubricant, he the prophylactics. Sometimes we're old-fashioned people doing the best we can.

Russell Banks

THE GULLY

The young man called Freckle Face, whose true name was Naldo de Arauja, was a bus driver with a dangerous route—through the Gully and along the waterfront to the airport and back, turning around at Central Square, where all the buses turn around, and doing it again, four times a day. He was only twenty years old, unmarried and making good money as a driver, and despite his many freckles and reddish hair, he was attractive to the women, possibly because he had lots of money to spend on taking them dancing, buying them Johnnie Walker Red and giving them little presents, such as nylons and stuffed animals. He lived for the women, as he himself often said, and when he was robbed in his bus in the Gully in the middle of the day twice in one week, he was angry enough to kill someone for it, especially after the cops laughed at him and the dispatcher at the bus depot told him that if he got robbed one more time this month he would be fired.

"It's company policy, Freckle Face," he said. "Three times in a month, and you're gone, man." The dispatcher stood in the garage holding his clipboard, waiting for the keys to the bus.

"Why?" Freckle Face asked. "What the hell good does it do to fire the driver? Tell me that."

"Sometimes the drivers are in cahoots with the thieves. Not that you'd do such a thing, but even so, the company's got to have a policy. You know how it is."

Freckle Face handed over the keys, stalked out of the garage, and went straight to a gambler he knew in the Gully two blocks from where he lived and bought a dark blue .45 and a box of bullets. He put the loaded gun inside his lunch bag, and when a few days later he stopped at the corner of Angelina and Fourteenth and picked up two men wearing rumpled tan safari jackets to cover the pistols stuck in their belts, Freckle Face simply waited until they had paid and sat down, one of them in the rear and the other directly behind him, as usual with thieves, and he reached down to his lunch bag on the floor, drew out the .45, spun around and shot the man behind him in the eye.

The other man leapt out the back door to the street and started running. Freckle Face grabbed the first one's pistol from where it had fallen to the floor, srepped over the man's body and jumped to the street, like Gary Cooper or Clint Eastwood, a gun in each hand. People in the bus and on the street and sidewalks, mostly women and children at this time of day, were terrified, a few were screaming, but when Freckle Face took off down the street after the second thief, everyone stepped back and cheered.

He caught the guy in a dead-end alley behind a Pakistani restaurant, and he shot him twice, first in the chest and then up close, in the head. He took his gun, too, and walked quickly back to the bus, which was still sitting at the corner of Angelina and Fourteenth with the doors open and the motor running. He climbed into the bus, dragged the body of the first thief out to the street, put all three guns into his lunch bag and continued down Angelina and on out to the airport.

He himself never mentioned the event to anyone, but in a short time everyone knew about it—the dispatcher, the other drivers, the people and merchants in the Gully, and the thieves. People started waiting especially for Freckle Face's bus, letting earlier buses go past. He was extremely popular with the women on his route, who smiled and hitched their dresses up their thighs a little as they climbed the steps of his bus and dropped their coins slowly, one by one, into his hand. No one, of course, mentioned to Freckle Face that they knew what he carried inside his lunch bag, and no one said anything to the police about it. When the police drove into the Gully to pick up the bodies of the two thieves, everyone on the street denied knowing how the men had died. "Who knows?" they shrugged. "Somebody just dumped the bodies there during the night or maybe this morning, when no one was looking. It happens all the time around here. You know that."

Over on the north side of the Gully, not far from the bus depot, a young man called Chink, whose real name was Felipe da Silva, worked in his parents' bakery with his mother, father and two younger sisters. One morning when he came into work late and hung over and expecting the usual harangue from his father, he met instead with the aftermath of a massacre. Moments before, robbers had walked into the shop and killed with guns and machetes all four members of Chink's family plus two customers, elderly ladies from the neighborhood. The white walls, floors, even the ceiling, were splattered with blood, grisly maps showing where the people had met their deaths and how. Chink's sisters had been shot in the front room of the shop, where they worked behind the counter, and the two old neighborhood ladies had been killed, each of them shot once behind the ear, just inside the door. They had probably walked in on the robbery. Chink's father had been cut down with a machete at the doorway leading from the back room, where the ovens were located, and his mother, also chopped practically in half by the machete, had been slain near the back door, evidently fleeing from the carnage.

Chink paused before each body, examined it for a second, stepped over it to the next, careful not to step into the huge spreading smears of thickening blood and flour, until he worked his way to the back, where he found his mother's body. Opening the door to the alley in back, he stepped out, and when he knelt down to the ground, as if to pray or vomit, he saw several pairs of white footprints that led down the alley toward the rear of the building.

Instantly, Chink set off in pursuit of whoever had laid down the tracks. He jogged down the alley, turned left behind the building and climbed over a ramshackle wood fence to another alley, passed through to a packed dirt yard shared by the backsides of a half-dozen tin-roof shanties, where he followed the white footprints across the yard to the rear of an old dark green panel truck sitting wheelless up on cinder blocks. He tiptoed to the rear door of the truck and listened and heard the men inside counting the few miserable dollars they had taken from the bakery. First, he dropped an old piece of iron pipe into the latch, jamming it. Then he walked out to the street to a filling station, boldly stole a five-gallon can of gasoline and brought it back to the panel truck, where he splashed the gasoline onto the packed dirt ground all around the truck, especially at the rear entrance, and poured more gas over the top and along the sides. Last, he lit a match, tossed it at the truck and ran.

People had watched the entire process from the beginning, and no one said or did a thing to stop Chink, and when the truck exploded in a fireball, the folks in the shanties, many of them mothers with babies on their hips, shouted with obvious pleasure. Later, when the firemen had put out the flames and opened the rear door of the truck, three charred, utterly unrecognizable bodies were discovered huddled inside. No one from the shanties knew who they were, how they got locked inside the truck or who doused the truck with gasoline and set it on fire. "We were inside cooking food," they said. And no one—that is, no one from the police or fire department—connected the bizarre incineration of the three young men in the panel truck to the massacre of the six people in the bakery two blocks away. In the Gully, however, everyone knew of the connection and spoke of Chink with sympathy and admiration, even those who used to think of him as a lazy, drunken playboy supported by his industrious family.

Then there was Saverio Gómez Macedo, called Tarzan, because of his great size and overdeveloped physique and the special way he cupped his hands around his mouth and yelled, which he liked to do at the start of every day. He would untangle himself from his hammock on the porch of his grandmother's shanty, step to the standpipe by the alley, where the people were already lining up to fill their pans and jars with water for cooking, and he'd give his yell and beat good-naturedly on his enormous chest.

In exchange for caring for his aged grandmother, who was crippled with arthritis, Tarzan was allowed to sleep on the porch of her cabin. Now and then he got himself hired for daywork, hauling bricks or laying sewer pipe down by the waterfront where the government was building hotels for foreigners, but most of the time he had no money and depended on his grandmother for everything. She, in turn, depended on her children, Tarzan's aunts and uncles, several of whom now lived in Florida and sometimes sent money.

The daughter who was Tarzan's mother had died of cancer many years before, and no one knew who his father was. Thus Tarzan and his grandmother were as close as mother and son. They spent most of their days and evenings sitting out on the shaded, tilted porch of the tiny cabin, where they watched the people pass on the street and chatted and gossiped about the old days and people they used to know. Despite his great size and obvious high spirits, Tarzan was in many ways like a little old man, which, of course, delighted his grandmother and amused everyone in the neighborhood who knew them.

For that reason most people were amazed by the transformation that Tarzan went through when his grandmother was killed. Her death was an unfortunate accident, and perhaps they expected him simply to accept it as such, as they certainly would have, but he treated it as if it were a cold-blooded murder. Two drug dealers in the neighborhood got into a scuffle over money, not an unusual event, and while chasing each other down the alleys and across the yards of the neighborhood, shooting whenever they caught sight of each other, one of them (it was never determined which one) shot Tarzan's grandmother, who was sitting on the porch waiting for Tarzan to come home from the store. She died instantly, shot in the throat, just as Tarzan rounded the corner and saw the pair of drug dealers dart between cars on the street, still shooting at one another, heading out of the neighborhood into another. He roared, pounded his chest in rage, frightening those who heard him, and took off after the drug dealers.

He caught up with them late that night in the back room of a bar out near the airport. Apparently they had settled their differences and were once again doing business with one another, when Tarzan, huge with his anger and his fearlessness, walked into the dingy room, grabbed the two scrawny punks and dragged them out to the street. It was raining, and the street was quiet and almost empty. The bartender and the few customers who were there at the time later described with a kind of horror, a horror oddly mixed with pride, the sound of the skulls cracking as the enormous young man slammed the two men's heads against one another. Then, when clearly they were dead in his hands, Tarzan tossed the pair like sacks of garbage into the gutter and walked off in the rain. After that, because for a while the drug dealers staved away, but also because of his pain, Tarzan was a hero in the neighborhood.

In the Gully, true heroes were almost nonexistent. Politicians and soldiers had lived off the people for generations, and athletes, singers, actors—figures whose famous faces were used to sell things people either did not otherwise want or could not afford—were, because of that, no longer trusted or admired or even envied. In the Gully, people had grown cynical. It was their only defense against being used over and over to fatten the already fat. They had learned long ago that it's the poor who feed the rich, not vice versa. And finally, when it was almost too late and they had almost nothing left to give to the rich, to the politicians, to the businessmen, to the foreigners, finally the people of the Gully had turned away from all projects and enterprises, all plans, all endeavors that depended for their completion on hope. And when you give up hope, and do it on principle—that is, when you do it because you have learned that hope is *bad* for you—then you give up on heroes as well.

That is why, when Freckle Face heard people praise Chink and then Tarzan and saw how people admired them for their pain and their rage, when, in short, he realized that he and the other two had become heroes, where before there were none, he determined to capitalize on it as swiftly as possible, before people settled back into their old ways of dismissing heroism as a trick.

He organized a meeting of the three in the back room of a café close to his rooming house, and when they had shaken hands, each of them slightly in awe of the other two, for they were as unused to genuine heroes as everyone else in the Gully, Freckle Face got quickly down to business. His plan was to build a watchtower in the center of the Gully and for one of them to be posted there at all times, and when he saw a robbery going on, to give the signal, and the others would chase down the robbers and kill them.

"What for?" Chink asked.

"For money," Freckle Face said.

"Who'd pay us?" Tarzan wanted to know.

"The robbers' victims," Freckle Face explained. "We just return what was stolen and ask for a percentage for our troubles."

"It's wrong to kill for money," Tarzan said.

"God kills. You just pull the trigger," Chink observed. He was definitely interested. Since the death of his parents and sisters, the bakery had been closed, and Chink was down to panhandling on Central Square with a sign around his neck that said, "Help the Avenger of the Bakery Massacre!"

Tarzan needed money, too. With his grandmother's death, his uncles and aunts had sold her shanty to a man on the Heights who rented out hundreds of shanties in the Gully. Consequently, Tarzan had lately been sleeping under two sheets of corrugated iron in back of a warehouse where he hoped to find work as a warehouseman, as soon as his aunt in Florida sent him the money he needed to bribe the foreman to hire him.

Freckle Face was not much better off. His popularity as a bus driver had cut into the income of the other drivers, and in recent weeks Freckle Face had come into work and found sugar in his gas tank one day, his tires slashed another, or a radiator hose cut, a distributor cap missing, every day another lengthy repair job that kept him in the garage, until he was taking home less than half of what he had been earning before the robberies. He'd stopped buying presents for his girlfriends, and they in turn had stopped turning down other guys. He used to be able to get several women to share him; now, despite being a hero, he could barely get one woman to wait for him to get off work and take her out dancing. A hero without money is just another man.

In short order, Freckle Face, Chink and Tarzan were making more money than they had ever imagined possible. Quickly they had specialized, Tarzan as lookout, because of his ability to call out the location and route of a thief spotted from the watchtower. He owned a voice so large and clear that every time he gave the alarm, the entire neighborhood became instantly involved in the pursuit and capture of the thief. Often, all Chink and Freckle Face had to do was follow along the pathway in the street that the crowd opened up for them and run directly down the alley people pointed at, enter the basement door indicated by an old woman with her chin, cross into the corner of the basement that stood exposed by a watchman with a flashlight, where Chink would take out the gun Freckle Face had given him and fire two bullets neatly into the man's head. That was Chink's specialty, shooting, and he did seem to believe that God did the killing, he only did the shooting.

Freckle Face's specialty might be called brokerage. It was he who unclamped the dead thief's fingers from the stolen money and delivered it back to the shopowner or pedestrian who'd been robbed, and he, therefore, who negotiated the price of the return, he who divided the fee three ways. Also, when it became clear that, if they wished, they could expand their business to other neighborhoods in the Gully, it was Freckle Face who arranged to have the new lookout towers built, he who hired the new lookouts, shooters and collectors and he who knew to put Tarzan in charge of all the lookouts and train them to cup their hands just so and call out exactly, clearly, as loud as a siren, where the thieves were running to. It was Freckle Face who put Chink in charge of procuring weapons for the shooters and training them to use their guns efficiently and responsibly, and of course it was he who trained the collectors, implemented the commission system based on the system used by the bus company and kept track of all the accounts.

By now, Tarzan owned his own house on the Heights, where he liked to throw wild, lavish parties by the pool, and Chink lived in a condominium on the waterfront, where he kept a forty-foot cabin cruiser anchored year round, and Freckle Face was sleeping with the daughter of the prime minister. They had come a long ways from the Gully and did not believe that they would ever have to return, especially Freckle Face, who had made a whole new set of friends who called him Naldo and barely knew where in the city the Gully was located.

Sometimes, though, late at night, Freckle Face would rise up from the bed he shared with the daughter of the prime minister, and he'd cross the parquet floor to the louvered doors that led to the terrace, and out on the terrace in the silvery moonlight, he'd lean over the balustrade, light a cigarette and look down and across the sleeping city all the way to the Gully. He'd stand there till dawn, smoking and

waiting for the sun to come up and for the people down in the Gully
to come out of their shanties and go for water, start up their cook fires,
head down to the waterfront looking for work or out to the airport to
panhandle tourists or over to Central Square just to hang out in the
shade of the mimosa trees. Freckle Face, miles away, up on his terrace,
wearing a blue silk robe and smoking French cigarettes, would say
over and over to himself, as if it were a magical charm, an incantation:
I don't live there anymore, and no one I know lives there. The people
who go on living there must want to live there, or they'd leave that
place. Look at Tarzan, look at Chink, look at me!

Then he'd go inside, shower, shave and dress, and walk down-
stairs for breakfast, where the first thing he'd do was read the morn-
ing newspaper for the names and addresses of thieves shot by his men
last night in the Gully. After breakfast, he'd drive out in his brown
Mercedes and call on the families of the dead thieves, offering first his
condolences and then his card and a special cut-rate coffin and burial
service from his Our Lady of the Gully Funeral Parlor chain. Later on,
he'd drop by the office and go over the figures. After that, lunch. Then
a workout and a massage. Then—who knows? Real estate, maybe.
Import-export. Hotels. Life is certainly surprising, he'd think.

Donald Barthelme

ME AND MISS MANDIBLE

13 SEPTEMBER

Miss Mandible wants to make love to me but she hesitates because I am officially a child; I am, according to the records, according to the gradebook on her desk, according to the card index in the principal's office, eleven years old. There is a misconception here, one that I haven't quite managed to get cleared up yet. I am in fact thirty-five, I've been in the Army, I am six feet one, I have hair in the appropriate places, my voice is a baritone, I know very well what to do with Miss Mandible if she ever makes up her mind.

In the meantime we are studying common fractions. I could, of course, answer all the questions, or at least most of them (there are things I don't remember). But I prefer to sit in this too-small seat with the desktop cramping my thighs and examine the life around me. There are thirty-two in the class, which is launched every morning with the pledge of allegiance to the flag. My own allegiance, at the moment, is divided between Miss Mandible and Sue Ann Brownly, who sits across the aisle from me all day long and is, like Miss Mandible, a fool for love. Of the two I prefer, today, Sue Ann; although between eleven and eleven and a half (she refuses to reveal her exact age) she is clearly a woman, with a woman's disguised aggression and a woman's peculiar contradictions.

15 SEPTEMBER

Happily our geography text, which contains maps of all the principal land-masses of the world, is large enough to conceal my clandestine journal-keeping, accomplished in an ordinary black composition book. Every day I must wait until Geography to put down such thoughts as I may have had during the morning about my situation and my fellows. I have tried writing at other times and it does not work. Either the teacher is walking up and down the aisles (during this period, luckily, she sticks close to the map rack in the front of the room) or Bobby Vanderbilt, who sits behind me, is punching me in the kidneys and wanting to know what I am doing. Vanderbilt, I have found out from certain desultory conversations on the playground, is hung up on sports cars, a veteran consumer of *Road & Track*. This explains the continual roaring sounds which seem to emanate from his desk; he is reproducing a record album called *Sounds of Sebring*.

19 SEPTEMBER

Only I, at times (only at times), understand that somehow a mistake has been made, that I am in a place where I don't belong. It may be that Miss Mandible also knows this, at some level, but for reasons not fully understood by me she is going along with the game. When I was first assigned to this room I wanted to protest, the error seemed obvious, the stupidest principal could have seen it; but I have come to believe it was deliberate, that I have been betrayed again.

Now it seems to make little difference. This life-role is as interesting as my former life-role, which was that of a claims adjuster for the Great Northern Insurance Company, a position which compelled me to spend my time amid the debris of our civilization: rumpled fenders, roofless sheds, gutted warehouses, smashed arms and legs. After ten years of this one has a tendency to see the world as a vast junkyard, looking at a man and seeing only his (potentially) mangled parts, entering a house only to trace the path of the inevitable fire. Therefore when I was installed here, although I knew an error had been made, I countenanced it, I was shrewd; I was aware that there might well be some kind of advantage to be gained from what seemed a disaster. The role of The Adjuster teaches one much.

22 SEPTEMBER

I am being solicited for the volleyball team. I decline, refusing to take unfair profit from my height.

23 SEPTEMBER

Every morning the roll is called: Bestvina, Bokenfohr, Broan, Brownly, Cone, Coyle, Crecelius, Darin, Durbin, Geiger, Guiswite, Heckler, Jacobs, Kleinschmidt, Lay, Logan, Masei, Mitgang, Pfeilsticker. It is like the litany chanted in the dim miserable dawns of Texas by the cadre sergeant of our basic training company.

In the Army, too, I was ever so slightly awry. It took me a fantastically long time to realize what the others grasped almost at once:

that much of what we were doing was absolutely pointless, to no purpose. I kept wondering why. Then something happened that proposed a new question. One day we were commanded to white-wash, from the ground to the topmost leaves, all of the trees in our training area. The corporal who relayed the order was nervous and apologetic. Later an off-duty captain sauntered by and watched us, white-splashed and totally weary, strung out among the freakish shapes we had created. He walked away swearing. I understood the principle (orders are orders), but I wondered: Who decides?

29 SEPTEMBER

Sue Ann is a wonder. Yesterday she viciously kicked my ankle for not paying attention when she was attempting to pass me a note during History. It is swollen still. But Miss Mandible was watching me, there was nothing I could do. Oddly enough Sue Ann reminds me of the wife I had in my former role, while Miss Mandible seems to be a child. She watches me constantly, trying to keep sexual significance out of her look; I am afraid the other children have noticed. I have already heard, on that ghostly frequency that is the medium of classroom communication, the words *"Teacher's pet!"*

2 OCTOBER

Sometimes I speculate on the exact nature of the conspiracy which brought me here. At times I believe it was instigated by my wife of former days, whose name was . . . I am only pretending to forget. I know her name very well, as well as I know the name of my former motor oil (Quaker State) or my old Army serial number (US 54109268). Her name was Brenda.

7 OCTOBER

Today I tiptoed up to Miss Mandible's desk (when there was no one else in the room) and examined its surface. Miss Mandible is a clean-desk teacher, I discovered. There was nothing except her gradebook (the one in which I exist as a sixth-grader) and a text, which was open at a page headed *Making the Processes Meaningful*. I read: "Many pupils enjoy working fractions when they understand what they are doing. They have confidence in their ability to take the right steps and to obtain correct answers. However, to give the subject full social significance, it is necessary that many realistic situations requiring the processes be found. Many interesting and lifelike problems involving the use of fractions should be solved . . ."

8 OCTOBER

I am not irritated by the feeling of having been through all this before. Things are done differently now. The children, moreover, are in some ways different from those who accompanied me on my first voyage through the elementary schools: *"They have confidence in their ability to take the right steps and to obtain correct answers."* This is surely true. When Bobby Vanderbilt, who sits behind me and has the great tactical advantage of being able to maneuver in my disproportionate shadow, wishes to bust a classmate in the mouth he first asks Miss Mandible to lower the blind, saying that the sun hurts his eyes. When she does so, *bip!* My generation would never have been able to con authority so easily.

13 OCTOBER

I misread a clue. Do not misunderstand me: it was a tragedy only from the point of view of the authorities. I conceived that it was

my duty to obtain satisfaction for the injured, for an elderly lady
(not even one of our policyholders, but a claimant against Big Ben
Transfer & Storage, Inc.) from the company. The settlement was
$165,000; the claim, I still believe, was just. But without my encour-
agement Mrs. Bichek would never have had the self-love to prize her
injury so highly. The company paid, but its faith in me, in my effi-
cacy in the role, was broken. Henry Goodykind, the district man-
ager, expressed this thought in a few not altogether unsympathetic
words, and told me at the same time that I was to have a new role.
The next thing I knew I was here, at Horace Greeley Elementary,
under the lubricious eye of Miss Mandible.

17 OCTOBER

Today we are to have a fire drill. I know this because I am a Fire
Marshal, not only for our room but for the entire right wing of the
second floor. This distinction, which was awarded shortly after my
arrival, is interpreted by some as another mark of my somewhat
dubious relations with our teacher. My armband, which is red and
decorated with white felt letters reading FIRE, sits on the little shelf
under my desk, next to the brown paper bag containing the lunch
I carefully make for myself each morning. One of the advantages
of packing my own lunch (I have no one to pack it for me) is that I
am able to fill it with things I enjoy. The peanut butter sandwiches
that my mother made in my former existence, many years ago, have
been banished in favor of ham and cheese. I have found that my diet
has mysteriously adjusted to my new situation; I no longer drink, for
instance, and when I smoke, it is in the boys' john, like everybody
else. When school is out I hardly smoke at all. It is only in the matter
of sex that I feel my own true age; this is apparently something that,

once learned, can never be forgotten. I live in fear that Miss Mandible will one day keep me after school, and when we are alone, create a compromising situation. To avoid this I have become a model pupil: another reason for the pronounced dislike I have encountered in certain quarters. But I cannot deny that I am singed by those long glances from the vicinity of the chalkboard; Miss Mandible is in many ways, notably about the bust, a very tasty piece.

24 OCTOBER

There are isolated challenges to my largeness, to my dimly realized position in the class as Gulliver. Most of my classmates are polite about this matter, as they would be if I had only one eye, or wasted, metal-wrapped legs. I am viewed as a mutation of some sort but essentially a peer. However Harry Broan, whose father has made himself rich manufacturing the Broan Bathroom Vent (with which Harry is frequently reproached, he is always being asked how things are in Ventsville), today inquired if I wanted to fight. An interested group of his followers had gathered to observe this suicidal undertaking. I replied that I didn't feel quite up to it, for which he was obviously grateful. We are now friends forever. He has given me to understand privately that he can get me all the bathroom vents I will ever need, at a ridiculously modest figure.

25 OCTOBER

"Many interesting and lifelike problems involving the use of fractions should be solved . . ." The theorists fail to realize that everything that is either interesting or lifelike in the classroom proceeds from what they would probably call interpersonal relations: Sue Ann Brownly kicking me in the ankle. How lifelike, how womanlike, is her tender solicitude after

the deed! Her pride in my newly acquired limp is transparent; everyone knows that she has set her mark upon me, that it is a victory in her unequal struggle with Miss Mandible for my great, overgrown heart. Even Miss Mandible knows, and counters in perhaps the only way she can, with sarcasm. "Are you wounded, Joseph?" Conflagrations smolder behind her eyelids, yearning for the Fire Marshal clouds her eyes. I mumble that I have bumped my leg.

30 OCTOBER

I return again and again to the problem of my future.

4 NOVEMBER

The underground circulating library has brought me a copy of *Movie-TV Secrets*, the multicolor cover blazoned with the headline "Debbie's Date Insults Liz!" It is a gift from Frankie Randolph, a rather plain girl who until today has had not one word for me, passed on via Bobby Vanderbilt. I nod and smile over my shoulder in acknowledgment; Frankie hides her head under her desk. I have seen these magazines being passed around among the girls (sometimes one of the boys will condescend to inspect a particularly lurid cover). Miss Mandible confiscates them whenever she finds one. I leaf through *Movie-TV Secrets* and get an eyeful. "The exclusive picture on these pages isn't what it seems. We know how it looks and we know what the gossipers will do. So in the interests of a nice guy, we're publishing the facts first. Here's what really happened!" The picture shows a rising young movie idol in bed, pajama-ed and bleary-eyed, while an equally blowzy young woman looks startled beside him. I am happy to know that the picture is not really what it seems; it seems to be nothing less than divorce evidence.

What do these hipless eleven-year-olds think when they come across, in the same magazine, the full-page ad for Maurice de Paree, which features "Hip Helpers" or what appear to be padded rumps? ("A real undercover agent that adds appeal to those hips and derriere, both!") If they cannot decipher the language the illustrations leave nothing to the imagination. "Drive him frantic . . ." the copy continues. Perhaps this explains Bobby Vanderbilt's preoccupation with Lancias and Maseratis; it is a defense against being driven frantic.

Sue Ann has observed Frankie Randolph's overture, and catching my eye, she pulls from her satchel no less than seventeen of these magazines, thrusting them at me as if to prove that anything any of her rivals has to offer, she can top. I shuffle through them quickly, noting the broad editorial perspective:

"Debbie's Kids Are Crying"
"Eddie Asks Debbie: Will You . . .?"
"The Nightmares Liz Has About Eddie!"
"The Things Debbie Can Tell About Eddie"
"The Private Life of Eddie and Liz"
"Debbie Gets Her Man Back?"
"A New Life for Liz"
"Love Is a Tricky Affair"
"Eddie's Taylor-Made Love Nest"
"How Liz Made a Man of Eddie"
"Are They Planning to Live Together?"
"Isn't It Time to Stop Kicking Debbie Around?"
"Debbie's Dilemma"
"Eddie Becomes a Father Again"
"Is Debbie Planning to Re-wed?"

"Can Liz Fulfill Herself?"

"Why Debbie Is Sick of Hollywood"

Who are these people, Debbie, Eddie, Liz, and how did they get themselves in such a terrible predicament? Sue Ann knows, I am sure; it is obvious that she has been studying their history as a guide to what she may expect when she is suddenly freed from this drab, flat classroom.

I am angry and I shove the magazines back at her with not even a whisper of thanks.

5 NOVEMBER

The sixth grade at Horace Greeley Elementary is a furnace of love, love, love. Today it is raining, but inside the air is heavy and tense with passion. Sue Ann is absent; I suspect that yesterday's exchange has driven her to her bed. Guilt hangs about me. She is not responsible, I know, for what she reads, for the models proposed to her by a venal publishing industry; I should not have been so harsh. Perhaps it is only the flu.

Nowhere have I encountered an atmosphere as charged with aborted sexuality as this. Miss Mandible is helpless; nothing goes right today. Amos Darin has been found drawing a dirty picture in the cloakroom. Sad and inaccurate, it was offered not as a sign of something else but as an act of love in itself. It has excited even those who have not seen it, even those who saw but understood only that it was dirty. The room buzzes with imperfectly comprehended titillation. Amos stands by the door, waiting to be taken to the principal's office. He wavers between fear and enjoyment of his temporary celebrity. From time to time Miss Mandible looks at me reproachfully, as if blaming me for the uproar. But I did not create this atmosphere, I am caught in it like all the others.

8 NOVEMBER

Everything is promised my classmates and me, most of all the future. We accept the outrageous assurances without blinking.

9 NOVEMBER

I have finally found the nerve to petition for a larger desk. At recess I can hardly walk; my legs do not wish to uncoil themselves. Miss Mandible says she will take it up with the custodian. She is worried about the excellence of my themes. Have I, she asks, been receiving help? For an instant I am on the brink of telling her my story. Something, however, warns me not to attempt it. Here I am safe, I have a place; I do not wish to entrust myself once more to the whimsy of authority. I resolve to make my themes less excellent in the future.

11 NOVEMBER

A ruined marriage, a ruined adjusting career, a grim interlude in the Army when I was almost not a person. This is the sum of my existence to dare, a dismal total. Small wonder that re-education seemed my only hope. It is clear even to me that I need reworking in some fundamental way. How efficient is the society that provides thus for the salvage of its clinkers!

14 NOVEMBER

The distinction between children and adults, while probably useful for some purposes, is at bottom a specious one, I feel. There are only individual egos, crazy for love.

15 NOVEMBER

The custodian has informed Miss Mandible that our desks are all the correct size for sixth-graders, as specified by the Board of Estimate and furnished the schools by the Nu-Art Educational Supply Corporation of Englewood, California. He has pointed out that if the desk size is correct, then the pupil size must be incorrect. Miss Mandible, who has already arrived at this conclusion, refuses to press the matter further. I think I know why. An appeal to the administration might result in my removal from the class, in a transfer to some sort of setup for "exceptional children." This would be a disaster of the first magnitude. To sit in a room with child geniuses (or, more likely, children who are "retarded") would shrivel me in a week. Let my experience here be that of the common run, I say, let me be, please God, typical.

20 NOVEMBER

We read signs as promises. Miss Mandible understands by my great height, by my resonant vowels, that I will one day carry her off to bed. Sue Ann interprets these same signs to mean that I am unique among her male acquaintances, therefore most desirable, therefore her special property as is everything that is Most Desirable. If neither of these propositions works out then life has broken faith with them.

I myself, in my former existence, read the company motto ("Here to Help in Time of Need") as a description of the duty of the adjuster, drastically mislocating the company's deepest concerns. I believed that because I had obtained a wife who was made up of wife-signs (beauty, charm, softness, perfume, cookery) I had found love. Brenda, reading the same signs that have now misled Miss

Mandible and Sue Ann Brownly, felt she had been promised that she would never be bored again. All of us, Miss Mandible, Sue Ann, myself, Brenda, Mr. Goodykind, still believe that the American flag betokens a kind of general righteousness.

But I say, looking about me in this incubator of future citizens, that signs are signs, and some of them are lies.

23 NOVEMBER

It may be that my experience as a child will save me after all. If only I can remain quietly in this classroom, making my notes while Napoleon plods through Russia in the droning voice of Harry Broan, reading aloud from our History text. All of the mysteries that perplexed me as an adult have their origins here. But Miss Mandible will not permit me to remain ungrown. Her hands rest on my shoulders too warmly, and for too long.

7 DECEMBER

It is the pledges that this place makes to me, pledges that cannot be redeemed, that will confuse me later and make me feel I am not *getting anywhere*. Everything is presented as the result of some knowable process; if I wish to arrive at four I get there by way of two and two. If I wish to burn Moscow the route I must travel has already been marked out by another visitor. If, like Bobby Vanderbilt, I yearn for the wheel of the Lancia 2.4-liter coupé, I have only to go through the appropriate process, that is, get the money. And if it is money itself that I desire, I have only to make it. All of these goals are equally beautiful in the sight of the Board of Estimate; the proof is all around us, in the no-nonsense ugliness of this steel and glass building, in the straightline matter-of-factness with which Miss Mandible handles some of our less reputable wars. Who points out that arrangements sometimes slip, that errors are made, that signs are misread? *"They have confidence in their ability to take the right steps and to obtain correct answers."*

8 DECEMBER

My enlightenment is proceeding wonderfully.

9 DECEMBER

Disaster once again. Tomorrow I am to be sent to a doctor, for observation. Sue Ann Brownly caught Miss Mandible and me in the cloakroom, during recess, Miss Mandible's naked legs in a scissors around my waist. For a moment I thought Sue Ann was going to choke. She ran out of the room weeping, straight for the principal's office, certain now which of us was Debbie, which Eddie, which Liz. I am sorry to be the cause of her disillusionment, but I know that she will recover. Miss Mandible is ruined but fulfilled. Although she will be charged with contributing to the delinquency of a minor, she seems at peace; *her* promise has been kept. She knows now that everything she has been told about life, about America, is true.

I have tried to convince the school authorities that I am a minor only in a very special sense, that I am in fact mostly to blame—but it does no good. They are as dense as ever. My contemporaries are astounded that I present myself as anything other than an innocent victim. Like the Old Guard marching through the Russian drifts, the class marches to the conclusion that truth is punishment.

Bobby Vanderbilt has given me his copy of *Sounds of Sebring*, in farewell.

Richard Bausch

UNJUST

One sunny morning in April, less than a week after he has been falsely accused of sexual harassment, Coleman finds a yellow jacket lazily circling and colliding with the surfaces in the spare room down in his basement. He kills it with a folded newspaper—striking it several times—then wads it in a paper towel and flushes it down the toilet, feeling a measure of disgust that surprises him. Just outside the door, he finds another walking up the wall, at eye level, and he kills that one, too, then checks the window that looks out on the uneven ground under the back porch, the sliding door to its right. No sign of entry. Back in the spare room, he parts the curtains over that window, and here are four others dead, lying on the sill. Looking down, he sees several on the carpet at the base of the wall. He disposes of them with another paper towel.

Upstairs in the kitchen his wife, Peg, sits drinking black coffee and gazing out at the sunny yard. When he enters she looks at him, then looks away. He says, "I think there's a yellow jackets' nest somewhere around the window in the spare room."

She doesn't respond for a beat, still staring off. Then: "I killed one in the downstairs hall yesterday."

"I hope they're not in the wall of that room."

She waves this away. "A few dead bees. They get in."

"If they are in the wall, it's better to know about it early rather than late. I don't want to find out by getting stung. Right?"

She says nothing.

"Right?" It's as if he's needling her, and he doesn't mean it that way. The gray in her hair has begun to show more lately, and it occurs to him that now they are no longer talking only about the bees. She's slightly stooped in the chair, her legs crossed at the knee, the cup of coffee on the saucer before her. A moment later, she lifts a hand to her face and rubs her eyes.

"Did you sleep at all?" he asks.

"Who can sleep? Maybe I dozed a little."

He did sleep, but kept waking in fright, unable to recall what he had dreamed. And for a long time, just before dawn, the two of them lay awake, aware of each other being awake and not speaking.

There isn't really much else to say.

The two women who lodged the charges against him are former employees of his in the sheriff's office. He had fired one of them for cause (the alcohol smell was all over her in the mornings, mingled with a too-heavy fragrance of peppermint), and the other, her close friend, quit in anger. After an interval of several weeks, the two of them retaliated: Coleman, they said, had consistently made threats, demanding sexual favors. They've hired a lawyer and the charges are official. It's been in the newspapers. He's going to have to answer for it, this lie. There has never been anything but a little lighthearted kidding, and in fact the two women did most of that. Nothing of their carefully coordinated story contains a shred of truth, yet Coleman has lain awake in the slow hours of night with a feeling of having trespassed, of having gone over some line. He has repeatedly searched his memory for any small thing that might tend to incriminate him, and there's nothing, and he still feels like a criminal.

Now his wife gets up from the table and takes her coffee cup and saucer to the dishwasher. He stands here, faintly sick, while she moves toward the entrance to the living room. "I'm so tired," she says.

"If they're in the wall," he tells her, "there isn't going to be any way to use that room until we get them out."

"Well, I don't know."

He's in his pajamas, and she's dressed. She has already done some work in the yard. The effect of everything, at least until now, has been to create a wordless haphazardness in her; the whole house is portioned out in unfinished tasks, all of them now carrying the weight and significance of full-blown projects, and these are things she would normally have taken care of as a matter of her daily routine: she has intermittently been cleaning in the kitchen and living room; ironing clothes in the upstairs hallway, running the washing machine, polishing furniture, dusting surfaces, and making a very bad job of everything—a streaked, unformed, slapdash confusion. If he tries to help her, or asks that she give him something to do, she shrugs and says there's nothing, he will only get in the way. Until last night, she kept to herself what she's actually going through, and he feels this as a kind of tacit indictment, though he hasn't expressed the thought, even to himself. After his initial outraged denials and his show of horror and repulsion at the cruel audaciousness of the assault on his integrity, his manner with her has been tentative, almost sheepish, as though he fears harming her by reminding her too much.

Once a charge like that is made, his lawyer told him, once that kind of poison is let into the air—well, it's tough to live down. It's very difficult even to live down in your own mind. Coleman has tried to explain all this to Peg, and in doing so has begun to realize how much she herself doubts him.

Last night, at last, she gave forth the words of her grief, her anger; holding the newspaper up and saying, "Everybody on this street takes this, thing! Everett. Up and down this street. They all know."

"If they read that, then they don't know a goddamn thing," he said. "Do they?"

"They know more about us than we know about any of them. They know what I do and they know what you do."

He heard the emphasis, and reacted. "They don't know what I do, Peg. They have no idea what I do, the way you mean it—because I didn't do anything. I didn't do anything but fire a goddamn drunk with no morals and no conscience. And when all this comes down to the truth, you're going to be ashamed of yourself for believing her and that other bitch."

"Don't call them bitches. Can't you hear what that does?"

"They are bitches. They're worse than bitches. They're sluts. A couple of ruthless vindictive . . . Look. There's a word for women like that, and I haven't used it yet. They're trying to ruin me, Peg. They're trying to take away my livelihood."

"You won't prove anything by using that language."

"I should call them ladies?"

"Just don't use that language. That shows an attitude."

"I have an attitude. I've got a right to have an attitude."

"Well, you can't afford it. We can't afford it. We have to show everyone you're innocent."

"How do we do that? We've been through this—it's their word against mine. I'm fucked. Christ, Peg, even you believe them a little. After all these years. Even you."

"I didn't say I believed them," Peg said. But then, in the next moment, half turning from him, sniffling, she went on: "You were so thick, the three of you. Going out for beers after work—all that. I *don't* believe them. I'm trying to make you see why I might—just for a second—why anyone might—oh. Christ—I don't know what I'm saying. I don't know anything anymore."

"Yeah," he told her. "And that's you—imagine what it is for all these other people."

"That's what I'm *saying*," she sobbed.

There was still the rest of the long night to do.

Now, glancing out the sliding doorway to his left, he sees the lawn mower with a pair of her garden gloves draped over the handle. It was the sound of the mower that awakened him this morning. There are zigzags in the grass, wide places where she missed.

"I'll finish the grass," he says.

She pauses at the doorway and turns. "What?" Her voice is almost irritable. "I did the grass."

"You missed a few places."

She leans forward and gazes questioningly out the window. "It doesn't matter."

"I guess I ought to get dressed first," he says.

"What about the bees?"

"I'll check outside."

Normally, on nights when he can't sleep, he goes down to the spare room, where he can read without keeping her awake. He went down there this morning to change the sheets, in preparation for the arrival of their only daughter, who's due in this evening from Los Angeles. Janine wants to be in movies. She attended college out there, and stayed, and recently changed her name. She's calling herself Anya Drake, now. The name change hasn't brought her any discernible benefit. There've been one or two callbacks after auditions, and one small part for her hands in a soap commercial. You see her hands in a large bowl of soapy water, and then you see them applying oil to the palms, a gentle motion that the camera light makes more sensual than applying oil to one's hands ever is. Coleman is unreasonably embarrassed by the thing, as if there's an element of shame about it all—she seems to be exhibiting something more private than her hands. He has been married twenty-six years and has never been unfaithful to his wife.

Janine, or Anya, as she now calls herself, intends this visit as a rest. She told her mother over the telephone that when she feels up to it, she wants to try getting stage work in New York. Her mother told her about the harassment charges, and Janine/Anya expressed nothing but indignation. But Coleman feels there is significance in the fact that her plans are fluid, now (they sounded anything but fluid before): traveling on to New York might come sooner rather than later.

Janine/Anya's old bedroom is crowded with Coleman's worktable and tools, and the unfinished cedar chest on which he has been working. Wood is an old passion. The spare room is where they moved her bed, and where she stays whenever she visits, though it's been three years since the last time.

He tries hard to concentrate on the matter at hand: there's a yellow jackets nest somewhere around the spare-room window, a way in for them through the casing. He'll have to attend to it. He puts on jeans and a T-shirt, goes back downstairs, and slowly traces along the seal of the window frame. He has to displace a lot of dust, and thick tangles of cobweb. The window seems sealed. He stands in the room and listens, but the sounds of the house are too loud to hear anything in the wall. He gets down on his hands and knees and follows along the baseboard, and here are two more dead bees, a third struggling sluggishly along the carpet. He kills it with his shoe, shuddering.

"I'll call the pest control people," Peg says from the door.

Her voice has startled him. If she's noticed this, she chooses not to remark it. "You think we can get somebody out here this afternoon?" he asks.

"Not likely."

"What about the room, then?"

"Anya Drake can sleep on the sofa for a few days."

He stands, and faces her. "You sound great."

"Well?"

"She's got a right to make her own way, Peg."

"Exactly."

"That doesn't mean without help. Listen to you."

"Tell me what you'd like in the circumstance," she says.

"I'd like us not to talk about it," he tells her.

She almost smiles. "You'd like us not to talk about what?"

.   .   .

It's a soft, clear, dry April day, with breezes starting and stopping. The curtains over the windows in the upstairs bedroom billow with a soundless rush, then fall still. Sitting on the bed to tie his shoes, he hears her running the tap down in the kitchen. He finishes tying the shoes, then brushes his hair. It's almost completely white now, and while he liked the streaks of gray when they began, about a dozen years ago, he has been unhappy with it for some time now, disliking the way it makes his eyes look—colorless, flat under the white eyebrows. For a time, he's even considered using one of those gradual dyes, to darken it. But the idea contains its own contradiction: since the purpose of the dye is to hide the gray, the only logical step, if he decides to use it, would be to move to another city, and never again see anyone who knows him as he has always been.

As he has always been.

"My God," he says, low.

How can he think of his appearance now, or ever again? It's as if his mind goes on its own track, separate from him, and there's something insinuating about his very vanity. It makes him recoil. He can't even look at himself in a mirror.

Downstairs once more, he stands behind Peg as she spoons more coffee into the machine. He wants to put his hands on her, but feels awkward about it. He stands close, not touching. "You wonder why you can't sleep."

"I can't stay awake in the days."

"You're all turned around."

"We both are." She looks at him.

"Peg," he says. But they've already said everything. Or that's how it feels. "I'll take care of everything today. I'll go pick up Janine. I'll finish the grass. I'll handle the bees. You try and get some sleep."

"I don't want to sleep now. I'd like to sleep tonight."

"You have to take it where and when you can get it, honey."

"Don't you have to see Rudy today, too?"

"Rudy's got all I can give him right now."

Rudy's their lawyer. Rudy has expressed how bad the situation is: Coleman and the two women were seen together on numerous occasions in a bar near the sheriff's office, drinking together and talking—and flirting. Yes, there was some of that, the kind of talk that happens in bars, adults together in the haze and good feeling of drinks and music. He never touched either one of them except in friendship, and that was never anything more than a pat on the shoulder, or a kiss on the cheek. *They* kissed *him* on the cheek. There were times, driving home, when he stumbled on the pleasant fact that indeed, he felt no physical enticement concerning them at all. They were attractive, and funny, and he liked them. He's twenty years older than they are. He worried and fretted over Deirdre, like a father, when her drinking spilled over into work hours, and the humor and ease between the three of them dwindled and became pure tension.

"You're certain there was never any talk about—say, how either one of them likes to have sex. That kind of thing?"

"Never."

"You're sure you never made a joke—even a joke—about sleeping with one of them?"

"Look, Rudy. Correct me if I'm wrong. Harassment is supposed to be I threaten them with their jobs if they don't screw me or blow me. Right?"

"You never made a joke about sleeping with one of them."

"I don't know—Jesus, I might've. Everybody jokes that way some-times, right? I might've said something in response. In response. But I never had a serious thought about it and never went one step any-where near it."

"You never made a pattern of jokes about sleeping with one of them."

"Never. No. There was no pattern."

"You never commented on their clothing or anything like that?"

"I'd say, you look nice today. With Deirdre I started having to say it because most days she came in looking like she'd spent the night out on the street doing tricks and got drugged up and left for dead. She was at the front desk, for Christ's sake. Can't I get some people to say how she looked? She looked terrible."

"She claims she was drinking because of the—the pressure you were putting her under. The—the harassment."

"It's a lie. Rudy, it's a fucking lie. And I'm going down the fucking drain with it and it's not right. It's not right."

The Colemans have had a very good marriage, that they seldom remarked on. It's been their life, and though to outsiders they might have seemed to take it for granted, they were often very grateful for each other in the nights, sometimes without quite being aware of it as gratitude. Neither can imagine, even now, how it might be to end up having to live without the other. They raised Janine. Or, rather, Anya. They went through the loneliness that followed upon her leaving them, and they had grown used to having her gone.

One of the manifestations of this loneliness was that Coleman took into his circle of affection the two young women who worked for him. Deirdre and Linda. They had gone to school together—they were only a couple of years older than Janine/Anya. Once he invited them to the house for a cook-out, with Peg and a few other people—neighbors, and some others from the sheriff's office. Everyone had a fine time until Deirdre, very drunk, began to cry for no reason. Linda helped her out to the little Toyota they had arrived in, and drove her away. Later that night, while the Colemans were undressing for bed, Peg said that Deirdre reminded her of Janine a little, and seeing her that way, crying, sloppy, falling all over herself, a spectacle, made her worry about Janine in a way she hadn't been accustomed to worrying particularly. Janine had been so well focused in her teen years. And now she was experiencing unsuccess and disappointment, all those miles away.

"It was as if I was given a vision of Janine acting like that on somebody's patio in Los Angeles County."

Coleman agreed. It was true.

And he worried all the more as Deirdre started coming to work late smelling of mint and alcohol. The rest of that summer and into the fall. There were days she never even bothered to call, and Linda would lie for her then, claiming that she *had* called.

"I'm gonna have to let her go," Coleman told Peg. "And it scares the hell out of me. Like I'm letting Janine go, somehow."

"You feel like you're firing Janine," Peg said.

"That must be," he told her. "Must be part of it."

It was during high school that Janine first showed serious interest in the performing arts. Peg had taken her to ballet classes and dance classes from the time she was a little girl, but a lot of little girls were in those classes. Janine, by the time she finished high school, was playing summer stock in the dinner theaters of the valley. Coleman still wonders if she really has any talent. He's not gifted with an ability to tell, has no ear for music, nor any sense of how acting happens. He likes to read, and rarely watches any television, and the movies seem too much the same: nudity, language, an excess of explosions. Noise. The ubiquitous bass voice whispering the words of the previews. It's always the last battle for humankind, the race to save the whole world, the future. Or else it's too cute or outrageous for words, with lots of quirky characters you wouldn't want to know. Janine/Anya wants to be a part of that, and her mother has always believed in her.

But privately Peg has expressed her conviction that Hollywood is politics, who you know—all those children of movie stars, starring in their own movies, with careers of their own: the sons of Lloyd Bridges; the Fondas, the daughters of Janet Leigh and Cliff Arquette and Blythe Danner. It's difficult for her to believe poor Janine/Anya has much of a chance. And the name change did hurt her feelings. Before Coleman's trouble broke upon them, she had resolved that during this visit she would question her daughter about settling down in a job here in Charlottesville.

Perhaps that won't come up now. Coleman doesn't want it to, knows it will lead to arguments and tension. Before Janine/Anya left for California there was plenty of that to go around.

Standing out on his porch, he looks across the road to the tall oaks bordering the field on that side. The sun blazes on the leaves, and above the trees a crow swoops and dives to avoid a darting blue jay. Perhaps the crow is looking for a meal in the blue jay's nest. Now it's a pair of blue jays, harassing the crow, making a racket that you can hear above the sound, in the near distance, of a lawn mower. Coleman steps down into his grass, which is striped with Peg's passes through it, and walks around the house, to the outside of the spare-room window. There's an abandoned bird's nest attached to the underside of the porch at this end, but no sign of a yellow jackets' nest. He goes farther along the wall, and around to the back of the house, crouching low, trying to see under the boards of the deck there. His back hurts. Behind him, over the sound of the lawn mower, comes the voice of the neighbor, Mr. Wilkins, shouting at his eleven-year-old son.

"Pull it back, you idiot. Back around. For Christ's sake. Pull it BACK."

Coleman looks at them, small in the distance, two acres away, the man standing there with his hands on his hips, and the boy trying to maneuver the lawn mower that's bigger than he is. The boy's trying to pull it back up the small incline beyond a shrub, and is not succeeding. His father shouts at him. "Pull it back, you *idiot*. BACK. Can't you understand English?"

The boy finally gets the mower level again, then tries leaning into it, facing it toward the lawn, away from the incline.

"Not that way. Use your head."

It goes on.

Coleman turns back to his house, and sees a bee float out from a crack in the plaster, just beneath the east-facing window of the spare room. He steps closer. Wilkins's shouted curses make him wince. He glances back and sees the boy struggling with the mower, Wilkins following close behind, poised as if about to strike. "You don't have the brains God gave green apples. *Look* at you. I swear you'd foul up a steel ball!"

Coleman tries to tune it out. He watches the place in the plaster, the seam where the house and the foundation meet. Another bee comes from there, and still another. In a minute or two, several come and settle close to it, then enter. After a time, Coleman goes up on the deck and in through the back door. Peg is working the puzzle.

"It's a nest, all right."

"I already called them," she says. "They can be here in a couple of hours."

"Can you hear what's going on out there? He's at it again. That poor scared little boy. I was sheriff, after all. I really ought to go over there."

"Stop talking about yourself in the past tense."

"Well, I *was*." He can't keep the anger out of his voice.

She says, "I'm sorry."

He looks out the window, at the scene of the boy struggling with the heavy machine, and the man moving along slow behind him—a tall, rounded figure of disapproval. Wilkins gesticulates, shouting. The boy works in a feverish, hopeless hurry to get it done.

"You know the terrible thing?" Peg says. "I used to talk to Mrs. Wilkins when Janine—when Anya—was in school. The librarian, his wife. I ought to be able to remember her first name. All they think about is that boy—they actually believe it's for his benefit. It's all out of love. Think of it. They believe they're doing it right. She yells at the poor kid, too. I've heard her over there letting him have it, the same way."

"Jesus," Coleman says. "Somebody ought to do something."

"How long have we been saying that?"

He occupies himself in the workroom, sanding the crest of the clock he's been building: yesterday, while cutting the wood according to its pattern, he allowed the blade to gouge it slightly at one edge. The inside of the mechanism, the weights, the chain, and the pendulum, are all connected and ready. He has finished the trunk, and the plinth, or base. The moon dial and the clock face are installed. As it has begun to look like itself, the hours he worked on it have increased.

Peg calls him when the pest control man drives up. She has spent the last hour out in front, pulling weeds out of the flower bed. Coleman finds them already walking around the house, to the site of the nest. Peg wears a red bandanna and white garden gloves, and she's carrying a trowel. She laughs at something the pest control man says, and in that sunny, grass-smelling instant, seems completely her old self. This tricks Coleman into forgetting the misery they're in. The pest control man is young, and dark, a quiet, shy-seeming boy, with round features and intelligent, humorous eyes. He knows his work, recognizes immediately that there is a nest in the wall, and that it will take a spraying of foam between the foundation of the house and the ribs of the inner walls to eradicate it. Also, the hole itself must be sealed with mortar.

"They can have a pretty good-sized nest built up in a day or so," the boy says. "They work fast this time of year."

He walks back to his truck, glancing toward the Wilkinses' house as he goes. Wilkins is alone there, now, weeding in his own garden patch. Peg stands a little to one side, gazing at the place where the yellow jackets lob themselves out, and come back.

"Does he have the stuff to spray now?" Coleman asks.

She shrugs. "It's getting time to go to the airport. Do you want me to do it?"

"I'll go," he says.

.   .   .

At the airport, he finds that Janine/Anya's arrival is delayed an hour. He waits at the gate. Perhaps some of the people gathered in the waiting area recognize him from the newspaper photographs. Perhaps they stare furtively, he can't be sure. He feels exposed, keeps to one side, beyond a bank of telephones, holding a magazine up. *Flight Lines.*

When her plane comes in at last, she's among the last ones out. He's surprised at how much weight she's gained. Her hair is a mass of crinkled curls as if she has just let it down from being braided, and she's dyed it bright red. She walks up to him, throws her arms around his neck, and hugs tight. "Dad," she says, stepping back from him. Then she turns slightly and with a gesture that looks like dismissal, says, "This here's Lucky Taylor."

"Lucky," he says, repeating it as if he's not certain he could've heard it right.

Standing at her side is a very small, thin, ragged-looking boy, with bad skin and a look of the street about him: holes in his jeans; a long tear in one sleeve of his shirt. His hair is unkempt and very long. The motion with which he pushes it back over his bony shoulders is decidedly feminine. "Hi," he says, offering a thin hand. There's something hangdog about him.

Coleman shakes it, glancing at his daughter, who gives him a look as if to say she means to explain. But no explanation comes. They go to the baggage carousel and wait for their bags, and Lucky chatters nervously, talking only to Coleman, about the turbulence they went through coming east. "It's the jet stream," he says. "It just buffets you."

"Lucky's supposed to spend a couple of days with us and then head on north."

Coleman clears his throat, and finds himself momentarily unable to say anything.

"I can always go on," Lucky says.

"No, we agreed."

"Well, actually, there is a little problem," says Coleman. "We've got a yellow jackets' nest in the spare room, Janine. You'll have to sleep on the sofa in the living room as it is."

She stares at him for a beat. "Nobody told me this."

"I just discovered it today, hon."

"And it's Anya, now," she says. "Remember?"

"I'm sorry."

"I can sleep on the floor," says Lucky.

"You can sleep on the roof, too."

"I said I'd go on."

"Just cool it."

For a few seconds, they stand watching the bags come by on the belt. Lucky reaches for one, and then another. They go on waiting.

"Lucky and I met in a theater group in Santa Monica," Janine/ Anya explains. "He's a future Broadway star." There's a note of sarcasm in her voice.

"Anya's very gifted, too," says Lucky, without any tone at all.

Coleman says, "Do you two want to tell me what's going on?"

"Nothing's going on," Janine/Anya says. "Is anything going on, Lucky?"

"Is Lucky your given name?" Coleman asks.

"No, sir."

They wait. Others step in, retrieve suitcases, and leave. The airport voices make their repeated pronouncements about unattended luggage. Lucky lifts another bag, the largest yet, from the belt, and steps back.

"Lot of stuff," says Coleman, wondering where he'll put it all.

"Anya thinks we shouldn't mention your trouble," Lucky says abruptly over Janine's protesting repetition of his adopted name.

"Well," Coleman gets out.

"I'm sorry if this makes you uncomfortable."

"Lucky has to have his own way in everything," Janine/Anya says. "Don't you, Lucky?"

"I'm being honest, okay?"

"Lucky puts a premium on honesty, like a badge everybody absolutely has to wear."

The young man looks at Coleman and shrugs. "I'm sorry if this makes you uncomfortable."

"I'm a little uncomfortable," Coleman says.

"Try sitting in a plane for five hours with him," says Janine/Anya.

They put the baggage on two carts, and push it out into the parking lot. There's a problem about where it will all fit into the car. It's far more than will go into the trunk alone. The two young people keep a low, muttering argument going all the way, seeming more and more like squabbling children. Janine/Anya decides that the only way they can accomplish getting the car packed is if she sits on Lucky's lap. "It's not that far home," she says.

They have to take everything out and start over again twice, and finally they succeed, with Janine/Anya on Lucky's lap in the front seat. Lucky perched on a stack of duffel bags, and Janine/Anya holding a box of books. The only avenue of vision Coleman possesses is out the windshield and to his immediate left. The passenger-side window is completely obscured by the box of books his daughter holds. He can't see Lucky's face for his daughter's bulk, and the box she holds, and anyway

Lucky has to report for him what is out that window. They make very slow and halting progress out of the airport parking lot. The simple matter of cooperation has stopped the bickering for a time.

"So what's happening," Janine/Anya asks. "Any more news?"

"There's no change from the last time we talked," says Coleman.

"Well, they can't get away with it. You have to attack their character."

"Let's not talk about it now," Coleman says. "It's been pretty hard on your mother. Rudy's handling it, lining up people to testify for me and all that. It's just that the air is sort of poisoned by it." The weight of this comes down on him anew, and he has to work to keep himself from uttering the phrases of his outrage. It is fairly certain that he'll never be able to go back to his job.

He drives on into the brightness, the traffic on the highway south, with its shifting lanes and blinking arrows. There's a lot of traffic; it's stop-and-go all the way. He reads the personalized license plate on the panel truck in front of them: BAD-ARSE. He thinks of the bar he used to go to with the two women, the loud talk and the laughs—Deirdre had a fund of remembered personalized plates, funny ones from her travels, she said, though Linda accused her of getting them off the Internet.

And perhaps there is no such thing as a completely innocent time.

But he stirs in himself and his heart hammers in his chest. He experiences a wave of nausea, scarcely hearing the other two as they negotiate in the small space for comfort, Janine/Anya shifting her weight and Lucky complaining that she's pinching the skin of his thighs. They come to a place where the traffic is at a standstill. BAD-ARSE is still in front of them. Lucky remarks about how odd it is to be stopped in the middle of a superhighway. No one answers. A moment later, he says, "My leg's going to sleep."

"You're such a whiner," Janine/Anya tells him.

"Can't you lift yourself a little?"

"Oh, for Christ's sake, Lucky. I'm not all that heavy."

"Tell my leg that."

Coleman grips the steering wheel. The traffic moves a little, and he swerves onto the shoulder of the road and heads to the exit, which is in sight up ahead.

"We're gonna get a ticket," Janine/Anya says in a singsong voice.

"Let the guy drive," Lucky says.

"Oh, shut up."

Coleman strives for a light tone: "Are you two gonna argue the whole time you're here?"

"My legs," says Lucky.

"Stop the car," Janine/Anya says. "This is ridiculous. I don't want to go another ten feet with him."

"That's fine with me," Lucky says.

"Look," says Coleman, feeling the blood rise to his face. "Both of you calm down, okay? I'm sure whatever it is you can settle it without acting like children."

They make the exit and he speeds a little, managing to beat the light at the first intersection. They are all quiet now, moving at a good clip.

"Will you stop the car?" Janine/Anya says.

"We're almost home," Coleman tells her. "Cut it out, I mean it."

"You can let me off anywhere," Lucky says.

Silence. Coleman's head is throbbing. When they reach the house, he walks around the car and opens their door.

"That was dicey," says Lucky.

The pest control truck is gone. Peg comes out and stands on the porch, arms folded in the slight chill that has come with the waning afternoon. "I thought something might've happened," she says.

Janine/Anya hugs her mother and then walks into the house, half turning to say, "The asshole there is somebody named Lucky."

Lucky offers his little white hand. "Forgive the confusion," he says. "'If I could use your phone to call a cab."

"I don't understand," Peg says. "Are you two—together?"

"Well, we were." He shakes his head, looking down.

"Janine, come out here," says Peg.

Janine/Anya comes to the door. "My name is *not* Janine anymore, God damn it."

"Hey, who do you think you're talking to?" Coleman says.

"We got in an argument on the plane," Lucky says. "It's stupid."

"No, I learned something about you," Janine/Anya says. "I learned that you have to have your own way in everything and that you think the truth happens always to coincide with whatever the hell you happen to be thinking at the time."

"Oh, and you're the only one who knows any truth, is that it?"

"Both of you shut *up*," Coleman says. "Jesus Christ."

For what seems an excruciatingly long moment, no one says anything.

"You want to use the phone?" he says to Lucky.

Janine/Anya storms back into the house, followed by her mother.

"I don't really have any money," Lucky says.

He and Coleman carry the bags into the house. It takes four trips. Peg and Janine/Anya remain upstairs for a long time. The two men sit in the living room, with all the luggage and the bags and boxes between them on the floor. They can hear the low murmur of the women contending with each other. Janine/Anya sobs, and curses.

Finally, Coleman says, "What happened?"

The other man is startled, and has to take a moment to breathe. "I don't even know. She's tense. She didn't want to come home."

Coleman is silent.

"I mean she didn't want to give up."

"Are you involved?"

The other man doesn't answer.

"I guess it's none of my business."

"No."

Coleman feels the blood rising in him. "Although this *is* my house, and I'm not gonna tolerate this kind of thing."

"We're married, sir. That's my wife up there."

He comes to his feet, but then sinks back down in the chair.

"And I'm this close to taking a taxicab out of here."

Peg comes downstairs, walks through the kitchen, and pours a glass of water. She brings it into the room and offers it to Lucky.

"No, thanks," he says.

"Take it," she says, with some force. "And cool off." Then she turns to Coleman, with the slightest motion of unsteadiness, as though she had suffered a sudden vertigo, and says, "I guess you've been told, too."

He nods.

She sighs. "The poor kid sprayed the foam as far as it would go. And then we found another entrance, under the side porch. He thinks it's the same nest and he's going to need some more foam and some other kind of equipment because of where it is. And he thinks the thing extends around in the wall to the opening we saw."

"So the room is out," Coleman says.

"I'll sleep on the floor," says Lucky.

"I wish somebody'd told me," Peg says. "It would've been nice if somebody had told me about it."

"Maybe I can move some things out of the workroom," Coleman says.

"I could go look for a motel or something," says Lucky.

"What's your name, anyway, son?"

"Lucky."

"Tell me your name, will you? First, middle, and last, okay?"

"Woodrow Warren Copley. But I don't think it matters because I'm leaving."

"You need a lift somewhere?" Coleman asks him.

"No," says Peg. "He's not going anywhere. Janine's going to have his baby."

Coleman stares at him. There is nothing he can think to say or do. His vision seems to be leaching out, light seeping from the pupils of his eyes. He thinks he might keel over out of the chair, and he holds on to the arms. "Okay," he says. "Now suppose you tell me what the hell is going on here."

"*She* just did," says Lucky, indicating Peg with a gesture.

"I want to hear it from you, boy."

"I'm not a boy. I'm twenty-nine years old."

"You look like you're about fifteen. And I don't mean it as a compliment either."

"Everett, that's enough," says Peg. "They're having an argument. Stay out of it."

He looks at his wife. The disbelief and unhappiness in her face makes him wince. "Jesus Christ," he says. "Jesus Christ."

Peg turns to Lucky. "*I'm* involved enough, though, to know that you brought our situation into the argument. Tell me, young man, what did you think that would do? Was it just to win? Was that it? Just to hurt your new wife and win your point?"

"What're you talking about?" Coleman says.

"I shouldn't have mentioned the—the charges," says Lucky. "She shouldn't've told you I mentioned it."

"I got it out of her," Peg says.

He gazes off, frowning, looking like a pouting boy. With that feminine motion he pushes the hair back over his shoulder. "We were—we were arguing about appearances. That was one of the things we were arguing about. We argue about absolutely every-thing."

Coleman stands. "Get out of here."

"No," says his wife. "That's not going to happen."

"If I decide to leave," Lucky mutters, "nothing will stop me."

Coleman hauls himself outside with a series of lurching strides, weak in the legs and fighting the sensation that he's about to col-lapse. He goes out onto the lawn, in the chilly sun, fists clenched, heart drumming. His own momentum seems part of a single stag-gering motion, and he's faintly surprised to find himself at the side of the house, peering in to where the foam drips down the wall. Across the way, Wilkins is shouting at his son again. The boy is attempting to lift a loaded wheelbarrow.

"Come on, *try*. You're not even *trying*."

Coleman turns, stares. Wilkins cuffs the boy on the back of the head, and stands there shouting at him. "When're you gonna stop being a baby!" The boy is crying. And for Coleman, now, suddenly something breaks inside, a shattering, deep. He starts across the wide space between the two lawns. He's halfway across the gravel lane before Wilkins turns from the boy. Wilkins seems curious, and not unfriendly, until he discerns the expression on Coleman's face. Then he draws himself inward slightly, stepping back. The boy looks frightened, white-faced, mouth agape, crying. Coleman hears his wife calling his name from the house behind him.

"What is it?" says Wilkins, raising one hand to protect himself.

Coleman strikes across the raised arm, hits the other man a glancing blow, but then steps in and connects with a straight left hand, feeling the bones of that fist crack on the jaw, and Wilkins goes down. Wilkins is writhing, dumbstruck, at Coleman's feet, then lies still, half-conscious, on the fresh-cut grass. There is the shouting coming from somewhere, and a small flailing force, clamoring at his middle. He takes hold of swinging arms and realizes it's the boy, trying to hit him, crying and swinging with everything he has, all the strength of his ten-year-old body.

"Stop," Coleman tells him. "Wait. Stop it, now. Quit—quit it." He grabs hold, and the boy simply glares at him, tears streaming from his eyes.

"Everett," Peg calls from the yard, standing at the edge of it, arms folded, her face twisted with fright. "Everett, please." A few feet behind her, holding tight to each other, his daughter and new son-in-law are approaching.

He lets the boy go, watches him kneel to help his father, crying, laying his head down on his father's chest, sobbing. Wilkins lifts one hand and gingerly places it on the back of the boy's head, a caress.

"Everett," Peg says, crying. *"Please."*

And now Wilkins's wife shouts from their porch, "I've called the police. Do you hear me, Everett Coleman? I've called the police. The police are on their way."

Coleman walks across to his own yard and on, toward the house. Wilkins is being helped up, wife on one side, the boy on the other. Peg, still crying, watches them, standing at the edge of the gravel lane. Janine/Anya and Lucky are a few feet behind her, arm in arm, looking like two people huddled against a cold wind. Peg turns and looks at him, and then the others do, too.

"I'm waiting here," he shouts, almost choking on the words. "Just let them come."

"God," Peg says.

"I'm waiting," he calls to her, to them. To all of them.

Ann Beattie

THE WORKING GIRL

This is a story about Jeanette, who is a working girl. She sometimes thinks of herself as a traveler, a seductress, a secret gourmet. She takes a one-week vacation in the summer to see her sister in Michigan, buys lace-edged silk underpants from a mail-order catalogue, and has improvised a way, in America, to make crème fraîche, which is useful on so many occasions.

Is this another story in which the author knows the main character all too well?

Let's suppose, for a moment, that the storyteller is actually mystified by Jeanette, and only seems to stand in judgment because words come easily. Let's imagine that in real life there is, or once was, a person named Jeanette, and that from a conversation the storyteller had with her, it could be surmised that Jeanette has a notion of freedom, though the guilty quiver of the mouth when she says "Lake Michigan" is something of a giveaway about how she really feels. If the storyteller is a woman, Jeanette might readily confide that she is a seductress, but if the author is a man, Jeanette will probably keep quiet on that count. Crème fraîche is crème fraîche, and not worth thinking about. But back to the original supposition: Let's say that the storyteller is a woman, and that Jeanette discusses the pros and cons of the working life, calling a spade a spade, and greenbacks greenbacks, and if Jeanette is herself a good storyteller, Lake Michigan sounds exciting, and if she isn't, it doesn't. Let's say that Jeanette talks about the romance in her life, and that the storyteller finds it credible. Even interesting. That there are details: Jeanette's lover makes a photocopy of his hand and drops the piece of paper in her in-box; Jeanette makes a copy of her hand and has her trusted friend Charlie hang it in the men's room, where it is allowed to stay until Jeanette's lover sees it, because it means nothing to anyone else. If the storyteller is lucky, they will exchange presents small enough to be put in a breast pocket or the pocket of a skirt. Also a mini French-English/English-French dictionary (France is the place they hope to visit); a finger puppet; an ad that is published in the "personals" column, announcing, by his initials, whom he loves (her), laminated in plastic and made useful as well as romantic by its conversion into a keyring. Let's hope, for the sake of a good story, they are wriggling together in the elevator, sneaking kisses as the bubbles rise in the watercooler, and she is tying his shoelaces together at night, to delay his departure in the morning.

Where is the wife?

In North Dakota or Memphis or Paris, let's say. Let's say she's out of the picture even if she isn't out of the picture.

No no no. Too expedient. The wife has to be there: a presence, even if she's gone off somewhere. There has to be a wife, and she has to be either determined and brave, vile and addicted, or so ordinary that with a mere sentence of description, the reader instantly knows that she is a prototypical wife.

There is a wife. She is a pretty, dark-haired girl who married young, and who won a trip to Paris and is therefore out of town.

Nonsense. *Paris?*

She won a beauty contest.

But she can't be beautiful. She has to be ordinary.

It suddenly becomes apparent that she is extraordinary. She's quite beautiful, and she's in Paris, and although there's no reason to bring this up, the people who sponsored the contest do not know that she's married.

If this is what the wife is like, she'll be more interesting than the subject of the story.

Not if the working girl is believable, and the wife's exit has been made credible.

But we know how that story will end.

How will it end?

It will end badly—which means predictably—because either the beautiful wife will triumph, and then it will be just another such story, or the wife will turn out to be not so interesting after all, and by default the working girl will triumph.

When is the last time you heard of a working girl triumphing?

They do it every day. They are executives, not "working girls."

No, not those. This is about a real working girl. One who gets very little money or vacation time, who periodically rewards herself for life's injustices by buying cream and charging underwear she'll spend a year paying off.

All right, then. What is the story?

Are you sure you want to hear it? Apparently you are already quite shaken, to have found out that the wife, initially ordinary, is in fact extraordinary, and has competed in a beauty pageant and won a trip to Paris.

But this was to be a story about the working girl. What's the scoop with her?

This is just the way the people in the office think: the boss wants to know what's going on in his secretary's mind, the secretary wonders if the mail boy is gay, the mail boy is cruising the elevator operator, and every day the working girl walks into this tense, strange situation. She does it because she needs the money, and also because it's the way things are. It isn't going to be much different wherever she works.

Details. Make the place seem real.

In the winter, when the light disappears early, the office has a very strange aura. The ficus trees cast shadows on the desks. The water in the watercooler looks golden—more like wine than water.

How many people are there?

There are four people typing in the main room, and there are three executives, who share an executive secretary. She sits to the left of the main room.

Which one is the working girl in love with?

Andrew Darby, the most recently hired executive. He has prematurely gray hair, missed two days of work when his dog didn't pull through surgery, and was never drafted because of a deteriorating disc which causes him much pain, though it is difficult to predict when the pain will come on. Once it seemed to coincide with the rising of a bubble in the watercooler. The pain shot up his spine as though mimicking the motion of the bubble.

And he's married?

We just finished discussing his wife.

He's really married, right?

There are no tricks here. He's been married for six years.

Is there more information about his wife?

No. You can find out what the working girl thinks of her, but as far as judging for yourself, you can't, because she is in Paris. What good would it do to overhear a phone conversation between the wife and Andrew? None of us generalizes from phone conversations. Other than that, there's only a postcard. It's a close-up of a column, and she says on the back that she loves and misses him. That if love could be embodied in columns, her love for him would be Corinthian.

That's quite something. What is his reaction to that?

He receives the postcard the same day his ad appears in the "personals" column. He has it in his pocket when he goes to laminate the ad, punch a hole in the plastic, insert a chain, and make a keyring of it.

Doesn't he go through a bad moment?

A bit of one, but basically he is quite pleased with himself. He and Jeanette are going to lunch together. Over lunch, he gives her the keyring. She is slightly scandalized, amused, and touched. They eat sandwiches. He can't sit in a booth because of his back. They sit at a table.

Ten years later, where is Andrew Darby?

Dead. He dies of complications following surgery. A blood clot that went to his brain.

Why does he have to die?

This is just reporting, now. In point of fact, he dies.

Is Jeanette still in touch with him when he dies?

She's his wife. Married men do leave their wives. Andrew Darby didn't have that rough a go of it. After a while, he and his former wife developed a fairly cordial relationship. She spoke to him on the phone the day he checked into the hospital.

What happened then?

At what point?

When he died.

He saw someone beckoning to him. But that isn't what you mean. What happened is that Jeanette was in a cab on her way to the hospital, and when she got there, one of the nurses was waiting by the elevator. The nurse knew that Jeanette was on her way, because she came at the same time every day. Also, Andrew Darby had been on that same floor, a year or so before, for surgery that was successful. That nurse took care of him then, also. It isn't true that the nurse you have one year will be gone the next.

This isn't a story about the working girl anymore.

It is, because she went right on working. She worked during the marriage and for quite a few years after he died. Toward the end, she wasn't working because she needed the money. She wanted the money, but that's different from needing the money.

What kind of a life did they have together?

He realized that he had something of a problem with alcohol and gave it up. She kept her figure. They went to Bermuda and meant to return, but never did. Every year she reordered perfume from a catalogue she had taken from the hotel room in Bermuda. She tried to find another scent that she liked, but always ended up reordering the one she was so pleased with. They didn't have children. He didn't have children with his first wife either, so that by the end it was fairly certain that the doctor had been right, and that the problem was with Andrew, although he never would agree to be tested. He had two dogs in his life, and one cat. Jeanette's Christmas present to him, the year he died, was a Rolex. He gave her a certificate that entitled her to twenty free tanning sessions and a monthly massage.

What was it like when she was a working girl?

Before she met him, or afterwards?

Before and afterwards.

Before, she often felt gloomy, although she entertained more in those days, and she enjoyed that. Her charge card bills were always at the limit, and if she had been asked, even at the time, she would have admitted that a sort of overcompensation was taking place. She read more before she met him, but after she met him he read the same books, and it was nice to have someone to discuss them with. She was convinced that she had once broken someone's heart: a man she dated for a couple of years, who inherited his parents' estate when they died. He wanted to marry Jeanette and take care of her. His idea was to commute into New York from the big estate in Connecticut. She felt that she didn't know how to move comfortably into someone else's life. Though she tried to explain carefully, he was bitter and always maintained that she didn't marry him because she didn't like the furniture.

Afterwards?

You've already heard some things about afterwards. Andrew had a phobia about tollbooths, so when they were driving on the highway, he'd pull onto the shoulder when he saw the sign for a tollbooth, and she'd drive through it. On the Jersey Turnpike, of course, she just kept the wheel. They knew only one couple that they liked equally well—they liked the man as well as they liked the woman, that is. They tended to like the same couples.

What was it like, again, in the office?

The plants and the watercooler.

Besides that.

That's really going back in time. It would seem like a digression at this point.

But what about understanding the life of the working girl?

She turned a corner, and it was fall. With a gigantic intake of breath, her feet lifted off the ground.

Explain.

Nothing miraculous happened, but still things did happen, and life changed. She lost touch with some friends, became quite involved in reading the classics. In Bermuda, swimming, she looked up and saw a boat and remembered very distinctly, and much to her surprise, that the man she had been involved with before Andrew had inherited a collection of ships in bottles from his great-great-grandfather. And that day, as she came out of the water, she cut her foot on something. Whatever it was was as sharp as glass, if it was not glass. And that seemed to sum up something. She was quite shaken. She and Andrew sat in the sand, and the boat passed by, and Andrew thought that it was the pain alone that had upset her.

In the office, when the light dimmed early in the day. In the winter. Before they were together. She must have looked at the shadows on her desk and felt like a person lost in the forest.

If she thought that, she never said it.

Did she confide in Charlie?

To some extent. She and Charlie palled around together before she became involved with Andrew. Afterwards, too, a little. She was always consulted when he needed to buy a new tie.

Did Charlie go to the wedding?

There was no wedding. It was a civil ceremony.

Where did they go on their honeymoon?

Paris. He always wanted to see Paris.

But his wife went to Paris.

That was just coincidence, and besides, she wasn't there at the same time. By then she was his ex-wife. Jeanette never knew that his wife had been to Paris.

What things did he not know?

That she once lost two hundred dollars in a cab. That she did a self-examination of her breasts twice a day. She hid her dislike of the dog, which they had gotten at his insistence, from the pound. The dog was a chewer.

When an image of Andrew came to mind, what was it?

Andrew at forty, when she first met him. She felt sorry that he had a mole on his cheekbone, but later came to love it. Sometimes, after his death, the mole would fill the whole world of her dream. At least that is what she thought it was—a gray mass like a mountain, seen from the distance, then closer and closer until it became amorphous and she was awake, gripping the sheet. It was a nightmare, obviously, not a dream. Though she called it a dream.

Who is Berry McKenn?

A woman he had a brief flirtation with. Nothing of importance.

Why do storytellers start to tell one story and then tell another?

Life is a speeding train. Storytellers get derailed too.

What did Andrew see when he conjured up Jeanette?

Her green eyes. That startled look, as if the eyes had a life of their own, and were surprised to be bracketing so long a nose.

What else is there to say about their life together?

There is something of an anecdote about the watercooler. It
disappeared once, and it was noticeably absent, as if someone had
removed a geyser. The surprise on people's faces when they stared
at the empty corner of the corridor was really quite astonishing.
Jeanette went to meet Andrew there the day the repairman took
it away. They made it a point, several times a day, to meet there
as if by accident. One of the other girls who worked there—think-
ing Charlie was her friend, which he certainly was not: he was Jea-
nette's friend—had seen the watercooler being removed, and she
whispered slyly to Charlie that it would be amusing when Jeanette
strolled away from her desk, and Andrew left his office moments
later with great purpose in his step and holding his blue pottery
mug, because they would be standing in an empty corridor, with
their prop gone and their cover blown.

What did Charlie say?

Jeanette asked him that too, when he reported the conversation.
"They're in love," he said. "You might not want to think it, but a
little thing like that isn't going to be a setback at all." He felt quite tri-
umphant about taking a stand, though there's room for skepticism,
of course. What people say is one thing, and what they later report
they have said is another.

T. Coraghessan Boyle

ZAPATOS

There is, essentially, one city in our country. It is a city in which everyone wears a hat, works in an office, jogs, and eats simply but elegantly, a city, above all, in which everyone covets shoes. Italian shoes, in particular. Oh, you can get by with a pair of domestically made pumps or cordovans of the supplest sheepskin, or even, in the languid days of summer, with huaraches or Chinese slippers made of silk or even nylon. There are those who claim to prefer running shoes—Puma, Nike, Saucony—winter and summer. But the truth is, what everyone wants—for the status, the cachet, the charm and refinement—are the Italian loafers and ankle boots, hand-stitched and with a grain as soft and rich as, well—is this the place to talk of the private parts of girls still in school?

My uncle—call him Dagoberto—imports shoes. From Italy. And yet, until recently, he himself could barely afford a pair. It's the government, of course. Our country—the longest and leanest

in the world—is hemmed in by the ocean on one side, the desert
and mountains on the other, and the government has leached and
pounded it dry till sometimes I think we live atop a stupendous,
three-thousand-mile-long strip of jerky. There are duties—prohibi-
tive duties—on everything. Or, rather, on everything we want.
Cocktail napkins. Band-Aids, Tupperware, crescent wrenches, and
kimchi come in practically for nothing. But the things we really
crave—microwaves, Lean Cuisine, CDs, leisure suits, and above
all, Italian shoes—carry a duty of two and sometimes three hun-
dred percent. The government is unfriendly. We are born, we die, it
rains, it clears, the government is unfriendly. Facts of life.

Uncle Dagoberto is no revolutionary—none of us are; let's face
it, we manage—but the shoe situation was killing him. He'd bring
his shoes in, arrange them seductively in the windows of his three
downtown shops, and there they'd languish, despite a markup so
small he'd have to sell a hundred pairs just to take his shopgirls out
to lunch. It was intolerable. And what made it worse was that the
good citizens of our city, vain and covetous as they are, paraded up
and down in front of his very windows in shoes identical to those he
was selling—shoes for which they'd paid half price or less. And how
were these shoes getting through customs and finding their way to
the dark little no-name shops in the ill-lit vacancies of waterfront
warehouses? Ask the Black Hand. Los Dedos Muertos, the fat and
corrupt Minister of Commerce.

For months, poor Uncle Dagoberto brooded over the situation,
while his wife (my mother's sister, Carmen, a merciless woman) and
his six daughters screamed for the laser facials, cellular phones, and
Fila sweats he could no longer provide for them. He is a heavyset
man. my uncle, and balding, and he seemed to grow heavier and

balder during those months of commercial despair. But one morning, as he came down to breakfast in the gleaming, tiled expanse of the kitchen our families share in the big venerable old mansion on La Calle Verdad, there was a spring in his step and a look on his face that, well—there is a little shark in the waters here, capable of smelling out one part of blood in a million parts of water, and when he does smell out that impossible single molecule of blood, I imagine he must have a look like that of Uncle Dagoberto on that sun-struck morning on La Calle Verdad.

"Tomás," he said to me, rubbing his hands over his Bran Chex, Metamusil, and decaffeinated coffee, "we're in business."

The kitchen was deserted at that hour. My aunts and sisters were off jogging. Dagoberto's daughters at the beach, my mother busy with aerobics, and my father—my late, lamented father—lying quiet in his grave. I didn't understand. I looked up at him blankly from my plate of microwave waffles.

His eyes darted round the room. There was a sheen of sweat on his massive, close-shaven jowls. He began to whistle—a tune my mother used to sing me, by Grandmaster Flash—and then he broke off and gave me a gold-capped smile. "The shoe business," he said. "There's fifteen hundred in it for you."

I was at the university at the time, studying semantics, hermeneutics, and the deconstruction of deconstruction. I myself owned two sleek pairs of Italian loafers, in ecru and rust. Still, I wasn't working, and I could have used the money. "I'm listening," I said.

What he wanted me to do was simple—simple, but potentially dangerous. He wanted me to spend two days in the north, in El Puerto Libre—Freeport. There are two free ports in our country, separated by nearly twenty-five hundred miles of terrain that looks from the air like the spine of some antediluvian monster. The southern port is called Calidad, or Quality. Both are what I imagine the great bazaars of Northern Africa and the Middle East to have been in the time of Marco Polo or Rommel, percolating cauldrons of sin and plenty, where anything known to man could be had for the price of a haggle. But there was a catch, of course. While you could purchase anything you liked in El Puerto Libre or Calidad, to bring it back to the city you had to pay duty—the same stultifying duty merchants like Uncle Dagoberto were obliged to pay. And why then had the government set up the free ports in the first place? In order to make digital audio tape and microwaves available to themselves, of course, and to set up discreet banking enterprises for foreigners, by way of generating cash flow—and ultimately, I think, to frustrate the citizenry. To keep us in our place. To remind us that government is unfriendly.

At any rate, I was to go north on the afternoon plane, take a room under the name "Chilly Buttons," and await Uncle Dagoberto's instructions. Fine. For me, the trip was nothing. I relaxed with a Glenlivet and Derrida, the film was *Death Wish VII*, and the flight attendants small in front and, well, substantial behind, just the way I like them. On arriving, I checked into the hotel he'd arranged for me—the girl behind the desk had eyes and shoulders like one of the amazons of the North American cinema, but she tittered and showed off her orthodontia when I signed "Chilly Buttons" in the register—and I went straight up to my room to await Uncle Dagoberto's call. Oh, yes, I nearly forgot: he'd given me an attaché case in which there were five hundred huevos—our national currency—and a thousand black-market dollars. "I don't anticipate any problems," he'd told me as he handed me onto the plane, "but you never know, eh?"

I ate veal medallions and a dry spinach salad at a brasserie frequented by British rock stars and North American drug agents, and then sat up late in my room, watching a rerun of the world cockfighting championships. I was just dozing off when the phone rang. "Bueno," I said, snatching up the receiver.

"Tomás?" It was Uncle Dagoberto.

"Yes," I said.

His voice was pinched with secrecy, a whisper, a rasp. "I want you to go to the customs warehouse on La Avenida Democracia at ten A.M. sharp." He was breathing heavily. I could barely hear him. "There are shoes there," he said. "Italian shoes. Thirty thousand shoes, wrapped in tissue paper. No one has claimed them and they're to be auctioned first thing in the morning." He paused and I listened to the empty hiss of the land breathing through the wires that separated us. "I want you to bid nothing for them. A hundred huevos. Two. But I want you to buy them. Buy them or die." And he hung up.

At quarter of ten the next morning. I stood outside the warehouse, the attaché case clutched in my hand. Somewhere a cock crowed. It was cold, but the sun warmed the back of my neck. Half a dozen hastily shaven men in sagging suits and battered domestically made oxfords gathered beside me.

I was puzzled. How did Uncle Dagoberto expect me to buy thirty thousand Italian shoes for two hundred huevos, when a single pair sold for twice that? I understood that the black-market dollars were to be offered as needed, but even so, how could I buy more than a few dozen pairs? I shrugged it off and buried my nose in Derrida.

It was past twelve when an old man in the uniform of the customs police hobbled up the street as if his legs were made of stone, produced a set of keys, and threw open the huge hammered-steel doors of the warehouse. We shuffled in, blinking against the darkness. When my eyes became accustomed to the light, the mounds of unclaimed goods piled up on pallets around me began to take on form. There were crates of crescent wrenches, boxes of Tupperware, a bin of door stoppers. I saw bicycle horns—thousands of them, black and bulbous as the noses of monkeys—and jars of kimchi stacked up to the steel crossbeams of the ceiling. And then I saw the shoes. They were heaped up in a small mountain, individually wrapped in tissue paper. Just as Uncle Dagoberto had said. The others ignored them. They read the description the customs man provided, unwrapped the odd shoe, and went on to the bins of churchkey openers and chutney. I was dazed. It was like stumbling across the treasure of the Incas, the Golden City itself, and yet having no one recognize it.

With trembling fingers, I unwrapped first one shoe, then another. I saw patent leather, suede, the sensuous ripple of alligator; my nostrils filled with the rich and unmistakable bouquet of newly tanned leather. The shoes were perfect, insuperable, the very latest styles, au courant, à la mode, and exciting. Why had the others turned away? It was then that I read the customs declaration: *Thirty thousand leather shoes*, it read, *imported from the Republic of Italy, port of Livorno. Unclaimed after thirty days. To be sold at auction to the highest bidder.* Beside the declaration, in a handscrawl that betrayed bureaucratic impatience—disgust, even—of the highest order, was this further notation: *Left feet only.*

It took me a moment. I bent to the mountain of shoes and began tearing at the tissue paper. I tore through women's pumps, stiletto heels, tooled boots, wing tips, deck shoes, and patent-leather loafers—and every single one, every one of those thirty thousand shoes, was half a pair. Uncle Dagoberto, I thought, you are a genius.

The auction was nothing. I waited through a dozen lots of number-two pencils, Cabbage Patch Dolls, and soft-white lightbulbs, and then I placed the sole bid on the thirty thousand left-footed shoes. One hundred huevos and they were mine. Later, I took the young amazon up to my room and showed her what a man with a name like Chilly Buttons can do in a sphere that, well—is this the place to gloat? We were sharing a cigarette when Uncle Dagoberto called. "Did you get them?" he shouted over the line.

"One hundred huevos," I said.

"Good boy," he crooned, "good boy." He paused a moment to catch his breath. "And do you know where I'm calling from?" he asked, struggling to keep down the effervescence in his voice.

I reached out to stroke the amazon's breasts—her name was Linda, by the way, and she was a student of cosmetology. "I think I can guess," I said. "Calidad?"

"Funny thing," Uncle Dagoberto said, "there are some shoes here, in the customs warehouse—fine Italian shoes, the finest, thirty thousand in a single lot—and no one has claimed them. Can you imagine that?"

There was such joy in his tone that I couldn't resist playing out the game with him. "There must be something wrong with them," I said.

I could picture his grin. "Nothing, nothing at all. If you're one-legged."

That was two years ago.

Today, Uncle Dagoberto is the undisputed shoe king of our city. He made such a killing on that one deal that he was able to buy his way into the cartel that "advises" the government. He has a title now—Undersecretary for International Trade—and a vast, brightly lit office in the President's palace.

I've changed too, though I still live with my mother on La Calle Verdad and I still attend the university. My shoes—I have some thirty pairs now, in every style and color those clever Italians have been able to devise—are the envy of all, and no small attraction to the nubile and status-hungry young women of the city. I no longer study semantics, hermeneutics, and the deconstruction of deconstruction, but have instead been pursuing a degree in business. It only makes sense. After all, the government doesn't seem half so unfriendly these days.

George Chambers
(I THOUGHT MY FATHER LOOKED LIKE FDR)

For a while I worked (another of my famous "jobs") as an occupational therapist at the Sunset Hill House. Every weekday at 2 pm I arrived to teach the "Golden Opportunities Workshop." A large, sunny room on the first floor. Scattered about were looms, workbenches, tool-boxes, painting easels, materials to knit and weave and crochet, several typewriters, a small hand-press with a set of type, and a boxing bag.

When I came through the door they were always there, waiting. Those who could still get about unassisted sat on the long pew-like bench. They sat quietly, disinterested, as if each were waiting to be called to some private inner office. Those who had come in wheelchairs always wheeled to the end of the room and sat there staring out the large bay window that overlooked the sawmill in the valley below. One man, who seemed to have been appointed the spokesman of the others, always began the "Golden Opportunities" hour with the same question. "What," he would commence, "have they told you to do to us today?" Neither he, nor anyone else waited for my reply. He, his name was Mr. Brekke, went to the boxing bag and began to fit on the thin leather practice gloves. The others remained silent.

I began the hour setting each person to some task. Mrs. Blead wheeled herself to the doll box to begin assembling the doll she never finished. Father Bane, a retired priest, was writing a book called *Stories from the Confessional*. Beside him, always in the same place, was Mrs. Brood, trying to knit. It was hard for her to work the needles with her stiff fingers. Soon, everyone was engaged in some task. Mr. Brekke, having fitted on his gloves, was punching the bag, slowly, rhythmically, as if he were keeping time to a funeral procession. Mrs. Brood, stumbling among her needles, would smile in Mr. Brekke's direction, call him "that nice man" and continue her work. Instead of saying "knit one, pearl two" as I had taught her to get the rhythm of the work, she kept repeating "shit fuck, piss cunt." Before she finished assembling the doll, Mrs. Blead, holding a soft plastic leg above her head to attract my attention, would ask if I had seen that bad little girl Suzie, her daughter. Yes, I would say, she is in the hall. That would satisfy her and she would spend the rest of the hour plugging and unplugging the doll's leg into the soft plastic torso in her left hand.

At 3:30 pm there was always the same crisis. Then the "Humpty-Dumpty" hour, a children's show with live animals, clowns, and cartoons, was on television. Most of the people in the Workshop wanted to watch it, but it was against Sunset Hill House regulations. Usually, one or two would start weeping. That time always provoked one man, whose name I forget, to speak seriously about the "great fall" that was the occasion of Humpty-Dumpty's demise. "It was" he would say, "a great fall." By then, most had stopped their work and sat where they were, waiting until 4 pm. Except for the slow slamming of Mr. Brekke's fists into the punching bag and the weeping for Humpty-Dumpty, the room was silent.

At 4 the steam-whistle from the saw mill down the valley could be heard as the white-suited attendants came to gather the people from the workshop. As they were conducted out of the room one could hear the attendants saying "and how are we today and we must be going along now and very soon we will be eating our supper."

John Cheever

THE WORLD OF APPLES

Asa Bascomb, the old laureate, wandered around his work house or study—he had never been able to settle on a name for a house where one wrote poetry—swatting hornets with a copy of *La Stampa* and wondering why he had never been given the Nobel Prize. He had received nearly every other sign of renown. In a trunk in the corner there were medals, citations, wreaths, sheaves, ribbons, and badges. The stove that heated his study had been given to him by the Oslo P.E.N. Club, his desk was a gift from the Kiev Writer's Union, and the study itself had been built by an international association of his admirers. The presidents of both Italy and the United States had wired their congratulations on the day he was presented with the key to the place. Why no Nobel Prize? Swat, swat. The study was a barny, raftered building with a large northern window that looked off to the Abruzzi. He would sooner have had a much smaller place with smaller windows but he had not been consulted. There seemed to be some clash between the altitude of the mountains and the disciplines of verse. At the time of which I'm writing he was eighty-two years old and lived in a villa below the hill town of Monte Carbone, south of Rome.

He had strong, thick white hair that hung in a lock over his forehead. Two or more cowlicks at the crown were usually disorderly and erect. He wet them down with soap for formal receptions, but they were never supine for more than an hour or two and were usually up in the air again by the time champagne was poured. It was very much a part of the impression he left. As one remembers a man for a long nose, a smile, birthmark, or scar, one remembered Bascomb for his unruly cowlicks. He was known vaguely as the Cézanne of poets. There was some linear preciseness to his work that might be thought to resemble Cézanne but the vision that underlies Cézanne's paintings was not his. This mistaken comparison might have arisen because the title of his most popular work was *The World of Apples*—poetry in which his admirers found the pungency, diversity, color, and nostalgia of the apples of the northern New England he had not seen for forty years.

Why had he—provincial and famous for his simplicity—chosen to leave Vermont for Italy? Had it been the choice of his beloved Amelia, dead these ten years? She had made many of their decisions. Was he, the son of a farmer, so naïve that he thought living abroad might bring some color to his stern beginnings? Or had it been simply a practical matter, an evasion of the publicity that would, in his own country, have been an annoyance? Admirers found him in Monte Carbone, they came almost daily, but they came in modest numbers. He was photographed once or twice a year for *Match* or *Epoca*—usually on his birthday—but he was in general able to lead a quieter life than would have been possible in the United States. Walking down Fifth Avenue on his last visit home he had been stopped by strangers and asked to autograph scraps of paper. On the streets of Rome no one knew or cared who he was and this was as he wanted it.

Monte Carbone was a Saracen town, built on the summit of a loaf-shaped butte of sullen granite. At the top of the town were three pure and voluminous springs whose water fell in pools or conduits down the sides of the mountain. His villa was below the town and he had in his garden many fountains, fed by the springs on the summit. The noise of falling water was loud and unmusical—a clapping or clattering sound. The water was stinging cold, even in midsummer, and he kept his gin, wine, and vermouth in a pool on the terrace. He worked in his study in the mornings, took a siesta after lunch, and then climbed the stairs to the village.

The tufa and pepperoni and the bitter colors of the lichen that takes root in the walls and roofs are no part of the consciousness of an American, even if he had lived for years, as Bascomb had, surrounded by this bitterness. The climb up the stairs winded him. He stopped again and again to catch his breath. Everyone spoke to him. *Salve, maestro, salve!* When he saw the bricked-up transept of the twelfth-century church he always mumbled the date to himself as if he were explaining the beauties of the place to some companion. The beauties of the place were various and gloomy. He would always be a stranger there, but his strangeness seemed to him to be some metaphor involving time as if, climbing the strange stairs past the strange walls, he climbed through hours, months, years, and decades. In the piazza he had a glass of wine and got his mail. On any day he received more mail than the entire population of the village. There were letters from admirers, propositions to lecture,

read, or simply show his face, and he seemed to be on the invitation
list of every honorary society in the Western world excepting, of
course, that society formed by the past winners of the Nobel Prize.
His mail was kept in a sack, and if it was too heavy for him to carry,
Antonio, the *postina*'s son, would walk back with him to the villa.
He worked over his mail until five or six. Two or three times a week
some pilgrims would find their way to the villa and if he liked their
looks he would give them a drink while he autographed their copy
of *The World of Apples*. They almost never brought his other books,
although he had published a dozen. Two or three evenings a week
he played backgammon with Carbone, the local padrone. They both
thought that the other cheated and neither of them would leave the
board during a game, even if their bladders were killing them. He
slept soundly.

Of the four poets with whom Bascomb was customarily grouped
one had shot himself, one had drowned himself, one had hanged
himself, and the fourth had died of delirium tremens. Bascomb had
known them all, loved most of them, and had nursed two of them
when they were ill, but the broad implication that he had, by choos-
ing to write poetry, chosen to destroy himself was something he
rebelled against vigorously. He knew the temptations of suicide
as he knew the temptations of every other form of sinfulness and
he carefully kept out of the villa all firearms, suitable lengths of
rope, poisons, and sleeping pills. He had seen in Z—the closest of
the four—some inalienable link between his prodigious imagina-
tion and his prodigious gifts for self-destruction, but Bascomb in
his stubborn, countrified way was determined to break or ignore
this link—to overthrow Marsyas and Orpheus. Poetry was a lasting
glory and he was determined that the final act of a poet's life should

not—as had been the case with Z—be played out in a dirty room with twenty-three empty gin bottles. Since he could not deny the connection between brilliance and tragedy he seemed determined to bludgeon it.

Bascomb believed, as Cocteau once said, that the writing of poetry was the exploitation of a substrata of memory that was imperfectly understood. His work seemed to be an act of recollection. He did not, as he worked, charge his memory with any practical tasks but it was definitely his memory that was called into play—his memory of sensation, landscapes, faces, and the immense vocabulary of his own language. He could spend a month or longer on a short poem but discipline and industry were not the words to describe his work. He did not seem to choose his words at all but to recall them from the billions of sounds that he had heard since he first understood speech. Depending on his memory, then, as he did, to give his life usefulness he sometimes wondered if his memory were not failing. Talking with friends and admirers he took great pains not to repeat himself. Waking at two or three in the morning to hear the unmusical clatter of his fountains he would grill himself for an hour on names and dates. Who was Lord Cardigan's adversary at Balaklava? It took a minute for the name of Lord Lucan to struggle up through the murk but it finally appeared. He conjugated the remote past of the verb *esse*, counted to fifty in Russian, recited poems by Donne, Eliot, Thomas, and Wordsworth, described the events of the Risorgimento beginning with the riots in Milan in 1812 up through the coronation of Vittorio Emanuele, listed the ages of prehistory, the number of kilometers in a mile, the planets of the solar system, and the speed of light. There was a definite retard in the responsiveness of his memory but he remained adequate, he thought. The only impairment was anxiety. He had seen time destroy so much that he wondered if an old man's memory could have more strength and longevity than an oak; but the pin oak he had planted on the terrace thirty years ago was dying and he could still remember in detail the cut and color of the dress his beloved Amelia had been wearing when they first met. He taxed his memory to find its way through cities. He imagined walking from the railroad station in Indianapolis to the memorial fountain, from the Hotel Europe in Leningrad to the Winter Palace, from the Eden-Roma up through Trastevere to San Pietro in Montori. Frail, doubting his faculties, it was the solitariness of this inquisition that made it a struggle.

His memory seemed to wake him one night or morning, asking him to produce the first name of Lord Byron. He could not. He decided to disassociate himself momentarily from his memory and surprise it in possession of Lord Byron's name but when he returned, warily, to this receptacle it was still empty. Sidney? Percy? James? He got out of bed—it was cold—put on some shoes and an overcoat and climbed up the stairs through the garden to his study. He seized a copy of *Manfred* but the author was listed simply as Lord Byron. The same was true of *Childe Harold*. He finally discovered, in the encyclopedia, that his lordship was named George. He granted himself a partial excuse for this lapse of memory and returned to his warm bed. Like most old men he had begun a furtive glossary of food that seemed to put lead in his pencil. Fresh trout. Black olives. Young lamb roasted with thyme. Wild mushrooms, bear, venison, and rabbit. On the other side of the ledger were all frozen foods, cultivated greens, overcooked pasta, and canned soups.

In the spring a Scandinavian admirer wrote, asking if he might have the honor of taking Bascomb for a day's trip among the hill towns. Bascomb, who had no car of his own at the time, was delighted to accept. The Scandinavian was a pleasant young man and they set off happily for Monte Felici. In the fourteenth and fifteenth centuries the springs that supplied the town with water had gone dry and the population had moved halfway down the mountain. All that remained of the abandoned town on the summit were two churches or cathedrals of uncommon splendor. Bascomb loved these. They stood in fields of flowering weeds, their wall paintings still brilliant, their façades decorated with griffins, swans, and lions with the faces and parts of men and women, skewered dragons, winged serpents, and other marvels of metamorphoses. These vast and fanciful houses of God reminded Bascomb of the boundlessness of the human imagination and he felt lighthearted and enthusiastic. From Monte Felici they went on to San Giorgio, where there were some painted tombs and a little Roman theater. They stopped in a grove below the town to have a picnic. Bascomb went into the woods to relieve himself and stumbled on a couple who were making love. They had not bothered to undress and the only flesh visible was the stranger's hairy backside. *Tanti, scusi*, mumbled Bascomb and he retreated to another part of the forest but when he rejoined the Scandinavian he was uneasy. The struggling couple seemed to have dimmed his memories of the cathedrals. When he returned to his villa some nuns from a Roman convent were waiting for him to autograph their copies of *The World of Apples*. He did this and asked his housekeeper, Maria, to give them some wine. They paid him the usual compliments—he had created a universe that seemed to welcome man; he had divined the voice of moral beauty in a rain wind—but all that he could think of was the stranger's back. It seemed to have more zeal and meaning than his celebrated search for truth. It seemed to dominate all that he had

seen that day—the castles, clouds, cathedrals, mountains, and fields
of flowers. When the nuns left he looked up to the mountains to raise
his spirits but the mountains looked then like the breasts of women.
His mind had become unclean. He seemed to step aside from its
recalcitrance and watch the course it took. In the distance he heard a
train whistle and what would his wayward mind make of this? The
excitements of travel, the *prix fixe* in the dining car, the sort of wine
they served on trains? It all seemed innocent enough until he caught
his mind sneaking away from the dining car to the venereal stalls of
the Wagon-Lit and thence into gross obscenity. He thought he knew
what he needed and he spoke to Maria after dinner. She was always
happy to accommodate him, although he always insisted that she take
a bath. This, with the dishes, involved some delays but when she left
him he definitely felt better but he definitely was not cured.

In the night his dreams were obscene and he woke several
times trying to shake off this venereal pall or torpor. Things were
no better in the light of morning. Obscenity—gross obscenity—
seemed to be the only fact in life that possessed color and cheer.
After breakfast he climbed up to his study and sat at his desk. The
welcoming universe, the rain wind that sounded through the
world of apples had vanished. Filth was his destiny, his best self,
and he began with relish a long ballad called The Fart That Saved
Athens. He finished the ballad that morning and burned it in the
stove that had been given to him by the Oslo P.E.N. The ballad
was, or had been until he burned it, an exhaustive and revolting
exercise in scatology, and going down the stairs to his terrace he
felt genuinely remorseful. He spent the afternoon writing a dis-
gusting confession called The Favorite of Tiberio. Two admirers—
a young married couple—came at five to praise him. They had

met on a train, each of them carrying a copy of his *Apples*. They had fallen in love along the lines of the pure and ardent love he described. Thinking of his day's work, Bascomb hung his head.

On the next day he wrote The Confessions of a Public School Headmaster. He burned the manuscript at noon. As he came sadly down the stairs onto his terrace he found there fourteen students from the University of Rome who, as soon as he appeared, began to chant "The Orchards of Heaven"—the opening sonnet in *The World of Apples*. He shivered. His eyes filled with tears. He asked Maria to bring them some wine while he autographed their copies. They then lined up to shake his impure hand and returned to a bus in the field that had brought them out from Rome. He glanced at the mountains that had no cheering power—looked up at the meaningless blue sky. Where was the strength of decency? Had it any reality at all? Was the gross bestiality that obsessed him a sovereign truth? The most harrowing aspect of obscenity, he was to discover before the end of the week, was its boorishness. While he tackled his indecent projects with ardor he finished them with boredom and shame. The pornographer's course seems inflexible and he found himself repeating that tedious body of work that is circulated by the immature and the obsessed. He wrote The Confessions of a Lady's Maid, The Baseball Player's Honeymoon, and A Night in the Park. At the end of ten days he was at the bottom of the pornographer's barrel; he was writing dirty limericks. He wrote sixty of these and burned them. The next morning he took a bus to Rome.

He checked in at the Minerva where he always stayed and telephoned a long list of friends, but he knew that to arrive unannounced in a large city is to be friendless, and no one was home. He wandered around the streets and, stepping into a public toilet, found himself

face to face with a male whore, displaying his wares. He stared at the
man with the naïveté or the retard of someone very old. The man's
face was idiotic—doped, drugged, and ugly—and yet, standing in
his unsavory orisons, he seemed to old Bascomb angelic, armed
with a flaming sword that might conquer banality and smash the
glass of custom. He hurried away. It was getting dark and that hell-
ish eruption of traffic noise that rings off the walls of Rome at dusk
was rising to its climax. He wandered into an art gallery on the Via
Sistina where the painter or photographer—he was both—seemed
to be suffering from the same infection as Bascomb, only in a more
acute form. Back in the streets he wondered if there was a univer-
sality to this venereal dusk that had settled over his spirit. Had the
world, as well as he, lost its way? He passed a concert hall where
a program of songs was advertised and thinking that music might
cleanse the thoughts of his heart he bought a ticket and went in. The
concert was poorly attended. When the accompanist appeared, only
a third of the seats were taken. Then the soprano came on, a splen-
did ash blonde in a crimson dress, and while she sang *Die Liebhaber
der Brücken* old Bascomb began the disgusting and unfortunate habit
of imagining that he was disrobing her. Hooks and eyes, he won-
dered? A zipper? While she sang *Die Feldspar* and went on to *Le temps
des lilas et le temps des roses ne reviendra plus* he settled for a zipper and
imagined unfastening her dress at the back and lifting it gently off
her shoulders. He got her slip over her head while she sang *L' Amore
Nascondere* and undid the hooks and eyes of her brassiere during *Les
Rêves de Pierrot*. His reverie was suspended when she stepped into
the wings to gargle but as soon as she returned to the piano he got
to work on her garter belt and all that it contained. When she took
her bow at the intermission he applauded uproariously but not for

her knowledge of music or the gifts of her voice. Then shame, limpid and pitiless as any passion, seemed to encompass him and he left the concert hall for the Minerva but his seizure was not over. He sat at his desk in the hotel and wrote a sonnet to the legendary Pope Joan. Technically it was an improvement over the limericks he had been writing but there was no moral improvement. In the morning he took the bus back to Monte Carbone and received some grateful admirers on his terrace. The next day he climbed to his study, wrote a few limericks and then took some Petronius and Juvenal from the shelves to see what had been accomplished before him in this field of endeavor.

Here were candid and innocent accounts of sexual merriment. There was nowhere that sense of wickedness he experienced when he burned his work in the stove each afternoon. Was it simply that his world was that much older, its social responsibilities that much more grueling, and that lewdness was the only answer to an increase of anxiety? What was it that he had lost? It seemed then to be a sense of pride, an aureole of lightness and valor, a kind of crown. He seemed to hold the crown up to scrutiny and what did he find? Was it merely some ancient fear of Daddy's razor strap and Mummy's scowl, some childish subservience to the bullying world? He well knew his instincts to be rowdy, abundant, and indiscreet and had he allowed the world and all its tongues to impose upon him some structure of transparent values for the convenience of a conservative economy, an established church, and a bellicose army and navy? He seemed to hold the crown, hold it up into the light, it seemed made of light and what it seemed to mean was the genuine and tonic taste of exaltation and grief. The limericks he had just completed were innocent, factual, and merry. They were also obscene, but when had the facts of life become obscene and what were the realities of this virtue he so painfully stripped from himself each morning? They seemed to be the realities of anxiety and love: Amelia standing in the diagonal beam of light, the stormy night his son was born, the day his daughter married. One could disparage them as homely but they were the best he knew of life—anxiety and love—and worlds away from the limerick on his desk that began: "There was a young consul named Caesar/Who had an enormous fissure." He burned his limerick in the stove and went down the stairs.

The next day was the worst. He simply wrote F - - k again and again covering six or seven sheets of paper. He put this into the stove at noon. At lunch Maria burned her finger, swore lengthily, and then said: "I should visit the sacred angel of Monte Giordano." "What is the sacred angel?" he asked. "The angel can cleanse the thoughts of a man's heart," said Maria. "He is in the old church at Monte Giordano. He is made of olive wood from the Mount of Olives and was carved by one of the saints himself. If you make a pilgrimage he will cleanse your thoughts." All Bascomb knew of pilgrimages was that you walked and for some reason carried a seashell. When Maria went up to take a siesta he looked among Amelia's relics and found a seashell. The angel would expect a present, he guessed, and from the box in his study he chose the gold medal the Soviet Government had given him on Lermontov's Jubilee. He did not wake Maria or leave her a note. This seemed to be a conspicuous piece of senility. He had never before been, as the old often are, mischievously elusive, and he should have told Maria where he was going but he didn't. He started down through the vineyards to the main road at the bottom of the valley.

As he approached the river a little Fiat drew off the main road and parked among some trees. A man, his wife, and three carefully dressed daughters got out of the car and Bascomb stopped to watch them when he saw that the man carried a shotgun. What was he going to do? Commit murder? Suicide? Was Bascomb about to see some human sacrifice? He sat down, concealed by the deep grass, and watched. The mother and the three girls were very excited. The father seemed to be enjoying complete sovereignty. They spoke a dialect and Bascomb understood almost nothing they said. The man took the shotgun from its case and put a single shell in the chamber. Then he arranged his wife and three daughters in a line and put their hands over their ears. They were squealing. When this was all arranged he stood with his back to them, aimed his gun at the sky, and fired. The three children applauded and exclaimed over the loudness of the noise and the bravery of their dear father. The father returned the gun to its case, they all got back into the Fiat and drove, Bascomb supposed, back to their apartment in Rome.

Bascomb stretched out in the grass and fell asleep. He dreamed that he was back in his own country. What he saw was an old Ford truck with four flat tires, standing in a field of buttercups. A child wearing a paper crown and a bath towel for a mantle hurried around the corner of a white house. An old man took a bone from a paper bag and handed it to a stray dog. Autumn leaves smoldered in a bathtub with lion's feet. Thunder woke him, distant, shaped, he thought, like a gourd. He got down to the main road where he was joined by a dog. The dog was trembling and he wondered if it was sick, rabid, dangerous, and then he saw that the dog was afraid of thunder. Each peal put the beast into a paroxysm of trembling and Bascomb stroked his head. He had never known an animal to be afraid of nature. Then the wind picked up the branches of the trees and he lifted his old nose to smell the rain, minutes before it fell. It was the smell of

damp country churches, the spare rooms of old houses, earth clos-
ets, bathing suits put out to dry—so keen an odor of joy that he
sniffed noisily. He did not, in spite of these transports, lose sight of
his practical need for shelter. Beside the road was a little hut for bus
travelers and he and the frightened dog stepped into this. The walls
were covered with that sort of uncleanliness from which he hoped
to flee and he stepped out again. Up the road was a farmhouse—one
of those schizophrenic improvisations one sees so often in Italy. It
seemed to have been bombed, spatch-cocked, and put together, not
at random but as a deliberate assault on logic. On one side there was
a wooden lean-to where an old man sat. Bascomb asked him for the
kindness of his shelter and the old man invited him in.

The old man seemed to be about Bascomb's age but he seemed
to Bascomb enviably untroubled. His smile was gentle and his face
was clear. He had obviously never been harried by the wish to write
a dirty limerick. He would never be forced to make a pilgrimage
with a seashell in his pocket. He held a book in his lap—a stamp
album—and the lean-to was filled with potted plants. He did not ask
his soul to clap hands and sing, and yet he seemed to have reached
an organic peace of mind that Bascomb coveted. Should Bascomb
have collected stamps and potted plants? Anyhow, it was too late.
Then the rain came, thunder shook the earth, the dog whined and
trembled, and Bascomb caressed him. The storm passed in a few
minutes and Bascomb thanked his host and started up the road.

He had a nice stride for someone so old and he walked, like all the
rest of us, in some memory of prowess—love or football, Amelia or a
good dropkick—but after a mile or two he realized that he would not
reach Monte Giordano until long after dark and when a car stopped
and offered him a ride to the village he accepted it, hoping that this

would not put a crimp in his cure. It was still light when he reached Monte Giordano. The village was about the same size as his own with the same tufa walls and bitter lichen. The old church stood in the center of the square but the door was locked. He asked for the priest and found him in a vineyard, burning prunings. He explained that he wanted to make an offering to the sainted angel and showed the priest his golden medal. The priest wanted to know if it was true gold and Bascomb then regretted his choice. Why hadn't he chosen the medal given him by the French Government or the medal from Oxford? The Russians had not hallmarked the gold and he had no way of proving its worth. Then the priest noticed that the citation was written in the Russian alphabet. Not only was it false gold; it was Communist gold and not a fitting present for the sacred angel. At that moment the clouds parted and a single ray of light came into the vineyard, lighting the medal. It was a sign. The priest drew a cross in the air and they started back to the church.

It was an old, small, poor country church. The angel was in a chapel on the left, which the priest lighted. The image, buried in jewelry, stood in an iron cage with a padlocked door. The priest opened this and Bascomb placed his Lermontov medal at the angel's feet. Then he got to his knees and said loudly: "God bless Walt Whitman. God bless Hart Crane. God bless Dylan Thomas. God bless William Faulkner, Scott Fitzgerald, and especially Ernest Hemingway." The priest locked up the sacred relic and they left the church together. There was a café on the square where he got some supper and rented a bed. This was a strange engine of brass with brass angels at the four corners, but they seemed to possess some brassy blessedness since he dreamed of peace and woke in the middle of the night finding in himself that radiance he had known when he was younger. Something seemed to shine in his mind and limbs and lights and vitals and he fell asleep again and slept until morning.

On the next day, walking down from Monte Giordano to the main road, he heard the trumpeting of a waterfall. He went into the woods to find this. It was a natural fall, a shelf of rock and a curtain of green water, and it reminded him of a fall at the edge of the farm in Vermont where he had been raised. He had gone there one Sunday afternoon when he was a boy and sat on a hill above the pool. While he was there he saw an old man, with hair as thick and white as his was now, come through the woods. He had watched the old man unlace his shoes and undress himself with the haste of a lover. First he had wet his hands and arms and shoulders and then he had stepped into the torrent, bellowing with joy. He had then dried himself with his underpants, dressed, and gone back into the woods and it was not until he disappeared that Bascomb had realized that the old man was his father.

Now he did what his father had done—unlaced his shoes, tore at the buttons of his shirt and knowing that a mossy stone or the force of the water could be the end of him he stepped naked into the torrent, bellowing like his father. He could stand the cold for only a minute but when he stepped away from the water he seemed at last to be himself. He went on down to the main road where he was picked up by some mounted police, since Maria had sounded the alarm and the whole province was looking for the maestro. His return to Monte Carbone was triumphant and in the morning he began a long poem on the inalienable dignity of light and air that, while it would not get him the Nobel Prize, would grace the last months of his life.

Charles D'Ambrosio

DRUMMOND & SON

Drummond opened the shop every morning at seven so he and his boy could eat breakfast while the first dropoffs were coming in. The boy liked cereal and sat at the workbench in back, slurping his milk, while Drummond occasionally hustled out to the curb to help a secretary haul a cumbersome IBM from the back seat of a car. The front of the store was a showroom for refurbished machines, displayed on shelves, each with a fresh sheet of white bond rolled into the platen, while the back was a chaos of wrecked typewriters Drummond would either salvage or cannibalize for parts someday. There were two stools and two lamps at the workbench for the rare times when the son felt like joining his father, cleaning keys, but generally after breakfast the boy spent the rest of the day sitting behind Drummond in an old Naugahyde recliner, laughing to himself and saying prayers, or wandering out to the sidewalk to smoke a cigarette. That he step outside to smoke was the only major request Drummond ever made of his son.

"Next week's your birthday," Drummond said.

"Next week." The boy finished his cereal, plunking the spoon against the empty bowl. He said, "I think I'll go outside."

"How about rinsing your bowl?"

"Oh, yeah."

"It's raining pretty hard out."

"That's okay," Pete said, grabbing a broken umbrella he'd found in the street, a batty contraption of bent spokes and torn black fabric.

A clear-plastic curtain separated the two parts of the store, and Drummond kept a careful eye on his son from the bench. Drummond had acquired sole ownership of the business after his father died of emphysema, and he still remembered those last months beside him on the bench, the faint whisper as the plastic tube fed the old man oxygen. He knew the tank was pumping air through his dad's nose and into his lungs, but day after day it sounded as though the life were leaking out of him. The elder Drummond had just cleaned his glasses with a purple shop rag and nudged them back on the bridge of his nose when he died, and it was as if, for a lingering moment, he were looking over the workbench, among a lifetime's clutter of keys and type bars, dental tools and unraveling ribbons, for his last breath.

Shortly after his dad died, Drummond had started bringing Pete to the shop, and he sometimes guessed that his wife, free of the boy for the first time in years, had discovered she liked living without the burden. She had hinted as much in a letter he recently received, postmarked from her new address in Portland, suggesting that he meet with a social worker to discuss "the future." He missed his wife tremendously when he opened the envelope and saw the beautiful loops of blue cursive running across the page. He hadn't written back yet, because he wasn't sure what to say to this woman whose absence rendered his life so strange. They had eloped during his senior year at West Seattle High, and this would have been their silver anniversary. Without her he felt lonely, but he wasn't angry, and he wondered if their marriage, after twenty-five years, had simply run its course.

The sheets of white paper in the twenty or so typewriters on display waved in unison when Pete opened the door after smoking his cigarette.

"Now is the time, now is the time, now is the time," the boy said, sweeping along the shelf and inspecting the sheets.

"You want to do some keys?" Drummond asked.

"Not now," Pete said, sitting in his brown recliner.

Drummond wore a blue smock and leaned under a bright fluorescent lamp like a jeweler or a dentist, dipping a Q-tip in solvent and dabbing inked dust off the type heads of an Olivetti Lettera 32. The machine belonged to a writer, a young man, about Pete's age, who worked next door, at La Bas Books, and was struggling to finish his first novel. The machine was a mess. Divots pocked the platen and the keys had a cranky, uneven touch, so that they punched through the paper or, on the really recalcitrant letters, the "A" or "Q," stuck midway and swung impotently at the empty air. Using so much muscle made a crescent moon of every comma, a pinprick of every period. Drummond offered to sell the young man an identical Olivetti, pristine, with case and original instruction manual, but was refused. Like a lot of writers, as Drummond had discovered, the kid believed a resident genie was housed inside his machine. He had to have this one. "Just not so totally fucked up," he'd said.

Hardly anybody used typewriters these days, but with the epochal change in clientele brought on by computers Drummond's business shifted in small ways and remained profitably intact. He had a steady stream of customers, some loyally held over from the old days, some new. Drummond was a good mechanic, and word spread among an emerging breed of hobbyist. Collectors came to him from around the city, mostly men, often retired, fussy and strange, a little contrary, who liked the smell of solvents and enjoyed talking shop and seemed to believe an unwritten life was stubbornly buried away in the dusty machines they brought in for restoration. His business had become more sociable as a growing tribe of holdouts banded together. He now kept a coffee urn and a stack of Styrofoam cups next to the register, for customers who liked to hang out. There were pockets of people who warily refused the future or the promise or whatever it was computers were offering and stuck by their typewriters. Some of them were secretaries who filled out forms, and others were writers, a sudden surge of them from all over Seattle. There were professors and poets and young women with colored hair who wrote for the local weeklies. There were aging lefties who made carbons of their correspondence or owned mimeographs and hand-cranked the ink drums and dittoed urgent newsletters that smelled of freshly laundered cotton for their dwindling coteries. Now and then, too, customers walked in off the street, a trickle of curious shoppers who simply wanted to touch the machines, tapping the keys and slapping back the carriage when the bell rang out, leaving a couple of sentences behind.

Drummond tore down the old Olivetti. While he worked, he could hear his son laughing to himself.

"What's so funny?" Drummond asked.

"Nothing," the boy said.

"You always say 'nothing,'" Drummond said, "but you keep on laughing. I'd sure like to know for once what you find so funny all the time."

The boy's face hadn't been moved by a real smile in years and he never cried. He had been quite close to Drummond's father—who doted on his only grandchild—but the boy's reaction at the funeral was unreadable: blanker and less emotional than that of a stranger, who at least might have reflected selfishly on his own death, or the death of friends, or death generally, digging up some connection.

But on the short drive from the church to the cemetary, Pete had only sat slumped in his seat, staring out at the rain-swept gray city, laughing.

"What are you laughing at?" Drummond had asked.

"Nothing."

Drummond had pressed the boy. On such a momentous day, the laughing had got to him.

"Tell me," he'd said impatiently.

"I just start to laugh when I see something sad," Pete had said.

"You think it's funny?"

"I don't think I find it funny. But I laugh anyway."

"Some of these are crooked as hell," Drummond said now, gently twisting the "T" with a pair of needle-nose pliers. "They'll never seat right in the guides, even if I could straighten them out. You see that?" He turned in his stool and showed the boy the bent type bar, just as his father had shown him ages ago. "Not with the precision you want, anyway. A good typewriter needs to work like a watch."

The boy couldn't carry his end of a conversation, not even with nods of feigned interest. His moods were a kind of unsettled weather, either wind-whipped and stormy with crazy words or becalmed by an overcasting silence. His face, blunt and drawn inward, was now and then seized by spasms, and his body, boggy and soft, was racked by jerky, purposeless movements. He wore slipshod saddle shoes that had flattened and grown wide at the toe like a clown's, collapsing under his monotonous tread. His button-down blue oxford shirt and his khakis were neatly pressed; Drummond ironed them every morning on a board built into a cupboard in the kitchen. He spritzed them as he'd seen his wife do, putting an orderly crease in slacks that were otherwise so deeply soiled with a greasy sheen that he was never able to wash the stain out.

"I think I'll go outside," Pete said.

"You sure smoke a lot," Drummond told him.

"Am I smiling?"

He wasn't, but Drummond smiled and said that he was. "I feel like I am inside," Pete said.

It was a gray Seattle day. There was a bus stop in front of the shop, and often the people who came in and browsed among the typewriters were just trying to escape the cold. A big, boxy heater with louvred vents hung from the ceiling on threaded pipe, warmly humming, and wet kids would gather in the right spot, huddled with upturned faces under the canted currents of streaming heat. Drummond let them be. He found the familiar moods and rhythms satisfying, the tapping keys enclosed in the larger tapping of the rain. Almost everyone who entered the shop left at least a word behind— their name, some scat, a quote. Even kids who typed a line of gobbledygook managed to communicate their hunger or hurt by an anemic touch or an angry jab. The sullen strokes of a stiffly pointing finger, the frustrated, hammering fist, the tentative, tinkering notes that opened to a torrent as the feel of the machine returned to the hand—all of it was like a single line of type, a continuous sentence. As far back as Drummond could recall, he'd had typewriter parts in his pockets and ink in the crevices of his fingers and a light sheen of Remington gun oil on his skin. His own stained hands were really just a replica of his father's, a version of the original he could still see, smeared violet from handling silk ribbons, the blunt blue-black nails squeezing soft white bread as the first team of Drummond & Son, taking a lunch break, ate their baloney-and-sweet-pickle sandwiches on Saturday afternoons.

A rosary of maroon beads dangled between the boy's legs, faintly ticking, as he rocked in his recliner and kept track of the decades. A silent prayer moved his lips.

"Jesus Christ was brain-dead," Pete said. "That's what I've been thinking lately."

Drummond turned on his stool. "Sometimes your illness tells you things, Pete. You know that." The smutted skin on the boy's hands was cracked and bleeding. "You need some lotion," Drummond said. Dead flakes sloughed to the floor, and a snow of scurf whitened the boy's lap. "You like that Vaseline, don't you?"

The boy didn't answer.

"You know I worry," Drummond said.

"Especially when I talk about God."

"Yeah, especially."

"You believe."

"I do," Drummond said, although of late he wasn't sure that was true. "But that's different."

"There's only one true God," the boy said.

"I know."

"I was thinking of writing a symphony to prove it."

"You want some classical?" Drummond asked, reaching for the radio knob.

"Don't," Pete said.

"Okay, okay."

"I'd show how many ways, how many ideas all lead to one idea. God. I'd get the main structure, and jam around it. The whole thing could be a jam."

Drummond futzed with the novelist's machine while he listened to the boy. The old platen's rubber, cracked and hard as concrete, was partially responsible for chewing up the paper and shredding the ribbons. Pressing his thumbnail into a new one, Drummond found that it was properly soft and pliant, in near-mint condition, and he began pulling out the old platen. Drummond had been one of those kids who, after taking apart an old clock or a radio, actually put it back together again, and his satisfaction at the end of any job still drew on the pleasure of that original competence.

"I'd rather record on a computer," the boy continued. "Instead of a static piece of stuff, like an album, you go right to the people, right into their brain. You can do that with a computer."

"You remember about your visitor?"

"Yeah."

"Today is going to be a little different," Drummond said. "We're not going to Dunkin' Donuts right away."

"I like the Dunkin' Donuts," Pete said.

"I know you do." Drummond took a deep breath and said firmly, "Today we're doing things just a little different from normal. You're having a visitor. She's a nice lady, and she wants to ask you some questions."

"I think I'd like to become a baker."

"What happened to being a janitor?"

"Maybe a janitor at a bakery."

"Now you're thinking." Drummond turned on his stool and looked his son in the eye. "Remember how Mom used to bake bread?"

"No," said the boy.

"No?" Drummond absently cleaned ink from a fingernail with the blade of a screwdriver. "Of course you do. She'd put a damp towel over the bowl, and you'd sing to her. She used to tell you that it was your singing that made the dough rise, remember?"

Drummond turned back to his workbench and listened to the rain and to the boy praying and telling the beads. The wall in front of his bench was covered with pinups of writers posed beside their typewriters. Drummond wasn't particularly well read but he knew a lot about literature through the machines that made it. This knowledge was handy in selling a Royal Quiet De Luxe to an aspiring writer whose hero was Hemingway or a Hermes Baby Rocket to a Steinbeck fan. A curiosity he'd never been able to figure out was that many of these writers didn't really know how to type. They hung like vultures over their machines, clawing at the keyboard with two fingers and sometimes a thumb, and while they were often hugely prolific, they went about it desperately, hunting and pecking, as though scratching sentences out of the dirt. Given their technique, it was a miracle some of them managed to say anything. An editorialist for the *Seattle Times* told Drummond that he just sat there and hit the machine until, letter by letter, it coughed up the words he wanted. Even Michener, a man

Drummond had read and esteemed highly, in part for having typed more than anyone on earth, except perhaps a few unsung women from the bygone era of the secretarial pool, was a clod at the keys.

"You had a really good voice," Drummond said.

At twenty-minute intervals, the sidewalk filled and then emptied, the shopwindow blooming with successive crops of black umbrellas as buses came and went. The hour for the appointment with the social worker approached, and Drummond found that he could no longer concentrate. He rolled two sheets of paper into the novelist's Olivetti, typing the date and a salutation to his wife, then sat with his elbows on the workbench, staring. He wondered if he should drop "Dear" and go simply with "Theresa," keeping things businesslike, a touch cold. Whenever Drummond opened a machine, he saw a life in the amphitheater of seated type bars, just as a dentist, peering into a mouth for the first time, probably understood something about the person, his age and habits and vices. Letters were gnawed and ground down like teeth, gunked up with ink and the plaque of gum erasers, stained with everything from coffee to nicotine and lipstick, but none of his knowledge helped him now. Drummond wanted to type a letter and update his wife, but the mechanic in him felt as though the soul of what he had to say just wasn't in the machine. He looked at the greeting again and noticed that the capital "T" in his wife's name was faintly blurred. That sometimes happened when the type bar struck the guide and slipped sideways on impact, indicating a slight misalignment.

Drummond had been expecting a rendition of his wife, but the woman who walked in the door shortly after noon was nothing like Theresa. She couldn't have been much older than Pete, and she wore faded jeans and a soft, sloppy V-necked sweater with the sleeves casually bunched up at her elbows. Her hair was long and her eyes were gray and her nose, though small, was bulbous. Drummond offered her a stool at the back of the shop and brought her a cup of coffee.

"So, Peter, I'm from Keystone," she said. "A halfway house in Fremont."

Pete squirmed in his recliner, rubbing his hands over the thighs of his soiled khakis.

"Nothing's been decided," Drummond assured the boy.

"Do you have many friends?" the social worker asked.

"No," Pete said.

"No one you see on a regular basis?"

The boy reached for the crumpled pack of cigarettes in his shirt pocket and then picked up his rosary beads instead. The long chain trembled in his trembling hands, and his mouth made smacking noises, as though he were slopping down soup.

"When I talked to your father, he said you were in a day program several years ago. Did you enjoy that?"

"It was okay."

"Why did you stop going?"

"I think I'll go outside."

"No," Drummond said. "Stay here and talk to the lady. She only has a few questions, and then we're done."

The copper cowbell above the shop door clattered and the sheets of paper in the typewriters waved and rustled, giving off the slight dry whisper of skittering leaves. Drummond half listened to the tapping keys and the ringing bells and the ratchet of the returning carriage until the cowbell clanged dully a second time as the customer left. In the ensuing quiet, the sound of his boy working the polished rosary beads between his rough scaly fingers distracted Drummond from the social worker's questions. The cowbell clapped a third time. A young mother was trying to ease a tandem carriage across the threshold without waking her twin babies. Drummond excused himself and went to help lift the front axle over the bump.

"My husband would love that," the woman said. Mindful of her babies, she spoke in a soft voice. "What is it?"

"That's a Remington Streamliner," Drummond said.

"Do you mind if I give it a try?"

"No, go right ahead."

He set the machine on a desk and held a chair for the woman. Perhaps the new world of computers had taught people timidity, schooling them in the possibility or threat of losing a thing irrevocably with the slightest touch. This woman's hand pressed the "H" so tentatively that the type bar fell back with an exhausted plop before it reached the paper.

"Go ahead," Drummond said. "Give it a good, clean stroke. You won't hurt it. With a manual typewriter you want a little bounce. You can put your shoulders into it."

"Now is the time for all good men now is the time," the woman typed on the black-lacquered machine, and when the bell rang out, happily ratifying what she'd written, she squealed and clapped her hands.

"This is the most beautiful typewriter I've ever seen," she said. "It's so—so noir! It's got Hollywood written all over it."

"It's prewar," Drummond said. "WWII, I mean. What's your husband do?"

"He's a lawyer," the woman said. "But he's got that midlife thing going on and wants to try his hand at screenplays. He's got lots of stories from his days as a public defender. His birthday's coming up, and I just know he's going to be depressed."

"Hold on," Drummond said, walking back to his workbench. He pulled a photo off the wall.

"If your mind's too great for you," Pete was saying, "you should just let God take it. That's what Christ did. He was brain-dead. He never thought on his own."

"I've never heard that before," the social worker said.

Drummond took the photograph and, somewhat chagrined at the wacky course the interview was taking, returned to the showroom. "That's Raymond Chandler," he said. Chandler wore large owlish glasses and sat with a pipe clenched between his teeth, in a bungalow on the Paramount lot. A sleek gleaming Streamliner rested on his desk.

The woman ran a slender hand lovingly over the polished casing, as though it were the hood of a car. Drummond told her the price, expecting her to balk, but instead she gave the machine a pat, ticking her wedding band against the metal, and then brought out a checkbook, paying for the machine and purchasing, in addition, extra ribbons, a bottle of Wite-Out, and a foam pad. "It's just too perfect," she said. The typewriter was added like a third sleeping baby to the carriage. Drummond helped the woman over the threshold again and watched her go. All the young mothers these days were so lovely in a casual, offhand way. Drummond still dressed like his father, who had always worn a shirt and tie under his smock, as though his job were on a par, in dignity and importance, with the work of a doctor.

Drummond returned to his son and the social worker.

"If I let God take my brain, I'd be laughing. I'd know where I was going."

The woman wrote something on a clipboard, which was beginning to crawl with tiny, antlike words.

"Where would you be going?" she asked.

"I'd be going down."

"Down?"

"I'm trying to figure my brain. What it wants me to do. I think to go down, but I can't figure out what it's good for. It's too much for me."

Pete's lips smacked grotesquely, and he stood up.

"I think I just want to be a son," he said. "Not a god." His elbow jerked involuntarily. "I have to go to the bathroom."

The boy vanished into the back of the shop. Drummond turned to the social worker, whose long straight hair framed a lovely, plain face.

"Is that typical?" she asked. "That kind of talk?"

Drummond sat on his stool. "Yeah," he said.

"And the dyskinesia?"

Drummond nodded—tardive dyskinesia. Half the words he needed to describe his son he couldn't spell, and all of them sounded as fantastic and as far away as the Mesozoic monsters he had loved so much as a child. He remembered paging through *The Big Golden Book of Dinosaurs* as if it were yesterday. The illustrations were lurid and the narrative encompassed the soupy advent and sad passing of an entire world. Now his boy was the incredible creature, and Drummond's vocabulary had become lumbering and dinosauric, plodding with polysyllables.

When the boy returned, he announced that he'd looked in the

bathroom mirror and couldn't see any love in his eyes. Without saying goodbye to the social worker, he picked up his broken umbrella, tapping the chrome spike across the carpeted floor on his way outside to smoke.

"Are you a believer?" Drummond asked.

"No," the young woman said.

"He suffers," Drummond said. "The suffering—"

The woman nodded. Drummond told her how the boy saw faces disintegrate before his eyes, faces that fell to pieces, then disappeared, leaving a hole. He told her how in the early days of the illness they'd taken the beloved family dog to the pound because it was talking to Pete and could read his mind and Pete was afraid the dog would tear him apart. Two weeks ago it was the shop radio, an old Philco that had been Drummond's father's—they couldn't listen anymore. When the announcers laughed, Pete thought they were laughing at him. They would say exactly what he was thinking, predicting his thoughts. Last week the boy was so afraid that he'd only walk backward in public, convinced that someone was following him. He stumbled in reverse up the steps of the bus, and walked backward down the aisle.

Drummond said, "It's Friday, so, what—Wednesday night, I guess—he smelled burning flesh in the house. I always check on him before I go to bed, just to make sure he's okay." He sighed. "When I went in that night, he had raw eggs all around his bed. So I thought it was time to call you."

"You said your wife is gone?"

"I think so," Drummond said. Even though he knew the interview was over, he let the matter drift because he was uncomfortable with sympathy. "If anything happened to me." he said, "I don't know—"

"That's got to have you worried," the woman said. She was very professional and understanding and Drummond realized how little conversation he'd had since his wife left. The interview, though, was a botch. When the social worker mentioned a waiting list, halfheartedly, Drummond saw that his growing need for help was exactly the thing disqualifying him for help from this woman.

"These things don't really bother me," he said feebly. "Because—because I understand him, you see."

Drummond taped a sign on the door and locked the shop. He and the boy walked in the rain to the drugstore. Pete twirled his ragged, useless umbrella over their heads.

"I decided against a halfway house," Drummond said.

"You have to forsake me," the boy said. "I see that eventually happening."

"You don't see, not if that's what you think."

"Maybe I just see better. I'm like a prophet. And you're sort of unevolved."

"Okay," Drummond said. "All right, maybe. I'm unevolved. Sure."

They picked up a bottle of hand lotion and then at the rack by the register Pete tried on a pair of glasses. The gold-rimmed frames sat cockeyed on his nose, and the left lens was stamped with the manufacturer's name: Optivision. The large square lenses themselves were neutral, as clear as windowpanes. Pete looked longingly at himself in the mirror, blinking his green eyes. Drummond wasn't sure whether to dissuade him; from a distance the boy, bespectacled, looked oddly more balanced, his elusive deranged face suddenly pulled into focus.

"You don't really need glasses," Drummond said.

"I do."

"Your eyes were fine last time we had them checked."

Pete said he wanted these glasses, these, with the gold frames, so that people would see the love. In the end, it was only another of the seemingly endless list of lunatic errands Drummond had grown accustomed to, and he gave up, paying for the glasses. They stepped next door and bought their usual lunch of doughnuts, of crullers and old-fashioneds, from the Greek. Drummond was still wary of the Greek, since the day, several months ago, when he'd asked Pete, rather loudly and obviously playing to an audience, if he wanted the psycho special. Drummond had been standing right beside Pete, but the Greek hadn't realized they were together. Pete's illness chipped away at the family resemblance and people often took them for strangers. The Greek had apologized, and Pete had forgotten the incident—if, indeed, he'd ever noticed it—but the day lingered in Drummond's mind, a slight defensive hitch, every time he walked through the door of Dunkin' Donuts.

"I love Seattle," Pete said, as they started back to the shop. He held the tattered umbrella in one hand and the white sack of doughnuts in the other. "I think Seattle's one of the most happening places on the face of the globe at this point in time. We're gonna determine civilization in the next century. I've never met so many movie stars—this is where it's at. Literally, one of the hot spots of the nation is Seattle, USA." He looked at his father through the rain-beaded, fogged lenses of his new glasses, which hung askew on the tip of his nose. "Just the other day, I ran into John Denver in the street. I said, 'Oh, John, I'm writing an album and mailing it to you. It's called *Donuts.*'"

Drummond let the conversation blow away in the rain. He hooked his arm through his son's and hurried him on, but Pete shrugged him off. People glanced sideways at the two men as they made their strange way down Second Avenue. The boy's umbrella was a blasted tangle of snapping fabric and flailing spokes. Drummond's smock flew out behind him. He lowered his head against the wind and the rain and the faces. His fondest boyhood memories were of walking down this same street with his father, strolling and waving as if the elder Drummond were the mayor of the avenue. Now his father was dead and he was the father, and this was his son.

"I love finding stuff in the street. Like this umbrella . . ." The boy lurched along, planting each foot directly in front of the other. "I went to a sculpture show. That's what the umbrella's all about. It didn't occur to me until I was walking up the street and it broke. I knew it was going to break, but I didn't know what I would do with it after. Then I thought. A sculpture. Of course. A sculpture. What else? I call it *Salvador*. After Salvador Allende, the city Salvador, and Salvador Dalí. It's a triumvirate piece of sculpture. Covering all three bases."

About a block from the shop, as they were crossing Bell Street, the boy knelt down in the intersection. He took up a storybook prayer posture, kneeling, his hands folded together in the shape of a candle flame and his head solemnly bowed with his lips touching the tips of his fingers. The sack of doughnuts split open in the rain and the umbrella skittered away in the wind. People paused to look down at the odd penitent praying in the crosswalk. Drummond saw a shiny patch on the asphalt turn from red to green, and then a few cars drove around, slowly. On either side of the crosswalk, a waiting crowd of pedestrians jostled one another at the curb for a view, and Drummond had a familiar passing urge to explain. It seemed the boy would never get up, but then suddenly he made the sign of the cross, rose, and resumed walking, contemplatively, toward the shop.

They had not made much progress when the boy again fell to the sidewalk, again crossing himself and praying, the whole thing repeated like a liturgical rite, as if the boy were kneeling for the Stations. A moment of prayer, the stream of people parting, the stares so blank they seemed to Drummond like pity or hatred, then the boy rising and picking his way cautiously along a fixed, narrow path, again dropping like a supplicant to the sidewalk. Drummond fell to his knees beside his son, imploring him to get up. The boy's glasses were gone and his thin, oily hair was pasted flat on his scalp. Drummond's long smock, saturated, clung darkly to his back. Pete rose again and put his foot down on a seam in the concrete and followed the cracked path and again began praying. Women in the beauty salon next to the shop watched at the window as Drummond knelt with his son in the rain. He tried to hoist him up by his armpits, but the boy was a heavy dead weight. He lugged him across the sidewalk, heaving him a few feet at a time, until they made it safely to the shop door.

Inside, Drummond snipped the twine on a new bundle of shop rags and began drying the boy off. He wiped his hair and ran the rag down his neck. He unbuttoned his shirt and toweled off his arms and chest, surprised, as always, to see the boy so hirsute. Drummond used to bathe him as an infant in the kitchen sink, and he remembered the yellow curtains Theresa had sewn, and the steamed window and the sill with the glossy green leaves of potted ivy. Drummond tried to bring back the feeling of those early winter twilights at the sink, he and the boy reflected in the window. He piled the wet rags, one after another, on the workbench, and when the boy was dry he said, "We're going to close up."

Pete nodded.

"Today's not working out," Drummond said. "Some days don't."

"My glasses," the boy said.

"Okay," Drummond said. "Okay." He sat the boy in the recliner and went out to the sidewalk. Someone had stepped on the glasses. Drummond stared, mystified, at the empty gold frames glinting in the rain. The lenses had popped out. Back at his workbench, he tweaked the bridge of the glasses until it returned to its symmetrical curve and then he gently pressured the right earpiece down so that it was again parallel with the left. He ran a bead of glue around the frames and inserted the lenses, wiping them clean with a cloth diaper. "That'll do you," he said, handing them to Pete. Drummond pulled out a pocket comb and neatly parted the boy's thinning hair and swept it back from his face. When the boy looked up at his father, faint stars of fluorescent light reflected off the glasses.

"Do your job now," Drummond said.

"I think I'll go outside," the boy said.

"Please," Drummond said under his breath. "Do your job first."

Pete began pulling the old paper from the typewriters. He stacked the sheets in a pile, squaring the edges with a couple of sharp taps against the counter. Then he fed blank sheets of paper into the platens, returned the carriages, and hit the tab buttons for the proper indentation, ready for a new paragraph, ready for the next day.

Drummond was nearly done with the Olivetti. He found the nameplate he needed—"Olivetti Lettera 32"—and glued it in place. He squeezed a daub of car wax on the cloth diaper and wiped down the case, drawing luster out of the old enamel. He called the bookstore and told the kid that he was closing shop but his typewriter was ready.

While Drummond waited, he straightened up his workbench. The blank letter to his wife lay there. He crumpled the empty sheet and tossed it into the wastebasket.

When the kid came over, he could hardly believe it was the same machine. He typed the words everyone typed: "now is the time for all good men to come to the aid of their—"

"Is it 'country' or 'party'?" he asked.

"I see it both ways," Drummond said.

He wrote up a sales slip while the kid tapped the keys a couple of times more and looked down doubtfully at the machine. There was something off in its rightness and precision, an old and familiar antagonism gone, a testiness his fingers wanted to feel. He missed the adversity of typing across a platen pitted like a minefield, the resistance of the querulous keys that would bunch and clog. Drummond had seen this before. The kid wasn't ready to say it yet, but half of him wanted the jalopy touch of his broken Olivetti back.

"It's different," he said.

"What's the plot of your novel?" Drummond said.

"It's hard to explain," the kid said.

"Well, is it sci-fi?" he asked. "Romance? Detective thriller?"

Somewhat snobbily, the kid said, "It doesn't really fit any of those categories."

Pete laughed. Drummond felt the entire length of the day settle in his bones. He said, "Take the machine back and monkey with it. See how it feels. Give yourself some time to get used to it."

"I don't know," the kid said.

"Look," Drummond said. "I kept all the old parts. I could restore it back to broken in ten minutes. Or if you don't like the way it works just throw it on the floor a few times. But first give it a fair chance." He pushed the handwritten bill across the counter.

"Can I pay you tomorrow? It's been a slow day."

"Sure," Drummond said. "Tomorrow."

Drummond and the boy boarded the bus and took their usual seats on the bench in back. Drummond wore an old snap-brim hat with a red feather in the band and a beige overcoat belted at the waist. He pulled a packet of salted nuts from the pocket, sharing them with the boy as the bus made its way slowly through the rush hour. His wife had taken their old green Fiat wagon, and Drummond sometimes wondered if he was supposed to feel foolish, letting her keep it. But he didn't really mind riding the bus, and during the past few months he and the boy had settled into a routine. They ate a snack and read what people had written during the day, and then, as they crossed the West Seattle Bridge, the boy would time the rest of the trip home, praying and telling the decades of his rosary.

"You want some?" Drummond asked, holding out the sort of small red box of raisins the boy liked. The boy shook his head indifferently, and Drummond slipped the box back into his pocket.

The boy pulled out the sheets of paper he'd taken from the typewriters. For the most part the sentences were nonsensical, the random crashing of keys, or the repetitive phrases people remembered from typing classes. But some were more interesting, when people typed tantalizing bits of autobiography or quoted a passage of meaningful philosophy. The boy slumped against the window and shuffled through the fluttering sheets while Drummond, looking over his shoulder, followed along.

"Now is the time for all good men."

"The quick brown fox jumped over."

"God is Dead."

"zrtiENsoina;ldu?/ng;'a!"

"Tony chief Tony Tony."

"Now is the time now."

"Jaclyn was here."

"???????????!!!!!!!"

"That interview didn't work out so great," Drummond said. The bus rose, crossing over the Duwamish River. A ferry on the Sound, its windows as bright as ingots of gold, seemed to be carting a load of light out of the city, making for the dark headlands of Bainbridge island. Drummond wondered if the boy would like a boat ride for his birthday, or maybe even to go fishing. His father had kept his tackle as meticulously as he had kept his typewriters, and it was still stored with his cane rod in the hall closet. After a trip to Westport or a day on the Sound, his father had sharpened his barbs with a hand file and dried and waxed the spoons and aught-six treble hooks until they shone as brightly as silverware. Nobody Drummond had ever known did that. Even now, a year after the old man's death, his gear showed no sign of rusting.

Drummond opened the bottle of lotion and squeezed a dollop into his palm. The lotion was cold, and he massaged it between his hands until it warmed to the touch.

"Give me your hand," he said to the boy.

He rubbed the boy's hands, smoothing the dry, dead skin between his fingers, feeling the flaking scales soften between his own hands.

"Your birthday's Monday," Drummond said.

Pete laughed.

"Any idea what you'd like?"

"No," the boy said.

Theresa would probably call home on Pete's birthday. She'd always been good that way, calling or writing nice thank-you notes to people. For months Drummond had expected his wife to have a realization, although he was never sure what she'd realize. When they had eloped during his senior year—her sophomore—she was six months pregnant and beginning to show. She had never had a real honeymoon or even, she had told him bitterly, a real life. The boy had been a tremendous, bewildering amount of work for a girl of sixteen. Drummond supposed that at forty-one she was still a young woman. Now that she was gone, he found most of his social life at church. He was in charge of the coffee urn, and he picked up pastries from a bakery on California Avenue whose owner was an old crony of his father's. He enjoyed the hour of fellowship after Mass, mingling with people he'd known all his life, people in whose aging faces he still recognized the shortstop from Catholic Youth ball or the remnant of a former May Day queen's smile. There was one particular lady he thought he might consider asking out on a possible date when the time was right.

The rain falling against the roof of the bus and the warm amber light inside were familiar. Drummond capped the lotion and put the bottle away. He turned down the brim of his hat anxiously and, checking his watch, realized it was still early. He wanted to stop by the corner store before it closed; he needed to pick up a frozen pizza and some pop and ice cream for dinner. As the bus wound around Alki Point, he looked again at his watch, a Hamilton pocket model, railroad grade, which he wore on a silver fob slipped through his belt. Resting in his palm, it had that satisfying heft well-made things often have, the weight falling just right. It had been his father's, and before that had belonged to his grandfather, an engineer for the old Great Northern. They'd never had to change the initials on the case, and the center wheel traveled four thousand miles, round and round, in the course of a year. His grandfather had told him that, and now Drummond often saw the image of the elderly frail man as he wound the stem in the morning.

"Tomorrow's Saturday," he said. "I've got some catching up to do.

"But Monday," he said, "I'll take the day off. How'd you like that? We'll do something, just me and you.

"You'll be twenty-five years old.

"Twenty-five years," he said.

Almost by way of acknowledgment the boy nudged his glasses up the bridge of his nose. Drummond fitted his old snap-brim hat on the boy's head and looked at him. But his face, reflected in the yellow glass, had already faded into its cryptic and strange cloister. His heavy purple lips were shaping the words to a prayer and the rosary was ticking in his lap as the maroon beads, one by one, slipped through his fingers.

"I love you," Drummond said, expecting the boy to laugh, but he only rested his head against the seat and looked out the window at the gray city going by.

Nicholas Delbanco

THE WRITERS' TRADE

Mark Fusco sold his novel when he was twenty-two. "You're a very fortunate young man," Bill Winterton proclaimed. They met in the editor's office, on the sixteenth floor. The walls were lined with photographs, book jackets, and caricatures. "You should be pleased with yourself."

He was. He had moved from apprentice to author with scarcely a hitch in his stride. It was 1967, and crucial to be young. One of the caricatures showed Hawthorne on a polo pony, meeting Henry James; their mallets were quill pens. They were swinging with controlled abandon at the letter A.

Bill Winterton took him to lunch. They ate at L'Armorique. The editor discoursed on luck; the luck of the draw, he maintained, comes to those who read their cards. He returned the first bottle of wine, a Pouilly Fumé. The sommelier deferred, but the second bottle also tasted faintly of garlic: the sommelier disagreed. They had words. "There's someone cooking near your glassware,"

Winterton declared. "Or you've got your glasses drying near the garlic pan."

He was proved correct. The maître d'hôtel apologized and congratulated him on his discerning nose. The meal was on the restaurant; they were grateful for Winterton's help. This pleased him appreciably; he preened. He spoke about the care and nurturing of talent, the ability to locate and preserve it. Attention to detail and standards—these were the tools of his trade. This was the be-all and end-all, the alpha and omega of publishing, he said.

Mark began his book in college, in a writing class. His father came from Florence and told tales about the family—the Barone P. P. who thought he had swallowed a sofa, the passion for clocks his aunt indulged obsessively, the apartment in Catania where they sent the younger sons. Of these characters he made his story, fashioning a treasure hunt: the grandmother from Agrigento whom the northern cousins spurned, the legacy she failed to leave but set her children hunting. He borrowed his father's inflections: his ear was good, eye accurate, and the book had pace. He completed a draft in six months. Then the work of revision began.

Bill Winterton was forty-five and given to hyperbole. He had been a black belt in karate in Korea; he had known Tallulah Bankhead well, and Blossom Dearie; he had heard Sam Beckett discourse on Jimmy Joyce. He drank and lived in Rhinecliff and was working on a novel of his own. Mark's book was slated to appear the second Sunday of July. "That's the first novelist season," Winterton informed him. "Coming out time for the debs. We want to get attention while the big boys are off at the beach. Not to worry . . ." He flourished his spoon.

·　　·　　·

Mark worked that summer in Wellfleet, at a bicycle rental garage by the harbor; he also served ice cream. He spent long hours clamming at low tide. He liked the brief defined conviviality of work, the casual commerce with strangers. He rented the upstairs apartment of what had been a captain's house. "Everybody was in whaling," said his landlady, Mrs. Newcombe. "All the men in Wellfleet." She meant, he learned later, in 1700. Her house had a large widow's walk, and furniture and ornaments from the China trade.

He was sleeping with the daughter of a real estate agent in town. Bonnie returned from her sophomore year at Simmons to find the local boys inadequate; they whistled and hooted at tourists, and lounged on the Town Office steps. They made peace signs and shouted "Flower Power!" and wore ponytails. They went drag racing on the sand and passed out drinking beer. She was small and blonde and sweetly submissive and had hazel eyes. Her father would kill her, she said.

Mark had read that writers lived along the ponds. He saw them on Main Street, buying papers or fish, wearing beards. He watched them strolling on the dock, wearing caps at jaunty angles, smoking pipes. He heard them at The Lighthouse, conversing over coffee, and at the public library, where they donated books. He told himself he too would be a man with a mission, aloof.

His room had a view of the dock. He had a double bed with a board beneath the mattress and brass bars painted white; he had a chest of drawers and a rolltop desk beneath the window. He organized the pigeonholes, the stacks of twenty-weight paper, the marmalade jar full of pens. The paraphernalia of habit codified, that summer, into ritual observance. He made himself strong coffee on a hot plate; he bought a blue tin cup. He played solitaire. This permitted him, he felt, to stay at his desk without restlessness; it engaged his hands but not attention. He could sit for hours, dealing cards.

He wrote his pages rapidly, then rewrote at length. The little ecstasy of correction, the page reworked if a syllable seemed inexact, or missing, the change of a comma that felt consequential, the tinkering and achieved finality: all this was new to Mark. He recited paragraphs aloud. He read chapters to the mirror, conscious of inflection, rhythm, emphasis. He blackened the blank pages with a sense of discovered delight.

Mrs. Newcombe's parlor shelf had Roger Tory Peterson and *Songs the Whalemen Sang*. An ancestor had figured in Thoreau's *Cape Cod*. She owned *The House of the Seven Gables* in a leather-bound edition; she had instruction books on quilting and *Just So Stories for Little Children* and *The Fountainhead*. He loved the smell and heft of books, the look of endpapers, the crackle of pages and literal flavor of print. He loved the way words edged against each other, the clashing, jangling sounds they made, the bulk of paragraphs and linear austerity of speech. He recited lines while driving or at Fort Hill gathering mussels; they formed his shoreline certainties while he watched the tide. A phrase like "shoreline certainties," for instance, seemed luminous with meaning; it served as his companion while he shuffled cards.

At Columbia he argued philosophy and baseball with his suite mates; he ate spareribs at midnight and went to double features at the Thalia and New Yorker and took his laundry home. His thesis had been focused on Karenin and Casaubon—the stiff unyielding husbands in *Anna Karenina* and *Middlemarch*. There were parallels, also, between Vronsky and Ladislaw, those weak romancing men. The question most urgently posed, he wrote, is how to live a life alone when urged by a secular power to succeed, a secular temptation to accede—or, as Lewis Carroll put it, "Will you, won't you join the dance?"

We each have known conviction, the sudden flush of rightness; Mark came to feel it then. His book had a blue cover and its title was handsomely lettered. A bird ascended—framed by temple columns—from the sea. The stages of production grew familiar. But that his work would be transformed—that strangers in another town would take his words and reproduce them—this careful rendering in multiples provided his first sense of public presence, the work existing elsewhere also. We grow used to the private response. When someone speaks our name we assume we are nearby to hear. We answer questions asked; we find ourselves aroused by provocation, flattered by flattery, angered by insult—part of a nexus of action and talk. But his career, he understood, was in the hands of strangers—someone who might read the book to whom he had not handed it, someone who might help or hinder from an indifferent distance. The recognition startled Mark. He was the master of his soul, perhaps, but not the captain of his fate. He was reading Joseph Conrad and could recite Henley's "Invictus"; such comparatives came readily to mind.

"I don't know you," Bonnie said.

"Of course you do."

"No. Not any longer."

"I haven't changed," he said.

"You're changing. Yes, you are."

She turned her back to him. It was beautiful, unblemished; he traced the white ridge of her spine. She shivered.

"I'll only be away three days."

"You won't come back."

"Of course I will."

"I mean you won't come back to me." She fingered the pillow.

"Make up something for your parents. That way you could come along."

"No."

"We'll figure something out."

"I wanted to be at the party. I'm so proud of you. A publication party. I did want to celebrate."

"You'll be there anyhow," he lied. "You go with me where I go."

"'Parting is sweet sorrow . . .'"

"'Such sweet sorrow,'" he corrected her. Mark flushed at his involuntary pedantry and—to counteract the rightness of her accusation—pressed her back down in the bed. She was all the more exciting when she cried.

His parents had scheduled a party. They were proud of his achievement and would celebrate on publication day. They lived in Rye, New York. His father took the train to Manhattan, working for an import-export firm. He dealt in bristles, hides, and furs; he placed orders for Kolinski, Chunking 2 1/4, Arctic fox, and seal. They were moderately prosperous and happy, they told him, to help. His job at the bicycle shop was therefore part time, a gesture; he drove an MG. It was British Racing Green, a graduation gift. "From here on," he promised his mother, "I'm enrolled in the school of real life."

She thought this phrase enchanting. Much of what he said enchanted her—his pronouncements on fashion, for instance, his sense of the cartographer as artist, mapping the imagined world

from its available features. She had two vodka martinis every after-
noon at five; he joined her on the porch.

"My son the poet," she said.

"Except it's fiction, Mom."

"You'll always be a poet." She swallowed the olive intact.

His mother liked occasions. She was not sociable and did not
attend parties herself. But she welcomed the caterers' bustle at
home, the porch festooned with lanterns, the garden sprouting
tables and white plastic chairs. She gave birthday and anniversary
parties, graduation parties, wedding parties. The house was large.
She felt less lonely entertaining, she explained; they should put the
place to use. She asked him for a guest list six weeks in advance.

He listed friends from Columbia, his editor, the publicity woman,
his cousin, a classmate from high school who was an all-night D.J.
His father invited business associates; his mother included the chil-
dren or parents of friends. She disliked a party at which everyone
knew everyone; a party ought to take you by surprise.

She made a habit of pronouncements, and then repeated them.
One such repeated assertion had to do with variety, the spice of life,
the way ingredients invariably vary. He humored her. He had come
to recognize his parents needed humoring; his father's politics, for
instance, had to be avoided when they met. His father admired
Judge Julius Hoffman. He wished the judge had thrown the book
at those impertinent Chicago-based conspirators; he was afraid of
Hoffman's leniency, he said. He trusted Mark. He knew his son
refused to bite the feeding hand.

On the Sunday of the party, he drove from Wellfleet to Rye. Trucks
rumbled past at speed. He reached the Sagamore Bridge in a sudden

cloudburst and pulled off the road to raise the convertible top. Tugs whistled in the canal; Mark saw the line squall receding. His book was coming out that day; he would celebrate that night. He opened his shirt to the rain.

There was much weekend traffic; he made New London by ten. He wondered if the tollbooth tenders worked eight-hour shifts. They would take coffee breaks. They would bring a heater with them in winter, soft drinks in Styrofoam cups; they would have portable radios for music and the news. They would have a grandson in Spokane. This grandson played the drums. Mark was learning to provide corroborative detail for his characters: birthday parties, a distaste for lima beans, a preference in socks. "Make a catalogue," his writing teacher had advised. "Make it on three-by-five cards. Know everything you can. Tell yourself the person despises lima beans. Try to decide if she likes snow peas or string beans better, and if she wears a girdle, and if she sleeps soundly at night."

He took the turnoff after Playland and reached his house by two. It was a sprawling half-timbered slate-roofed structure; there was a three-car garage. His mother met him at the kitchen door. "Congratulations," she said.

"I made it," Mark said, stretching. "Six hours on the nose."

"It's a wonderful review."

"What is?"

"You didn't know?"

He shook his head.

"A beautiful review," she said. "In this morning's Sunday *Times*. I thought they would have told you."

"No."

"They must have planned to make it a surprise. It's wonderful. You'll see."

The pantry was filled with salads. There were trays of deviled eggs. The review was prominent, and generous; he had heard of the reviewer, and she made much of his book. "Classic and unmannered cadences," she wrote. "Fidelity of mind and spirit, a tale told with economy and grace." The novel avoided those pitfalls young writers so rarely avoid; she hailed "an auspicious debut." His mother clapped her hands. "They've been calling all day long," she said. "We tried you up in Wellfleet but you'd gone already. Everyone who's anyone reads the Sunday *Times*."

We all have been assessed in public, whether by report card, hiring, or review. Our system incorporates rank. We are used to reading how we've done, what we are doing, and in which percentile. But this was new and newly exciting—far more so than the notice in trade journals earlier. He had never heard of the *Library Journal* or *The Kirkus Reviews* prior to their praise. To read himself described as "brilliantly inventive," "persuasively original," was a "heady, yet heartfelt experience": he took his duffel to his room, and then he showered and changed.

His parents knew an author who wrote children's books. Ernest the dog was anything but earnest—was, in fact, mischief itself. Ernest got into and barely escaped from trouble; he was a cross between a dachshund and Dalmatian—known as a dachmatian to his friends. Mark, nine, disliked the books. His parents thought them cute, however, and gave him *Ernest in the Monkeyhouse*, *Ernest Goes to Boarding School*, *Ernest and the Alligator Swamp*. There were elaborate inscriptions from the author for his birthday, for Christmas, or when he was sick. Ernest had a pal called Busy Bee. They helped each other out—when Ernest was being chased by the men from the dog pound, for instance, Busy Bee distracted them: when Busy Bee was slated for the honeymill, Ernest picked the lock.

One day the author came to lunch. His name was Harold Weber, and he had a big white beard and was completely bald. Like one of his own characters, he wore a blue velvet vest. His wife, who died three years before, had been Mark's mother's cousin; they kept distantly in touch. Harold Weber drove a Lancia; his father admired the car. "This is your biggest fan," he said, presenting Mark. "He knows *Ernest Goes to Boarding School* by heart. And *The Frying Pan and Fire*. It's his favorite."

That November had been blustery: the last dark leaves of the Japanese maple beat at the bay window. Branches blew past. His father said, "Let's have a fire," and a voice from the chimney said, "Wait!" "What's that?" his father asked. "Wait, won't you?" called the voice. "I have to get my family out first. We fell asleep."

Mark approached the fireplace and put his ear to the wall. "Hello, little boy; what's your name?" He turned to his parents, shocked. "I've got it—you must be Mark. Ernest told me all about you. You're his favorite person on all Echo Lane." Then the voice changed register, grew gruff. "Hello, Mark. How've you been? Tell them not to start that fire till I get Busy Bee out."

Harold Weber leaned against the mantelpiece. He was smiling; his mouth moved slightly, and his Adam's apple worked. Yet the voice came from the chimney, not where he stood beneath it. Mark said, "You're doing that," and Harold Weber bent, shaking his bald head, raking his beard with his fingers, looking up the fireplace and saying from what seemed like the window, "He's not."

Then there were drinks. There were cheese biscuits and shrimp with plastic toothpicks impaling them on a cabbage, so it looked as if the cabbage grew multicolored quills. "Don't poke me," said the cabbage. "I get ticklish if you poke." Then the cabbage giggled, and Harold Weber laughed. "I guess we'll have that fire," he said to Mark's father. "I guess Ernest helped old Busy Bee to get his family out." "I guess," agreed Mark's father, and they laughed and swallowed shrimp.

That day he knew he'd witnessed magic—not the poor ventriloquy but the invented voice. A creature from a page had spoken to him, Mark, from a familiar place. He adored Harold Weber through lunch.

The party started at six. His father's business partners, his uncle from Arezzo, his neighbors arrived. They congratulated him. They offered wine and a leather-bound notebook and a subscription to *The New York Review of Books* and champagne. His sister's plane was late. She took a taxi from LaGuardia and clattered in, exuberant, embracing him. "I knew you could do it," she said. She told him that Johns Hopkins was a prison, and medical school like some sort of boot camp or jail; she hadn't slept in weeks, and then just for an hour with the surgeon on the cot. She laughed with the openmouthed braying hilarity that meant she did not mean it. "I love the place," she said. "Seriously, kid."

The caterers served drinks. They set out food. There were several pâtés and salmon mousse and sliced roast beef and a whole ham and veal in aspic and caviar and water chestnuts and vegetable dip. Bill Winterton drove down from Rhinecliff. He accepted scotch. "It's quite a spread," he said. Mark was uncertain if he referred to the tables piled with food or to the house itself. "It's a question of proportion," Winterton observed. "Your folks are spending more for this than we paid for the book."

His friends appeared. They drove from Manhattan and Riverdale and Westport and Larchmont and Barnegat Light. They arrived in pairs or carloads and three of them came on the train. Betty Allentuck traveled alone. She had been living with Sam Harwood, his close friend; she and Sam had broken up that spring. Sam was on a Fulbright in Brazil.

Betty had thick chestnut hair, long legs and high wide hips. Her breasts were full. She smoked and drank and swore with what he thought of as erotic frankness; he had envied Sam. They brushed against each other in the foyer, and she kissed him happily. "Your big night," she said.

"I'm glad you're here."

She kissed him again. "Later," she promised, and they went out on the porch.

That promise hovered where she stood in the gathering dark on the lawn. Spotlights in the oak trees lit the far stone wall. There were lanterns and torches as well. There were aromatic candles in glass jars. His father moved among the guests, wearing a pinstriped blazer, looking like a politician, pumping hands. The punch was good.

His friends attended him. They asked about the Cape, they praised his tan, they asked for free copies or where they could buy one or if he would sign books they brought. They talked about themselves. They were in law school and business school and advertising agencies; they were moving to Los Angeles and Spain. There was a rope hammock, slung between two maples; Betty lay inside it, swinging, sandals off. His father's accountant said, "Mazel tov," pointing in what seemed to be her direction; his uncle asked about his plans, what he was planning next. There were checkered tablecloths and helium balloons in clusters anchored by his book. The balloons were blue and white.

Then there were toasts. Bill Winterton said he was pleased, and Mark should get to work. He hoped and trusted this was the beginning of a long career. There was applause. Mark's sister said, I want to tell you, everyone, his handwriting is rotten. Scribble, scribble, scribble, Mr. Gibbon. People laughed. There was a toast to the reviewer for the *Times*: may her judgment be repeated. I'm proud of you. Mark's father said, I'm grateful you folks came. Imagine what this food will look like in the morning, said his mother; please everybody take seconds. Help yourselves.

By the time dessert arrived, he had grown impatient. A party in your honor is supposed to be more fun than this, he told Betty in the hammock; it was nine o'clock. Dessert was cake. His mother said, "You cut it, dear," and led him to the serving table. They made space. The cake was large, rectangular, its icing fashioned in a perfect likeness of the cover of his novel. The blue sky and the bird outstretched against it and the pillars with his name inscribed—all were reproduced. He was embarrassed. "Beautiful," they chorused. "It's magnificent." "The word made sugar," said Billy the D.J. "Take of my body. Eat, eat."

There were photographs. Flashbulbs popped repeatedly while he smiled and blinked. His mother provided a knife. "You cut the first slice, author."

"I can't."

"It's the book's birthday. We made it a cake."

"I don't want to."

"Please," she said.

He took the knife and flourished it, then stabbed the air. He wielded it as if it were a saber, impaling, conducting. In the angle of his vision he saw his mother's face, shocked. He advanced as might a fencer, left arm curled above the shoulder, wrist cocked, thrusting. She would construct indulgence yet again. There were a hundred portions, and he hacked.

"You were wonderful," said Betty.

"When?"

"With the cake. I loved it."

"You're in the minority."

She put her hand on his arm. "When the party's over would you take me home?"

"Is that a proposition?"

"Yes."

The guests dispersed. They took their leave of him as if he were a host. There were pots of coffee for those who had to drive. The caterers cleaned up. His parents and his sister rocked companionably on the porch. "You'd never make a surgeon, Mark," she said. "Look what you did to that cake."

He told them he was taking Betty to New York. He claimed a bottle of champagne, said thank you to his parents, and promised to return by dawn. "Drive carefully," they said. "To the victor," said his sister, and they laughed.

The MG's top was down. The seats were wet. He dried them with his handkerchief, and Betty leaned against him, and they kissed. Headlights from a turning car illuminated their embrace; she did not turn away.

What followed was delight. They drove into Manhattan in their own created wind; she rested her hand on his thigh. The city spread beneath them like a neon maze through which he knew the track, a necklace suspended from the dark neck of the river. At the Triboro Bridge toll booth the attendant said, "Fine night." He found a parking space in front of her apartment, and they closed the car. "I've wanted this all year," she said. "Haven't we been virtuous? It seems like I've waited all spring."

The sex was a promise delivered. Betty took him into her with a high keening wail, a fierce enfolding heat; she flailed against him in the bed, repeating to his rhythm, "God, my God, my God." He was proving something, celebrating, displacing his friend in her flesh; he battered at her till she cried, "I love you, Mark." He wondered, was that true. They drank champagne. The ache in his knees, in his back, the plenitude of travel and arrival and release, the long day waning, the radio's jazz, the whites of her eyes rolling back—all this was bounty, a gift. Each time he entered her she begged him, "Stop. Don't stop."

On Tuesday he and Winterton met again for lunch. This time they ate at Lutèce. "Word is the *Newsweek* is good. And *The Saturday Review*." He handed Mark *The Saturday Review*. There was his photograph, and a review entitled "Timeless Parable." Again he had heard of the critic; again the assessment was kind. "I wish I could have written a book this good at twenty-two. I could not, and very few do. There's a major talent here. Hats off."

"Publicity is ringing off the hook," said Winterton. "Don't let it go to your head."

The bumblebee, he said, is by all scientific measure too slow and fat to fly. Cheerfully ignorant of this, however, and to the dismay of scientists, the bumblebee just flies. Winterton flapped his arms. He drank. You've got to learn, he said, to be like that bumblebee flying: just go ahead and buzz.

"I'm working on a story," Mark announced.

"Good."

"It's about discovery. Self-discovery. A boy who sleeps with his best friend's girlfriend, then finds out she's the Muse."

"Don't spoil it by analysis."

"I'm not. I'm only telling you."

"Well, don't." He pressed his palms to his temples and then extracted glasses from his coat. He had not worn glasses before in Mark's presence; he studied the menu with care. "There's nothing that can happen now," he said, "that's anything but a distraction to your work. If the praise continues, if it dies down or changes or stops. All of this"—he waved his hand—"it's beside the point. The point is to keep working, to not stop."

He said this with bitterness, smiling. The first course arrived. Thereafter the mood lightened, and Winterton grew expansive. Ernest Hemingway drank rum, and Scott drank French 75's, and Bill Faulkner drank Jack Daniels; he emulated them all. You can tell a writer's models by which drink he orders, at which bar.

His tennis game was off. He had lost his backhand and his overhead. His marriage was a warring truce, his boy a diabetic, and his secretary couldn't tell the difference between Tolstoi and Mickey Spillane if her raise depended on it; his eyes hurt. No one read Galsworthy now. No book buyer in this room—he raised his arm, inclusive—could tell him, he was certain, where "The apple tree, the singing and the gold," came from, and what was its original.

Mark too recited a verse. "Samuel Smith he sells good beer / His company will please. / The way is lit and very near / It's just beyond the trees."

"What's that?" asked Winterton, incurious, and Mark said he read it in Wellfleet. It was a tavern motto from a tavern washed away. The whalers weighed anchor off Jeremy Point—but all they found was pewter now, a bowl or two, some spoons.

"Mine's Sophocles," said Winterton, "in the Gilbert Murray translation. 'Apples and singing and gold . . .'"

The garden room was full. Light slanted through the windows; women laughed. Mark had taken the train to Manhattan and would take it home again; his car was being serviced in the garage at Rye. They drank Italian wines, to honor what Bill Winterton described as his true provenance; it seemed important, somehow, to pretend they were in Italy. This went against the decor's grain; the waiters spoke in French. "You know where Napoleon comes from? It's a riddle." Winterton coughed. "The question is what nationality was Napoleon at birth? I ask you, 'Can you answer?' and the answer's, 'Cors-I-can.'"

This seemed uproarious to Mark—witty, learned, apt. They celebrated lengthily, and there was nothing he could not attain, no prospect unattainable. Walking to Grand Central he breathed deeply, weaving. He made the 4:18.

Between self-pity and aggrandisement, there is little room to maneuver. His stomach churned; his shirt felt rank. The train was old. Mark wandered to the forward car; the conductor waved him in. The gray seats were unoccupied, the windows dark. He sat sprawling in the windowseat while the train filled up.

A woman with two shopping bags settled beside him. She wore a pink knit suit and had a purple handbag and white hair. He made space. She produced *The Saturday Review*. The train lurched and rumbled forward, and he told himself his father made this trip five hundred times a year. They stopped at 125th Street, and then they gathered speed.

He needed water. He wanted to sleep. His neighbor read the magazine with absorbed attention and came, on page 23, to his photograph. He was sitting on a rock in front of Long Island Sound. His tie had blown over his shoulder, his hair was engagingly tousled by the propitious breeze. He wanted to tell her, "That's me." He wanted her to know that she was sitting next to Mark Fusco, novelist, whose first book earned such praise. He imagined her shocked disbelief, then recognition. She would tell her husband, when she got off the train at Pelham or Greenwich or wherever she was getting off, "Guess who I sat next to, guess who I met on the train?"

Mark was on the verge of telling her, clearing his throat to begin, when the train braked. Momentum threw him forward; he jerked back. They had no scheduled stop. His neighbor had her handbag open, and its contents spilled. "What was that?" she asked. The whistle shrieked. He bent to help her gather pens, a tube of lipstick, Kleenex, keys. "What was that?" she asked again, as if he might have known.

They remained there without explanation. The train lights flickered, dimmed. He tried to open his window, but it had been sealed shut. Brown grime adhered to his hands. His head hurt. He excused himself to drink from the water dispenser, but there were no paper cups. He pressed the lever nonetheless, and water trickled out. In the space between the cars conductors huddled, conferring. They looked at their logbooks, their watches. The next stop was Larchmont, he knew. He tried to see the Larchmont station down along the track; he saw the New England Thruway and apartment buildings and gas stations and what looked like a supermarket and a lumberyard. The train had been stopped in its tracks. He understood, of a sudden, the force of that expression; he returned to his seat and repeated it. "The train has been stopped in its tracks."

Then there were rumors. The train had hit a dog. It had hit a car. It had narrowly avoided a collision with a freight; the switching devices failed. The President was on his way to New Rochelle, and traffic had therefore been halted. There was trouble ahead with the switches, and they would wait it out here. There were work slowdowns, strikes. The woman to his right protested the delay. Her husband would be worried silly; he was a worrier. He liked to feed the cat and canary just so, in sequence, and if there was some change in the schedule, some reason to feed the canary first, he worried for the cat.

Her husband would be waiting at Mamaroneck. He would keep the motor running and fret about the wasted gas and fret about the timer oven since this was the maid's Tuesday off; since her husband had retired, she called him worrywart. She went to New York once a week. It wasn't for the shopping, really, it was to escape—a freedom spree, she called it, not a shopping spree.

Mark drifted, nodding, sweating. They would know him at Lutèce. He would buy a pipe and captain's hat and lounge along the dock.

The grandmother from Agrigento buried donkey bones. She told her children there was treasure at the temple site, and they ought to dig. They were greedy; they vied for attention. She lay dying by the seawall, seeing her progeny fight, watching them swing shovels and threaten each other with picks.

Her favorite nephew watched too. He had flown to Sicily on a visit from the north; he was torn between two women—a big city sophisticate and the girl next door. The grandmother stretched out a finger like a claw. He mopped her brow with flannel soaked in lemon water; he ground rosemary and garlic and fed her moistened mouthfuls of bread and olive oil. Her house was bright with broken glass embedded in cement. Barbed wire clung to the doorframe like a climbing rose.

"Giovanni?" she said.

"Grandmother?"

Her voice was as the sea on gravel. "When there's treasure, *stupido*, you look for it here." She scratched at her ribcage, then nodded. "You understand, *caro*, the heart?"

He understood, he said. Dolphins played in the white surf. This teetered on the verge of sentiment, said Winterton, but it might be profound.

Then the conductor appeared. His hair was brown, and he wore a handlebar moustache. He stood at the front of the car, expectant, gathering an audience. They quieted. "We're sorry to inform you"— he cleared his throat, repeated it—"I'm sorry to inform you of the cause of our delay. There has been an accident. A person or persons unknown has been discovered on the track. That's all I can reliably report." His voice was high. He relished the attention, clearly, and refused to answer questions. "That's the statement, folks."

Police appeared beneath the window, with leashed dogs. There were stretcher-bearers and photographers; it was beginning to rain. He said to the woman beside him, "I need air." Then he followed the conductor to the space between the cars. "Can I get out and walk?" he asked. "I'm late. I know the way." They would not let him leave. "I might be sick," he said. They pointed to the bathroom door, unlocked.

The bathroom reeked of urine; the toilet would not flush. He held his nose and gagged. He braced himself upon the sink and stared at his reflection—hawking, blear-eyed, pinched. "'The apple tree . . .'" he mouthed. What was out there on the track found him irrelevant; it proceeded at its chosen pace, and Mark was not a witness they would call.

In the next two hours, waiting, he learned what he could of the story. He heard it in bits and fragments, the narrative disjunct. A body was found on the tracks. It had been covered with branches and pine boughs and leaves. It had been a suicide, perhaps, or murder. It was female and, judging by hair color, young. The engineer had noticed the leaf pile ahead and slowed but failed to stop. By the time he identified clothing underneath the branches, and what looked like a reaching hand, he could not halt the train. No blame attached to his action. The body had been crushed. There were few identifying marks. Bone and flesh and clothing shreds were scattered on the engine, spattered on the crossties and beneath the first two cars. If the act were suicide imagine the anticipation, the self-control awaiting death; if murder, the disposal of the corpse. Forensic experts had arrived to gather evidence. Police were searching the approach roads to the overpass, and all nearby foliage. Traffic was delayed in both directions, therefore, while they combed the tracks.

"I'm leaving tomorrow," he said to his parents that night.

"For the Cape?" his father asked.

"So soon?" his mother asked.

"I need to get to work again."

"We wouldn't bother you," she said. "We'd leave a tray at the door."

"We'd screen your calls," his father said. "We'd say, 'No interviews.'"

"I didn't mean it that way. I left my work in Wellfleet."

"Coffee?"

"Please."

They settled in the living room. He tried to tell them, and could not, what had happened on the train—how his blithe assumption of the primacy of art was made to seem ridiculous by fact. It was flesh and not Karenina that spread across the track. It was rumor, not a cry for help, he heard. What impressed itself upon him was his picture in a magazine, and Betty's lush compliance in, enactment of his fantasy, was how much money they might spend for lunch. Mrs. Newcombe's ancestor spat in the coal grate. Bonnie will not take him back, will work in the Town Library; she runs off with the drummer from Spokane.

He would write it down, of course. Mark made notes. It would become his subject; he would squeeze and absorb and digest it— as might have, once, the Barone P. P. He would throw his voice. It would take him time, of course, but if it took him twenty years he'd balance the account. He would feed the canary, then cat.

Junot Díaz

EDISON, NEW JERSEY

The first time we try to deliver the Gold Crown the lights are on in the house but no one lets us in. I bang on the front door and Wayne hits the back and I can hear our double drum shaking the windows. Right then I have this feeling that someone is inside, laughing at us.

This guy better have a good excuse, Wayne says, lumbering around the newly planted rosebushes. This is bullshit.

You're telling me, I say but Wayne's the one who takes this job too seriously. He pounds some more on the door, his face jiggling. A couple of times he raps on the windows, tries squinting through the curtains. I take a more philosophical approach; I walk over to the ditch that has been cut next to the road, a drainage pipe half filled with water, and sit down. I smoke and watch a mama duck and her three ducklings scavenge the grassy bank and then float downstream like they're on the same string. Beautiful, I say but Wayne doesn't hear. He's banging on the door with the staple gun.

.   .   .

At nine Wayne picks me up at the showroom and by then I have
our route planned out. The order forms tell me everything I need to
know about the customers we'll be dealing with that day. If some-
one is just getting a fifty-two-inch card table delivered then you
know they aren't going to give you too much of a hassle but they
also aren't going to tip. Those are your Spotswood, Sayreville and
Perth Amboy deliveries. The pool tables go north to the rich sub-
urbs—Livingston, Ridgewood, Bedminster.

You should see our customers. Doctors, diplomats, surgeons, presi-
dents of universities, ladies in slacks and silk tops who sport thin watches
you could trade in for a car, who wear comfortable leather shoes. Most
of them prepare for us by laying down a path of yesterday's *Washington
Post* from the front door to the game room. I make them pick it all up. I
say: Carajo, what if we slip? Do you know what two hundred pounds of
slate could do to a floor? The threat of property damage puts the chop-
chop in their step. The best customers leave us alone until the bill has
to be signed. Every now and then we'll be given water in paper cups.
Few have offered us more, though a dentist from Ghana once gave us a
six-pack of Heineken while we worked.

Sometimes the customer has to jet to the store for cat food or
a newspaper while we're in the middle of a job. I'm sure you'll be
all right, they say. They never sound too sure. Of course, I say. Just
show us where the silver's at. The customers ha-ha and we ha-ha and
then they agonize over leaving, linger by the front door, trying to
memorize everything they own, as if they don't know where to find
us, who we work for.

Once they're gone, I don't have to worry about anyone both-
ering me. I put down the ratchet, crack my knuckles and explore,

usually while Wayne is smoothing out the felt and doesn't need help. I take cookies from the kitchen, razors from the bathroom cabinets. Some of these houses have twenty, thirty rooms. On the ride back I figure out how much loot it would take to fill up all that space. I've been caught roaming around plenty of times but you'd be surprised how quickly someone believes you're looking for the bathroom if you don't jump when you're discovered, if you just say, Hi.

After the paperwork's been signed, I have a decision to make. If the customer has been good and tipped well, we call it even and leave. If the customer has been an ass—maybe they yelled, maybe they let their kids throw golf balls at us—I ask for the bathroom. Wayne will pretend that he hasn't seen this before; he'll count the drill bits while the customer (or their maid) guides the vacuum over the floor. Excuse me, I say. I let them show me the way to the bathroom (usually I already know) and once the door is shut I cram bubble bath drops into my pockets and throw fist-sized wads of toilet paper into the toilet. I take a dump if I can and leave that for them.

Most of the time Wayne and I work well together. He's the driver and the money man and I do the lifting and handle the assholes. Tonight we're on our way to Lawrenceville and he wants to talk to me about Charlene, one of the showroom girls, the one with the blow-job lips. I haven't wanted to talk about women in months, not since the girlfriend.

I really want to pile her, he tells me. Maybe on one of the Madisons.

Man, I say, cutting my eyes towards him. Don't you have a wife or something?

He gets quiet. I'd still like to pile her, he says defensively.

And what will that do?

Why does it have to *do* anything?

Twice this year Wayne's cheated on his wife and I've heard it all, the before and the after. The last time his wife nearly tossed his ass out to the dogs. Neither of the women seemed worth it to me. One of them was even younger than Charlene. Wayne can be a moody guy and this is one of those nights; he slouches in the driver's seat and swerves through traffic, riding other people's bumpers like I've told him not to do. I don't need a collision or a four-hour silent treatment so I try to forget that I think his wife is good people and ask him if Charlene's given him any signals.

He slows the truck down. Signals like you wouldn't believe, he says.

On the days we have no deliveries the boss has us working at the showroom, selling cards and poker chips and mankala boards. Wayne spends his time skeezing the salesgirls and dusting shelves. He's a big goofy guy—I don't understand why the girls dig his shit. One of those mysteries of the universe. The boss keeps me in the front of the store, away from the pool tables. He knows I'll talk to the customers, tell them not to buy the cheap models. I'll say shit like, Stay away from those Bristols. Wait until you can get something real. Only when he needs my Spanish will he let me help on a sale. Since I'm no good at cleaning or selling slot machines I slouch behind the front register and steal. I don't ring anything up, and pocket what comes in. I don't tell Wayne. He's too busy running his fingers through his beard, keeping the waves on his nappy head in order. A hundred-buck haul's not unusual for me and back in the day, when the girlfriend used to pick me up, I'd buy her anything she wanted, dresses, silver rings, lingerie. Sometimes I blew it all on her. She didn't like the stealing but hell, we weren't made out of loot and I liked going into a place and saying, Jeva, pick out anything, it's yours. This is the closest I've come to feeling rich.

Nowadays I take the bus home and the cash stays with me. I sit next to this three-hundred-pound rock-and-roll chick who washes dishes at the Friendly's. She tells me about the roaches she kills with her water nozzle. Boils the wings right off them. On Thursday I buy myself lottery tickets—ten Quick Picks and a couple of Pick 4s. I don't bother with the little stuff.

The second time we bring the Gold Crown the heavy curtain next to the door swings up like a Spanish fan. A woman stares at me and Wayne's too busy knocking to see. Muñeca, I say. She's black and unsmiling and then the curtain drops between us, a whisper on the glass. She had on a t-shirt that said *No Problem* and didn't look like she owned the place. She looked more like the help and couldn't have been older than twenty and from the thinness of her face I pictured the rest of her skinny. We stared at each other for a second at the most, not enough for me to notice the shape of her ears or if her lips were chapped. I've fallen in love on less.

Later in the truck, on the way back to the showroom Wayne mutters, This guy is dead. I mean it.

The girlfriend calls sometimes but not often. She has found herself a new boyfriend, some zángano who works at a record store. *Dan* is his name and the way she says it, so painfully gringo, makes the corners of my eyes narrow. The clothes I'm sure this guy tears from her when they both get home from work—the chokers, the rayon skirts from the Warehouse, the lingerie—I bought with stolen money and I'm glad that none of it was earned straining my back against hundreds of pounds of raw rock. I'm glad for that.

The last time I saw her in person was in Hoboken. She was with *Dan* and hadn't yet told me about him and hurried across the street in her high clogs to avoid me and my boys, who even then could sense me turning, turning into the motherfucker who'll put a fist through anything. She flung one hand in the air but didn't stop. A month before the zángano, I went to her house, a friend visiting a friend, and her parents asked me how business was, as if I balanced the books or something. Business is outstanding, I said.

That's really wonderful to hear, the father said.

You betcha.

He asked me to help him mow his lawn and while we were dribbling gas into the tank he offered me a job. A real one that you can build on. Utilities, he said, is nothing to be ashamed of.

Later the parents went into the den to watch the Giants lose and she took me into her bathroom. She put on her makeup because we were going to a movie. If I had your eyelashes, I'd be famous, she told me. The Giants started losing real bad. I still love you, she said and I was embarrassed for the two of us, the way I'm embarrassed at those afternoon talk shows where broken couples and unhappy families let their hearts hang out.

We're friends, I said and Yes, she said, yes we are.

There wasn't much space so I had to put my heels on the edge of the bathtub. The cross I'd given her dangled down on its silver chain so I put it in my mouth to keep it from poking me in the eye. By the time we finished my legs were bloodless, broomsticks inside my rolled-down baggies and as her breathing got smaller and smaller against my neck, she said, I do, I still do.

Each payday I take out the old calculator and figure how long it'd take me to buy a pool table honestly. A top-of-the-line, three-piece slate affair doesn't come cheap. You have to buy sticks and balls and chalk and a score keeper and triangles and French tips if you're a fancy shooter. Two and a half years if I give up buying underwear and eat only pasta but even this figure's bogus. Money's never stuck to me, ever.

Most people don't realize how sophisticated pool tables are. Yes, tables have bolts and staples on the rails but these suckers hold together mostly by gravity and by the precision of their construction. If you treat a good table right it will outlast you. Believe me. Cathedrals are built like that. There are Incan roads in the Andes that even today you couldn't work a knife between two of the cobblestones. The sewers that the Romans built in Bath were so good that they weren't replaced until the 1950s. That's the sort of thing I can believe in.

These days I can build a table with my eyes closed. Depending on how rushed we are I might build the table alone, let Wayne watch until I need help putting on the slate. It's better when the customers stay out of our faces, how they react when we're done, how they run fingers on the lacquered rails and suck in their breath, the felt so tight you couldn't pluck it if you tried. Beautiful, is what they say and we always nod, talc on our fingers, nod again, beautiful.

The boss nearly kicked our asses over the Gold Crown. The customer, an asshole named Pruitt, called up crazy, said we were *delin-*

quent. That's how the boss put it. Delinquent. We knew that's what the customer called us because the boss doesn't use words like that. Look boss, I said, we knocked like crazy. I mean, we knocked like federal marshals. Like Paul Bunyan. The boss wasn't having it. You fuckos, he said. You butthogs. He tore us for a good two minutes and then *dismissed* us. For most of that night I didn't think I had a job so I hit the bars, fantasizing that I would bump into this cabrón out with that black woman while me and my boys were cranked but the next morning Wayne came by with that Gold Crown again. Both of us had hangovers. One more time, he said. An extra delivery, no overtime. We hammered on the door for ten minutes but no one answered. I jimmied with the windows and the back door and I could have sworn I heard her behind the patio door. I knocked hard and heard footsteps.

We called the boss and told him what was what and the boss called the house but no one answered. OK, the boss said. Get those card tables done. That night, as we lined up the next day's paperwork, we got a call from Pruitt and he didn't use the word delinquent. He wanted us to come late at night but we were booked. Two-month waiting list, the boss reminded him. I looked over at Wayne and wondered how much money this guy was pouring into the boss's ear. Pruitt said he was *contrite* and *determined* and asked us to come again. His maid was sure to let us in.

What the hell kind of name is Pruitt anyway? Wayne asks me when we swing onto the parkway.

Pato name, I say. Anglo or some other bog people.

Probably a fucking banker. What's the first name?

Just an initial, C. Clarence Pruitt sounds about right.

Yeah, Clarence, Wayne yuks.

Pruitt. Most of our customers have names like this, court case names: Wooley, Maynard, Gass, Binder, but the people from my town, our names, you see on convicts or coupled together on boxing cards.

We take our time. Go to the Rio Diner, blow an hour and all the dough we have in our pockets. Wayne is talking about Charlene and I'm leaning my head against a thick pane of glass.

Pruitt's neighborhood has recently gone up and only his court is complete. Gravel roams off this way and that, shaky. You can see inside the other houses, their newly formed guts, nailheads bright and sharp on the fresh timber. Wrinkled blue tarps protect wiring and fresh plaster. The driveways are mud and on each lawn stand huge stacks of sod. We park in front of Pruitt's house and bang on the door. I give Wayne a hard look when I see no car in the garage.

Yes? I hear a voice inside say.

We're the delivery guys, I yell.

A bolt slides, a lock turns, the door opens. She stands in our way, wearing black shorts and a gloss of red on her lips and I'm sweating.

Come in, yes? She stands back from the door, holding it open.

Sounds like Spanish, Wayne says.

No shit, I say, switching over. Do you remember me?

No, she says.

I look over at Wayne. Can you believe this?

I can believe anything, kid.

You heard us didn't you? The other day, that was you.

She shrugs and opens the door wider.

You better tell her to prop that with a chair. Wayne heads back to unlock the truck.

You hold that door, I say.

We've had our share of delivery trouble. Trucks break down. Customers move and leave us with an empty house. Handguns get pointed. Slate gets dropped, a rail goes missing. The felt is the wrong color, the Dufferins get left in the warehouse. Back in the day, the girlfriend and I made a game of this. A prediction game. In the mornings I rolled onto my pillow and said, What's today going to be like?

Let me check. She put her fingers up to her widow's peak and that motion would shift her breasts, her hair. We never slept under any covers, not in spring, fall or summer and our bodies were dark and thin the whole year.

I see an asshole customer, she murmured. Unbearable traffic. Wayne's going to work slow. And then you'll come home to me.

Will I get rich?

You'll come home to me. That's the best I can do. And then we'd kiss hungrily because this was how we loved each other.

The game was part of our mornings, the way our showers and our sex and our breakfasts were. We stopped playing only when it started to go wrong for us, when I'd wake up and listen to the traffic outside without waking her, when everything was a fight.

She stays in the kitchen while we work. I can hear her humming. Wayne's shaking his right hand like he's scalded his fingertips. Yes, she's fine. She has her back to me, her hands stirring around in a full sink, when I walk in.

I try to sound conciliatory. You're from the city?

A nod.

Where about?

Washington Heights.

Dominicana, I say. Quisqueyana. She nods. What street?

I don't know the address, she says. I have it written down. My mother and my brothers live there.

I'm Dominican, I say.

You don't look it.

I get a glass of water. We're both staring out at the muddy lawn.

She says, I didn't answer the door because I wanted to piss him off.

Piss who off?

I want to get out of here, she says.

Out of here?

I'll pay you for a ride.

I don't think so, I say.

Aren't you from Nueva York?

No.

Then why did you ask the address?

Why? I have family near there.

Would it be that big of a problem?

I say in English that she should have her boss bring her but she stares at me blankly. I switch over.

He's a pendejo, she says, suddenly angry. I put down the glass, move next to her to wash it. She's exactly my height and smells of liquid detergent and has tiny beautiful moles on her neck, an archipelago leading down into her clothes.

Here, she says, putting out her hand but I finish it and go back to the den.

Do you know what she wants us to do? I say to Wayne.

.   .   .

Her room is upstairs, a bed, a closet, a dresser, yellow wallpaper. Spanish *Cosmo* and *El Diario* thrown on the floor. Four hangers' worth of clothes in the closet and only the top dresser drawer is full. I put my hand on the bed and the cotton sheets are cool.

Pruitt has pictures of himself in his room. He's tan and probably has been to more countries than I know capitals for. Photos of him on vacations, on beaches, standing beside a wide-mouth Pacific salmon he's hooked. The size of his dome would have made Broca proud. The bed is made and his wardrobe spills out onto chairs and a line of dress shoes follows the far wall. A bachelor. I find an open box of Trojans in his dresser beneath a stack of boxer shorts. I put one of the condoms in my pocket and stick the rest under his bed.

I find her in her room. He likes clothes, she says.

A habit of money, I say but I can't translate it right; I end up agreeing with her. Are you going to pack?

She holds up her purse. I have everything I need. He can keep the rest of it.

You should take some of your things.

I don't care about that vaina. I just want to go.

Don't be stupid, I say. I open her dresser and pull out the shorts on top and a handful of soft bright panties fall out and roll down the front of my jeans. There are more in the drawer. I try to catch them but as soon as I touch their fabric I let everything go.

Leave it. Go on, she says and begins to put them back in the dresser, her square back to me, the movement of her hands smooth and easy.

Look, I say.

Don't worry. She doesn't look up.

I go downstairs. Wayne is sinking the bolts into the slate with the Makita. You can't do it, he says.

Why not?

Kid. We have to finish this.

I'll be back before you know it. A quick trip, in out.

Kid. He stands up slowly; he's nearly twice as old as me.

I go to the window and look out. New gingkoes stand in rows beside the driveway. A thousand years ago when I was still in college I learned something about them. Living fossils. Unchanged since their inception millions of years ago. You tagged Charlene, didn't you?

Sure did, he answers easily.

I take the truck keys out of the toolbox. I'll be right back, I promise.

My mother still has pictures of the girlfriend in her apartment. The girlfriend's the sort of person who never looks bad. There's a picture of us at the bar where I taught her to play pool. She's leaning on the Schmelke I stole for her, nearly a grand worth of cue, frowning at the shot I left her, a shot she'd go on to miss.

The picture of us in Florida is the biggest—shiny, framed, nearly a foot tall. We're in our bathing suits and the legs of some stranger frame the right. She has her butt in the sand, knees folded up in front of her because she knew I was sending the picture home to my moms; she didn't want my mother to see her bikini, didn't want my mother to think her a whore. I'm crouching next to her, smiling, one hand on her thin shoulder, one of her moles showing between my fingers.

My mother won't look at the pictures or talk about her when I'm around but my sister says she still cries over the breakup. Around me my mother's polite, sits quietly on the couch while I tell her about what I'm reading and how work has been. Do you have anyone? she asks me sometimes.

Yes, I say.

She talks to my sister on the side, says, In my dreams they're still together.

We reach the Washington Bridge without saying a word. She's emptied his cupboards and refrigerator; the bags are at her feet. She's eating corn chips but I'm too nervous to join in.

Is this the best way? she asks. The bridge doesn't seem to impress her.

It's the shortest way.

She folds the bag shut. That's what he said when I arrived last year. I wanted to see the countryside. There was too much rain to see anything anyway.

I want to ask her if she loves her boss, but I ask instead, How do you like the States?

She swings her head across at the billboards. I'm not surprised by any of it, she says.

Traffic on the bridge is bad and she has to give me an oily fiver for the toll. Are you from the Capital? I ask.

No.

I was born there. In Villa Juana. Moved here when I was a little boy.

She nods, staring out at the traffic. As we cross over the bridge I drop my hand into her lap. I leave it there, palm up, fingers slightly curled. Sometimes you just have to try, even if you know it won't work. She turns her head away slowly, facing out beyond the bridge cables, out to Manhattan and the Hudson.

Everything in Washington Heights is Dominican. You can't go a block without passing a Quisqueya Bakery or a Quisqueya Supermercado or a Hotel Quisqueya. If I were to park the truck and get out nobody would take me for a deliveryman; I could be the guy who's on the street corner selling Dominican flags. I could be on my way home to my girl. Everybody's on the streets and the merengue's falling out of windows like TVs. When we reach her block I ask a kid with the sag for the building and he points out the stoop with his pinkie. She gets out of the truck and straightens the front of her sweatshirt before following the line that the kid's finger has cut across the street. Cuídate, I say.

Wayne works on the boss and a week later I'm back, on probation, painting the warehouse. Wayne brings me meatball sandwiches from out on the road, skinny things with a seam of cheese gumming the bread.

Was it worth it? he asks me.

He's watching me close. I tell him it wasn't.

Did you at least get some?

Hell yeah, I say.

Are you sure?

Why would I lie about something like that? Homegirl was an animal. I still have the teeth marks.

Damn, he says.

I punch him in the arm. And how's it going with you and Charlene?

I don't know, man. He shakes his head and in that motion I see him out on his lawn with all his things. I just don't know about this one.

We're back on the road a week later. Buckinghams, Imperials, Gold Crowns and dozens of card tables. I keep a copy of Pruitt's paperwork and when the curiosity finally gets to me I call. The first time I get the machine. We're delivering at a house in Long Island with a view of the Sound that would break you. Wayne and I smoke a joint on the beach and I pick up a dead horseshoe crab by the tail and heave it in the customer's garage. The next two times I'm in the Bedminster area Pruitt picks up and says, Yes? But on the fourth time she answers and the sink is running on her side of the phone and she shuts it off when I don't say anything.

Was she there? Wayne asks in the truck.

Of course she was.

He runs a thumb over the front of his teeth. Pretty predictable. She's probably in love with the guy. You know how it is.

I sure do.

Don't get angry.

I'm tired, that's all.

Tired's the best way to be, he says. It really is.

He hands me the map and my fingers trace our deliveries, stitching city to city. Looks like we've gotten everything, I say.

Finally. He yawns. What's first tomorrow?

We won't really know until the morning, when I've gotten the paperwork in order but I take guesses anyway. One of our games. It passes the time, gives us something to look forward to. I close my eyes and put my hand on the map. So many towns, so many cities to choose from. Some places are sure bets but more than once I've gone with the long shot and been right.

You can't imagine how many times I've been right.

Usually the name will come to me fast, the way the numbered balls pop out during the lottery drawings, but this time nothing comes: no magic, no nothing. It could be anywhere. I open my eyes and see that Wayne is still waiting. Edison, I say, pressing my thumb down. Edison, New Jersey.

Andre Dubus

DELIVERING

Jimmy woke before the alarm, his parents' sounds coming back to him as he had known they would when finally three hours ago he knew he was about to sleep: their last fight in the kitchen, and Chris sleeping through it on the top bunk, grinding his teeth. It was nearly five now, the room sunlit; in the dark while they fought Jimmy had waited for the sound of his father's slap, and when it came he felt like he was slapping her and he waited for it again, wished for it again, but there was only the one clap of hand on face. Soon after that, she drove away.

Now he was ashamed of the slap. He reached down to his morning hardness which always he had brought to the bathroom so she wouldn't see the stain; he stopped once to turn off the alarm when he remembered it was about to ring into his quick breath. Then he stood and gently shook Chris's shoulder. He could smell the ocean. He shook Chris harder: twelve years old and chubby and still clumsy about some things. Maybe somebody else was Chris's father. No. He would stay with what he heard last night; he would not start making up more. Somewhere his mother was naked with that son of a bitch, and he squeezed Chris's shoulder and said: 'Wake up.' Besides, their faces looked alike: his and Chris's and his father's. Everybody said that. Chris stared at him.

'Come with me.'

'You're crazy.'

'I need you to.'

'You didn't say anything last night.'

'Come on.'

'You buying the doughnuts?'

'After we swim.'

In the cool room they dressed for the warm sun, in cut-off jeans and T-shirts and sneakers, and went quietly down the hall, past the closed door where Jimmy stopped and waited until he could hear his father's breath. Last night after she left, his father cried in the kitchen. Chris stood in the doorway, looking into the kitchen; Jimmy looked over his head at the table, the beer cans, his father's bent and hers straight, the ashtray filled, ashes on the table and, on the counter near the sink, bent cans and a Seagram's Seven bottle.

'Holy shit,' Chris said.

'You'd sleep through World War III.'

He got two glasses from the cupboard, reaching over the cans and bottle, holding his breath against their smell; he looked at the two glasses in the sink, her lipstick on the rim of one, and Chris said: 'What's the matter?'

'Makes me sick to smell booze in the morning.'

Chris poured the orange juice and they drank with their backs to the table. Jimmy picked up her Winston pack. Empty. Shit. He took a Pall Mall. He had learned to smoke by watching her, had started three years ago by stealing hers. He was twelve then. Would he and Chris see her alone now, or would they have to go visit her at that son of a bitch's house, wherever it was? They went out the back door and around to the front porch where the stacked papers waited, folded and tied, sixty-two of them, and a note on top saying Mr. Thompson didn't get his paper yesterday. 'It's his Goddamn dog,' he said, and cut the string and gave Chris a handful of rubber bands. Chris rolled and banded the papers while Jimmy stood on the lawn, smoking; he looked up the road at the small houses, yellow and brown and grey, all of them quiet with sleeping families, and the tall woods beyond them and, across the road, houses whose back lawns ended at the salt marsh that spread out to the northeast where the breeze came from. When he heard the rolling papers stop, he turned to Chris sitting on the porch and looking at him.

'Where's the car?'

'Mom took it.'

'This early?'

He flicked the cigarette toward the road and kneeled on the porch and started rolling.

'Where'd she go so early?'

'Late. Let's go.'

He trotted around the lawn and pushed up the garage door and went around the pickup; he did not look at Chris until he had unlocked the chain and pulled it from around the post, coiled it under his bicycle seat, and locked it there. His hands were ink-stained.

'You can leave your chain. We'll use mine at the beach.'

He took the canvas sack from its nail on the post and hung it from his right side, its strap over his left shoulder, and walked his bicycle past the truck and out into the sun. At the front porch he stuffed the papers into the sack. Then he looked at Chris.

'We're not late,' Chris said.

'She left late. Late last night.' He pushed down his kickstand. 'Hold on. Let's get these papers out.'

'She left?'

'Don't you start crying on me. Goddamnit, don't.'

Chris looked down at his handlebar.

'They had a fight,' Jimmy said.

'Then she'll be back.'

'Not this time. She's fucking somebody.'

Chris looked up, shaking his head. Shaking it, he said: 'No.'

'You want to hear about it or you just going to stand there and tell me I didn't hear what I heard.'

'Okay, tell me.'

'Shit. I was going to tell you at the beach. Wait, okay?'

'Sixty-two papers?'

'You know she's gone. Isn't that enough for a while?' He kicked up his stand. 'Look. We've hardly ever lived with both of them. It'll be like Pop's aboard ship. Only it'll be her.'

'That's not true.'

'What's not.'

'About hardly ever living with both of them.'

'It almost is. Let's go.'

Slowly across the grass, then onto the road, pumping hard, shifting gears, heading into the breeze and sun, listening for cars to their rear, sometimes looking over his shoulder at the road and

Chris's face, the sack bumping his right thigh and sliding forward but he kept shoving it back, keeping the rhythm of his pedalling and his throws: the easy ones to the left, a smooth motion across his chest like second to first, snapping the paper hard and watching it drop on the lawn; except for the people who didn't always pay on time or who bitched at him, and he hit their porches or front doors, a good hard sound in the morning quiet. He liked throwing to his right better. The first week or so he had cheated, had angled his bicycle toward the houses and thrown overhand; but then he stopped that, and rode straight, leaning back and throwing to his right, sometimes having to stop and leave his bicycle and get a paper from under a bush or a parked car in the driveway, but soon he was hitting the grass just before the porch, unless it was a house that had a door or wall shot coming, and he could do that with velocity too. Second to short. He finished his road by scaring himself, hitting Reilly's big front window instead of the wall beside it, and it shook but didn't break and when he turned his bicycle and headed back he grinned at Chris, who still looked like someone had just punched him in the mouth.

He went left up a climbing road past a pine grove, out of its shade into the warmth on his face: a long road short on customers, twelve of them scattered, and he rode faster, thinking of Chris behind him, pink-cheeked, breathing hard. Ahead on the right he saw Thompson's collie waiting on the lawn, and he pulled out a paper and pushed the sack behind his leg, then rose from the seat pumping toward the house, sitting as he left the road and bounced on earth and grass: he threw the paper thumping against the open jaws, his front tire grazing the yelping dog as it scrambled away, and he lightly hand-braked for his turn then sped out to the road again.

He threw two more to his left and started up a long steep hill for the last of the route: the road cut through woods, in shade now, standing, the bicycle slowing as the hill steepened near the hardest house of all: the Claytons' at the top of the hill, a pale green house with a deep front lawn: riding on the shoulder, holding a paper against the handlebar, standing, his legs hot and tight, then at the top he sat to throw, the bicycle slowing, leaning, and with his left hand he moved the front wheel from side to side while he twisted to his right and cocked his arm and threw; he stood on the pedals and gained balance and speed before the paper landed sliding on the walk. The road wound past trees and fifteen customers and twice that many houses. He finished quickly. Then he got off his bicycle, sweating, and folded the sack and put it in his orange nylon saddlebag, and they started back, Chris riding beside him.

From one house near the road he smelled bacon. At another he saw a woman at the kitchen window, her head down, and he looked away. Some of the papers were inside now. At Clayton's house he let the hill take him down into the shade to flat land and, Chris behind him now, he rode past the wide green and brown salt marsh, its grass leaning with the breeze that was cool and sea-tanged on his face, moving the hair at his ears. There were no houses. A fruit and vegetable stand, then the bridge over the tidal stream: a quick blue flow, the tide coming in from the channel and cove beyond a bend to the north, so he could not see them, but he knew how the cove looked this early, with green and orange charter boats tied at the wharves. An hour from now, the people would come. He and Chris and his father went a few afternoons each summer, with sandwiches and soft drinks and beer in the ice chest, and his father drank steadily but only a six-pack the whole afternoon, and they stood abreast at the rail, always near the bow, the boat anchored a mile or two out, and on lucky days filled a plastic bag with mackerel slapping tails till they died, and on unlucky ones he still loved the gentle rocking of the boat and the blue sea and the sun warmly and slowly burning him. Twice in late summer they had bottom-fished and pulled up cusks from three hundred feet, tired arm turning the reel, cusk breaking the surface with eyes pushed outward and guts in its mouth. His mother had gone once. She had not complained, had pretended to like it, but next time she told them it was too much sun, too smelly, too long. Had she been with that son of a bitch when they went fishing again? The boats headed in at five and his father inserted a cleaning board into a slot in the gunwale and handed them slick cool mackerel and he and Chris cleaned them and threw their guts and heads to the sea gulls that hovered and cried and dived until the boat reached the wharf. Sometimes they could make a gull come down and take a head from their fingers.

They rode past beach cottages and up a one-block street to the long dune that hid the sea, chained their bicycles to a telephone pole, and sprinted over loose sand and up the dune; then walking, looking at the empty beach and sea and breakers, stopping to take off sneakers and shirts. Jimmy stuffing his three bills into a sneaker, then running onto wet hard sand, into the surf cold on his feet and ankles. Chris beside him, and they both shouted at once, at the cold but to the sea as well, and ran until the water pushed at their hips and they walked out toward the sea and low sun, his feet hurting in the cold. A wave came and they turned their backs to it and he watched over his shoulder as it rose; when it broke they dived and he was riding it fast, swallowing water, and in that instant of old sea-panic he saw his father crying; he opened his eyes to the sting, his arms stretched before him, hands joined, then he was lying on the sand and the wave was gone and he stood shouting: 'All *right*.' They ran back into the sea and body-surfed until they were too cold, then walked stiffly up to higher sand. He lay on his back beside his clothes, looked at the sky; soon people would come with blankets and ice chests. Chris lay beside him. He shut his eyes.

'I was listening to the ball game when they came home. With the ear plug. They won, three to two. Lee went all the way. Rice drove in two with a double—' Bright field and uniforms under the lights in Oakland, him there too while he lay on his bunk, watching Lee working fast, Remy going to his left and diving to knock it down, on his knees for the throw in time when they came in talking past the door and down the hall to the kitchen— 'They talked low for a long time; that's when they were drinking whiskey and mostly I just heard Pop getting ice, then I don't know why but after a while I knew it was trouble, all that ice and quiet talk and when they popped cans I figured they'd finished the whiskey and they were still talking that way so I started listening. She had already told him. That's what they were talking about. Maybe she told him at the Chief's Club. She was talking nice to him—'

'What did she say?'

'She said—shit—' He opened his eyes to the blue sky, closed them again, pressed his legs into the warm sand, listened to the surf. 'She said I've tried to stop seeing him. She said Don't you believe I've tried? You think I want to hurt you? You know what it's like. I can't stop. I've tried and I can't. I wish I'd never met him. But I can't keep lying and sneaking around. And Pop said Bullshit: you mean you can't keep living here when you want to be fucking him. They didn't say anything for a minute and they popped two more cans, then she said You're right. But maybe I don't have to leave. Maybe if you'd just let me go to him when I wanted to. That's when he started yelling at her. They went at it for a long time, and I thought you'd wake up. I turned the game up loud as I could take it but it was already the ninth, then it was over, and I couldn't stop hearing them anyway. She said Jason would never say those things to her, that's all I know about that son of a bitch, his name is Jason and he's a civilian somewhere and she started yelling about all the times Pop was aboard ship he must have had a lot of women and who did he think he was anyway and she'd miss you and me and it broke her heart how much she'd miss you and me but she had to get out from under his shit, and he was yelling about she was probably fucking every day he was at sea for the whole twenty years and she said You'll never know you bastard you can just think about it for another twenty. That's when he slapped her.'

'Good.'

'Then she cried a little, not much, then they drank some more beer and talked quiet again. He was trying to make up to her, saying he was sorry he hit her and she said it was her fault, she shouldn't have said that, and she hadn't fucked anybody till Jason—'

'She said that?'

'What.'

'Fuck.'

'Yes. She was talking nice to him again, like he was a little kid, then she went to their room and packed a suitcase and he went to the front door with her, and I couldn't hear what they said. She went outside and he did too and after she drove off he came back to the kitchen and drank beer.' He raised his head and looked past his feet at a sea gull bobbing on the water beyond the breakers. 'Then he cried for a while. Then he went to bed.'

'He did?'

'Yes.'

'I've never heard him cry.'

'Me neither.'

'Why didn't you wake me up?'

'What for?'

'I don't know. I wish you had.'

'I did. This morning.'

'What's going to happen?'

'I guess she'll visit us or something.'

'What if they send Pop to sea again and we have to go live with her and that guy?'

'Don't be an asshole. He's retiring and he's going to buy that boat and we'll fish like bastards. I'm going to catch a big fucking tuna and sell it to the Japanese and buy you some weights.'

He squeezed Chris's bicep and rose, pulling him up. Chris turned his face, looking up the beach. Jimmy stepped in front of him, still holding his arm.

'Look: I heard Pop cry last night. For a long time. Loud. That's all the fucking crying I want to hear. Now let's take another wave and get some doughnuts.'

They ran into the surf, wading coldly to the wave that rose until there was no horizon, no sea, only the sky beyond it.

Dottie from tenth grade was working the counter, small and summer-brown.

'Wakefield boys are here,' Jimmy said. 'Six honey dip to go.'

He only knew her from math and talking in the halls, but the way she smiled at him, if it were any other morning, he would stay and talk, and any other day he would ask her to meet him in town tonight and go on some of the rides, squeeze her on the roller coaster, eat pizza and egg rolls at the stands, get somebody to buy them a six-pack, take it to the beach. He told her she was foxy, and got a Kool from her. Cars were on the roads now, but so many that they were slow and safe, and he and Chris rode side by side on the shoulder; Chris held the doughnut bag against the handlebar and ate while Jimmy smoked, then he reached over for the bag and ate his three. When they got near the house it looked quiet. They chained their bicycles in the garage and crept into the kitchen and past the closed door, to the bathroom. In the shower he pinched Chris's gut and said: 'No shit, we got to work on that.'

They put on gym shorts and sneakers and took their gloves and ball to the backyard.

'When we get warmed up I'm going to throw at your face, okay?'

'Okay.'

'You're still scared of it there and you're ducking and you'll get hurt that way.'

The new baseball smooth in his hand and bright in the sun, smacking in Chris's glove, coming back at him, squeezed high in the pocket and webbing, then he heard the back door and held the ball and watched his father walking out of the shade into the light. He squinted at his father's stocky body and sunburned face and arms, his rumpled hair, and motioned to Chris and heard him trotting on the grass. He was nearly as tall as his father, barely had to tilt his head to look into his eyes. He breathed the smell of last night's booze, this morning's sleep.

'I heard you guys last night,' he said. 'I already told him.'

His father's eyes shifted to Chris, then back.

'She'll come by tomorrow, take you boys to lunch.' He scratched his rump, looked over his shoulder at the house, then at Jimmy. 'Maybe later we'll go eat some lobsters. Have a talk.'

'We could cook them here,' Chris said.

'Sure. Steamers too. Okay: I'll be out in a minute.'

They watched him walk back to the house, then Jimmy touched Chris, gently pushed him, and he trotted across the lawn. They threw fly balls and grounders and one-hop throws from the outfield and straight ones to their bare chests, calling to each other, Jimmy listening to the quiet house too, seeing it darker in there, cooler, his father's closet where in a corner behind blue and khaki uniforms the shotgun leaned. He said, 'Here we go,' and threw at Chris's throat, then face, and heard the back door, his breath quickened, and he threw hard: the ball grazed the top of Chris's glove and struck his forehead and he bent over, his bare hand rubbing above his eye, then he was crying deeply and Jimmy turned to his running father, wearing his old glove, hair wet and combed, smelling of after-shave lotion, and said: 'He's all right, Pop. He's all right.'

Stuart Dybek

SAUERKRAUT SOUP

couldn't eat. Puking felt like crying. At first, I almost enjoyed it the way people do who say they had a good cry. I had a good puke or two. But I was getting tired of sleeping in a crouch.

"It's not cancer; it's not even flu," the doctor told me.

"What is it?"

"Are you nervous?"

"Puking makes me nervous."

"It's not nerves. It's lack of nerve," Harry, my best friend, a psych major, told me.

He'd come over to try exorcising it—whatever it was—with a gallon of Pisano. Like all *its*, it swam in the subconscious, that flooded sewer pipe phosphorescent with jellyfish. We believed in drink the way saints believed in angels.

It took till four in the morning to kill the Pisano, listening to Harry's current favorites, the "Moonlight Sonata" and "Ghost Trio," over and over on the little Admiral stereo with speakers unfolded like wings. We were composing a letter to a girl Harry had met at a parapsychology convention. All he'd say about her is that she lived in Ohio and had told him, "Ectoplasm is the come of the dead."

He opened the letter: "In your hair the midnight hovers. . . ."

"Take 'the' out, at least," I said.

"Why? It sounds more poetic."

"It's melodramatic."

"She's from Ohio, man. She craves melodrama."

Working on that theory, we wrote he was alone, listening to the "Moonlight Sonata," sipping wine, waiting for dawn, thinking of her far away across the prairie in Ohio, thinking of the moonlight entering her bedroom window and stealing across her body, her breasts, her thighs. We ended with the line "My dick is a moonbeam."

I watched him lick the envelope and suddenly my mouth seemed full of glue and the taste of stamps. My tongue was pasted to the roof of my mouth. I gagged. From dawn till noon I heaved up wine while Harry lay passed out on the floor, the needle clicking at the end of the record. It felt like weeping.

After a week's hunger strike against myself I still didn't know what I was protesting. Nothing like this had ever happened to me before. I did remember my father telling me he'd had an ulcer in his twenties. It was during the war. He'd just been married and was trying to get his high-school diploma in night school, working at a factory all day. Once, climbing the stairs to the El, the pain hit him so hard he doubled up and couldn't make it to the platform. He sat on the stairs groaning, listening to the trains roar overhead while rush-hour crowds shoved by him. Nobody tried to help.

"Must have figured me for a drunk," he said.

It was one of his few good stories, the only one except for the time he'd ridden a freight to Montana during the Depression, when I could imagine him young.

You're getting melodramatic, I told myself. I had begun lecturing myself, addressing myself by name. Take it easy, Frank, old boy. I would have rather said, Tony, old boy. Tony was my middle name, after a favorite uncle, a war hero at nineteen, shot up during a high-altitude bombing mission over Germany. He'd returned from the war half deaf and crazy. He'd perfected a whistle as piercing as a siren and all he did for three years was whistle and drink. He had hooded, melancholy eyes like Robert Mitchum's. His name was Anthony, but everybody called him Casey. Franklin is a name I'd never especially liked. My father said he'd given it to me because it sounded like a good business name. I'd never been successful in getting people to call me Tony. You're a Frankie, not a Tony, they'd say. Finally, I regressed to what they'd called me in the neighborhood: Marzek. Nobody used first names there, where every last name could be spit out like an insult. There was no melodrama in a last name. People are starving in this world, Marzek, and you aren't eating. Famine. War. Madness. What right do you have to suffer? Trying to hold your guts together on the Western Avenue bus riding to work. At your age Casey was taking flak over Germany.

I worked part time for an ice-cream company on Forty-seventh. Supposedly, I was going to school during the day and so I didn't get to the factory till after three, when the lines were already shut down. It was October. The lines that ran overtime in summer shut down early in fall.

A few of the production crew were usually still around, the ones who'd gotten too sticky to go home without showering, and the Greeks who'd worked in the freezers since seven A.M. still trying to thaw dry ice from their lungs and marrow. The locker room stank of piled coveralls marinating in sweat, sour milk, and the sweet ingredients of ice cream. I opened my locker and unhooked my coveralls from the handle of the push broom. That terrible lack of sympathy pervading all locker rooms hung in the air.

"Look how awful he looks," Nick said to Yorgo. "Skin and bones."

I quickly tugged on my coveralls.

"Moves like he got a popsicle up the ass," Yorgo said.

"It's a fudgsicle. Greek cure for hemorrhoids."

"He got morning sickness," Nick said.

"It's punishment for being a smartass. God is punishing you. You think you don't pay sooner or later," Yorgo said.

"I'm paying."

"You only think you're paying. Just wait. You won't believe how much more expensive it gets."

I pushed my broom along the darkened corridors, a dune of dust and green floor-cleaning compound forming before me. The floor compound reminded me of nuns. They'd sprinkle it on vomit whenever someone got sick in class. Vomit filled my thoughts and memories.

Has it come to this, Marzek?

It's what Harry had kept mumbling as I barfed up Pisano. It was his favorite expression. *Has it come to this*, he'd ask at the subway window as he paid his fare, at restaurants when they brought the check, at the end of the first movement of the "Moonlight Sonata," in letters to Ohio.

A month ago it had been summer. I'd worked production,

overtime till six P.M., saving money for school. At night I'd played softball—shortstop for a team called the Jokers. I hadn't played softball since early in high school. This was different, the city softball league. Most of the guys were older, playing after work. The park was crowded with girlfriends, wives, and kids. They spread beach blankets behind the backstop, grilled hotdogs, set out potato salad, jugs of lemonade. Sometimes, in a tight game with runners on, digging in at short, ready to break with the ball, a peace I'd never felt before would paralyze the diamond. For a moment of eternal stillness I felt as if I were cocked at the very heart of the Midwest.

We played for keggers and after the game, chaperoned by the black guys on the team, we made the rounds of the blues bars on the South Side, still wearing our black-and-gold-satin Joker jerseys. We ate slabs of barbecued ribs with slaw from smoky little storefront rib houses or stopped at takeout places along the river for shrimp. Life at its most ordinary seemed rich with possibility.

In September we played for the division championship and lost 10–9. Afterward there was a party that went on all night. We hugged and laughed and replayed the season. Two of the wives stripped their blouses off and danced in bras. The first baseman got into a fist fight with the left fielder.

When I woke hung over it was Monday. I knew I'd never see any Jokers again. I lay in bed feeling more guilty than free about not going to work. I'd worked full time all summer and had decided to take the last week off before school began. I wanted to do nothing but lie around for a solid week. My tiny apartment was crammed with books I'd been wanting to read and wouldn't have a chance to read once school started. I'd been reading Russians all summer and wanted now to concentrate on Dostoevsky.

"Anybody who spells his name so many different ways has got to be great," Harry said.

I started with *Notes from the Underground*, then read *The Possessed* and *The Idiot*. The night before school reopened I read *Crime and Punishment* in a single sitting. It was early in the morning when I closed the book, went straight to the bathroom, and threw up. That was the first time it felt like crying.

In high school the priests had cautioned us about the danger of books.

"The wrong ones will warp your mind more than it is already, Marzek."

I tried to find out what the wrong ones were so I could read them. I had already developed my basic principle of Catholic education—the Double Reverse: *(1) suspect what they teach you; (2) study what they condemn.*

My father had inadvertently helped lay the foundation of the Double Reverse. Like the priests, he'd tried to save me.

"Math," he'd say. "Learn your tables. Learn square roots!"

On Christmas and birthdays he'd shower me with slide rules, T squares, drafting kits, erector sets. Each Sunday he pored over the want ads while I read the comics. He was resigned to his job at the factory, but he was looking for jobs for me—following trends, guiding my life by the help-wanteds the way some parents relied on Dr. Spock. By the time I was in sixth grade he'd begun keeping tally sheets, statistics, plotting graphs.

"Engineers! They are always looking for engineers—electrical engineers, chemical engineers, mechanical engineers."

It was what he'd wanted to be, but he'd never had the chance to go to college.

I enrolled in drafting class, machine shop, wood shop, math. When I became the first person in the history of Holy Angels High to fail wood shop without even completing the first project, a sanding block, he became seriously concerned.

"You gotta be more practical. Get your mind on what's real. I used to read Nick Carter mysteries all the time when I was a kid. I read hundreds. Then, one day I asked myself, Is this practical or just another way they make a sucker out of you? Who's it helping? Me or Nick Carter? I never read another."

"But Shakespeare," I said.

"Shakespeare? Don't you see that one well-designed bridge is worth more than everything Shakespeare ever wrote?"

I swept my broom past the lunchroom. I thought about my first day working the production line. When they relieved me I got my lunch, thinking it was noon. It was only the ten-fifteen break. Sweeping floors seemed like relaxation after production. But people endured the line year after year. Except in Dostoevsky's novels I couldn't think of having ever met anyone purified by suffering. I didn't want Siberia. The freezers were bad enough. People were condemned to them every day—without plotting against the czar.

The cleanup shift was in the lunchroom taking one of several breaks. The men worked after the bosses had gone and were pretty much on their own so long as the machines were clean in the morning. Unlike for the production crew, a break for cleanup didn't mean a ten-cent machine coffee. It meant feasting. Most of them were Slavs, missing parts of hands and arms that had been chewed off while trying to clean machines that hadn't been properly disconnected. I could never exactly identify where in Eastern Europe any of them were from.

"Russian?" I'd ask.

No, no—vigorous denial.

"Polish?"

No. They'd smile, shaking their heads in amusement. "Lithuanian?"

Ho, ho, ho. Much laughter and poking one another. "Bohemian?"

Stunned amazement that I could suggest such a thing.

The lunch table was spread as for a buffet. Swollen gray sausages steaming garlic, raw onions, dark bread, horseradish, fish roe.

Still, despite the banquet, a sullen, suspicious air pervaded the room. Next to the cleanup crew, the Greeks from the freezer were cheerful. Not that they weren't always friendly toward me, though they were distressed that I was sweeping floors, as that had previously been "a colored's job."

"Want *y'et*?" the burly, red-bearded man missing the index fingers of both hands asked, offering rye bread spread with pigs' brains from the communal can.

Cleanup always offered me food, urging *y'et, y'et*. It rhymed with *nyet*, but I suspected it was one of those foreign words actually manufactured out of English—some contraction of "you" and "eat." They'd been concerned with my eating habits since the time they'd seen me plunge my arm up to the elbow into the whey and scoop out a handful of feta cheese from the barrel the Greeks kept in the fruit cooler.

"*Nyet, nyet*," they'd groaned then, screwing up their faces in disgust.

"*Nyet, nyet*," I said apologetically now, declining the brains, pointing to my stomach and miming the heaves. "Can't eat . . . sick . . . stomach . . ." I explained, lapsing into broken English as if they'd understand me better.

"Have to *y'et*. No *y'et*, no live."

"That's true."

"*Y'et* ice cream? Dixie cup? Creamsicle?"

"*Y'et* ice cream!" The idea startled me. After a summer of production, ice cream seemed no more edible than machinery. I wanted to sit down at this cleanup banquet table and discuss it. To find out how it had remained food for them; what it was like to work in after-hours America. They knew something they were hiding. I wanted to explore paradox with them: how was vomiting the same as crying? Dostoevsky like softball? Were factory wounds different from war wounds? We could discuss ice cream. How did working transmute it from that delight of childhood into a product as appetizing as lead? But my broom seemed to be drawing me away as if on gliders, down unswept, dark, waxed corridors.

Besides, the engineering of ice cream is another problem. This is about soup. Or *zupa*, as cleanup called it. They called it after me, the words echoing down the corridor like their final pronouncement as I glided away: *y'et zupa . . . zupa . . . zupa . . .*

I stood before my locker stripping off my coveralls, gagging on the sweaty-sweet effluvia of flavors hovering around the laundry bin—strawberry, burgundy cherry, black walnut, butter brickle. *Zupa*—chicken broth, beef barley, cream of celery—sounded like an antidote, the way black olives and goat cheese could counterbalance a morning of working with chocolate marshmallow, or pigs' brains on rye neutralize tutti-frutti.

It was six when I punched out; the deceptive light of Indian summer was still pink on the sidewalks. I walked, paycheck in my pocket, along the grassy median of Western Boulevard, traffic whizzing on both sides like sliding, computerized walls of metal and glass. Workers were racing away from the factories that lined Western, down streets that resembled nothing so much as production lines, returning to resume real lives, trailing the dreams they survived by like exhaust fumes—promotions, lotteries, jackpots, daily doubles, sex, being discovered by Hollywood, by New York, by Nashville, sex, going back to school, going into real estate, stocks, patents, sex, embezzlements, extortions, hijackings, kidnappings, wills of distant millionaire uncles, sex . . .

These were things we'd talked about all summer while the ice cream filed by. Now I was free of it, weaving slightly as I followed the wavy trails of strawlike cuttings the mowers had left. I could still feel the envy I'd had all summer for the guys riding the mowers over the boulevards, shirts off, tanning, ogling sunbathing girls while grass tossed through the almost musical rotary blades. It had seemed like freedom next to working in a factory, but those were city jobs and you had to know somebody to get one.

The factory had changed my way of thinking more in one summer than my entire education had. Beneath the *who-gives-a-shit* attitude there was something serious about it I couldn't articulate even to myself, something everyone seemed to accept, to take for granted, finally to ignore. It had to do with the way time was surrendered—I knew that, and also knew it was what my father, who'd worked in a factory all his life, had wanted to tell me. But he'd never been able to find the words either, had never heard them or read them anywhere, and so distrusted language.

My stomach was knotted. I was feeling dizzy and for a moment thought it might be because the line of grass cuttings I was following was crooked. When I stood still the colors of the trees looked ready to fly apart like the points of unmixed pigment in the van Gogh self-portrait I'd stare at every time I went to the Art Institute trying to provoke that very sensation. It wasn't a sensation I wanted to be feeling now. I sat down in the grass and lowered my head, trying to clear the spots from my eyes. I tried breathing rhythmically, looking away from the trees to the buildings across the street. The flaring light slanted orange along the brick walls in a way that made them appear two-dimensional, faked. The sky looked phony too, flat clouds like cutouts pasted on rather than floating. It looked possible to reach up and touch the sky, and poke a finger through.

I was starting to go nuts. It was one of those moments when the ordinariness is suddenly stripped away and you feel yourself teetering between futures. Then, at a restaurant across the street, under a Coca-Cola sign, I ate a bowl of soup and was reprieved.

A week later I doubt if I thought much about any of it—the weepy, wrenching heaves that felt like spitting out the name Raskolnikov, the involuntary fast, the universe turning to tissue on Western Boulevard. It was a near-miss and near-misses are easy to forget if we notice them at all. In America one takes a charmed life for granted.

Casey once told me that's what had seemed strange to him when he first got back from the war. People seemed unaware they were about to die. It took him the next three years of whistling like a siren to readjust. By then he'd drunk himself into an enlarged liver, having settled back into the old neighborhood, where the railroad viaduct separated the houses from the factories and every corner was a tavern. His entire life had become a near-miss at nineteen.

When I try to recall the times I almost died I get bogged down in childhood—repeated incidents like Swantek (who at age twelve was more psychotic than any other person I've ever met) demonstrating a new switchblade by flinging it at my head, grazing an ear as it twanged into a door. But my closest call would come a few years after that day I opted for *zupa* on Western Boulevard. It was as Casey had observed—I had no awareness of death at the time, though certainly there were strong hints.

By then the ice-cream factory was only a memory. I'd finished college and was working for the Cook County Department of Public Aid on the South Side. I was living on the North Side in an efficiency apartment half a block from the lake. It was August, hot, and for the last few days there'd been a faint, sweetly putrid smell around the refrigerator. For the first time since I'd lived there I stripped the shelves and scrubbed everything with Kitchen Klenzer. While I was at it I even cleaned under the burners on the stove.

The smell only got stronger, except now it was tinged with bleach. I tried moving the refrigerator, but it was one of those types in a recess in the wall and I couldn't budge it.

I went downstairs and rang the manager's bell. No answer. By the time I got back to my apartment the smell had permeated the entire room. I got a towel and blanket and left to sleep the night out on the beach.

As soon as I hit the street I knew something was wrong. Police and ambulance flashers whirled blue and scarlet at the end of the block, fusing into a violet throb. Shadows hurried away from the beach in the dark, cutting across lawns where sprinklers whipped under streetlights.

At the end of the sidewalk a couple of cops had a kid pinned down, his face grinding in sand, eyes rolling as if he were having a fit. Flashlights moved slowly across the dark beach and groans and crying echoed over the hollow lapping of water. I hung around long enough to find out what had happened. A local gang, ripped on drugs, had made a lightning raid with bats, knives, and chains. Apparently they were after a rival gang, but anyone out on the beach had been attacked.

Back in my apartment I smoked an old cigar, trying to smother the smell long enough to fall asleep. I was still tossing, half awake, sweating, trying to suck breath through a cold towel without smelling, when the buzzer rang around two A.M. It was Harry with a fifth of old Guckenheimer.

"What the hell's the stench in here?" he asked.

"BO?"

"No." He sniffed. "I know that smell. It's death! Yeah, death, all right—rotting, decomposing flesh . . . decay, rot, putrescence . . . . maggots, worms . . . that's it, all right, the real stuff. Where'd you hide the body?"

"Behind the fridge."

"Don't worry. You can cop an insanity plea. I'll get you a nice wing. Something quiet with the seniles—take a lot of naps. No, it gets too petty there. Maybe the hydrocephalics. You'd have to drink a lot more water to fit in. Aaaiiiyyyeee!" he suddenly screamed. "See them? There! Giant, swollen heads!" He was pointing at the window, eyes wild. "Whiskey, I need whiskey," he rasped, slugging from the bottle, then wiping his mouth with the back of his hand. "Aaaiiiyyyeee." He shuddered quietly.

Aaaiiiyyyeee had replaced *Has it come to this* in his lexicon since he'd been working at Dunning, the state mental hospital. He claimed to see hydrocephalics everywhere.

We walked out along the cooling streets, away from the lake, into a deserted neighborhood where blue neon Stars of David glowed behind grated shop windows. We were passing the old Guckenheimer, washing it down at water fountains, trading stories on our usual subjects—poverty, madness, slums, asylums—laughing like crazy. Harry kept breaking into the childhood song he'd started singing in my apartment:

> *"The worms crawl in,*
> *The worms crawl out,*
> *They turn your guts*
> *To sauerkraut. . . ."*

About four in the morning we found an open liquor store and bought another bottle. We sat drinking on a bench on the Howard Street El platform. Howard was the end of the line. El cars were stacked on the tracks, paralyzed, darkened, in lines that crossed the border into Evanston.

"We could probably walk to the next station before the train comes," Harry said.

We jumped down on the tracks and started walking, stepping carefully along the ties. The tracks looked down on the streetlights. We were even with roofs and windows reflecting moonlight. It was lovely, but we kept checking behind us for the single headlight that meant the train was coming. Then we'd have to jump the electric rail to the next set of tracks. The only danger was if we caught trains coming in both directions. We weren't saying much, our ears straining to hear the distant roar of the El, but it was perfectly still.

"This is the feeling I sometimes get in flying dreams," I said.

It was in that mood of ecstasy that I decided to piss on the third rail. It suddenly seemed like something I'd always wanted to do. I straddled it carefully and unzipped my fly. I was just ready to let go when Harry split the silence with an *Aaaiiiyyyeee*.

"What's the matter—train coming?"

"Aaaiiiyyyeee!" he repeated.

"Hydrocephalics?"

"Suppose the current goes upstream and zaps you in the dick?"

I carefully unstraddled the rail, zipping up my pants.

We were staggering now, which made it hard walking on ties, but made it to Fargo, the next station, with time to spare. When the train came we rode it three more stops, then walked east to the beach. By then a metallic sheen had spread from the auras of streetlights to the sky. In the faint blue light over the lake we were amazed at how filthy the beach was before the early crews arrived to clean it. Wire baskets overflowed. Piles of smashed cartons, cans, and bags littered the sand. It looked like the aftermath of a battle.

We began mounding garbage at the lapping edge of water the way kids mound sand for castles. A disk of new sun was rising across the lake from the general direction of Indiana. Two nuns, dressed in white with wimples like wings sprouting from their heads, glided past us and smiled.

"And the dawn comes up like thunder," Harry was singing.

We took our clothes off and lit the pyre of paper and cartons. Its flames flicked pale and fragile-looking against the sun and foil of water. We sprinkled on the last swallow of whiskey and danced around the fire, then took turns starting back in the sand and running through the blazing paper into the lake.

The squad car came jouncing over the sand just as I was digging in for another sprint. One of the cops was out before the car even stopped. He missed a tackle as I raced by him into the flames, splashing out into the water. I stayed under as long as I could, then just kept stroking out. They followed me in the car along the breakwater, loudspeaker announcing that if I would come back we could talk it over.

When I woke it was noon. I was on my bathroom floor with the mat tucked over me. In the next room Harry was saying to the landlord, "Death . . . It stinks of death in here . . . corruption . . . putrescence . . . rotting flesh . . . abandoned bones. . . . What kind of charnel house are you running here anyway?"

The janitor arrived and removed a mouse from behind the refrigerator. And sometime later a coroner told me one of the most awful deaths he'd seen was that of a man who'd urinated on the third rail.

As far as I could see, the restaurant didn't have a name except maybe Drink Coca-Cola. I went in because it had an awning—forest green with faded silver stripes. It was cranked down, shading the plate-glass window from the corona of setting sun. Forty-seventh had a number of places like it, mostly family-owned, bars that served hot lunches, little restaurants different ethnics ran, almost invisible amid McDonald's arches and Burger King driveways.

I sat on the padded stool, revolving slightly, watching the traffic go by on Western, knowing if I could eat I'd get my rhythm back and things would be all right. I picked the mimeographed menu from between the napkin dispenser and catsup bottle. Nothing unusual: hamburgers, hot beef sandwich and mashed potatoes, pork chops. Handwritten under soups was *Homemade Sauerkraut Soup*.

I'd never had sauerkraut soup before. I'd been thinking of *zupa*, but of something more medicinal, like chicken rice. "Homemade" sounded good. How could sauerkraut soup be otherwise, I thought. Who would can it?

"Yeah, ready?" the waitress asked. She was too buxom to be grandmotherly.

"Sauerkraut soup."

She brought it fast, brimming to the lip of the heavy bowl, slopping a little onto the plate beneath it. It was thick and reddish, not the blond color of sauerkraut I'd expected. The kind of soup one cuts into with the edge of the spoon. Steaming. The spoon fogging as if with breath. The peppery smell of soup rising like vapor to open the bronchial tubes. I could smell the scalded pepper and also another spice and then realized what colored the soup—paprika.

After a few sipped spoonfuls I sprinkled in more salt and oyster crackers for added nourishment. The waitress brought them in a separate bowl.

Sometimes I wonder if that place is still there on the corner of Forty-seventh. I like to think it is—hidden away like a hole card. I daydream I could go back. Drive all night, then take the bus to the factory. Open my old locker and my coveralls with STEVE stitched over the pocket would be hanging on the handle of the push broom. Walk in the grass down Western Boulevard. Sit at the counter sipping soup.

Outside, the crepe-paper colors were fading into a normal darkness. A man with a hussar's mustache, wearing a cook's apron, was cranking up the awning with a long metal rod. Neon lights were blinking on. I ordered a second bowl. I was never happier than in the next two years after I'd eaten those bowls of soup. Perhaps I was receiving a year of happiness per bowl. There are certain mystical connections to these things. Only forty cents a bowl. With my paycheck in my pocket, I could have ordered more, maybe enough for years, for a lifetime perhaps, but I thought I'd better stop while I was feeling good.

Deborah Eisenberg

THE FLAW IN THE DESIGN

float back in.

The wall brightens, dims, brightens faintly again—a calm pulse, which mine calms to match, of the pale sun's beating heart. Outside, the sky is on the move—windswept and pearly—spring is coming from a distance. In its path, scraps of city sounds waft up and away like pages torn out of a notebook. Feather pillows, deep carpet, the mirror a lake of pure light—no imprints, no traces; the room remembers no one but us. "Do we have to be careful about the time?" he says.

The voice is exceptional, rich and graceful. I turn my head to look at him. Intent, reflective, he traces my brows with his finger, and then my mouth, as if I were a photograph he's come across, mysteriously labeled in his own handwriting.

I reach for my watch from the bedside table and consider the dial—its rectitude, its innocence—then I understand the position of the hands and that, yes, rush-hour traffic will already have begun.

I pull into the driveway and turn off the ignition. Evening is descending, but inside no lights are on. The house looks unfamiliar.

It looks to me much the way it did when I saw it for the first time, years ago, before it was ours, when it was just a house the Realtor brought us to look at, all angles and sweep—flashy, and rather stark. John took to it immediately—I saw the quick alliance, his satisfaction as he ran his hand across the granite and steel. I remember, now, my faint embarrassment: I'd been taken by surprise to discover that this was what he wanted, that this was something he must have more or less been longing for.

I can just make out the shadowy figure upstairs in our bedroom. I allow myself to sit for a minute or so, then I get out of the car and close the door softly behind me.

John is at the roll-top desk, going over some papers. He might have heard me pull into the drive, or he might not have. He doesn't turn as I pause in the bedroom doorway, but he glances up when I approach to kiss him lightly on the temple. His tie is loosened: he's still in his suit. The heavy crystal tumbler is nearly full.

I turn on the desk light. "How can you see what you're doing?" I say.

I rest my hand on his shoulder and he reaches up to pat it. "Hello, sweetheart," he says. He pats my hand again, terminating, and I withdraw it. "Absolutely drowning in this stuff . . ." He rubs the bridge of his nose under his glasses frames, then directs a muzzy smile my way.

"Wouldn't it be wonderful to live in a tree," I say. "In a cave, with no receipts, no bills, no records—-just no paper at all . . ." I close my eyes for a moment. Good. Eclipsed—the day has sealed up behind me. "Oh, darling—did you happen to feed Pod?"

John blinks. "No one told me."

"It's all right. I didn't expect to be so late. Maybe Oliver thought to."

Gingerly, I stroke back John's thin, pale hair. He waits rigidly. "Any news?" I ask.

"News," he says. "Nothing to speak of, really." He turns back to the desk.

"John," I say.

"Hello, darling," he says.

"Lamb chops," Oliver observes pleasantly.

"I'm sorry, sweetie," I say. "I'm sure there's a plain pizza in the freezer, and there's some of that spinach thing left. If I had thought you'd be home tonight, I would have made something else."

"Don't I always come home, Mom?"

"'Always'?" I smile at him. "I assumed you'd be at Katie's again tonight."

"But don't I always *actually* come home? Don't I always come home *eventually*, Mom, to you?"

He seems to want me to laugh, or to pretend to, and I do. I can't ever disguise the pleasure I take in looking at him. How did John and I ever make this particular child, I always wonder. He looks absolutely nothing like either of us, with his black eyes and wild, black hair—though he does bear some resemblance to the huge oil portrait of John's grandfather that his parents have in their hallway. John's father once joked to me, are you sure you're the mother? I remember the look on John's face then—his look of reckoning, the pure coldness, as if he were calculating his disdain for his father in orderly columns. John's father noted that look, too—with a sort of gratification, I thought—then turned to me and winked.

"You're seriously not going to have any of these?" John says.

Oliver looks at the platter.

This only started recently, after Oliver went off to school. "You don't have to, darling," I say.

"You don't know what you're missing," John says.

"Hats off, Dad." Oliver nods earnestly at his father. "Philosophically watertight."

Recently, John has developed an absent little laugh to carry him past these moments with Oliver, and it does seem to me healthier, better for both of them, if John at least appears to rise above provocation.

"But don't think I'm not grateful, Mom, Dad, for the fact that we can have this beautiful dinner, in our beautiful, architecturally unimpeachable open-plan . . . *area*. And actually, Dad, I want to say how grateful I am to you in general. Don't think, just because I express myself awkwardly and my vocabulary's kind of fucked up—"

John inclines his head, with the faint, sardonic smile of expectations met.

"—Sorry, Dad. That I'm not grateful every single day for how we're able to preside as a *family* over the things of this world, and that owing to the fantastic education you've secured for me, I'll eventually be able—I mean of course with plenty of initiative and hard work or maybe with a phone call to someone from you—to follow in your footsteps and assume my rightful place on the planet, receiving beautiful Mother Earth's bounty—her crops, her oil, her precious metals and diamonds, and to cast my long, dark shadow over—"

"Darling," I say. "All right. And when you're at home, you're expected to feed Pod. We've talked about this."

Oliver clasps my wrist. "Wow, Mom, don't you find it poignant, come to think of it? I really think there's a poignancy here in this divergence of paths. Your successful son, home for a flying visit from his glamorous institution of higher education, and Pod, the companion of your son's youth, who stayed on and turned into a dog?"

"That's why you might try to remember to feed him," I say.

Oliver flashes me a smile, then ruffles grateful Pod's fur. "Poor old Pod," he says, "hasn't anyone fed you since I went away?"

"Not when you're handling food, please, Oliver," John says.

"Sorry, Dad," Oliver says, holding up his hands like an apprehended robber. "Sorry, Mom, sorry, Pod."

And there's the radiant smile again. It's no wonder that the girls are crazy about Oliver. His phone rings day and night. There are always a few racy, high-tech types running after him, as well as the attractive, well-groomed girls, so prevalent around here, who absolutely shine with poise and self-confidence—perfect girls, who are sure of their value. And yet the girls he prefers always seem to be in a bit of disarray. Sensitive, I once commented to John. "Grubby," he said.

"Don't you want the pizza?" I say. "I checked the label *scrupulously*—I promise."

"Thanks, Mom. I'm just not really hungry, though."

"I wish you would eat something," I can't help saying.

"Oh—but listen, you guys!" Oliver says. "Isn't it sad about Uncle Bob?"

"Who?" John says. He gets up to pour himself another bourbon.

"Uncle Bob? Bob? Uncle Bob, your old friend Bob Alpers?"

"Wouldn't you rather have a glass of wine, darling?" I ask.

"No," John says.

"Was Alpers testifying today?" I ask John. "I didn't realize. Did you happen to catch any of it?"

John shrugs. "A bit. All very tedious. When did this or that memo come to his attention, was it before or after such and such a meeting, and so on."

"Poor Bob," I say. "Who can remember that sort of thing?"

"Who indeed," John says.

"We used to see so much of Uncle Bob and Aunt Caroline," Oliver says.

"That's life," John says. "Things change."

"That's a wise way to look at things, Dad," Oliver nods seriously. "It's, really, I mean . . . *wise*."

"I'm astonished that you remember Bob Alpers," I say. "It's been a long time since he and your father worked together. It's been years."

"We never did work together," John says. "Strictly speaking."

Oliver turns to me. "That was back when Uncle Bob was in the whatsis, Mom, right? The private sector? And Dad used to consult?"

John's gaze fixes on the table as if he were just daring it to rise.

"But I guess you still do that, don't you. Dad—don't you still consult?"

"As you know, I consult. People who know something about something 'consult,' if you will. People hire people who know things about things. What are we saying here?"

"I'm just saving, poor Uncle Bob—"

"Where did this 'uncle' business come from?" John says.

"Let me give you some salad at least, darling. You'll eat some salad, won't you?" I put a healthy amount on Oliver's plate for him.

"I mean, picture the future, the near, desolate future," Oliver says. He shakes his head and trails off, then reaches over, sticks a finger absently right into a trickle of blood on the platter, and resumes. "There's Uncle Bob, wandering around in the night and fog, friendless and alone . . ."

John's expression freezes resolutely over as Oliver walks his fingers across the platter, leaving a bloody track.

"A pariah among all his former friends," Oliver continues, getting up to wash his hands. "Doors slam in his face, the faithless sycophants flee . . . How is poor Uncle Bob supposed to live? He can't get a job, he can't get a job bussing tables! And all just because of these . . . phony *allegations*." John and I reflexively look over at one another, but our glances bounce apart. "I mean, wow, Dad, you must know what it's like out there! You must be keeping up with the unemployment stats! Its *fierce*. Of course *I'll* be fine, owing to my outrageous abundance of natural merit or possibly to the general, um, esteem, Dad, in which you're held, but gee whiz, I mean, some of my ridiculous friends are worried to the point of throwing really up about what they're all going to do when they graduate, and yet their problems pale in comparison to Uncle Bob's."

"Was there some dramatic episode I missed today?" I say.

"Nothing," John says. "Nothing at all. Just nonsense."

"I just don't see that Bob could have been expected to foresee the problems," I say.

"Well, that's the *reasonable* view," John says. "But some of the regulations are pretty arcane, and if people are out to get you, they can make fairly routine practices look very bad."

"Oh, dear," I say. "What Caroline must be going through!"

"There's no way this will stick," John says. "It's just grandstanding."

"Gosh, Dad, that's great. Because I was somehow under the impression, from the—I mean, due to the—That is, because of the—"

"Out with it, Oliver," John says. "We're all just people, here."

"—the *evidence*, I guess is what I mean, Dad, that Bob *knew* what that land was being used for. But I guess it was all, just, what did you call that, Dad? 'Standard practice,' right?"

John looks at him. "What I said was—"

"Oops, right, you said '*routine practices*,' didn't you. Sorry, that's *different*! And anyhow, you're right. How on earth could poor Bob have guessed that those silly peasants would make such a fuss, when KGS put the land to such better use than they ever had? *Beans?* I mean, *please*. Or that KGS would be so sensitive about their lousy, peasant sportsmanship and maybe overreact a bit? You know what? We should console Uncle Bob in his travails, open up our family to receive him in the warmth of our love, let him know that we feel his pain. Would Uncle Bob ever hurt a fly? He would not! Things just have a way of *happening*, don't they! And I think we should invite Uncle Bob over, for one last piece of serious *meat*, before he gets hauled off to the slammer."

John continues simply to look at Oliver, whose eyes gleam with excitement. When I reach over and touch John's hand, he speaks. "I applaud your compassion, Oliver. But no need to squander it. I very much doubt it's going to come to that."

"Really?" Oliver says. "You do? Oh, I see what you mean. That's great, Dad. You mean that if it seems like Uncle Bob might start naming names, he'll be able to retire in style, huh."

"*Ooooo*kay," John says. "*All* right," and a white space cleaves through my brain as if I'd actually slapped Oliver, but in fact Oliver is turning to me with concern, and he touches my face. "What's the matter, Mom? Are you all right?"

"I'm fine, darling," I say. He reaches for my hand and holds it.

"You went all pale," he says.

"I applaud your interest in world affairs," John says. "But as the situation is far from simple, and as neither you nor I were *there* at the time, perhaps we should question, just this once—this once!—whether we actually have the right to sit in judgment. This will blow over in no time, Oliver, I'm happy to be able to promise you, and no one will be the worse for it. And should the moment arrive in which reason reasserts its check on your emotions, you will see that this spectacle is nothing more than a witch hunt."

"Well, *that's* good," Oliver says. "I mean, it's bad. Or it's good, it's bad, it's—"

"Do you think we might cross off and move on?" John says.

"Sure thing, Dad," Oliver says, dropping my hand.

John and Oliver appear to ripple briefly, and then a cottony silence drops over us. Even if I tried, I doubt I would be able to remember what we'd just been saying.

Oliver prongs some salad, and John and I watch as he lifts it slowly toward his mouth. It actually touches his lips, when he puts it down abruptly, as if he's just remembered something important. "So!" He beams at us. "What did you gentle people do today?"

John pauses, then gathers himself. "The office, naturally. Then I caught a bit of the hearings, as I have to surmise that you and Kate did."

"We did, Dad, that's very astute." Oliver nods seriously again, then turns to me with that high-watt smile. "Your turn, Mom."

"I went into town," I say. I stand up suddenly and walk over to the fridge, balancing myself on my fingertips against the reflective steel surface, in which I appear as a smudge. "I had an urge to go to the museum." I open the fridge as if I were looking for something, let the cool settle against me for a moment, close the door, and return to the table.

"You look so pretty, Mom!" Oliver says childishly. "Isn't Mom pretty, Dad?"

"Your mother was the prettiest girl at all the schools around," John says wearily. For a moment, we all just sit there again, as if someone had turned off the current, disengaging us.

"And what about you, Oliver?" John asks. "What news?"

"None," Oliver says, spearing some salad again.

"None?" John says. "Nothing at all happened today."

Oliver rests the fork on his plate and squints into the distance. "Gosh, Dad." He turns to John, wide-eyed. "I think that's right—nothing at all! Oh, unless you count my killing spree in Katie's physics class."

"Seriously not funny," John says.

"Whoops, sorry," Oliver says, standing up and stretching. "Anyhow, don't worry, Dad—I cleaned your gun and put it nicely back in the attic."

"*Enough*," John says.

"You bet, Dad." Oliver bends down to kiss first John and then me. "I'm going upstairs now, to download some pornography. See you fine folks later."

The moon is a cold, sizzling white tonight, caustically bright. Out the window everything looks like an X-ray; the soft world of the day is nowhere to be seen.

"When did you last talk to him about seeing Molnar?" John is sitting at the desk again. I glance at him then turn back to the window.

"He won't," I say.

"What are you looking at?" John says.

I close the blinds. "He won't see Dr. Molnar. He won't agree to see anyone. He doesn't want to take anything. He seems to be afraid it will do something to his mind." I sit down on the bed. Then I get up and sit down at the dressing table.

"Do something to his mind?" John says. "Isn't that desirable? I treat him with kid *gloves*. I'm *concerned*. But this is getting out of hand, don't you think? The raving, the grandiosity, the needling—wallow, wallow, atone, atone, avenge, avenge. And this morbid obsession with the hearings! Thank you, I do not understand what this is all about—what are we all supposed to be so tainted with? We may none of us be perfect, but one tries; one does, in my humble opinion, one's best. And explain to me, please, what the kid is doing here—what's his excuse? He should be at school."

"Darling, it's normal for a college student to want to come home from time to time."

"He's hardly 'home' in any case. For the last three days he's been with Kate every second she's not at school or asleep. I wouldn't be surprised if he actually did go to her physics class today. Why the Ericksons put up with it, I can't imagine. Have you seen that girl lately? She looks positively, what . . . *furtive*. Furtive and drained, as though she were . . . feeding some beast on the sly. What does he do to them? These wounded birds of his! It's as if he's running a hospital, providing charity transfusions to ailing vampires. That

Schaeffer girl last year—my god! And before her that awful creature who liked to take razor blades to herself."

"Darling," I say. "Darling? This is a hard world for young people."

"If any human being leads an easy life, it's that boy. Attention, education, privilege—what does he lack? He lacks nothing. The whole planet was designed for his well-being."

"Well, it's stressful to be away at school. To be studying all the time and encountering so many new ideas. And all young people like to dramatize themselves."

"I didn't," John says. "And you didn't."

That's true, I realize. John took pains, in fact, to behave unexceptionably; and I was so shy I would hardly have wanted to call attention to myself with so much as a hair ribbon. I certainly didn't want drama! I wanted a life very much like the one I'd grown up with, a life like my parents'—a cozy old house on a sloping lawn, magnolias and lilacs, the sun like a benign monarch, the fragrance of a mown lawn, the pear tree a gentle torch against the blue fall sky, sleds and the children's bicycles out front, no more than that, a music box life, the chiming days.

"Young people go through things. I don't think we should allow ourselves to become alarmed. He hasn't lost his sense of humor, after all, and—"

"His—ex*cuse* me?"

"—and his grades certainly don't reflect a problem. I know you're thinking of what's best for him. I know you've benefited, but he's very afraid of medication. I don't think he should be forced to—"

"No one's forcing anyone to do anything here," John says. "*Jesus.*"

"John, we don't really have a gun in the house, do we?"

"Oh for god's sake," John says. "We don't even *really* have an attic."

"Just try to be patient with him," I say. "He loves you, darling—he respects you."

"I rue the day I ever agreed to work outside of the country," John says.

"Oh, John, don't say that, darling! Even when it was difficult, it was a fascinating life for us all. And Oliver was very happy."

"I *curse* the day," John says.

Strange . . . Yes, strange to think that we used to move around so much. And then we came back and settled down here, in a government town, where everyone else is always moving. Every four years, every eight years, a new population. And yet, everyone who arrives always looks just the same as the ones who left—as if it were all a giant square dance.

"What?" John says.

"How did Bob look?" I ask.

"Bob?" he says. "Older."

Driving back along the highway this afternoon, flowing along in the reflections on the windshield, the shadows of the branches—it was like being underwater. Morning, evening, from one shore to the oilier, the passage between them is your body.

I stroke Oliver's hair, but his jaw is clamped tightly shut and he's staring up at the ceiling, his eyes glazed with tears.

When he was little, he and I used to be on his bed like this and often I'd read to him, or tell him stories, and he liked to pretend that he and I were characters from the stories—an enchanted prince and a fairy, the fairy who put the spell on him or the one who removes it, or Hansel and Gretel, and we would hide under the covers from whatever wicked witch. His imagination was so vivid that sometimes I even became frightened myself.

Yesterday I was sorting through some papers upstairs at my desk, when I noticed him and Kate outside on the lawn. He was holding the lapels of her jacket and they were clearly talking, as they always seem to be, with tremendous seriousness, as if they were explorers calculating how to survive on their last provisions. I could see Kate's round, rather sweet face—at least it's sweet when its not flickering with doubts, worries, fears—and then Oliver held her to him, and all I could see of her was her shiny, taffy-colored hair, pinned loosely up.

It's an affecting romance. It's not likely to last long, though—none of Oliver's romances do, however intense they seem to be. Oliver is way too young. In any case, I can't help imagining a warm young woman as a daughter-in-law, someone who would be glad for my company, rather than someone beset, as Kate always seems to be, by suspicion and resentment.

They came inside, and I could hear Oliver talking. The house was so silent I didn't have to make any effort to hear the story he was telling, a story I'd certainly never told him myself, which he must have heard from the help someplace we'd lived or stayed during our time away, a strange, winding folk tale, it seemed to be, about a man who had been granted the power to understand the language of the animals.

Oliver spoke slowly, in a searching way, as if vivid but puzzling events were being disclosed to him one by one. Kate said not a word, and I was sure that the two of them were touching in some way, lying on the sofa feet to feet, or holding hands, or clasped together, looking over one another's shoulders into the glimmering mist that fans out from a story. And in the long silences I could feel her uneasiness as she waited for him to find the way to proceed. It was as if they were sleeping, making something together in their sleep—an act of memory. But I was a stranger to it, following on my own as morning after morning the poor farmer discovers the broken pots, the palm wine gone—as finally one night he waits in the dark, watching, then chases the thieving deer through the fields and hills all the way to the council of the animals—as the Leopard King, in reparations, grants him the spectacular power on condition that he never reveal it—as the farmer and his wife prosper from this power, year after year.

The story spiraled in until the farmer, now wealthy, is forced to face an enraged accuser: "I was not laughing at you," he says in desperation. "I laughed because I heard a little mouse say, *I'm so hungry—I'm going into the kitchen to steal a bit of the master's grain.*"

Oliver paused to let the story waver on its fulcrum and the shame of eavesdropping broke over me in a wave, but before I could get up and shut the door of the room or make some other alerting noise, Kate spoke. Her voice was blurred and sorrowful. "What happened then?" she said, but it was clearly less a question than a ritual acknowledgment of the impending.

"Then?" Oliver said. "So—" He seemed to awaken, and shed the memory. "—then, as all the people of the village watched, the man's lifeless body fell to the ground."

All that time we were away, during his childhood—which seems as remote to me now as the places where we were—and John was working so hard, Oliver was my companion, my darling, my *heart*. And I was shocked, I suppose, to be reminded yesterday that his childhood could not have been more different from mine, that he and I—who hardly even have to speak, often, to understand one another completely—are divided by that reality, by the differences between our earliest, most fundamental sense of the world we live in. I had never stopped to think, before, that he had heard stories from beyond the boundaries of my world. And I was really *shocked*, actually, that it was one of those stories, a story I never could have told him, that he had chosen to recount to Kate.

My gaze wanders around his pristine room, as orderly as a tribute. When he's away, no one would think of disturbing anything he has here, of course, any of his possessions. But I do sometimes come in and sit on his bed.

He's still focused at the ceiling as though he were urgently counting. "Shall I leave you alone, darling?" I say. "Would you like me to leave you alone?" But he reaches for my hand.

"Oliver?" I say. "Darling?"

He blinks. His startling, long, thick eyelashes sweep down and up; his eyes glisten. "Darling, Katie is a dear girl, but sometimes I worry that she's too dependent on you. You can't be responsible for her, you know."

He draws a breath and licks his dry lips. "I can't be responsible for anything, Ma, haven't you noticed?"

"That's not true, darling. You're a very responsible person. But I just want to be sure that you and Katie are using protection."

He laughs, without lifting his head or closing his eyes, and I can tell how shallowly he's breathing. "Protection against what, Ma? Protection against Evildoers?"

"I don't want to pry, darling. I just want to set myself at ease on that score."

"Be at ease, Ma. Be very at ease. You can put down your knitting, because whatever you're fantasizing just isn't the case."

Well, I don't know. I remember, when we returned to the States, how it seemed to me, the onslaught of graphic images that are used to sell things—everywhere the perfect, shining, powerful young bodies, nearly naked, the flashing teeth, the empty, perfect, predatory faces, the threat of sexual ridicule, the spectre of sexual inadequacy if you fail to buy the critical brand of plastic wrap or insurance or macaroni and cheese. Either the images really had proliferated and coarsened during our absence or else I had temporarily lost something that had once kept the assault from affecting me.

I became accustomed to it again soon enough, though, and I don't know that I would have remembered the feeling now, that feeling of being battered and soiled, unless I'd just been reminded of Oliver's expression when, for example, we would turn on the television and that harsh, carnal laughter would erupt.

Maybe Oliver's fastidiousness, his severity, is typical of his generation. These things come in waves, and I know that many of Oliver's friends have seen older brothers and sisters badly damaged by all sorts of excesses. And it is a fact that Oliver spent his early childhood in places where there was a certain amount of hostility toward us—not us personally, of course, but toward our culture, I suppose, as it was perceived, and it wouldn't be all that remarkable, I suppose, if his view of his native country had been tarnished before he ever really came to live in it.

There were a lot of changes occurring in all the places where John had to go, and foreigners, like ourselves, from developed countries, were seen to represent those changes. Fortunately, most of the people we encountered personally received us, and the changes that accompanied us, with great enthusiasm.

In time, it came to feel to me as though we were standing in a shrinking pool of light, with shapes moving at the edges, but, especially at first, I was delighted by the kindness, the hospitality of the local officials, by parties at the embassies. Everyone was always kind to Oliver, in any case—more than kind.

And there were always children around for Oliver to play with, the children of other people who had come to help, the engineers and agronomists and contractors of various sorts and people who were conducting studies or surveys, and children of the government officials to whose parties we went and so on, who invariably spoke English. And sometimes there would he a maid on the premises, or a gardener, who had children. But when we would drive by local markets or compounds, or even fenced-off areas, Oliver would cry—he would *scream*—to play with the children he saw outside the car window.

John would explain, quietly and tirelessly, about languages, about customs, about illnesses. We brought Oliver up to share—naturally—but how does a child *share* with another child who has nothing at all? I always thought, and I still think, that John was absolutely right to be cautious, but the fact is, when Oliver was a bit older and John was away for some days, I would sometimes relent and let Oliver play with some of the children whom, for whatever reason, he found so alluring.

Oliver had spent so little time on the planet, so all those places we went were really his life—his entire life until we came back—and maybe I didn't take adequate account of that. Sometimes now, when I hear one of those names—Nigeria, or Burma, or Ecuador—any of the names of places where we spent time—it is as lustrous to me as it was before I had ever traveled. But usually what those names bring to my mind now are only the houses where we stayed, all the houses, arranged for us by the various companies John was attached to, similarly well equipped and comfortable, where I spent so much time waiting for John and working out how to bring up a child in an unfamiliar place.

Oh, there were beautiful things, of course—many beautiful and exciting things. Startling landscapes, and the almost physical thrill of encountering unaccustomed languages and unaccustomed people, their music, their clothing, their faces, the food—the sharp, dizzying flash of possibilities revealed—trips into the hectic, noisy, astonishing towns and cities.

Sometimes, on a Sunday afternoon, when he wasn't traveling around, John liked to go to a fancy hotel if there was one in our area, and have a comically lavish lunch. Or, if we were someplace where the English had had a significant presence, a tea—which was Oliver's favorite, because of the little cakes and all the different treats and the complicated silver services.

There was the most glamorous hotel, so serene, so grand. The waiters were handsome—truly glorious—all in white linen uniforms that made their skin look like satin, dark satin. And their smiles—well, those smiles made you feel that life was worth living! And of course they were charming to Oliver, they could not have been more charming.

And there were elegant, tall windows overlooking the street, with heavy, shining glass that was very effective against the heat and noise, with long, white drapes hanging at their sides. It was really bliss to stop at that hotel, such a feeling of well-being to sip your tea, watching the silent bustle of the street outside the window. And then one afternoon, beyond the heavy glass—I was just pouring John a second cup, which I remember because I upset it, saucer and all, and could never get the spot out of my lovely yellow dress—there was a sort of explosion, and there was that dull, vast, sound of particles, unified, rising like an ocean wave, and everyone on the street was running.

Well, we were all a bit paralyzed, apparently, transfixed in our velvety little chairs—but immediately there was a *whoosh*, and the faint high ringing of the drapery hardware as the waiters rushed to draw the long, white drapes closed.

Early on, John would sometimes describe to me his vision of the burgeoning world—lush mineral fields that lie beneath the surface of the earth and the plenitude they could generate, great arteries of oil that could be made to flow to every part of the planet, immense hydroelectric dams producing cascades of energy. A degree of upheaval was inevitable, he said, painful adjustments were inevitable, but one had to keep firmly in mind the long-term benefits—the inevitable increases in employment and industry, the desperately needed revenues.

Well, in practice things are never as clear, I suppose, as they are in the abstract; things that are accomplished have to *get* accomplished in one way or another. And in fairly fluid situations, certain sorts of people will always find opportunities. And that, of course, is bound to affect everyone involved, to however slight a degree.

In any case, eventually there was a certain atmosphere. And there were insinuations in the press and rumors about the company John was working with, and it just wasn't fun for John anymore.

It was an uncomfortable, silent ride to the airport when we finally did come back for good. I remember Oliver staring out the window at the shanties and the scrub and the barbed wire as John drove. There was a low, black billowing in the sky to one side of us, fire in the distance, whether it was just brush or something more—crops or a village or an oil field, I really don't know. And after we returned, there was a very bad patch for John, for all of us, though John certainly had done well enough financially. Many people had done very well.

"What is it, darling?" I ask Oliver. "Please tell me. Is one of your courses troubling you?"

He turns to gaze at me. "One of my courses?" His face is damp.

"You're not eating at all. I'm so worried about you, sweetheart."

"Ma, can't you see me? I can see you. I can see everything, Ma. Sometimes I feel like I can see through skin, through bone, through the surface of the earth. I can see cells doing their work, Ma—I can see thoughts as they form. I can hear everything, everything that's happening. Don't you hear the giant footfalls, the marauder coming, cracking the earth, shaking the roots of the giant trees? What can we do, Ma? We can't hide."

"Darling, there's nothing to be frightened of. We're not in any danger."

"His brain looks like a refinery at night, Ma. The little bolts of lightning combusting, shooting between the towers, all the lights blinking and moving . . ."

"Darling—" I smile, but my heart is pounding. "Your father loves you dearly."

"Mother!" He sits bolt upright and grabs me by the shoulders. "Mother, I've got one more minute—can't you see me, there, way off in the distance, coming apart, flailing up the hill, all the gears and levers breaking apart, falling off—flailing up the hill at the last moment, while the tight little ball of fire hisses and spits and falls toward the sea? He'll close his fist. Ma, he'll snuff it out. Are you protected by a magic cloak? The cloak of the prettiest girl at school?"

"Please, darling—" I try to disengage myself gently, and he flops back down.

"Oh, God," he says.

"What, darling? Tell me. Please try to tell me so that I can understand. So that I can understand what is happening. So I can try to help you."

"It's all breaking up, Ma. How long do I have? I'm jumping from floe to floe. Do I have a minute? Do I have another minute after that? Do I have another minute after that?"

I run my hands over his face, to clear the tears and sweat. "This is a feeling, darling," I say. My heart is lodged high up near my throat, pounding, as if it's trying to exit my body. "It's just a feeling of pressure. We've all experienced something like it at one time or another. You have to remember that it's not possible for you to fix every problem in the world. Frankly, darling, no one has appointed you king of the planet." I force myself to smile.

"Every breath I take is a theft," he says.

"Oliver!" I say. "Please! Oh, darling, listen. Do you want to stay home for a while? Do you want to drop one of your courses. Tell me how to help you, sweetheart, and I will."

"It's no use, Ma. There's no way out. It was settled for me so long ago, and now here's your poor boy, his head all in pieces, just howling at the moon."

During that whole, long time, when we were away, I used to dream that I was coming home. Almost every night, for a long time. I dreamed that I was coming home. I still dream that I am coming home.

I stand, for a moment, outside the bedroom door.

"Well, there you are," John says, when I bring myself to open it. "I was calling for you. Didn't you hear me?"

"I was . . . Do we have any aspirin?"

"Come in," he says. "Why don't you come in?"

The blinds are drawn, the house is a thin shell. The acid moonlight pours down, scalding.

"Talking to your son?" he asks.

"John?" I say. "Do you remember if Oliver ever had a nurse—maybe in Africa—who told him stories?"

"A 'nurse'?" John says. "Is he having some sort of nineteenth-century European colonial hallucination?"

I sit down at the dressing table. In the mirror, I watch John pacing slowly back and forth. "He needs reassurance from you, darling," I say. "He needs your approval."

"My approval? Actually, it seems that I need *his* approval. After all, I'm an arch criminal, he must have mentioned it—he's not one to let the opportunity slip by. I'm responsible for every ill on the planet, didn't he spell it out for you? Poverty? My fault. Injustice? My fault. War somewhere? Secret prisons? Torture? My fault. Falling rate of literacy? Rising rate of infant mortality? Catastrophic climate change? New lethal viruses? My fault, whatever is wrong, whatever might someday go wrong, whatever some nut thinks might someday go wrong, it's all my fault, did he not happen to mention that? The whole world, the future, whose fault can any of it be? Must be dear old Dad's."

I rest my head in my hands and close my eyes. When I open them again, John is looking at me in the mirror.

After a moment, he shakes his head and looks away. "I noticed we're running low on coffee," he says.

I turn around, stricken, to face him. A neat, foil packet, weighing exactly a pound—such a simple thing to have failed at! "I meant to pick some up today—I completely forgot. I'm so sorry, darling. But there's enough for you in the morning."

He looks back at me, sadly, almost pityingly, as if he had just read a dossier describing all my shortcomings. "Enough for me?" he says. "But what about you? What will you do?"

"I don't mind," I say. "It doesn't matter—it's fine. I'll get some later—I have to do a big shop tomorrow, anyhow."

"No," he says. "I'll go out now. Someplace will still be open."

John's car pulls out. The sound shrinks into a tiny dot and I feel it vanish with a little, inaudible *pop*. I listen, but I can't hear a thing from Oliver's room—no music, or sounds of movement. I'll check on him later, after John has gone to sleep. I begin to brush my hair. It's surprisingly soothing—it always has been; it's like an erasure.

It's extreme to say, "I do my best." That can never quite be true, and in my opinion it's often just a pretext for self-pity, or self-congratulation—an excuse to give yourself leeway. Still, I do *try*. I try reasonably hard to be sincerely cheerful, and to do what I can. Of course I understand Oliver's feeling—that he's lashed to the controls of some machine that eats up whatever is in its path. But this is something he'll grow out of. As John says, this is some sort of performance Oliver is putting on for himself, some melodrama. And ultimately, people learn to get on with things. At least in your personal life, your life among the people you know and live with, you try to live responsibly. And when you have occasion to observe the difficult lives that others have to bear, you try to feel gratitude for your own good fortune.

I did manage to throw out his card. I couldn't help seeing the name; the address of his office twinkled by. But I made an effort to cleanse them from my mind right away, and I think I'd succeeded by the time the card landed in the trash basket.

There's no chance that he would turn out to be the person who appeared to me this afternoon, really no chance at all. And I doubt I'm the person he was imagining, either—which for all I know, actually, was simply a demented slut. And the fact is, that while I might not be doing Oliver or John much good, I'm certainly in a position to do them both a great deal of harm.

I'd intended to stay in today, to run some errands, to get down to some paperwork myself. But there we are. The things that are hidden! I felt such a longing to go into town, to go to the museum. It's not something I often do, but it's been a difficult week, grueling, really, with Oliver here, ranging about as if he were in a cage, talking talking talking about those hearings and heaven only knows what—and I kept picturing the silent, white galleries.

Looking at a painting takes a certain composure, a certain resolve, but when you really do look at one it can be like a door swinging open, a sensation, however brief, of vaulting freedom. It's as if, for a moment, you were a different person, with different eyes and different capacities and a different history—a sensation, really, that's a lot like hope.

It was probably around eleven when I parked the car and went down into the metro. There was that awful, artificial light, like a disinfectant, and the people, silhouettes, standing and walking, the shapeless, senseless sounds. The trains pass through in gray streaks, and it's as if you've always been there and you always will be. You can sense the cameras, now, too—that's all new, I think, or relatively new—and you can even see some of them, big, empty eyes that miss nothing. You could be anywhere, anywhere at all; you could be an unknowing participant in a secret experiment. And with all those lives streaking toward you and streaking away, you feel so strongly, don't you, the singularity and the accidentalness of your own life.

We passed each other on the platform. I hadn't particularly noticed him until that second, and yet in some way he'd impressed himself so forcibly upon me it was as if I'd known him elsewhere.

I walked on for what seemed to be a long interval before I allowed myself to turn around—and he was turning, too, of course, at just the same instant. We looked at each other, and we smiled, just a little, and then I turned and went on my way again.

When I reached the end of the platform, I turned back, and he was waiting.

He was handsome, yes, and maybe that was all it was about, really. And maybe it was just that beautiful appearance of his that caused his beautiful clothing, too, his beautiful overcoat and scarf and shoes to seem, themselves, like an expression of merit, of integrity, of something attended to properly and tenderly, rather than an expression of mere vanity, for instance, or greed.

Because, there are a lot of attractive men in this world, and if one of them happens to be standing there, well, that's nice, but that's that. This is a different thing. The truth is that people's faces contain specific messages, people's faces are secret messages for certain other people. And when I saw this particular face, I thought, oh, yes—so that's it.

The sky was scudding by out the taxi window, and we hardly spoke—just phrases, streamers caught for an instant as they flashed past in the bright, tumultuous air. And no one at the reception desk looked at us knowingly or scornfully, despite the absence of luggage and the classically suspect hour. It was as solemn and grand, in its way, as a wedding.

We had taken the taxi, had stood at the desk; *we had done it*—the thought kept tumbling over me like pealing bells as we rose up in the elevator, our hands lightly clasped. And we were solemn, and so happy, or at least I was, as we entered our room, the beautiful room that we might as well have been the first people ever to see—elated as if by some solution, when just minutes before we'd been on the metro platform, clinging fiercely, as if before a decisive separation, the way lovers do in wartime.

Jeffrey Eugenides

GREAT EXPERIMENT

I f you're so smart, how come you're not rich?"

It was the city that wanted to know. Chicago, refulgent in early-evening, late-capitalist light. Kendall was in a penthouse apartment (not his) of an all-cash building on Lake Shore Drive. The view straight ahead was of water, eighteen floors below. But if you pressed your face to the glass, as Kendall was doing, you could see the biscuit-colored beach running down to Navy Pier, where they were just now lighting the Ferris wheel.

The gray Gothic stone of the Tribune Tower, the black steel of the Mies building just next door—these weren't the colors of the new Chicago. Developers were listening to Danish architects who were listening to nature, and so the latest condominium towers were all going organic. They had light-green façades and undulating rooflines, like blades of grass bending in the wind.

There had been a prairie here once. The condos told you so.

Kendall was gazing at the luxury buildings and thinking about the people who lived in them (not him) and wondering what they knew that he didn't. He shifted his forehead against the glass and heard paper crinkling. A yellow Post-it was stuck to his forehead. Piasecki must have come in while Kendall was napping at his desk and left it there.

The Post-it said: "Think about it."

Kendall crumpled it up and threw it in the wastebasket. Then he went back to staring out the window at the glittering Gold Coast.

For sixteen years now, Chicago had given Kendall the benefit of the doubt. It had welcomed him when he arrived with his "song cycle" of poems composed at the Iowa Writers' Workshop. It had been impressed with his medley of high-I.Q. jobs the first years out: proofreader for *The Baffler*; Latin instructor at the Latin School. For someone in his early twenties to have graduated summa cum laude from Amherst, to have been given a Michener grant, and to have published, one year out of Iowa City, an unremittingly bleak villanelle in the *T.L.S.*, all these things were marks of promise, back then. If Chicago had begun to doubt Kendall's intelligence when he turned thirty, he hadn't noticed. He worked as an editor at a small publishing house, Great Experiment, which published five titles per year. The house was owned by Jimmy Dimon, now eighty-two. In Chicago, people remembered Jimmy Dimon more from his days as a State Street pornographer back in the sixties and seventies and less from his much longer life as a free-speech advocate and publisher of libertarian books. It was Jimmy's penthouse that Kendall worked out of, Jimmy's high-priced view he was taking in. He was still mentally acute, Jimmy was. He was hard of hearing but if you shouted in his ear the old man's blue eyes gleamed with mischief and undying rebellion.

Kendall pulled himself away from the window and walked back to his desk, where he picked up the book that was lying there. The book was Alexis de Tocqueville's "Democracy in America." Tocqueville, from whom Jimmy had got the name for Great Experiment Books, was one of Jimmy's passions. One evening six months ago, after his nightly Martini, Jimmy had decided that what the country needed was a super-abridged version of Tocqueville's seminal work, culling all of the predictions the Frenchman had made about America, but especially those that showed the Bush Administration in its worst light. So that was what Kendall had been doing for the past week, reading through "Democracy in America" and picking out particularly tasty selections. Like the opening, for instance: "Among the novel objects that attracted my attention during my stay in the United States, nothing struck me more forcibly than the general equality of condition among the people."

"How damning is that?" Jimmy had shouted, when Kendall read the passage to him over the phone. "What could be less in supply, in Bush's America, than equality of condition!"

Jimmy wanted to call the little book "The Pocket Democracy." After his initial inspiration, he'd handed off the project to Kendall. At first, Kendall had tried to read the book straight through, but now he skipped around in Volumes I and II. Lots of parts were unspeakably boring: methodologies of American jurisprudence, examinations of the American system of townships. Jimmy was interested only in the prescient bits. "Democracy in America" was like the stories parents told their grown children about their toddler days, recalling early signs of business acumen or religious inclination, describing speech impediments that had long ago disappeared. It was curious to read a Frenchman writing about America when America was small, unthreatening, and admirable, when it was still something underappreciated that the French could claim as their own and champion, like serial music or the novels of John Fante.

> In these, as in the forests of the Old World, destruction was perpetually going on. The ruins of vegetation were heaped upon one another; but there was no laboring hand to remove them, and their decay was not rapid enough to make room for the continual work of reproduction. Climbing plants, grasses, and other herbs forced their way through the mass of dying trees; they crept along their bending trunks, found nourishment in their dusty cavities and a passage beneath the lifeless bark. Thus decay gave its assistance to life.

How beautiful that was! How wonderful to imagine what America had been like in 1831, before the strip malls and the highways, before the suburbs and the exurbs, back when the lake shores were "embosomed in forests coeval with the world." What had the country been like in its infancy? Most important, where had things gone wrong and how could we find our way back? How did decay give its assistance to life?

A lot of what Tocqueville described sounded nothing like the America Kendall knew. Other judgments seemed to part a curtain, revealing American qualities too intrinsic for him to have noticed before. The growing unease Kendall felt at being an American, his sense that his formative years, during the Cold War, had led him to unthinkingly accept various national pieties, that he'd been propagandized as efficiently as a kid growing up in Moscow at the time, made him want, now, to get a mental grip on this experiment called America.

Yet the more he read about the America of 1831, the more Kendall became aware of how little he knew about the America of today, 2005, what its citizens believed, and how they operated.

Piasecki was a perfect example. At the Coq d'Or the other night, he had said, "If you and I weren't so honest we could make a lot of money."

"What do you mean?"

Piasecki was Dimon's accountant. He came on Fridays, to pay bills and handle Dimon's books. He was pale, perspirey, with limp blond hair combed straight back from his oblong forehead.

"He doesn't check anything, O.K.?" Piasecki said. "He doesn't even know how much money he has."

"How much does he have?"

"That's confidential information," Piasecki said. "First thing they teach you at accounting school. Zip your lips."

Kendall didn't press. He was leery of getting Piasecki going on the subject of accounting. When Arthur Andersen had imploded, in 2002, Piasecki, along with eighty-five thousand other employees, had lost his job. The blow had left him slightly unhinged. His weight fluctuated, he chewed diet pills and Nicorette. He drank a lot.

Now in the shadowy, red-leather bar, crowded with happy-hour patrons, Piasecki ordered a Scotch. So Kendall did, too.

"Would you like the executive pour?" the waiter asked.

Kendall would never be an executive. But he could have the executive pour. "Yes," he said.

For a moment they were silent, staring at the television screen, tuned to a late-season baseball game. Two newfangled Western

Division teams were playing. Kendall didn't recognize the uniforms. Even baseball had been adulterated.

"I don't know," Piasecki said. "It's just that, once you've been screwed like I've been, you start to see things different. I grew up thinking that most people played by the rules. But after everything went down with Andersen the way it did—I mean, to scapegoat an entire company for what a few bad apples did on behalf of Ken Lay and Enron . . ." He didn't finish the thought. His eyes grew bright with fresh anguish.

The tumblers, the mini-barrels of Scotch, arrived at their table. They finished the first round and ordered another. Piasecki helped himself to the complimentary hors d'oeuvres.

"Nine people out of ten, in our position, they'd at least think about it," he said. "I mean, this fucking guy! How'd he make his money in the first place? On twats. That was his angle. Jimmy pioneered the beaver shot. He knew tits and ass were over. Didn't even bother with them. And now he's some kind of saint? Some kind of political activist? You don't buy that horseshit, do you?"

"Actually," Kendall said, "I do."

"Because of those books you publish? I see the numbers on those, O.K.? You lose money every year. Nobody reads that stuff."

"We sold five thousand copies of 'The Federalist Papers,'" Kendall said in defense.

"Mostly in Wyoming," Piasecki countered.

"Jimmy puts his money to good use. What about all the contributions he makes to the A.C.L.U.?" Kendall felt inclined to add, "The publishing house is only one facet of what he does."

"O.K., forget Jimmy for a minute," Piasecki said. "I'm just saying, look at this country. Bush-Clinton-Bush-maybe Clinton. That's not a democracy, O.K.? That's a dynastic monarchy. What are people like us supposed to do? What would be so bad if we just skimmed a little cream off the top? Just a little skimming. I'm telling you I think about it sometimes. I fucking hate my life. Do I think about it? Yeah. I'm already convicted. They convicted all of us and took away our livelihood, whether we were honest or not. So I'm thinking, if I'm guilty already, then who gives a shit?"

When Kendall was drunk, when he was in odd surroundings like the Coq d'Or, when someone's misery was on display in front of him, in moments like this, Kendall still felt like a poet. He could feel the words rumbling somewhere in the back of his mind, as though he still had the diligence to write them down. He took in the bruise-colored bags under Piasecki's eyes, the addict-like clenching of his jaw muscles, his bad suit, his corn-silk hair, and the blue Tour de France sunglasses pushed up on his head.

"Let me ask you something," Piasecki said. "How old are you?"

"Forty-five," Kendall said.

"You want to be an editor at a small-time place like Great Experiment the rest of your life?"

"I don't want to do anything for the rest of my life," Kendall said, smiling.

"Jimmy doesn't give you health care, does he?"

"No," Kendall allowed.

"All the money he's got and you and me are both freelance. And you think he's some kind of social crusader."

"My wife thinks that's terrible, too."

"Your wife is smart," Piasecki said, nodding with approval. "Maybe I should be talking to her."

·   ·   ·

The train out to Oak Park was stuffy, grim, almost penal in its depri-
vation. It rattled on the tracks, its lights flickering. During moments
of illumination Kendall read his Tocqueville. "The ruin of these
tribes began from the day when Europeans landed on their shores;
it has proceeded ever since, and we are now witnessing its comple-
tion." With a jolt, the train reached the bridge and began crossing
the river. On the opposite shore, glass-and-steel structures of breath-
taking design were cantilevered over the water, all aglow. "Those
coasts, so admirably adapted for commerce and industry; those
wide and deep rivers; that inexhaustible valley of the Mississippi;
the whole continent, in short, seemed prepared to be the abode of a
great nation yet unborn."

His cell phone rang and he answered it. It was Piasecki, calling
from the street on his way home.

"You know what we were just talking about?" Piasecki said.
"Well, I'm drunk."

"So am I," Kendall said. "Don't worry about it."

"I'm drunk," Piasecki repeated, "but I'm serious."

Kendall had never expected to be as rich as his parents, but he'd
never imagined that he would earn so little or that it would bother
him so much. After five years working for Great Experiment, he and
his wife, Stephanie, had saved just enough money to buy a big fixer-
upper in Oak Park, without being able to fix it up.

Shabby living conditions wouldn't have bothered Kendall in the
old days. He'd liked the converted barns and under-heated garage
apartments Stephanie and he had lived in before they were married,
and he liked the just appreciably nicer apartments in questionable

neighborhoods they lived in after they were married. His sense of their marriage as countercultural, an artistic alliance committed to the support of vinyl records and Midwestern literary quarterlies, had persisted even after Max and Eleanor were born. Hadn't the Brazilian hammock as diaper table been an inspired idea? And the poster of Beck gazing down over the crib, covering the hole in the wall?

Kendall had never wanted to live like his parents. That had been the whole idea, the lofty rationale behind the snow-globe collection and the flea-market eyewear. But as the children got older, Kendall began to compare their childhood unfavorably with his own, and to feel guilty.

From the street, as he approached under the dark, dripping trees, his house looked impressive enough. The lawn was ample. Two stone urns flanked the front steps, leading up to a wide porch. Except for paint peeling under the eaves, the exterior looked fine. It was with the interior that the trouble began. In fact, the trouble began with the word itself: interior. Stephanie liked to use it. The design magazines she consulted were full of it. One was even *called* it: *Interiors*. But Kendall had his doubts as to whether their home achieved an authentic state of interiority. For instance, the outside was always breaking in. Rain leaked through the master-bathroom ceiling. The sewers flooded up through the basement drain.

Across the street, a Range Rover was double-parked, its tailpipe fuming. As he passed, Kendall gave the person at the wheel a dirty look. He expected a businessman or a stylish suburban wife. But sitting in the front seat was a frumpy, middle-aged woman, wearing a Wisconsin sweatshirt, talking on her cell phone.

Kendall's hatred of S.U.V.s didn't keep him from knowing the base price of a Range Rover: seventy-five thousand dollars. From the official Range Rover Web site, where a husband up late at night could build his own vehicle, Kendall also knew that choosing the "Luxury Package" (preferably cashmere upholstery with navy piping and burled-walnut dash) brought the price tag up to eighty-two thousand dollars. This was an unthinkable, a testicle-withering sum. And yet, pulling into the driveway next to Kendall's was another Range Rover, this belonging to his neighbor Bill Ferret. Bill did something relating to software; he devised it, or marketed it. At a back-yard barbecue the previous summer, Kendall had listened with a serious face as Bill explained his profession. Kendall specialized in a serious face. This was the face he'd trained on his high-school and college teachers from his seat in the first row: the ever-alert, A-student face. Still, despite his apparent attentiveness, Kendall didn't remember what Bill had told him about his job. There was a software company in Canada named Waxman, and Bill had shares in Waxman, or Waxman had shares in Bill's company, Duplicate, and either Waxman or Duplicate was thinking of "going public," which apparently was a good thing to do, except that Bill had just started a third software company, Triplicate, and so Waxman, or Duplicate, or maybe both, had forced him to sign a "non-compete," which would last a year.

Munching his hamburger, Kendall had understood that this was how people spoke, out in the world—in the real world he himself lived in, though, paradoxically, had yet to enter. In this real world, there were things like custom software and ownership percentages and Machiavellian corporate struggles, all of which resulted in the ability to drive a heartbreakingly beautiful forest-green Range Rover up your own paved drive.

Maybe Kendall wasn't so smart.

He went up his front walk and into the house, where he found Stephanie in the kitchen, next to the open, glowing stove.

"Don't get mad," she said. "It's only been on a few minutes."

Stephanie wore her hair in the same comp-lit pageboy she'd had the day they met, twenty-two years earlier, in an H.D. seminar. In college, Kendall had had a troubling habit of falling in love with lesbians. So imagine his relief, his utter joy, when he learned that Stephanie wasn't a lesbian but only looked like one.

She'd dumped the day's mail on the kitchen table and was flipping through an architecture magazine.

"How's this for our kitchen?" Stephanie said.

Kendall bent to look. It didn't cost anything to look. An old house, like theirs, had been expanded by ripping off the rear wall and replacing it with a Bauhaus extension.

Kendall asked, "Where are the kids?"

"Max is at Sam's," Stephanie said. "Eleanor says it's too cold here. So she's sleeping over at Olivia's."

"Sixty-five isn't that cold," Kendall said emphatically.

"If you're here all day, it is."

Instead of replying, Kendall opened the refrigerator and stared in. There were bottles and cartons, most nearly empty. There was something greenish black in a produce bag.

"Piasecki said something interesting to me today," Kendall said.

"Piasecki who?"

"Piasecki the accountant. From work." Kendall poked the greenish-black thing with his forefinger. "Piasecki said it's unbelievable that Jimmy doesn't give me any health insurance."

"*I've* told you that," Stephanie said.

"Piasecki agrees with you."

Stephanie raised her eyes. "What are you looking for in there?"

"All we have are sauces," Kendall said. "What are all these sauces for? They wouldn't be to put on food, would they? Because we have no food."

Stephanie had gone back to flipping through her magazine. "If we didn't have to pay for our own health insurance," she said, "we might have some money for renovations."

"Or we could waste heat," Kendall said. "Eleanor would like that. What temperature do Olivia's parents keep their house at?"

"Not sixty-five," Stephanie said.

"I've got my head in the refrigerator and it's not even that cold," Kendall said.

Abruptly, he straightened up and slammed the refrigerator door. He sighed once, satisfyingly, and headed out of the room and up the front stairs.

He came down the hall into the master bedroom. And here he stopped again.

He wondered if Alexis de Tocqueville had ever envisaged a scene like this. An American bedroom quite like this.

It wasn't the only master bedroom of its kind in Chicago. Across the country, the master bedrooms of more and more two-salaried, stressed-out couples were taking on the bear-den atmosphere of Kendall and Stephanie's bedroom. In this suburban cave, this commuter-town hollow, two large, hirsute mammals had recently hibernated. Or were hibernating still. That twisted mass of bedsheet was where they slept. The saliva stains on the denuded pillows were evidence of a long winter spent drooling and dreaming. The socks and underpants scattered on the floor resembled the skins of rodents recently consumed.

In the far corner of the room was a hillock rising three feet in the air. This was the family wash. They'd used a hamper for a while and, for a while, the kids had dutifully tossed their dirty clothes in. But the hamper soon overflowed and the family had begun tossing their dirty clothes in its general direction. The hamper could still be there, for all Kendall knew, buried beneath the pyramid of laundry.

How had it happened in one generation? His parents' bedroom had never looked like this. Kendall's father had a dresser full of folded laundry, a closet full of tailored suits, and, every night, a neat, clean bed to climb into. Nowadays, if Kendall wanted to live as his own father had lived, he was going to have to hire a cleaning lady and a seamstress and a social secretary. He was going to have to hire a wife. Wouldn't that be great? Stephanie could use one, too. Everybody needed a wife, and no one had one anymore.

But to hire a wife Kendall needed to make more money. The alternative was to live as he did, in middle-class squalor, in married bachelorhood.

Like most honest people, Kendall sometimes fantasized about committing a crime. In the following days, however, he found himself indulging in criminal fantasies to a criminal extent. How did one embezzle if one wanted to embezzle well? What kind of mistakes did the rank amateurs make? How could you get caught and what were the penalties?

Quite amazing, to an embezzler-fantasist, was how instructive the daily newspapers were. Not only the lurid Chicago *Sun-Times*, with its stories of gambling-addicted accountants and Irish "minority" trucking companies. Much more instructive were the business pages of the *Tribune* or the *Times*. Here you found the pension-fund manager who'd siphoned off five million, or the Korean-American hedge-fund genius who vanished with a quarter billion of Palm Beach retiree money and who turned out to be a Mexican guy named Lopez. Turn the page to read about the Boeing executive sentenced to four months in jail for rigging contracts with the Air Force. The malfeasance of Bernie Ebbers and Dennis Kozlowski claimed the front page, but it was the short articles on A21 or C15 detailing the quieter frauds, the scam artists working in subtler pigments, in found objects, that showed Kendall the extent of the national deceit.

At the Coq d'Or the next Friday, Piasecki said, "You know the mistake most people make?"

"What?"

"They buy a beach house. Or a Porsche. They red-flag them-selves. They can't resist."

"They lack discipline," Kendall said.

"Right."

"No moral fibre."

"Exactly."

Wasn't scheming the way America worked? The real America that Kendall, with his nose stuck in "Rhyme's Reason," had failed to notice? How far apart were the doings of these minor corporate embezzlers from the accounting fraud at Enron? And what about all the business people who were clever enough not to get caught, who wriggled free from blame? The example set on high wasn't one of probity and full disclosure. It was anything but.

When Kendall was growing up, American politicians denied that the United Stales was an empire. But they weren't doing that anymore. They'd given up. Everyone knew about the empire now. Everyone was pleased.

And in the streets of Chicago, as in the streets of L.A., New York, Houston, and Oakland, the message was making itself known. A few weeks back, Kendall had seen the movie "Patton" on TV. He'd been reminded that the general had been severely punished for slapping a soldier. Whereas now Rumsfeld ran free from responsibility for Abu Ghraib. Even the President, who'd lied about W.M.D., had been reelected. In the streets, people took the point. Victory was what counted, power, muscularity, doublespeak if necessary. You saw it in the way people drove, in the way they cut you off, gave you the finger, cursed. Women and men alike, showing rage and toughness. Everyone knew what he wanted and how to get it. Everybody you met was nobody's fool.

One's country was like one's self. The more you learned about it, the more you were ashamed of.

Then again, it wasn't pure torture, living in the plutocracy. Jimmy was still out in Montecito, and every weekday Kendall had the run of his place. There were serf-like doormen, invisible porters who hauled out the trash, a squad of Polish maids who came Wednesday and Friday mornings to pick up after Kendall and scrub the toilet in the Moorish bathroom and tidy up the sunny kitchen where he ate his lunch. The co-op was a duplex. Kendall worked on the second floor. Downstairs was Jimmy's "Jade Room," where he kept his collection of Chinese jade in museum-quality display cases. The carvings were made from single pieces of jade and were usually of horses' heads, enfolded upon themselves. Jimmy kept what he couldn't show off in specially built, curatorial drawers. (If you had criminality in mind, a good place to start would be the Jade Room.)

In his office, when Kendall looked up from his Tocqueville, he could see the opalescent lake spreading out in all directions. The surround of water at this altitude made for a fish-tank sensation. Water, water, everywhere. The curious emptiness Chicago confronted, the way it just dropped off into nothing, especially at sunset or in the fog, this void was responsible for all the activity. The land had been waiting to be exploited. These shores so suited to industry and commerce had raised a thousand factories. The factories had sent vehicles of steel throughout the world, and now these vehicles, in armored form, were clashing for control of the petroleum that powered the whole operation.

The phone rang. It was Jimmy, calling from Montecito.

"Hello, Jimmy, how are you?"

"Not bad," Jimmy said. "It's only three in the afternoon and I've already had my cock out three times."

One nice thing about being obscenely rich was the liberty it afforded you to utter sentences such as this. But Jimmy's impropriety predated his money. It was the reason for his money.

"Sounds like retirement agrees with you," Kendall said.

"What are you talking about?" Jimmy said, laughing. "I'm not retired. I've got more going on now than when I was thirty. Speaking of which, I'm returning *your* call. What's up, kiddo?"

"Right," Kendall said, gearing up. "I've been running the house for six years now and I think you've been happy with my work."

"I have been," Jimmy said. "No complaints."

"So I was wondering, given my tenure here, and my performance, if it might be possible to work out some kind of health-insurance coverage."

"Can't do it," Jimmy answered abruptly. The suddenness with which he spoke suggested he was defending himself against his feelings. "That was never part of your package. I'm running a non-profit here, kiddo. Piasecki just sent me the statements. We're in the red this year. We're in the red every year. All these books we publish, important, foundational, patriotic books—truly patriotic books—and nobody buys them! The people in this country are asleep! We've got an entire nation on Ambien. Sandman Rove is blowing dust in everybody's eyes."

He went off on a tear, anathematizing Bush and Wolfowitz and Perle, but then he must have felt bad about avoiding the subject at hand because he came back to it, softening his tone. "Listen, I know you've got a family. You've got to do what's best for you. If you wanted to test your value out in the marketplace, I'd understand. I'd hate to lose you, Kendall, but I'd understand if you have to move on."

There was silence on the line.

Jimmy said, "You think about it." He cleared his throat. "So, tell me. How's 'The Pocket Democracy' coming?"

Kendall wished he could remain businesslike, professional. He tried his best to keep bitterness out of his voice. He'd been a pouter as a kid, however, and the pleasures of pouting were still enticing.

He said nothing.

"When do you think you'll have something to show me?" Jimmy asked.

"No idea."

"What was that?"

"I've got no answer at the moment," Kendall said.

"I'm running a business, Kendall," Jimmy said before hanging up. "I'm sorry."

The sun was setting. The water reflected the gray-blue of the darkening sky, and the lights of the water-pumping stations had come on, making them look like a line of floating gazebos. Kendall's mood had dimmed, too. He slumped in his office chair, the Xeroxed pages of "Democracy in America" spread out around him. His left temple throbbed. He winced and, rubbing his forehead, looked down at the page in front of him:

> I do not mean that there is any lack of wealthy individuals in the United States; I know of no country, indeed, where the love of money has taken stronger hold on the affections of men and where a profounder contempt is expressed for the theory of the permanent equality of property. But wealth circulates with inconceivable rapidity, and experience shows that it is rare to find two succeeding generations in the full enjoyment of it.

He swivelled in his chair and violently grabbed the phone off its hook. He stabbed out the number and after a single ring Piasecki answered. Kendall told Piasecki to meet him at the Coq d'Or.

This was how you did it. This was taking action. In an instant, everything could change.

At the Coq d'Or, they sat in their usual booth in the back room. Kendall stared across the table at Piasecki and said, "About that idea you had the other day."

Piasecki gave Kendall a sideways look, suspicious. "You serious or you just playing around?"

"I'm curious," Kendall said.

"Don't fuck with me," Piasecki cautioned.

"I'm not." Kendall was blinking rapidly. "I was just wondering how it would work. Technically speaking." Piasecki leaned closer to Kendall and lowered his voice. "I never said what I'm about to say, O.K.?"

"O.K."

"If you do something like this, what you do is you set up a dummy company. You create invoices from this company, O.K.? Great Experiment pays these invoices. After a few years, you close the account and liquidate the company."

Kendall didn't understand exactly. It couldn't be that complicated, but he was unclear on a few points.

"But the invoices won't be for anything. Won't that be obvious?"

"When's the last time Jimmy checked the invoices? He's eighty-two, for Christ sake. He's out in California taking Viagra so he can bang some hooker. He's not thinking about the invoices. His mind is occupied."

"What if we get audited?"

Here Piasecki smiled. "I like how you say 'we.' That's where I come in. If we get audited, who handles that? I do. I show the I.R.S. the bills and the payments. Since our payments into the dummy company match the bills, everything looks fine. If we pay the right taxes on income, how is the I.R.S. going to complain?"

It wasn't all that complicated. Kendall wasn't used to thinking this way, not just criminally but financially, but as his executive pour went down, he saw how it could work. He looked around the bar, at the businessmen boozing, making deals.

"I'm not talking about that much," Piasecki was saying. "Jimmy's worth, like, eighty million. I'm talking maybe half a million for you, half for me. Maybe, if things go smooth, a million each. Then we shut it down, cover our tracks, and move to Bermuda."

Piasecki leaned forward and with burning, needy eyes, said, "Jimmy makes more than a million in the markets every four months. It's nothing to him."

"What if something goes wrong? I've got a family."

"And I don't? It's my family I'm thinking of. It's not like things are fair in this country. Things are unfair. Why should a smart guy like you not get a little piece of the pie? Are you scared?"

"Yes," Kendall said.

"Listen to me. I'll be honest. If we do this, you should be a little scared. Just a little. But, statistically, I'd put the chances at our getting caught at about one per cent. Maybe less."

For Kendall it was exciting, somehow, just to be having this conversation. Everything about the Coq d'Or, from the fatty appetizers to the Tin Pan Alley entertainment to the faux-Napoleonic décor, suggested it was 1926. Under the influence of the atmosphere, it seemed to Kendall that he and Piasecki were leaning conspiratorially together, foreheads almost touching. They'd seen the Mafia movies, so they knew how to do it. Kendall wanted to laugh. He'd thought this kind of thing was over. He thought that because of the rise of postmodern irony the durable street rackets and shady backroom dealing had gone out of style. But he was wrong. Kendall was so smart he was stupid. He'd figured criminality was like academia, progressive, built on one movement succeeding another. But the same scheming that had gone on eighty years ago was going on now. This was especially true in Chicago, where even the bar decor colluded to promote an underworld effect.

"I'm telling you, we could be in and out in two years," Piasecki was saying. "We do it nice and easy and leave no trail. Then we invest our money and do our part for the G.D.P."

What was an intellectual but a guy who thought? Who thought instead of did. What would it be like to do? To apply his brain to the small universe of money instead of the battle between Jefferson and the Federalists?

This made Kendall contemplate how Stephanie would view all this. He would never be able to tell her about it. He'd have to say he'd been given a raise. Simultaneous with this thought was another: renovating your kitchen wasn't a red flag. They could do the whole house without attracting attention.

In his mind he saw his fixer-upper all fixed up, a gleaming, wood-polished house, a stop on the Oak Park landmark tour, and, sliding down the bannister, into his providing, fatherly arms, Eleanor.

Wealth circulates with inconceivable rapidity . . .

The full enjoyment of it . . .

"O.K., I'm in," Kendall said.

"You're in?"

"Let me think about it," Kendall said.

That was sufficient for Piasecki for now. He lifted his glass. "To Ken Lay," he said. "My hero."

"What sort of business is this you're opening?"

"It's a storage facility."

"And you're?"

"The president. Co-president."

"With Mr."—the lawyer, a squat woman with thatchlike hair, searched on the incorporation form—"with Mr. Piasecki."

"That's right," Kendall said.

It was a Saturday afternoon. Kendall was in downtown Oak Park, in the lawyer's meagre, diploma-showy office. Max was outside on the sidewalk, catching autumn leaves, staring up at the sky with hands outstretched.

"I could use some storage," the lawyer joked. "We've got three kids and our house is stuffed."

"We mainly do commercial storage," Kendall said. "We don't have a lot of little storage lockers but just a few big ones. Sorry."

He hadn't even seen the place, which was up in the sticks, outside Kewanee. Piasecki had driven up and leased the land. There was nothing on it but an old, weed-choked Esso station. But it had a legal address, and soon, as Midwestern Storage, a steady income.

Great Experiment, since it sold few books, had a lot of books on hand. In addition to storing them in their usual warehouse, in Schaumburg, Kendall would now send a phantom number of books up to the facility in Kewanee. Midwestern Storage would charge Great Experiment for this service, and Piasecki would send the company checks. As soon as the incorporation forms were filed, Piasecki planned to open a bank account in Midwestern Storage's name. Signatories to this account: Michael J. Piasecki and Kendall Wallis.

It was all quite elegant. Kendall and Piasecki owned a legal company. The company earned money legally, paid its taxes; the two of them split the profit and claimed it as business income on their tax returns. That the warehouse was a broken-down gas station, that it housed no books—who was ever to know?

"I just hope the old guy doesn't kick," Piasecki had said. "We've got to pray for the health of Jimmy's prostate."

When Kendall had signed the required forms, the lawyer said, "O.K., I'll file these papers for you Monday. And that's all there is to it. Congratulations, you're the proud new owner of a corporation in the state of Illinois."

Outside, Max was still whirling beneath the falling leaves.

"How many did you catch, buddy?" Kendall asked his son.

"Sixty-two!" Max shouted.

Kendall, copies of the papers tucked under his arm, looked up at the sky to watch the leaves, red and gold, spinning down toward the earth. The air smelled of autumn, of leaf raking, of the dependable and virtuous Midwest.

And now it was a Monday morning in January, start of a new week, and Kendall was on the train again, reading about America: "There is one country in the world where the great social revolution that I am speaking of seems to have nearly reached its natural limits." Kendall had a new pair of shoes on, two-tone cordovans from the Allen Edmonds store on Michigan Avenue. Otherwise, he looked the way he always did, same chinos, same shiny-elbowed corduroy jacket. Nobody on the train would have guessed that he wasn't the mild, bookish figure he appeared to be. No one would have imagined Kendall making his weekly drop-off at the mailbox outside the all-cash building (to keep the doormen from noticing the deposit envelopes addressed to the Kewanee bank). Seeing Kendall jotting figures in his newspaper, most riders assumed he was working out a Sudoku puzzle instead of estimating potential earnings from a five-year C.D. Kendall in his editor-wear had the perfect disguise. He was like Poe's purloined letter, hiding in plain sight.

Who said he wasn't smart?

The fear had been greatest the first few weeks. Kendall would awaken at 3 A.M. with what felt like a battery cable hooked to his navel. The current surged through him, as he sweated and twitched. What if Jimmy noticed the printing, shipping, and warehouse costs for the phantom books? What if Piasecki drunkenly confessed to a Ukrainian barmaid whose brother was a cop? Kendall's mind whirled with potential mishaps and dangers. How had he got into something like this with someone like that? In their transforming bedroom, with Stephanie sleeping beside him, unaware that she was bedding down with a criminal, Kendall lay awake for hours, jittery with visions of jail time and perp walks and the loss of his children.

It got easier after a while. Fear was like any other emotion. From an initial passionate stage, it slowly ebbed until it became routine and then barely noticeable. Plus, things had gone so well. Kendall drew up separate checks, one for the books they actually printed and another for the books he and Piasecki pretended to. On Friday, Piasecki entered these debits in his accounts against weekly income. "It looks like a profit-loss," he told Kendall. "We're actually saving Jimmy taxes. He should thank us."

"Why don't we let him in on it then?" Kendall said.

Piasecki only laughed. "Even if we did, he's so out of it he wouldn't remember."

Kendall kept to his low-profile plan, too. As the bank account of Midwestern Storage slowly grew, the same beaten-up old Volvo remained in his driveway. The money stayed away from prying eyes. It showed only inside. In the interior. Kendall said the word now. He said it every night, inspecting the work of the plasterers and carpenters and carpet installers. He was looking into additional interiors as well: the walled gardens of college-savings funds (the garden of Max, the garden of Eleanor); the inner sanctum of a SEP-I.R.A

And there was something else hidden away in the interior: a wife. Her name was Arabella. She was from Venezuela and spoke no English. She'd cried with true alarm upon seeing the mountain of laundry in the master bedroom for the first time. But she'd hauled it away to the basement, load by load. Kendall and Stephanie were thrilled.

At the all-cash building, Kendall did something he hadn't done in a long time: he did his job. He finished abridging "Democracy in America" and Fed-Exed the color-coded manuscript to Jimmy in Montecito. He buried Jimmy under a flurry of new reprint proposals, writing one up every other day and shipping the nominated texts west. Instead of waiting for Jimmy to call the office, Kendall called Jimmy daily, sometimes twice a day, pestering him with questions. Just as Kendall had expected, Jimmy had at first taken his calls and then begun to complain about them and finally had told Kendall to stop bothering him with minutiae and to deal with things himself. Jimmy hardly called the office at all anymore.

Swamping Jimmy with work had been a clever idea. You could learn a lot about human nature, it turned out, from reading books.

The train deposited him at Union Station. Coming out onto Madison Street, Kendall could smell snow. There was a graininess to the air, which had itself warmed and grown windless, as it always did before a storm. Kendall took a cab (paying with untraceable cash) and had the driver let him out a block from the all-cash building. From there he trudged around the corner, looking as though he'd come on foot. With Mike, the doorman on duty, Kendall exchanged a proletarian greeting (they both worked here, after all) on his way to the gilded elevator.

The penthouse was empty. Not even a maid around. Passing the Jade Room, Kendall stepped in to admire the lighted display cases. He pulled open a custom drawer and found a horse's head. He'd thought jade was meant to be dark green. But that wasn't so. Jimmy had told him the best jade, the most rare, was light green in color, almost white. As was this equine example. For a moment, the beauty of the thing hit Kendall with full force. A thousand years ago, an artisan had carved this horse from a single piece of jade, rendering the animal in sinuous, pythonic form. Being able to appreciate an object of this kind was what Kendall had always appreciated about himself. What had counted as true riches.

The windows of his office showed the storm moving in across the lake. In front of the building, the sky was still blue. On Kendall's desk sat "The Pocket Democracy," just back from the (real) printer. It was as small and sleek as an iPod, easily slipped into a pocket: a concealed weapon of a book. Kendall was staring at it for the hundredth time, with disquiet, when the telephone rang.

"How's the weather up there?" It was Jimmy.

"Tolstoyan," Kendall said. "Snowstorm coming in."

"You like that sort of thing, right? Invigorating."

Soon Jimmy got around to business. "The 'Pocket Democracy,'" Jimmy said. "Just got it. I love it. Nice job."

"Thank you," Kendall said.

"What do the orders look like?"

"Good, actually."

"I think it's priced right. What about getting some reviews?"

"It's difficult getting reviews for a two-hundred-year-old book."

"Well, we should do some advertising then," Jimmy said. "Send me a list of places you think would be best. Not the fucking *New York Review of Books*. That's preaching to the converted. I want this book to get *out* there."

"Let me think a little," Kendall said.

"What else was there? Oh yeah! The bookmark! That's a great idea. Let's print bookmarks with the Great Experiment quote on them. Put one in every book. Maybe we can do posters, too. We might sell some books for once."

"That's the idea," Kendall said.

"If this book does as well as I hope it will, I tell you what," Jimmy said. "I'll give you health insurance."

Kendall hesitated only an instant. "That would be great."

"I don't want to lose you, kiddo. Plus, I'll be honest. It's a headache finding someone else."

The light in the room changed, dimmed. Kendall turned to see the wall of cloud approaching the shoreline. Snow flurries swirled against the windows.

This late generosity wasn't grounds for reappraisal and regret. Jimmy had taken his sweet time, hadn't he? And the promise was phrased in the conditional. No, let's wait and see how things turn out. If Kendall got insurance and a nice raise, then maybe he'd think about shutting Midwestern Storage down.

"Oh," Jimmy said. "One more thing."

Kendall waited, looking at the snow. It was like being in a submarine passing through a school of fish.

"Piasecki sent me the accounts. The numbers look funny."

"What do you mean?"

"What are we doing printing thirty thousand copies of Thomas Paine?" Jimmy said. "And why are we using two printers?"

At congressional hearings, in courtrooms, the accused C.E.O.s and C.F.O.s followed one of two strategies: either they said they didn't know, or they said they didn't remember.

"I don't remember why we printed thirty thousand," Kendall said. "I'll have to check the orders. I don't know anything about the printers. Piasecki handles that. Maybe someone offered us a better deal."

"The new printer is charging us a higher rate."

Piasecki hadn't told Kendall that. Piasecki had become greedy and kept it to himself.

"Listen," Jimmy said, "send me the contact info for the new printer. And for that storage place. I'm going to have my guy out here look into this."

The smart thing was to act nonchalant. But Kendall said, "What guy?"

"My accountant. You think I'd let Piasecki operate without oversight? No way! Everything he does gets double-checked out here. If he's pulling anything, we'll find out. And then Mr. Piasecki's up shit's creek."

Kendall sat up straighter in his desk chair, making the springs cry out.

"Listen, kiddo, I'm going to London next week," Jimmy said. "The house'll be empty. Why don't you bring your family out here for a long weekend? Get out of that cold weather."

When Kendall didn't reply, Jimmy said, "Don't worry. It's a nice house. I'll hide the porn."

Kendall's laugh sounded false to him. He wondered if it sounded false to Jimmy. Far below, in the storm's wash cycle, a faint glimmer revealed rush-hour headlights along the Drive.

"Anyway, you did good, kiddo. You boiled Tocqueville down to his essence. I remember when I first read this book. Blew me away."

In his vibrant, scratchy voice, Jimmy began to recite a passage of "Democracy in America." It was the passage they were putting on the bookmarks. Out in Montecito, bald, liver-spotted, in a tank top and shorts probably, the old libertine and libertarian crowed out his favorite lines: "In that land the great experiment of the attempt to construct society upon a new basis was to be made by civilized man," Jimmy read, "and it was there, for the first time, that theories hitherto unknown, or deemed impracticable, were to exhibit a spectacle for which the world had not been prepared by the history of the past."

Snow pummelled the glass. The lakefront was obscured, the water too. Kendall was enclosed in a dark space high above a city rising from a coast engulfed in darkness.

"That fucking kills me," Jimmy said. "Every time."

Richard Ford

UNDER THE RADAR

O n the drive over to the Nicholsons' for dinner—their first in some time—Marjorie Reeves told her husband, Steven Reeves, that she had had an affair with George Nicholson (their host) a year ago, but that it was all over with now and she hoped he—Steven— would not be mad about it and could go on with life.

At this point they were driving along Quaker Bridge Road where it leaves the Perkins Great Woods Road and begins to border the Shenipsit Reservoir, dark and shadowy and calmly mirrored in the late spring twilight. On the right was dense young timber, beech and alder saplings in pale leaf, the ground damp and cakey. Peepers were calling out from the watery lows. Their turn onto Apple Orchard Lane was still a mile on.

Steven, on hearing this news, began gradually and very carefully to steer their car—a tan Mercedes wagon with hooded yellow headlights—off of Quaker Bridge Road and onto the damp grassy shoulder so he could organize this information properly before going on.

They were extremely young. Steven Reeves was twenty-eight. Marjorie Reeves a year younger. They weren't rich, but they'd been lucky. Steven's job at Packard-Wells was to stay on top of a small segment of a larger segment of a rather small prefabrication intersection that serviced the automobile industry, and where any sudden alteration, or even the rumor of an alteration in certain polymer-bonding formulas could tip crucial down-the-line demand patterns, and in that way affect the betting lines and comfort zones of a good many meaningful client positions. His job meant poring over dense and esoteric petrochemical-industry journals, attending technical seminars, flying to vendor conventions, then writing up detailed status reports and all the while keeping an eye on the market for the benefit of his higher-ups. He'd been a scholarship boy at Bates, studied chemistry, was the only son of a hard-put but upright lobstering family in Pemaquid, Maine, and had done well. His bosses at Packard-Wells liked him, saw themselves in him, and also in him saw character qualities they'd never quite owned—blond and slender callowness tending to gullibility, but backed by caution, ingenuity and a thoroughgoing, compact toughness. He was sharp. It was his seventh year with the company—his first job. He and Marjorie had been married two years. They had no children. The car had been his bonus two Christmases ago.

When the station wagon eased to a stop, Steven sat for a minute with the motor running, the salmon-colored dash lights illuminating his face. The radio had been playing softly—the last of the news, then an interlude for French horns. Responding to no particular signal, he pressed off the radio and in the same movement switched off the ignition, which left the headlights shining on the empty, coun-trified road. The windows were down to attract the fresh spring air, and when the engine noise ceased the evening's ambient sounds were waiting. The peepers. A sound of thrush wings fluttering in the brush only a few yards away. The noise of something falling from a small distance and hitting an invisible water surface. Beyond the stand of saplings was the west, and through the darkened trunks, the sky was still pale yellow with the day's light, though here on Quaker Bridge Road it was nearly dark.

When Marjorie said what she had just said, she'd been look-ing straight ahead to where the headlights made a bright path in the dark. Perhaps she'd looked at Steven once, but having said what she'd said, she kept her hands in her lap and continued look-ing ahead. She was a pretty, blond, convictionless girl with small demure features—small nose, small ears, small chin, though with a surprisingly full-lipped smile which she practiced on everyone. She was fond of getting a little tipsy at parties and lowering her voice and sitting on a flowered ottoman or a burl table top with a glass of something and showing too much of her legs or inappropriate amounts of her small breasts. She had grown up in Indiana, studied art at Purdue. Steven had met her in New York at a party while she was working for a firm that did child-focused advertising for a large toymaker. He'd liked her bobbed hair, her fragile, wispy features, translucent skin and the slightly husky voice that made her seem more sophisticated than she was, but somehow convinced her she was, too. In their community, east of Hartford, the women who knew Marjorie Reeves thought of her as a bimbo who would not stay married to sweet Steven Reeves for very long. His second wife would be the right wife for him. Marjorie was just a starter.

Marjorie, however, did not think of herself that way, only that she liked men and felt happy and confident around them and assumed Steven thought this was fine and that in the long run it would help his career to have a pretty, spirited wife no one could pigeonhole. To set herself apart and to take an interest in the community she'd gone to work as a volunteer at a grieving-children's center in Hartford, which meant all black. And it was in Hartford that she'd had the chance to encounter George Nicholson and fuck him at a Red Roof Inn until they'd both gotten tired of it. It would never happen again, was her view, since in a year it hadn't happened again.

For the two or possibly five minutes now that they had sat on the side of Quaker Bridge Road in the still airish evening, with the noises of spring floating in and out of the open window, Marjorie had said nothing and Steven had also said nothing, though he realized that he was saying nothing because he was at a loss for words. A loss for words, he realized, meant that nothing that comes to mind seems very interesting to say as a next thing to what has just been said. He knew he was a callow man—a boy in some ways, still—but he was not stupid. At Bates, he had taken Dr. Sudofsky's class on *Ulysses*, and come away with a sense of irony and humor and the assurance that true knowledge was a spiritual process, a quest, not a storage of dry facts—a thing like freedom, which you only fully experienced in practice. He'd also played hockey, and knew that knowledge and aggressiveness were a subtle and surprising and uncommon combination. He had sought to practice both at Packard-Wells.

But for a brief and terrifying instant in the cool padded semi-darkness, just when he began experiencing his loss for words, he entered or at least nearly slipped into a softened fuguelike state in which he began to fear that he perhaps *could* not say another word;

that something (work fatigue, shock, disappointment over what Marjorie had admitted) was at that moment causing him to detach from reality and to slide away from the present, and in fact to begin to lose his mind and go crazy to the extent that he was in jeopardy of beginning to gibber like a chimp, or just to slowly slump sideways against the upholstered door and not speak for a long, long time—months—and then only with the aid of drugs be able merely to speak in simple utterances that would seem cryptic, so that eventually he would have to be looked after by his mother's family in Damariscotta. A terrible thought.

And so to avoid that—to save his life and sanity—he abruptly just said a word, any word that he could say into the perfumed twilight inhabiting the car, where his wife was obviously anticipating his reply to her unhappy confession.

And for some reason the word—phrase, really—that he uttered was "ground clutter." Something he'd heard on the TV weather report as they were dressing for dinner.

"Hm?" Marjorie said. "What was it?" She turned her pretty, small-featured face toward him so that her pearl earrings caught light from some unknown source. She was wearing a tiny green cocktail dress and green satin shoes that showed off her incredibly thin ankles and slender, bare brown calves. She had two tiny matching green bows in her hair. She smelled sweet. "I know this wasn't what you wanted to hear, Steven," she said, "but I felt I should tell you before we got to George's. The Nicholsons', I mean. It's all over. It'll never happen again. I promise you. No one will ever mention it. I just lost my bearings last year with the move. I'm sorry." She had made a little steeple of her fingertips, as if she'd been concentrating very hard as she spoke these words. But now she put her hands again calmly in her minty green lap. She had bought her dress especially for this night at the Nicholsons'. She'd thought George would like it and Steven, too. She turned her face away and exhaled a small but detectable sigh in the car. It was then that the headlights went off automatically.

George Nicholson was a big squash-playing, thick-chested, hairy-armed Yale lawyer who sailed his own Hinckley 61 out of Essex and had started backing off from his high-priced Hartford plaintiffs' practice at fifty to devote more time to competitive racket sports and senior skiing. George was a college roommate of one of Steven's firm's senior partners and had "adopted" the Reeveses when they moved into the community following their wedding. Marjorie had volunteered Saturdays with George's wife, Patsy, at the Episcopal Thrift Shop during their first six months in Connecticut. To Steven, George Nicholson had recounted a memorable, seasoning summer spent hauling deep-water lobster traps with some tough old sea dogs out of Matinicus, Maine. Later, he'd been a Marine, and sported a faded anchor, ball and chain tattooed on his forearm. Later yet he'd fucked Steven's wife.

Having said something, even something that made no sense, Steven felt a sense of glum and deflated relief as he sat in the silent car beside Marjorie, who was still facing forward. Two thoughts had begun to compete in his reviving awareness. One was clearly occasioned by his conception of George Nicholson. He thought of George Nicholson as a gasbag, but also a forceful man who'd made his pile by letting very little stand in his way. When he thought about George he always remembered the story about Matinicus, which then put into his mind a mental picture of his own father and himself hauling traps somewhere out toward Monhegan. The reek of the bait, the toss of the ocean in late spring, the consoling monotony of the solid, tree-lined shore barely visible through the mists. Thinking through that circuitry always made him vaguely admire George Nicholson and, oddly, made him think he liked George even now, in spite of everything.

The other compering thought was that part of Marjorie's character had always been to confess upsetting things that turned out, he believed, not to be true: being a hooker for a summer up in Saugatuck; topless dancing while she was an undergraduate; heroin experimentation; taking part in armed robberies with her high-school boyfriend in Goshen, Indiana, where she was from. When she told these far-fetched stories she would grow distracted and shake her head, as though they were true. And now, while he didn't particularly think any of these stories was a bit truer, he did realize that he didn't really know his wife at all; and that in fact the entire conception of knowing another person—of trust, of closeness, of marriage itself—while not exactly a lie since it existed *someplace* if only as an idea (in his parents' life, at least marginally) was still completely out-of-date, defunct, was something typifying another era, now unfortunately gone. Meeting a girl, falling in love, marrying her, moving to Connecticut, buying a fucking house, starting a life with her and thinking you really knew anything about her—the last part was a complete fiction, which made all the rest a joke. Marjorie might as well have *been* a hooker or held up 7-Elevens and shot people, for all he really knew about her. And what was more, if he'd said any of this to her, sitting next to him thinking he would never know what, she either would not have understood a word of it or simply would've said, "Well, okay, that's fine." When people talked about the bottom line, Steven Reeves thought, they weren't talking about money, they were talking about what *this* meant, *this* kind of fatal ignorance. Money—losing it, gaining it, spending it, hoarding it—all that was only an emblem, though a good one, of what was happening here right now.

At this moment a pair of car lights rounded a curve somewhere out ahead of where the two of them sat in their station wagon. The lights found both their white faces staring forward in silence. The lights also found a raccoon just crossing the road from the reservoir shore, headed for the woods that were beside them. The car was going faster than might've been evident. The raccoon paused to peer up into the approaching beams, then continued on into the safe, opposite lane. But only then did it look up and notice Steven and Marjorie's car stopped on the verge of the road, silent in the murky evening. And because of that notice it must've decided that where it had been was much better than where it was going, and so turned to scamper back across Quaker Bridge Road toward the cool waters of the reservoir, which was what caused the car—actually it was a beat-up Ford pickup—to rumble over it, pitching and spinning it off to the side and then motionlessness near the opposite shoulder. "Yaaaa-haaaa-yipeeee!" a man's shrill voice shouted from inside the dark cab of the pickup, followed by another man's laughter.

And then it became very silent again. The raccoon lay on the road twenty yards in front of the Reeveses' car. It didn't struggle. It was merely there.

"Gross," Marjorie said.

Steven said nothing, though he felt less at a loss for words now. His eyes, indeed, felt relieved to fix on the still corpse of the raccoon.

"Do we do something?" Marjorie said. She had leaned forward a few inches as if to study the raccoon through the windshield. Light was dying away behind the slender young beech trees to the west of them.

"No," Steven said. These were his first words—except for the words he took no responsibility for—since Marjorie had said what she'd importantly said and their car was still moving toward dinner.

It was then that he hit her. He hit her before he knew he'd hit her, but not before he knew he wanted to. He hit her with the back of his open hand without even looking at her, hit her straight in the front of her face, straight in the nose. And hard. In a way, it was more a gesture than a blow, though it was, he understood, a blow. He felt the soft tip of her nose, and then the knuckly cartilage against the hard bones of the backs of his fingers. He had never hit a woman before, and he had never even thought of hitting Marjorie, always imagining he *couldn't* hit her when he'd read newspaper accounts of such things happening in the sad lives of others. He'd hit other people, been hit by other people, plenty of times—tough Maine boys on the ice rinks. Girls were out, though. His father always made that clear. His mother, too.

"Oh, my goodness" was all that Marjorie said when she received the blow. She put her hand over her nose immediately, but then sat silently in the car while neither of them said anything. His heart was not beating hard. The back of his hand hurt a little. This was all new ground. Steven had a small rosy birthmark just where his left sideburn ended and his shaved face began. It resembled the shape of the state of West Virginia. He thought he could feel this birthmark now. His skin tingled there.

And the truth was he felt even more relieved, and didn't feel at all sorry for Marjorie, sitting there stoically, making a little tent of her hand to cover her nose and staring ahead as if nothing had

happened. He thought she would cry, certainly. She was a girl who
cried—when she was unhappy, when he said something insensitive,
when she was approaching her period. Crying was natural. Clearly,
though, it was a new experience for her to be hit. And so it called
upon something new, and if not new then some strength, resilience,
self-mastery normally reserved for other experiences.

"I can't go to the Nicholsons' now," Marjorie said almost patiently.
She removed her hand and viewed her palm as if her palm had her
nose in it. Of course it was blood she was thinking about. He heard
her breathe in through what sounded like a congested nose, then the
breath was completed out through her mouth. She was not crying
yet. And for that moment he felt not even sure he *had* smacked her—
if it hadn't just been a thought he'd entertained, a gesture somehow
uncommissioned.

What he wanted to do, however, was skip to the most impor-
tant things now, not get mired down in wrong, extraneous details.
Because he didn't give a shit about George Nicholson or the particu-
lars of what they'd done in some shitty motel. Marjorie would never
leave him for George Nicholson or anyone like George Nicholson,
and George Nicholson and men like him—high rollers with Hinck-
leys—didn't throw it all away for unimportant little women like
Marjorie. He thought of her nose, red, swollen, smeared with sticky
blood dripping onto her green dress. He didn't suppose it could be
broken. Noses held up. And, of course, there was a phone in the car.
He could simply make a call to the party. He pictured the Nichol-
sons' great rambling white-shingled house brightly lit beyond the
curving drive, the original elms exorbitantly preserved, the foot-
lights, the low-lit clay court where they'd all played, the heated pool,
the Henry Moore out on the darkened lawn where you just stum-

bled onto it. He imagined saying to someone—not George Nichol-
son—that Marjorie was ill, had thrown up on the side of the road.

The *right* details, though. The right details to ascertain from her
were: *Are you sorry?* (he'd forgotten Marjorie had already said she
was sorry) and *What does this mean for the future?* These were the
details that mattered.

Surprisingly, the raccoon that had been cartwheeled by the
pickup and then lain motionless, a blob in the near-darkness, had
come back to life and was now trying to drag itself and its useless
hinder parts off of Quaker Bridge Road and onto the grassy verge
and into the underbrush that bordered the reservoir.

"Oh, for God's sake," Marjorie said, and put her hand over her
damaged nose again. She could see the raccoon's struggle and
turned her head away.

"Aren't you even sorry?" Steven said.

"Yes," Marjorie said, her nose still covered as if she wasn't think-
ing about the fact that she was covering it. Probably, he thought, the
pain had gone away some. It hadn't been so bad. "I mean no," she
said.

He wanted to hit her again then—this time in the ear—but he
didn't. He wasn't sure why not. No one would ever know. "Well,
which is it?" he said, and felt for the first time completely furious.
The thing that made him furious—all his life, the very maddest—
was to be put into a situation in which everything he did was wrong,
when right was no longer an option. Now felt like one of those situ-
ations. "Which is it?" he said again angrily. "Really." He should just
take her to the Nicholsons', he thought, swollen nose, bloody lips, all
stoppered up, and let her deal with it. Or let her sit out in the car, or
else start walking the 11.6 miles home. Maybe George could come

out and drive her in his Rover. These were only thoughts, of course. "Which is it?" he said for the third time. He was stuck on these words, on this bit of barren curiosity.

"I was sorry when I told you," Marjorie said, very composed. She lowered her hand from her nose to her lap. One of the little green bows that had been in her hair was now resting on her bare shoulder. "Though not very sorry," she said. "Only sorry because I had to tell you. And now that I've told you and you've hit me in my face and probably broken my nose, I'm not sorry about anything—except that. Though I'm sorry about being married to you, which I'll remedy as soon as I can." She was still not crying. "So *now*, will you as a gesture of whatever good there is in you, get out and go over and do something to help that poor injured creature that those motherfucking rednecks maimed with their motherfucking pickup truck and then because they're pieces of shit and low forms of degraded humanity, laughed about? Can you do that, Steven? Is that in your range?" She sniffed back hard through her nose, then expelled a short, deep and defeated moan. Her voice seemed more nasal, more midwestern even, now that her nose was congested.

"I'm sorry I hit you," Steven Reeves said, and opened the car door onto the silent road.

"I know," Marjorie said in an emotionless voice. "And you'll be sorrier."

When he had walked down the empty macadam road in his tan suit to where the raccoon had been struck then bounced over onto the road's edge, there was nothing now there. Only a small circle of dark blood he could just make out on the nubbly road surface and that might've been an oil smudge. No raccoon. The raccoon with its last reserves of savage, unthinking will had found the strength to pull itself off into the bushes to die. Steven peered down into the dark, stalky confinement of scrubs and bramble that separated the road from the reservoir. It was very still there. He thought he heard a rustling in the low brush where a creature might be, getting itself settled into the soft grass and damp earth to go to sleep forever. Someplace out on the lake he heard a young girl's voice, very distinctly laughing. Then a car door closed farther away. Then another sort of door, a screen door, slapped shut. And then a man's voice saving "Oh no, oh-ho-ho-ho-ho, no." A small white light came on farther back in the trees beyond the reservoir, where he hadn't imagined there was a house. He wondered about how long it would be before his angry feelings stopped mattering to him. He considered briefly why Marjorie would admit this to him now. It seemed so odd.

Then he heard his own car start. The muffled-metal diesel racket of the Mercedes. The headlights came smartly on and disclosed him. Music was instantly loud inside. He turned just in time to see Marjorie's pretty face illuminated, as his own had been, by the salmon dashboard light. He saw the tips of her fingers atop the arc of the steering wheel, heard the surge of the engine. In the woods he noticed a strange glow coming through the trees, something yellow, something out of the low wet earth, a mist, a vapor, something that might be magical. The air smelled sweet now. The peepers stopped peeping. And then that was all.

Edward P. Jones

THE STORE

'd been out of work three four months when I saw her ad in the *Daily News*; a few lines of nothing special, almost as if she really didn't want a response. On a different day in my life I suppose I would have passed right over it. I had managed to squirrel away a little bit of money from the first slave I had, and after that change ran out, I just bummed from friends for smokes, beer, the valuables. I lived with my mother, so rent and food weren't a problem, though my brother, when he came around with that family of his, liked to get in my shit and tell me I should be looking for another job. Usually, my mother was okay, but I could tell when my brother and his flat-butt wife had been around when I wasn't there, because for days after that my mother would talk that same shit about me getting a job, like I'd never slaved a day before in my life.

That first slave I had had just disappeared out from under me, despite my father always saying that the white people who gave me that job were the best white people he'd known in his life.

My father never had a good word to say about anybody white, and I believed him when he said I could go far in that place. I started working there—the Atlas Printing Co. ("75 YEARS IN THE SAME LOCATION")—right after I graduated from Dunbar, working in the mailroom and sometimes helping out the printers when the mail work was slow. My father had been a janitor there until he got his third heart attack, the one that would put him in the ground when I was in my sophomore year at Dunbar.

At twenty I was still in the mailroom: assistant chief mail clerk or something like that, still watching the white boys come in, work beside me, then move on. My mother always said that every bullfrog praises his own poem, but I know for a natural fact that I was an excellent worker. Never late, never talked back, always volunteering; the product of good colored parents. Still . . . In the end, one bitching cold day in January, the owner and his silly-ass wife, who seemed to be the brains of the outfit, came to me and said they could no longer afford to keep me on. Times were bad, said the old man, who was so bald you could read his thoughts. They made it sound like I was the highest-paid worker in the joint, when actually I was making so little the white guys used to joke about it.

I said nothing, just got my coat and took my last check and went home. Somewhere along K Street, I remembered I'd left some of my personal stuff back there—some rubbers I'd bought just that morning at Peoples, a picture of the girl I was going with at the time, a picture of my father, my brother, and me at four years old on one of our first fishing trips. I had the urge to go back—the girl was already beginning not to mean anything to me anymore, so I didn't care about her picture, but the fishing trip picture was special. But I didn't turn back because, first of all, my balls were beginning to freeze.

My father always said that when the world pisses on you, it then spits on you to finish the job. At New York Avenue and 5th I crossed on the red light. A white cop twirling his billy club saw me and came to spit on me to finish up what Atlas had done: He asked me if I didn't know it was against D.C. and federal law to cross on the red light. I was only a few blocks from home and maybe heat and thawing out my nuts were the only things on my mind, because I tried to be funny and told him the joke my father had always told—that I thought the green light was for white folks and the red light was for colored people. His face reddened big-time.

When my brother and I were in our early teens, my mother said this to us with the most seriousness she had ever said anything: "Never even if you become kings of the whole world, I don't want yall messin with a white cop." The worst that my mother feared didn't happen to her baby boy that day. The cop only made me cross back on the green light and go all the way back to 7th Street, then come back to 5th Street and cross again on the green light. Then go back to 7th to do it all over again. Then I had to do it twice more. I was frozen through and through when I got back to 5th the second time and as I waited for the light to change after the fourth time and he stood just behind me I became very afraid, afraid that doing all that would not be enough for him, that he would want me to do more and then even more after that and that in the end I would be shot or simply freeze to death across the street from the No. 2 police precinct. Had he told me to deny my mother and father, I think I would have done that too.

I got across the street and went on my way, waiting for him to call me back. I prayed, "Just get me back to one fifteen New York Avenue safely and I'll never come to their world again. . . . Just get me back to one fifteen New York Avenue safely. . . ." For days after that I just hung out at home. My mother believed that a day had the best foundation if you had breakfast, so after she fixed our breakfast, and went off to work, I went back to bed and slept to about noon.

When I got some heart back, I started venturing out again, but I kept to my own neighborhood, my own world. Either my ace-boon, Lonney McCrae, would come get me or I would go looking for him and we'd spend the rest of the afternoon together until our friends got off work. Then all of us would go off and fuck with the world most of the night.

Lonney was going to Howard, taking a course here and there, doing just enough to satisfy his father. I'd seen his old man maybe once or twice in all the time I knew Lonney, and I'd been knowing him since kindergarten. His father had been one of the few big-shot Negro army officers in the Korea war, and Lonney was always saying that after the war his father would be home for good. He was still saying it that January when Kennedy was inaugurated.

Lonney liked to fuck bareback and that was how he got Brenda Roper pregnant. I think he liked her, maybe not as much as she liked him, but just enough so it wasn't a total sacrifice to marry her.

I was to be his best man. One night, all of us—me and Lonney and his mother and Brenda and her parents—were sitting around his living room, talking about the wedding and everything. Someone knocked on the door and Lonney opened it. It was his old man, standing there tall and straight as a lamppost in his uniform. You know something's wrong when a man doesn't even have a key to his own house.

The soldier didn't say Hello or Good to see you, son. He just stood in the doorway and said—and I know he could see everybody else in the room— "You don't have anything better to do with your time than marrying this girl?" Lonney's mother stood up, in that eager, happy way women do when they want to greet their husbands home from a foreign land. Brenda's father stood up too, but he had this goofy look on his face like he wanted to greet his soon-to-be in-law. "I asked you something," Lonney's father said. Lonney said nothing, and his father walked by him, nodded at Mrs. McCrae, and went on upstairs with his suitcase. The next morning he was gone again.

Lonney married Brenda that March, a few weeks before I saw the ad in the *Daily News*. I think that he wanted to make things work with Brenda, if only to push the whole thing in his father's face, but the foundation, as my mother would have said, was built on shifting sand. In about a year or so he had separated from her, though he continued to be a good father to the child, a chubby little girl they named after his mother. And some two years after he married, he had joined the army and before long he himself was in a foreign land, though it was a different one from where his father was.

The day before I saw the ad I spent the evening at Lonney and Brenda's place. They fought, maybe not for the first time as newly-weds, but for the first rime in front of me. I felt as if I were watching my own folks arguing, as if the world I knew and depended on was now coming apart. I slept till one the next day, then went down to Mojo's near North Capitol and Florida Avenue and hung out there for most of the day. Late in the day, someone left a *Daily News* at a table and over my second beer, with nothing better to do, I read the want ads. Her ad said:

> STORE HELPER. *Good pay. Good hours.*
> *Good Opportunity for Advancement.*

Then she had the store's location—5th and O streets North-
west. The next morning I forced myself to stay awake after my
mother had left, then went off about eight o'clock to see what the
place was about. I didn't want any part of a white boss and I stood
outside the store, trying to see just who ran the place. Through
the big windows I could see a colored woman of fifty or so in an
apron, and she seemed to be working alone. Kids who attended
Bundy Elementary School down the street went in and out of the
store buying little treats. I walked around the block until about
nine, then went in. A little bell over the door tinkled and the
first thing I smelled was coal oil from the small pump just inside
the door. The woman was now sitting on a tall stool behind the
counter, reading the *Post*, which she had spread out over the glass
counter.

She must have known I was there, but even after I was halfway
to her, she just wet a finger and turned the page. I was inches from
the counter, when she looked up. "Somethin you want?" she said.
Oh shit, I thought, she's one of those bitches. I could feel my balls
trying to retreat back up into my body.

"I come about the job in the paper," I said.

"Well, you pass the first test: At least you know how to read.
What else you know how to do? You ever work in a store before? A
grocery store like this?"

I gave her my work history, such as it was, and all the while she
looked like she wanted to be someplace else. She kept reading and
turning those pages. She seemed skeptical that the printing com-
pany had let me go without just cause.

"What you been doin since you lost that job?" she said.

"Lookin. I just never found anything I liked."

That was not the right answer, I could see that right away, but by then I didn't care. I was ready to start mouthing off like somebody was paying me to do it.

"The job pays thirty a week," she said finally. "The work is from eight in the mornin till eight in the evenin. Every day but Sunday and maybe a holiday here and there. Depends. You got questions?" But she didn't wait for me to ask, she just went on blubbering. "I'll be interviewin everybody else and then make my decision. Affix your name and phone number and if you're crowned queen of the ball, I'll let you know, sweetie." She tossed a pencil across the counter and pointed to the top of a newspaper page where she wanted me to put my telephone number. I wrote down my name and number, and just before I opened the door to leave, I heard her turn the next page.

The next day was Tuesday, and I spent most of that morning and the next few mornings cleaning up what passed for the backyard of Al's and Penny's Groceries. I had been surprised when she called me Monday night, too surprised to even tell her to go to hell. Then, after she hung up, I figured I just wouldn't show up, but on Tuesday morning, way long before dawn, I woke up and couldn't get back to sleep. And so for a change I was up when my mother rose and I fixed our breakfast. She did days work for some white people in Chevy Chase, and that morning I noticed how fast she ate, "wolfing down" her food, she would have called it.

For the first time in a long while, I stood at the window and watched her skinny legs take her down New York Avenue to hop the first of two D.C. Transits that would take her to Chevy Chase. Maybe it was watching her that sent me off that morning to the store. Or maybe it was that I came back to the table and saw that she hadn't finished all of her coffee. My mother would have sold me back into slavery for a good cup of coffee, and no one made it to her satisfaction the way she did.

"Good," the store owner said to me after she parked her lavender Cadillac and was opening the store's door. "You passed the second test: You know how to show up on time." It was about 7:30 and I'd been waiting about fifteen minutes.

She took me straight to the backyard, through the store itself, through a smaller room that served mostly as a storage area, to the back door, which took a hell of an effort for us to open. In the yard, two squirrels with something in their hands stood on their hind legs, watching us. No one had probably been in the yard for a coon's age and the squirrels stood there for the longest time, perhaps surprised to see human beings. When they realized we were for real, they scurried up the apple tree in a corner of the yard. The store owner brought out a rake, shovel, wheelbarrow, everything I needed to do to the yard what no one had done for years. I hadn't worn any good clothes and I was glad of that. Right off I took my tools and went to the far end of the yard to begin.

"By the way," she said, standing in the back door, "my name's Penelope Jenkins. Most people call me Penny. But the help call me Mrs. Jenkins, and you, buddy boy, you the help."

Beyond the high fence surrounding the yard there were the sounds of schoolchildren getting into their day. Well into the second hour of work, after I knew I was getting dirty and smelly as hell, after the children were all in school, I started throwing stones at the damn squirrels, who, jumping back and forth from tree to fence, seemed to be taunting me. Just like on the cold evening of the green light, I began to feel that I would be doing that shit forever.

The first thick layer of crap in the yard was slimy dead leaves from the autumn before, maybe even years before, and the more I disturbed the leaves the more insects and slugs crawled out from the home they had created and made a run for it under the fence and to other parts of the yard. The more spiteful and stupid bugs crawled up my pants legs. Beneath the layer of leaves there was a good amount of soda bottles, candy wrappers, the kind of shit kids might have thrown over the fence. But I didn't get to that second layer until Thursday morning, because the yard was quite large, big enough for little kids to play a decent game of kickball. Sometimes, when I heard voices on the other side of the fence, I would pull myself up to the top and look over.

My father always told the story of working one week for an undertaker in Columbia, South Carolina, one of his first jobs. He didn't like the undertaker and he knew the undertaker didn't like him. But, and maybe he got this from his old man, my father figured that he would give the undertaker the best goddamn week of work a fourteen-year-old was capable of. And that's what he did—for seven days he worked as if that business was his own. Then he collected his pay and never went back. The undertaker came by late one evening and at first, thinking my father wasn't showing up because he was just lazy, the undertaker acted big and bad. Then, after my father told him he wouldn't be coming back, the undertaker promised a raise, even praised my father's work, but my father had already been two days at a sawmill.

I didn't think Mrs. Jenkins was the kind of woman who would beg me to come back, but I did like imagining her sitting on her high stool, reading her damn paper and thinking of what a good worker she had lost. That was the image I took home each evening that week, so sore and depressed I could not think of fucking the world or anybody else. My mother would fix me dinner and I would sit hunched down in my chair close to the food because I had little strength left to make the long distance from the plate to my mouth if I sat up straight. Then, before I could fall asleep in the chair, my mother would run water for me to take a bath, the same thing I had seen her do for my father so often when I was a child that I didn't notice it anymore.

In the late mornings that week, after she thought I had done enough in the yard, Mrs. Jenkins would have me sweep the area around the front of the store or provide some order to the merchandise in the storage room. On Tuesday she wanted the boxes of stuff arranged just so, but then, as if she had some revelation during the night, she wanted everything rearranged on Wednesday. Then on Thursday I had to do things different again, and then different still again on Friday. And because she claimed she planned to repaint, she also had me up on a ladder, scraping away the peeling orange paint of the store's exterior. The paint chips would fly off into my eyes and hair, and it took me until Thursday to get smart about wearing a stocking cap and the goggles my father had once used.

Saturday morning I woke up happy. Again, I was there waiting for her to open up and again I did all the shit work while she chatted and made nice-nice with all the customers. I had already planned my weekend, had, in my mind, spent every dollar I was to be paid. But I was also prepared to get cheated. Cheating folks was like some kind of religion with people like Mrs. Jenkins—they figured that if they didn't practice it they'd go to hell. Actually, I was kind of hoping she would cheat me, just so I could come back late that night and break all the fucking windows or something.

At the end of the day, after she had locked the front door to any more customers and pulled down the door's shade with the little

CLOSED sign on it, she opened the cash register and counted out my money. It came to about twenty-five dollars after she took out for taxes and everything. She explained where every dollar I wasn't getting was going, then she gave me a slip with that same information on it.

"You did a good job," she said. "You surprised me, and no one in the world surprises me anymore."

The words weren't much and I had heard better in my time, but as I stood there deliberately counting every dollar a second and third time, I found I enjoyed hearing them, and it came to me why some girls will give their pussys to guys who give them lines full of baby this and baby that and I'll do this and I'll be that forever and ever until the end of time. . . .

I just said yeah and good night and thanks, because my mother had always taught me and my brother that the currency of manners didn't cost anything. Mrs. Jenkins had untied her apron, but she still had it on and it hung loosely from her neck. She followed me to the door and unlocked it. "I'll see you bright and early Monday mornin," she said, like that was the only certainty left in my whole damn life. I said yeah and went out. I didn't look back.

Despite my aches, I went dancing with Mabel Smith, a girl I had gone to Dunbar with. We stepped out with Lonney and Brenda. I didn't get any trim that night, and it didn't bother me, because there was something satisfying in just dancing. I danced just about every dance, and when Mabel said she was tired, couldn't take it anymore, I took Brenda out on the dance floor, and when I had worn her out, I danced away what was left of the night with girls at other tables.

I got home about six that Sunday morning. In the dark apartment, I could see that slice of light along the bottom of my mother's closed door.

.   .   .

I didn't go back to the store on Monday. In fact, I slept late and spent the rest of the day running the streets. Tuesday, I couldn't get back to sleep after my old lady left, and about ten I wandered over to the store, then wandered in. She didn't act mad and she sure didn't act like she was glad to see me. She just put me to work like the week before had been a rehearsal for the real thing. And she enjoyed every bad thing that happened to me. Tuesday I restocked the cereal section of shelves behind the counter with the cash register. As I bent down to dust the bottom shelves, a box of oatmeal fell on my head from three or four shelves up. Hit me so hard I'm sure some of my descendants will be born dumb because of it. Mrs. Jenkins went into a laugh that went on and on for minutes, and throughout the rest of the day she'd come up behind me and shout "Oatmeal!" and go into that laugh again.

"In the grocery business," she said after I replaced the box, "the first law of supply in them shelves is to supply em so that nothin falls over."

And late that Friday afternoon, as I was checking the coal oil pump to see how much was in it, a customer rushed in and the door pushed me against the pump, soiling a good shirt with oily dirt and dust. None of Mrs. Jenkins's aprons fit me and she had said she was ordering one for me. "Sorry, sport," the customer said.

"The first law of customer relations," Mrs. Jenkins said after the guy was gone, "is to provide your customers with proper egress to and from your product." Such bullshit would have been enough in itself, but then, for the rest of that day, she'd look at me and ask, "What am I thinkin?" And before I could say anything, she would say, "Wrong! Wrong! I'm thinkin oil." Then the laugh again.

·   ·   ·

That was how it was for months and months. But each Monday morning, like a whipped dog that stayed because he didn't know any other master but the one that whipped him, I was at the store's front door, waiting for her to open up. And a thousand times during the week I promised myself I would give her a week of work that only my father could surpass and then, come Saturday night, get my pay and tell her to kiss my ass. But always there was something during the week to bring me back on Monday—she allowed me, for example, to wait on customers (but didn't allow me to open the cash register and make change); and I got two new aprons with my name stitched in script over the left pocket; and I got a raise of one dollar more a week after I had been there six months; and eventually she allowed me to decide how much of what things we had to reorder. Often, at home in the evening, I would go over the day and rate it according to how many times Mrs. Jenkins had laughed at me, and it became a challenge to get through the next day and do things as perfectly as possible. By the time I got my raise I felt comfortable enough to push that laugh back in her face whenever she slipped up on something. I'd say, "The first law of bein a grocery store boss is to be perfect."

Then, too, I found that there was something irresistible to girls about a man in an apron with his name stitched on it. I had to suffer with a lot of giggly little girls from Bundy, who would hang around the store just to look at me, but there were also enough high school and older girls to make working there worth my while. Before my first year was out, I was borrowing from next week's pay to finance the good life of the current week.

The first time I waited on Kentucky Connors was just after Lonney separated from Brenda and went back to a room in his father's house. Mrs. Jenkins didn't tolerate the type of friendliness with customers that led to what she called "exploiratation," so when I wanted a date with someone who came into the store, I'd arrange to set up things after I got off. The night Kentucky came in that first time, I purposely failed to put her pack of gum in the bag and ran after her.

"Why, of all the men on this earth," she said after I caught up with her and boldly told her to clear her calendar for that Saturday night, "would I think of going out with someone like you?" You can tell when girls are just being coy and want you to lay it on just a little thicker before they say yes. But there are others who have no facade, who are not seeking to be wooed, who give out smiles like each time they do it takes them a mile farther from heaven. And after they speak you're a year older and a foot shorter. That was Kentucky.

She actually stood there for several long seconds as if waiting for me to give her some kind of fucking resume. Then she said, "I thought so," and walked away. A thousand and one comebacks came much later, when I was trying to go to sleep.

You do manage to go on with your life. Over the next weeks and months, I had to put up with her coming in a few times a week, but for her there seemed to be no memory of me asking her out and she acted as though I was no more or less than the fellow who took her money and bagged her groceries. But her you're welcome in response to my thanking her for her purchases contained no sense of triumph, of superiority, as I would have expected. I learned in bits and pieces over time that she lived in an apartment on Neal Place a few doors from 5th Street, was a year out of Dunbar, was a secretary with the government people, that her family lived in a house on N Street that her mother's parents had bought. . . .

About a fifth of Mrs. Jenkins's customers bought things on credit and each purchase was carefully noted. On a chain beside the cash register she kept an elongated accounting book for nonmeat credit purchases. The meat case, with its small array of dressed chickens and parts, wrapped hamburger and stew beef, rolls of lunch meats, pork chops, etc., was catty-corner to the counter with the register. The meats had their own credit book, and perhaps no one—except maybe Mrs. Gertrude Baxter—had a longer bill than the Turner family. I rarely ever saw the father of the two Turner children and I came to know that he worked as a night watchman. The mother seemed to live and die for her stories on television, and I rarely saw her either. The boy and girl were in and out all the time.

"My mama said gimme a small box of soap powder," one of them would say. "Gimme" meant the mother wanted it on credit. "My mama said give her a pound of baloney and a loaf a Wonda Bread." "My mama said give her two cans a spaghetti. The kind with the meatballs, not the other kind. She said you gave me the wrong kind the last time." If you got a please with any of that, it was usually from the little girl, who was about seven or so. Mrs. Jenkins had a nice way with every customer as long as they didn't fuck with her, but the Turner girl seemed to have a special place in her heart. Which is why, despite what Mrs. Baxter went about telling the whole world, I know that Penny Jenkins would have done anything to avoid killing the Turner girl.

The ten-year-old Turner boy, however, was an apprentice thug. He never missed a chance to try me, and he was particularly fond of shaking the door just to hear that tinkling bell. He never messed with Mrs. Jenkins, of course, but he seemed to think God had put me on the earth just for his amusement. He also liked to stand at the cooler with the sodas and move his hand about, knocking the bottles over and getting water on the floor. Whenever I told him to get a soda and get out of the box, he would whine, "But I want a *reeaal* cold one. . . ." He would persist at the box and I usually had to come and pull his arm out, and he'd back away to the door.

He'd poke his tongue out at me and, no matter how many old church ladies were in the store, would say in his loudest voice: "You don't tell me what to do, mothafucka!" Then he'd run out.

Just before he dashed out, his sister, Patricia, who often came with him, would say, "Ohh, Tommy. I'm gonna tell Mama you been cursin." Then she would look up at me with this exasperated look as if to say, "What can you do?"

"Where me and you gonna retire to?" was the standard question Mrs. Jenkins would ask the girl after she had bagged the girl's stuff.

"To Jamaica," Patricia would say, giggling that standard little-girl giggle.

"Now don't you grow up and run off somewhere else," Mrs. Jenkins said. "There's some fine, fine men in Jamaica, and we gon get us some."

"Oh, no," Patricia said as if Mrs. Jenkins had implied that the girl was capable of doing something horrible.

"And how we gon get to Jamaica?"

"On a slow boat by way a China."

None of that meant very much to me then, of course. It was just so much bullshit heard over the hours of a long day.

·   ·   ·

By the summer of 1962 I was making forty dollars a week and that November I had enough to buy a used Ford from a longtime friend of my parents. "Always know where the seller lives in case the thing turns out to be a piece of junk," my father once said. The first long trip I took in the car was to Fort Holabird in Baltimore, where Lonney was inducted into the man's army. I came back to Washington and dropped his mother off at her house and then went back to work, though Penny had said I could take the day off. Perhaps it was the effort of trying to get through the day, of trying not to think about Lonney, that made me feel reckless enough to ask Kentucky out again.

Penny had waited on her, and I followed Kentucky out of the store. I waited until we were across O Street and asked with words that would have done my mother proud if I could take her to Howard Theater to see Dinah Washington that Saturday night.

"I'd like that," she said without much hesitation. And because she was the kind of woman she was, I knew it was the simple truth, no more, no less. She set down her bag of stuff and pulled a pen and a slip of paper from her pocketbook. She began to write. "This is my telephone number. If you're going to be late," she said, "I'd like the courtesy of knowing. And if you are late and haven't called, don't come. I love Dinah Washington, but I don't love her that much."

I found her family a cold and peculiar lot, except for her little sisters, who were as passionate about the Washington Senators as I was. A few times a month we had dinner at their place on N Street. Her father was a school principal and talked as if every morning when he got up, he memorized an awfully big word from the dictionary and forced himself to use that word in his conversations throughout the day, whether the word actually fit what he was saying or not. Kentucky's mother was the first Negro supervisor at some office in the Department of Commerce. She was a bit better to take than her husband, but she was a terrible cook and I seemed to be the only person at her dinner table who realized this.

The first time we slept together was that January. I had waited a long time, something quite unusual for me. I had started to think I would be an old man with a dick good for nothing but peeing before she would let me get beyond heavy petting. So when she turned to me as we were sitting at the counter at Mile Long one Sunday night, I didn't think anything was up.

She turned to look at me. "Listen," she said and waited until I had chewed up and swallowed the bite of steak sandwich I had in my mouth. "Listen: Thou shall have no other woman before me. I can take a lot but not that." Which didn't mean anything to me until we got back to her apartment. We had just gotten in and shut the door. She took my belt in both her hands and pulled me to her until our thighs and stomachs met. Until then I'd made all the moves, and so what she did took my breath away. She kissed me and said again, "Thou shall have no other woman before me." Then she asked if I wanted to stay the night.

A very mischievous wind came through Washington that night and the rattling windows kept waking us, and each time we woke we would resettle into each other's arms, to drift away with sleep and return with another rattling. I can be twenty-two forever as long as I can remember that evening and that night.

When you work in a grocery store the world comes to buy: tons of penny candy and small boxes of soap powder because the next size up—only pennies more—is too expensive and rubbing alcohol and baby formula and huge sweet potatoes for pies for church socials and spray guns and My Knight and Dixie Peach hair grease and Stanback ("snap back with Stanback") headache powder and all colors of Griffin shoe polish and nylon stockings and twenty-five cents worth of hogshead cheese cut real thin to make more sandwiches and hairnets for practically bald old women trudging off to work at seventy-five and lard and Argo starch not for laundry but to satisfy a pregnant woman's craving and mousetraps and notebook paper for a boy late with his what-I-did-on-my-summer-vacation paper and Kotex and clothespins and Bat 'N' Balls and coal oil for lamps in apartments where landlords decline to provide electricity and Sneaky Pete dream books and corn flakes with the surprise in the box and light bulbs for a new place and chocolate milk and shoestrings and Wonder Bread to help "build strong bodies 12 ways" and RC Cola and Valentine's Day specials to be given with all your heart and soul and penny cookies and enough chicken wings to feed a family of ten and bottles of bluing. . . .

By the time I came on the scene, Penelope Jenkins had been selling all that and more for about fifteen years. She and her husband ("the late Mr. Al Jenkins") had bought the place from a Jewish family not long after World War II. Al had died ten years before I showed up, and Penny had had a succession of helpers, including a son who went off and died in Korea, never to come back to Al's and Penny's Groceries.

Because of my life at the store, my sense of neighborhood began to expand; then, too, it's easier to love a neighborhood when you love the girl in it. My allegiances had always been to the world around New York Avenue and 1st Street, around Dunbar, because that was

Home. In fact, I hadn't much cared for the world around 5th and O; when I was still in junior high I'd gotten my ass whipped by a boy who lived around 5th and O. Lonney and I and people from our world had always associated the whole 5th and O area with punk fighters, and the boy I fought turned out to be one of the biggest punks around. From the get-go, this guy went for my privates with a hard kick and it took everything out of me; you never recover from shit like that, so even though I lost, I didn't lose fair.

The second time I realized my allegiances were expanding, that I was making room in my soul for more than one neighborhood, was when I was asked to be godfather to two babies within one month; Penny got to be the godmother and I stood beside her as the god-father. The first time, though, was the afternoon Penny gave me the combination to the safe she kept in the little room off the main room. She had me practice the combination that afternoon until I knew it by heart. After a few turns I got tired of that and ended up looking through some of what was in the safe. There was a stack of pictures Al Jenkins had taken in those early years, mostly pictures of people in the 5th and O Street neighborhood. Many of the people in the pictures still lived around there; having served them in the store for so long, I recognized them despite what time had done to them. I sat on the floor and read what Al had written on the backs of the black-and-white pictures. One picture showed Joy Lambert, the mother of Patricia and Tommy Turner. Surrounded by several girlfriends, Joy was standing on what must have been a sunny day in front of the store in her high-school graduation cap and gown. Al had written on the back of the picture, "June 1949. The world awaits." This picture, above all the others, captivated me. You could tell that they were innocents, with good hearts. And the more I looked at those smiling girls, especially Joy, the more I wanted only good things for them, the way I wanted only good things for my nieces and nephews. Perhaps it was tiredness, but I began to feel that I was looking at a picture of the dead, people who had died years and years before, and now there was nothing I could do.

"Now you know why I keep all those in the safe." Penny had come up behind me and was looking down on me and the pictures spread out before me. "Out of harm's way," she said, "way in back, behind the money."

Kentucky and I fell into an easy, pleasant relationship, which is not to say that I didn't tip out on her now and again. But it was never anything to upset what we had, and, as far as I know, she never found out about any of it. More and more I got to staying at her place, sleeping at my mother's only a few times a month. "I hope you know what you doin'," my mother would say sometimes. Who knew? Who cared?

In fact, my mother said those very words that August Thursday night when I went to get clean clothes from her place. That Friday was hot, but bearably humid, and the next day would be the same. The weather would stay the same for a week or so more. After that, I remember nothing except that it stayed August until it became September. The air-conditioning unit installed over the front door, which Penny had bought second-hand, had broken down again that Wednesday, and we had managed to get the repairman, a white man with three fingers missing on one hand, to come out on Thursday and do his regular patch-up job. In the summer, we had two, sometimes three, deliveries a week of sodas and stuff like Popsicles and Creamsicles that the kids couldn't seem to do without. For years and years after that, my only dreams of the store were of a summer day and of children coming to buy those sodas and ice cream. We always ran out of the product in my dreams and the delivery men were either late or never showed up and a line of nothing but children would form at the door, wanting to buy the stuff that we didn't have, and the line would go on down 5th Street, past N, past M, past New York Avenue, past F, past Pennsylvania Avenue, all the way down into Southwest, until it went on out Washington and into another land. In the dreams I would usually be yelling at Penny that I wanted her to do something about that line of children, that we weren't in business to have a line like that, that I wanted it gone pretty damn soon. Eventually, in the dreams, she would do something to placate me—sometimes, she would disappear into the back and return with a nib of sniff that I recognized immediately as the homemade ice cream my mother said her parents always made when she was a little girl.

About a half hour or so before closing that Friday, Kentucky came by. She had bought a new stereo and all week I had been borrowing records from friends because we planned a little party, just the two of us, to break in the stereo. Penny left the locking up to me and got ready to go.

"Who's the man tonight?" Kentucky asked Penny. I think she must have had more boyfriends than Carter had liver pills. I had just finished covering the meat for the night, something Penny and I called putting the chickens to bed.

"Ask me no questions . . . ," Penny said and winked. She whispered in Kentucky's ear, and the two laughed. Then Kentucky, looking dead at me, whispered to Penny, and they laughed even louder. Finally, Penny was ready to leave.

If the sign said we closed at nine, that was precisely the time Penny wanted the store closed and I wasn't allowed to close any sooner. I could close later for a late-arriving customer, but not any sooner. And as it happened, someone did come in at the last minute and I had to pull out some pork chops. Penny said good night and left. I locked the door after the pork chop customer. I may or may not have heard the sound of a car slamming on brakes, but I certainly heard little Carl Baggot banging at the door.

"You little squirt," I said to him. "If you break that window, I'm gonna make your daddy pay for it." I'd pulled down the door shade to an inch or so of where the glass ended, and I could see the kid's eyes beaming through that inch of space. "Can't you read, you little punk. We closed. We closed!" and I walked away. Kentucky was standing near the door and the more the kid shouted, the closer she got to the door.

"He's hysterical, honey," she said, unlocking the door. She walked out, and I followed.

Penny's lavender Cadillac was stopped in the middle of 5th Street, one or two doors past O Street. From everywhere people were running to whatever had happened. Penny was standing in front of the car. I pushed my way through the crowd, and as I got closer I saw that her fists were up, shaking, and she was crying.

"She hit my sista," Tommy Turner was saying, pounding away at Penny's thigh. "This bitch hit my sista! This bitch hit my sista!" Some stranger picked the boy up. "All right, son," the man said, "thas anough of that."

Patricia Turner lay in the street, a small pool of blood forming around her head. She had apparently been chasing a rolling Hula Hoop, and she and the hoop, now twisted, had fallen in such a way that one of her arms was embracing the toy. Most of what light there was came from the street lamps, but there were also the Cadillac's headlights, shining out on the crowd on the other side of the girl. "You should watch where you goin with that big ole car," Mrs. Baxter said to Penny. "Oh, you know it was a accident," a man said. "I don't know no such thing," Mrs. Baxter said.

The girl's eyes were open and she was looking at me, at the people around her, at everything in the world, I suppose. The man still had hold of Tommy, but the boy was wiggling violently and still cursing Penny. Penny, crying, bent down to Patricia and I think I heard her tell the child that it would be all right. I could tell that it wouldn't be. The girl's other arm was stretched out and she had a few rubber bands around the wrist. There was something about the rubber bands on that little wrist and they, more than the blood perhaps, told me, in the end, that none of it would be all right.

Soon Joy, the girl's mother, was there. "You murderin fuckin monster!" she kept yelling at Penny, and someone held her until she said that she wanted to go to her baby. "Look what that murderin monster did to my baby!"

The police arrived, but they did not know what else to do except handcuff Penny and threaten to arrest the man who held Tommy if he didn't control the boy. Then the ambulance arrived and in little or no time they took the girl and her mother away, the flashing light on the roof shining on all the houses as it moved down 5th Street. A neighbor woman took Tommy from the stranger and took the boy inside. Wordlessly, the crowd parted to let them by, as it had parted to let the ambulance through. The police put Penny in the back of the scout car and I followed, with Kentucky holding tight to my arm. Through the rolled down window, she said to me, "Bail me out, if they'll let me go." But most of what she said was just a bunch of mumbles, because she hadn't managed to stop crying. I reached in the window and touched her cheek.

I opened the store as usual the next day, Saturday. The child died during the night. No one, except people from out of the neighborhood, spoke when they came in the store; they merely pointed or got the items themselves and set them on the counter. I sold no meat that day. And all that day, I kept second-guessing myself about even the simplest of things and kept waiting for Penny to come and tell me what to do. Just before I closed, one girl, Snowball Patterson, told me that Mrs. Baxter was going about saying that Penny had deliberately killed Patricia.

Penny called me at Kentucky's on Sunday morning to tell me not to open the store for two weeks. "We have to consider Pat's family," she said. I had seen her late that Friday night at No. 2 police precinct, but she had said little. I would not see her again for a month. I had parked the Cadillac just in front of the store, and sometime over the next two weeks, the car disappeared, and I never found out what happened to it, whether Penny came to get it late one night or whether it was stolen. "Pay it no mind," Penny told me later.

She called me again Monday night and told me she would mail me a check for two thousand dollars, which I was to cash and take the money to Patricia's family for her funeral. The police were satisfied that it had been an accident, but on the phone Penny always talked like old lady Baxter, as if she had done it on purpose. "Her mother," Penny said, "wouldn't let me come by to apologize. Doesn't want me to call anymore." All that month, and for some months after, that was the heart of the phone conversation, that the mother wouldn't allow her to come to see her and the family.

Joy came in one day about three months after Pat died. Tommy came with her, and all the time they were in the store, the boy held his mother's hand.

"You tell her to stop callin me," Joy said to me. "You tell her I don't want her in my life. You tell her to leave me alone, or I'll put the law on her. And you"—she pointed at me—"my man say for you not to bring me no more food." Which is what Penny had been instructing me to do. The boy never said a word the whole time, just stood there close to his mother, with his thumb in his mouth and blinking very, very slowly as if he were about to fall asleep on his feet.

About once a week for the next few years, Penny would call me at Kentucky's and arrange a place and time to meet me. We always met late at night, on some fairly deserted street, like secret lovers. And we usually met in some neighborhood in far, far Northeast or across the river in Anacostia, parts of the world I wasn't familiar with. I would drive up, park, and go to her car not far away. She wanted to know less about how I was operating the store than what was going on with the people in the neighborhood. She had moved from her apartment in Southwest, and because I had no way of getting in touch with her, I always came with beaucoup questions about this and that to be done in the store. She dispensed with all the questions as quickly as possible, and not always to my satisfaction. Then she wanted to know about this one and that one, about so-and-so and whoever. Because it was late at night, I was always tired and not always very talkative. But when I began to see how important our meetings were, I found myself learning to set aside some reserve during the day for that night's meeting, and over time, the business of the store became less important in our talks than the business of the people in the neighborhood.

And over time as well, nearly all the legal crap was changed so that my name, just below hers, was on everything—invoices, the store's bank account, even the stuff on the door's window about who to call in case of emergency. After she had been gone a year or so, I timidly asked about a raise because I hadn't had one in quite a while. "Why ask me?" she said. We were someplace just off Benning Road and I didn't know where I would get the strength to drive all the way back to Kentucky's. "Why in the world are you askin me?"

I went about my days at first with tentativeness, as if Penny would show up at any moment in her dirty apron and make painful jokes about what I had done wrong. When she was there, I had, for example, always turned the bruised fruit and vegetables bad side up so people could see from jump what was what, but Penny always kept the bruised in with all the healthy pieces and sold the good and the not-so-good at the same price. Now that she was not there, I created a separate bin for the bruised and sold it at a reduced price, something she had always refused to do. But the dividing line of that separate bin was made of cardboard, something far from permanent. Every week or so the cardboard would wear out and I had to replace it.

Because there were many nights when I simply was too exhausted to walk the two blocks or so to Kentucky's, I made a pallet for myself in the back room, which would have been an abomination to Penny. "Work is work, and home is home," she always said, "and never should those trains meet."

When Mrs. Baxter came in to buy on credit, which was about twice a day, she would always ask, "How the murderer doin?" I tried to ignore it at first, but began trying to get back at her by reminding her of what her bill was. Generally, she owed about a hundred dollars; and rarely paid more than five dollars on the bill from month to month. Since Penny had told me to wipe the slate clean for Patricia's mother, Old Lady Baxter became the biggest deadbeat. Baxter always claimed that her retirement check was coming the next day. After I started pressing her about the bill, she stopped bad-mouthing Penny, but I found out that that was only in the store, where I could hear.

When I told her that I wouldn't give her any more credit until she paid up, she started crying. My mother once told me that in place of muscles God gave women the ability to cry on a moment's notice.

"I'll tell," Mrs. Baxter boo-hooed. "I'm gonna tell."

"Oh, yeah," I said, loud enough for everyone in the store to hear. "Who you gonna tell? Who you gonna go to?"

"Penny," she said. "I'll tell Penny. She oughta know how you runnin her sto into the ground. I'm a tell her you tryin to starve me to death."

Within a few weeks her account was settled down to the last penny, but I still told her never to step foot in the store again. Surprisingly, the old lady took it like a man. It was a full month before I got the courage to tell Penny what I had done. I could see that she did not approve, but she only had this look that my mother had the day my brother came home with the first piece of clothing my parents allowed him to buy on his own. A look of resignation—Thank God I don't have to live with it.

At first, with Penny's blessing, I hired my more trustworthy friends or cousins or a few people in the neighborhood, but either they could only work part time or they didn't do the job well enough to suit me. Kentucky even helped out some, but after she got into an executive training program at what she called her "real job," she didn't want to work in the store anymore.

Then, in the spring of 1965, I lucked onto a Muslim who lived on 6th Street. She was on public assistance and had three children, which made me skeptical about her working out, but I gave her a one-week tryout, then extended it another week. Then extended two weeks more, then I took her on full time, permanent, and gave her two aprons with her named stitched over the left pockets. I was always afraid that I'd find the place overrun with her kids every day, but in all the time I knew her, despite the fact that she lived only a block away, I met her kids only a few times and came to know them only by the pictures she showed me. Her name was Gloria 5X, but before she lost her slave name, the world—and she seemed to know three fourths of it—had called her Puddin. And that was what I learned to call her.

After I got where I could leave things in Puddin's hands, I was able to take off now and again and spend more time than I had been with Kentucky. We did two weeks in Atlantic City in the summer of 1965, back when the only rep the city had was what the ocean gave it, and that seemed to revive what we had had. That fall I set about redoing the store—repainting, rearranging shelves, and, at long last, getting a new meat case. The renovations left me, again, spending more and more nights on the pallet in the back. There were fewer people buying coal oil and I wanted to tear out the pump, but Penny vetoed that. "Wait," she said. "Wait till the day after the very last person comes to buy some, then you tear it out."

I passed the halfway mark in the new work before the end of winter and wanted to celebrate with a good meal and a movie. I was to meet Kentucky at her office one evening in February, but I was late getting there for a reason I don't remember, for a reason that, when it is all said and done, will not matter anyway. When I did get there, she iced me out and said she was no longer interested in going out, which pissed me off. I kept telling her we could have a good evening, but she insisted we go home.

"You know," she said as I continued trying to coax her to go, "you spend too much time at that damn store. You act like you own it or something." I was making $110 a week, had a full-time employee and one part-time worker, and I didn't particularly want to hear that shit.

"It's my job," I said. "You don't hear me complainin and everything when you come home and sit all evening with your head in those books."

"It's not every single day, not like you do. Maybe once every three weeks. You come first, and you know it."

When we got home, she began to thaw.

"Why are we letting all this come between you and me?" she said. "Between us?" She repeated that "us" three or four times and put her arms around me.

Because she was thawing, I felt I was winning. And I think I got to feeling playful, because the first thing that came to mind after all those *uses* was that joke about Tonto and the Lone Ranger looking up to see a band of Indians bearing down on them: "What they gonna do to us, Tonto?" "Whatcha mean 'us,' Kemo Sabe?"

I don't think I said that line out loud. Maybe I did. Or maybe she just read my mind. In any case, she withdrew from me, then went to the window, her arms hugging her body. "I thought so," she said after a bit. "Clean your things out of here," she said, in the same quiet way she used to tell me to remember to set the clock's alarm. "Clean everything out as soon as possible."

Despite what she had said, I left her place feeling pretty cocky and went to Mojo's. After four beers, I called Kentucky to say we should wipe the slate clean. She calmly told me not to call her again. "You fuckin bitch!" I said. "Who the fuck do you think you are!" After a while I went to my mother's place. For the most part, I had sobered up by the time I got there. I found my mother at the kitchen table, listening to gospel on the radio. I don't recall what conversation we had. I do remember noticing that she had lost, somewhere in time, three or four of her teeth, and it pained me that I did not even know when it had happened.

It took me three days to clean out my life from Kentucky's place. She stayed at work until I had finished each day. And on each of those days, I left a note telling her I wanted to stay.

I suppose any man could take rejection by any woman as long as he knew that the morning after he was cast out, the woman would be bundled up with her best memories of him and taken away to a castle in the most foreign of lands to live there forever, guarded by a million eunuchs and by old women who had spent their lives equating sex with death. No, no, the woman would have to say to the old women for the rest of her life, I remember different.

If you approached Al's and Penny's Groceries coming down O Street from 6th you could see the bright new orange color I myself put on, a color announcing to the world an establishment of substance, a place I tried to make as friendly as a customer's own home. Joy and Tommy and Tommy's father moved away when the paint was still fresh and bright. And it was still bright when Mrs. Baxter went on to her reward, and though she had not been in the store since the day I told her not to come back, Penny had me send flowers to the funeral home in both our names. The paint was still radiant when the babies I was godfather to learned to walk in the store on their own and beg for candy from me.

One evening—the season it was is gone from my mind now—I let Puddin go home early. Alone in the store, I sat on my high stool behind the counter, reading the *Afro*, a rare treat. At one point I stood to stretch and looked out the O Street window to see Penny, with shorter hair and in her apron, looking in at me. I smiled and waved furiously and she smiled and waved back. I started from behind the counter and happened to look out the 5th Street window and saw my father coming toward me. When I saw that he too had on an apron, I realized that my mind, exhausted from a long day, was only playing tricks.

I do not know what would have happened had Penny not decided to sell. Perhaps I would be there still, and still going home each evening with the hope that I would not see, again, Kentucky arm-in-arm with someone else. Penny and I had continued to meet in her car about once a week. The night she told me she was selling the place, we met on Q Street, between 5th and 6th. And the very last meeting was on O Street, in front of Bundy's playground. From meetings far, far from the neighborhood, we had now come to one that was just down the street from the store. I came out of the store about midnight, locked it, stepped back to take one final look at the place as I usually did, and walked only a few yards. In a few minutes, Penny drove up.

"You been a good friend to me," she said as soon as I got in the car. She handed me two envelopes—one with a month's pay for

Puddin and the other with four thousand dollars for me. "Severin pay," she said. "Don't spend it on all the whores, for a man does not live on top of whores alone."

She hugged me, kissed me hard on the cheek. After a while, I got out and watched her make a U turn and go back down the way she had come. I had a feeling that that would be the last time I would ever see her and I stood there with my heart breaking, watching her until I lost her in the night.

The next week I took the G2 bus all the way down P Street, crossing 16th Street into the land of white people. I didn't drive because my father had always told me that white people did not like to see Negroes driving cars, even a dying one like my Ford. In the fall, I was sitting in classes at Georgetown with glad-handing white boys who looked as if they had been weaned only the week before. I was twenty-seven years old, the age my mother was when she married. Sometimes, blocks before my stop on my way home from Georgetown in the evening, I would get off the G2 at 5th Street. I would walk up to O and sit on the low stone wall of the apartment building across the street from what had been Al's and Penny's Groceries. The place became a television repair shop after it stopped being a store, then it became a church of Holy Rollers. But whatever it was over the years, I could, without trying very hard, see myself sitting in the window eating my lunch the way I did before I knew Kentucky, before Pat was killed. In those early days at the store, I almost always had a lunch of one half smoke heavy with mustard and a large bottle of Upper 10 and a package of Sno-Ball cupcakes. I sat on the stone wall and watched myself as I ate my lunch and checked out the fine girls parading past the store, parading as if for me and me alone.

Jhumpa Lahiri

INTERPRETER OF MALADIES

At the tea stall Mr. and Mrs. Das bickered about who should take Tina to the toilet. Eventually Mrs. Das relented when Mr. Das pointed out that he had given the girl her bath the night before. In the rearview mirror Mr. Kapasi watched as Mrs. Das emerged slowly from his bulky white Ambassador, dragging her shaved, largely bare legs across the back seat. She did not hold the little girl's hand as they walked to the rest room.

They were on their way to see the Sun Temple at Konarak. It was a dry, bright Saturday, the mid-July heat tempered by a steady ocean breeze, ideal weather for sightseeing. Ordinarily Mr. Kapasi would not have stopped so soon along the way, but less than five minutes after he'd picked up the family that morning in front of Hotel Sandy Villa, the little girl had complained. The first thing Mr. Kapasi had noticed when he saw Mr. and Mrs. Das, standing with their children under the portico of the hotel, was that they were very young, perhaps not even thirty. In addition to Tina they had two boys, Ronny and Bobby, who appeared very close in age and had teeth covered in a network of flashing silver wires. The family looked Indian but dressed as foreigners did, the children in stiff, brightly colored clothing and caps with translucent visors. Mr. Kapasi was accustomed to foreign tourists; he was assigned to them regularly because he could speak English. Yesterday he had driven an elderly couple from Scotland, both with spotted faces and fluffy white hair so thin it exposed their sunburnt scalps. In comparison, the tanned, youthful faces of Mr. and Mrs. Das were all the more striking. When he'd introduced himself, Mr. Kapasi had pressed his palms together in greeting, but Mr. Das squeezed hands like an American so that Mr. Kapasi felt it in his elbow. Mrs. Das, for her part, had flexed one side of her mouth, smiling dutifully at Mr. Kapasi, without displaying any interest in him.

As they waited at the tea stall, Ronny, who looked like the older of the two boys, clambered suddenly out of the back seat, intrigued by a goat tied to a stake in the ground.

"Don't touch it," Mr. Das said. He glanced up from his paperback tour book, which said "INDIA" in yellow letters and looked as if it had been published abroad. His voice, somehow tentative and a little shrill, sounded as though it had not yet settled into maturity.

"I want to give it a piece of gum," the boy called back as he trotted ahead.

Mr. Das stepped out of the car and stretched his legs by squatting briefly to the ground. A clean-shaven man, he looked exactly like a magnified version of Ronny. He had a sapphire blue visor, and was dressed in shorts, sneakers, and a T-shirt. The camera slung around his neck, with an impressive telephoto lens and numerous buttons and markings, was the only complicated thing he wore. He frowned, watching as Ronny rushed toward the goat, but appeared to have no intention of intervening. "Bobby, make sure that your brother doesn't do anything stupid."

"I don't feel like it," Bobby said, not moving. He was sitting in the front seat beside Mr. Kapasi, studying a picture of the elephant god taped to the glove compartment.

"No need to worry," Mr. Kapasi said. "They are quite tame." Mr. Kapasi was forty-six years old, with receding hair that had gone completely silver, but his butterscotch complexion and his unlined brow, which he treated in spare moments to dabs of lotus-oil balm, made it easy to imagine what he must have looked like at an earlier age. He wore gray trousers and a matching jacket-style shirt, tapered at the waist, with short sleeves and a large pointed collar, made of a thin but durable synthetic material. He had specified both the cut and the fabric to his tailor — it was his preferred uniform for giving tours because it did not get crushed during his long hours behind the wheel. Through the windshield he watched as Ronny circled around the goat, touched it quickly on its side, then trotted back to the car.

"You left India as a child?" Mr. Kapasi asked when Mr. Das had settled once again into the passenger seat.

"Oh, Mina and I were both born in America," Mr. Das announced with an air of sudden confidence. "Born and raised. Our parents live here now, in Assansol. They retired. We visit them every couple years." He turned to watch as the little girl ran toward the car, the wide purple bows of her sundress flopping on her narrow brown shoulders. She was holding to her chest a doll with yellow hair that looked as if it had been chopped, as a punitive measure, with a pair of dull scissors. "This is Tina's first trip to India, isn't it, Tina?"

"I don't have to go to the bathroom anymore," Tina announced.

"Where's Mina?" Mr. Das asked.

Mr. Kapasi found it strange that Mr. Das should refer to his wife by her first name when speaking to the little girl. Tina pointed to where Mrs. Das was purchasing something from one of the shirtless men who worked at the tea stall. Mr. Kapasi heard one of the shirtless men sing a phrase from a popular Hindi love song as Mrs. Das walked back to the car, but she did not appear to understand the words of the song, for she did not express irritation, or embarrassment, or react in any other way to the man's declarations.

He observed her. She wore a red-and-white-checkered skirt that stopped above her knees, slip-on shoes with a square wooden heel, and a close-fitting blouse styled like a man's undershirt. The blouse was decorated at chest-level with a calico appliqué in the shape of a strawberry. She was a short woman, with small hands like paws, her frosty pink fingernails painted to match her lips, and was slightly plump in her figure. Her hair, shorn only a little longer than her husband's, was parted far to one side. She was wearing large dark brown sunglasses with a pinkish tint to them, and carried a big straw bag, almost as big as her torso, shaped like a bowl, with a water bottle poking out of it. She walked slowly, carrying some puffed rice tossed with peanuts and chili peppers in a large packet made from newspapers. Mr. Kapasi turned to Mr. Das.

"Where in America do you live?"

"New Brunswick, New Jersey."

"Next to New York?"

"Exactly. I teach middle school there."

"What subject?"

"Science. In fact, every year I take my students on a trip to the Museum of Natural History in New York City. In a way we have a lot in common, you could say, you and I. How long have you been a tour guide, Mr. Kapasi?"

"Five years."

Mrs. Das reached the car. "How long's the trip?" she asked, shutting the door.

"About two and a half hours," Mr. Kapasi replied.

At this Mrs. Das gave an impatient sigh, as if she had been traveling her whole life without pause. She fanned herself with a folded Bombay film magazine written in English.

"I thought that the Sun Temple is only eighteen miles north of Puri," Mr. Das said, tapping on the tour book.

"The roads to Konarak are poor. Actually it is a distance of fifty-two miles," Mr. Kapasi explained.

Mr. Das nodded, readjusting the camera strap where it had begun to chafe the back of his neck.

Before starting the ignition, Mr. Kapasi reached back to make sure the cranklike locks on the inside of each of the back doors were secured. As soon as the car began to move the little girl began to play with the lock on her side, clicking it with some effort forward and backward, but Mrs. Das said nothing to stop her. She sat a bit slouched at one end of the back seat, not offering her puffed rice to anyone. Ronny and Tina sat on either side of her, both snapping bright green gum.

"Look," Bobby said as the car began to gather speed. He pointed with his finger to the tall trees that lined the road. "Look."

"Monkeys!" Ronny shrieked. "Wow!"

They were seated in groups along the branches, with shining black faces, silver bodies, horizontal eyebrows, and crested heads.

Their long gray tails dangled like a series of ropes among the leaves. A few scratched themselves with black leathery hands, or swung their feet, staring as the car passed.

"We call them the hanuman," Mr. Kapasi said. "They are quite common in the area."

As soon as he spoke, one of the monkeys leaped into the middle of the road, causing Mr. Kapasi to brake suddenly. Another bounced onto the hood of the car, then sprang away. Mr. Kapasi beeped his horn. The children began to get excited, sucking in their breath and covering their faces partly with their hands. They had never seen monkeys outside of a zoo, Mr. Das explained. He asked Mr. Kapasi to stop the car so that he could take a picture.

While Mr. Das adjusted his telephoto lens, Mrs. Das reached into her straw bag and pulled out a bottle of colorless nail polish, which she proceeded to stroke on the tip of her index finger.

The little girl stuck out a hand. "Mine too. Mommy, do mine too."

"Leave me alone," Mrs. Das said, blowing on her nail and turning her body slightly. "You're making me mess up."

The little girl occupied herself by buttoning and unbuttoning a pinafore on the doll's plastic body.

"All set," Mr. Das said, replacing the lens cap.

The car rattled considerably as it raced along the dusty road, causing them all to pop up from their seats every now and then, but Mrs. Das continued to polish her nails. Mr. Kapasi eased up on the accelerator, hoping to produce a smoother ride. When he reached for the gearshift the boy in front accommodated him by swinging his hairless knees out of the way. Mr. Kapasi noted that this boy was slightly paler than the other children. "Daddy, why is the driver sitting on the wrong side in this car, too?" the boy asked.

"They all do that here, dummy," Ronny said. "Don't call your brother a dummy," Mr. Das said. He turned to Mr. Kapasi. "In America, you know . . . it confuses them."

"Oh yes, I am well aware," Mr. Kapasi said. As delicately as he could, he shifted gears again, accelerating as they approached a hill in the road. "I see it on *Dallas*, the steering wheels are on the left-hand side."

"What's *Dallas*?" Tina asked, banging her now naked doll on the seat behind Mr. Kapasi.

"It went off the air," Mr. Das explained. "It's a television show."

They were all like siblings, Mr. Kapasi thought as they passed a row of date trees. Mr. and Mrs. Das behaved like an older brother and sister, not parents. It seemed that they were in charge of the children only for the day; it was hard to believe they were regularly responsible for anything other than themselves. Mr. Das tapped on his lens cap, and his tour book, dragging his thumbnail occasionally across the pages so that they made a scraping sound. Mrs. Das continued to polish her nails. She had still not removed her sunglasses. Every now and then Tina renewed her plea that she wanted her nails done, too, and so at one point Mrs. Das flicked a drop of polish on the little girl's finger before depositing the bottle back inside her straw bag.

"Isn't this an air-conditioned car?" she asked, still blowing on her hand. The window on Tina's side was broken and could not be rolled down.

"Quit complaining," Mr. Das said. "It isn't so hot."

"I told you to get a car with air-conditioning," Mrs. Das continued. "Why do you do this, Raj, just to save a few stupid rupees. What are you saving us, fifty cents?"

Their accents sounded just like the ones Mr. Kapasi heard on American television programs, though not like the ones on *Dallas*.

"Doesn't it get tiresome, Mr. Kapasi, showing people the same thing every day?" Mr. Das asked, rolling down his own window all the way. "Hey, do you mind stopping the car. I just want to get a shot of this guy."

Mr. Kapasi pulled over to the side of the road as Mr. Das took a picture of a barefoot man, his head wrapped in a dirty turban, seated on top of a cart of grain sacks pulled by a pair of bullocks. Both the man and the bullocks were emaciated. In the back seat Mrs. Das gazed out another window, at the sky, where nearly transparent clouds passed quickly in front of one another.

"I look forward to it, actually," Mr. Kapasi said as they continued on their way. "The Sun Temple is one of my favorite places. In that way it is a reward for me. I give tours on Fridays and Saturdays only. I have another job during the week."

"Oh? Where?" Mr. Das asked.

"I work in a doctor's office."

"You're a doctor?"

"I am not a doctor. I work with one. As an interpreter."

"What does a doctor need an interpreter for?"

"He has a number of Gujarati patients. My father was Gujarati, but many people do not speak Gujarati in this area, including the doctor. And so the doctor asked me to work in his office, interpreting what the patients say."

"Interesting. I've never heard of anything like that," Mr. Das said.

Mr. Kapasi shrugged. "It is a job like any other."

"But so romantic," Mrs. Das said dreamily, breaking her extended silence. She lifted her pinkish brown sunglasses and arranged them on top of her head like a tiara. For the first time, her eyes met Mr.

Kapasi's in the rearview mirror: pale, a bit small, their gaze fixed but drowsy.

Mr. Das craned to look at her. "What's so romantic about it?"

"I don't know. Something." She shrugged, knitting her brows together for an instant. "Would you like a piece of gum, Mr. Kapasi?" she asked brightly. She reached into her straw bag and handed him a small square wrapped in green-and-white-striped paper. As soon as Mr. Kapasi put the gum in his mouth a thick sweet liquid burst onto his tongue.

"Tell us more about your job, Mr. Kapasi," Mrs. Das said.

"What would you like to know, madame?"

"I don't know," she shrugged, munching on some puffed rice and licking the mustard oil from the corners of her mouth. "Tell us a typical situation." She settled back in her seat, her head tilted in a patch of sun, and closed her eyes. "I want to picture what happens."

"Very well. The other day a man came in with a pain in his throat."

"Did he smoke cigarettes?"

"No. It was very curious. He complained that he felt as if there were long pieces of straw stuck in his throat. When I told the doctor he was able to prescribe the proper medication."

"That's so neat."

"Yes," Mr. Kapasi agreed after some hesitation.

"So these patients are totally dependent on you," Mrs. Das said. She spoke slowly, as if she were thinking aloud. "In a way, more dependent on you than the doctor."

"How do you mean? How could it be?"

"Well, for example, you could tell the doctor that the pain felt like a burning, not straw. The patient would never know what you had told the doctor, and the doctor wouldn't know that you had told the wrong thing. It's a big responsibility."

"Yes, a big responsibility you have there, Mr. Kapasi," Mr. Das agreed.

Mr. Kapasi had never thought of his job in such complimentary terms. To him it was a thankless occupation. He found nothing noble in interpreting people's maladies, assiduously translating the symptoms of so many swollen bones, countless cramps of bellies and bowels, spots on people's palms that changed color, shape, or size. The doctor, nearly half his age, had an affinity for bell-bottom trousers and made humorless jokes about the Congress party. Together they worked in a stale little infirmary where Mr. Kapasi's smartly tailored clothes clung to him in the heat, in spite of the blackened blades of a ceiling fan churning over their heads.

The job was a sign of his failings. In his youth he'd been a devoted scholar of foreign languages, the owner of an impressive collection of dictionaries. He had dreamed of being an interpreter for diplomats and dignitaries, resolving conflicts between people and nations, settling disputes of which he alone could understand both sides. He was a self-educated man. In a series of notebooks, in the evenings before his parents settled his marriage, he had listed the common etymologies of words, and at one point in his life he was confident that he could converse, if given the opportunity, in English, French, Russian, Portuguese, and Italian, not to mention Hindi, Bengali, Orissi, and Gujarati. Now only a handful of European phrases remained in his memory, scattered words for things like saucers and chairs. English was the only non-Indian language he spoke fluently anymore. Mr. Kapasi knew it was not a remarkable talent. Sometimes he feared that his children knew better English than he did, just from watching television. Still, it came in handy for the tours.

He had taken the job as an interpreter after his first son, at the age of seven, contracted typhoid — that was how he had first made the acquaintance of the doctor. At the time Mr. Kapasi had been teaching English in a grammar school, and he bartered his skills as an interpreter to pay the increasingly exorbitant medical bills. In the end the boy had died one evening in his mother's arms, his limbs burning with fever, but then there was the funeral to pay for, and the other children who were born soon enough, and the newer, bigger house, and the good schools and tutors, and the fine shoes and the television, and the countless other ways he tried to console his wife and to keep her from crying in her sleep, and so when the doctor offered to pay him twice as much as he earned at the grammar school, he accepted. Mr. Kapasi knew that his wife had little regard for his career as an interpreter. He knew it reminded her of the son she'd lost, and that she resented the other lives he helped, in his own small way, to save. If ever she referred to his position, she used the phrase "doctor's assistant," as if the process of interpretation were equal to taking someone's temperature, or changing a bedpan. She never asked him about the patients who came to the doctor's office, or said that his job was a big responsibility.

For this reason it flattered Mr. Kapasi that Mrs. Das was so intrigued by his job. Unlike his wife, she had reminded him of its intellectual challenges. She had also used the word "romantic." She did not behave in a romantic way toward her husband, and yet she had used the word to describe him. He wondered if Mr. and Mrs. Das were a bad match, just as he and his wife were. Perhaps they, too, had little in common apart from three children and a decade of their lives. The

signs he recognized from his own marriage were there — the bicker-
ing, the indifference, the protracted silences. Her sudden interest in
him, an interest she did not express in either her husband or her chil-
dren, was mildly intoxicating. When Mr. Kapasi thought once again
about how she had said "romantic," the feeling of intoxication grew.

He began to check his reflection in the rearview mirror as he
drove, feeling grateful that he had chosen the gray suit that morning
and not the brown one, which tended to sag a little in the knees. From
time to time he glanced through the mirror at Mrs. Das. In addition to
glancing at her face he glanced at the strawberry between her breasts,
and the golden brown hollow in her throat. He decided to tell Mrs.
Das about another patient, and another: the young woman who had
complained of a sensation of raindrops in her spine, the gentleman
whose birthmark had begun to sprout hairs. Mrs. Das listened atten-
tively, stroking her hair with a small plastic brush that resembled an
oval bed of nails, asking more questions, for yet another example. The
children were quiet, intent on spotting more monkeys in the trees,
and Mr. Das was absorbed by his tour book, so it seemed like a private
conversation between Mr. Kapasi and Mrs. Das. In this manner the
next half hour passed, and when they stopped for lunch at a roadside
restaurant that sold fritters and omelette sandwiches, usually some-
thing Mr. Kapasi looked forward to on his tours so that he could sit in
peace and enjoy some hot tea, he was disappointed. As the Das family
settled together under a magenta umbrella fringed with white and
orange tassels, and placed their orders with one of the waiters who
marched about in tricornered caps, Mr. Kapasi reluctantly headed
toward a neighboring table.

"Mr. Kapasi, wait. There's room here," Mrs. Das called out. She
gathered Tina onto her lap, insisting that he accompany them. And

so, together, they had bottled mango juice and sandwiches and plates of onions and potatoes deep-fried in graham-flour batter. After finishing two omelette sandwiches Mr. Das took more pictures of the group as they ate.

"How much longer?" he asked Mr. Kapasi as he paused to load a new roll of film in the camera. "About half an hour more."

By now the children had gotten up from the table to look at more monkeys perched in a nearby tree, so there was a considerable space between Mrs. Das and Mr. Kapasi. Mr. Das placed the camera to his face and squeezed one eye shut, his tongue exposed at one corner of his mouth. "This looks funny. Mina, you need to lean in closer to Mr. Kapasi."

She did. He could smell a scent on her skin, like a mixture of whiskey and rosewater. He worried suddenly that she could smell his perspiration, which he knew had collected beneath the synthetic material of his shirt. He polished off his mango juice in one gulp and smoothed his silver hair with his hands. A bit of the juice dripped onto his chin. He wondered if Mrs. Das had noticed.

She had not. "What's your address, Mr. Kapasi?" she inquired, fishing for something inside her straw bag.

"You would like my address?"

"So we can send you copies," she said. "Of the pictures." She handed him a scrap of paper which she had hastily ripped from a page of her film magazine. The blank portion was limited, for the narrow strip was crowded by lines of text and a tiny picture of a hero and heroine embracing under a eucalyptus tree.

The paper curled as Mr. Kapasi wrote his address in clear, careful letters. She would write to him, asking about his days interpreting at the doctor's office, and he would respond eloquently, choosing only the most entertaining anecdotes, ones that would make her laugh out loud as she read them in her house in New Jersey. In time she would reveal the disappointment of her marriage, and he his. In this way their friendship would grow, and flourish. He would possess a picture of the two of them, eating fried onions under a magenta umbrella, which he would keep, he decided, safely tucked between the pages of his Russian grammar. As his mind raced, Mr. Kapasi experienced a mild and pleasant shock. It was similar to a feeling he used to experience long ago when, after months of translating with the aid of a dictionary, he would finally read a passage from a French novel, or an Italian sonnet, and understand the words, one after another, unencumbered by his own efforts. In those moments Mr. Kapasi used to believe that all was right with the world, that all struggles were rewarded, that all of life's mistakes made sense in the end. The promise that he would hear from Mrs. Das now filled him with the same belief.

When he finished writing his address Mr. Kapasi handed her the paper, but as soon as he did so he worried that he had either misspelled his name, or accidentally reversed the numbers of his postal code. He dreaded the possibility of a lost letter, the photograph never reaching him, hovering somewhere in Orissa, close but ultimately unattainable. He thought of asking for the slip of paper again, just to make sure he had written his address accurately, but Mrs. Das had already dropped it into the jumble of her bag.

They reached Konarak at two-thirty. The temple, made of sandstone, was a massive pyramid-like structure in the shape of a chariot. It was dedicated to the great master of life, the sun, which struck three sides of the edifice as it made its journey each day across the sky. Twenty-four giant wheels were carved on the north and south sides of the plinth. The whole thing was drawn by a team of seven horses, speeding as if through the heavens. As they approached, Mr. Kapasi explained that the temple had been built between A.D. 1243 and 1255, with the efforts of twelve hundred artisans, by the great ruler of the Ganga dynasty, King Narasimhadeva the First, to commemorate his victory against the Muslim army.

"It says the temple occupies about a hundred and seventy acres of land," Mr. Das said, reading from his book.

"It's like a desert," Ronny said, his eyes wandering across the sand that stretched on all sides beyond the temple.

"The Chandrabhaga River once flowed one mile north of here. It is dry now," Mr. Kapasi said, turning off the engine.

They got out and walked toward the temple, posing first for pictures by the pair of lions that flanked the steps. Mr. Kapasi led them next to one of the wheels of the chariot, higher than any human being, nine feet in diameter.

"The wheels are supposed to symbolize the wheel of life," Mr. Das read. "'They depict the cycle of creation, preservation, and achievement of realization.' Cool." He turned the page of his book. "'Each wheel is divided into eight thick and thin spokes, dividing the day into eight equal parts. The rims are carved with designs of birds and animals, whereas the medallions in the spokes are carved with women in luxurious poses, largely erotic in nature.'"

What he referred to were the countless friezes of entwined naked bodies, making love in various positions, women clinging to the necks of men, their knees wrapped eternally around their lovers' thighs. In addition to these were assorted scenes from daily life, of hunting and trading, of deer being killed with bows and arrows and marching warriors holding swords in their hands.

It was no longer possible to enter the temple, for it had filled with rubble years ago, but they admired the exterior, as did all the tourists Mr. Kapasi brought there, slowly strolling along each of its sides. Mr. Das trailed behind, taking pictures. The children ran ahead, pointing to figures of naked people, intrigued in particular by the Nagamithunas, the half-human, half-serpentine couples who were said, Mr. Kapasi told them, to live in the deepest waters of the sea. Mr. Kapasi was pleased that they liked the temple, pleased especially that it appealed to Mrs. Das. She stopped every three or four paces, staring silently at the carved lovers, and the processions of elephants, and the topless female musicians beating on two-sided drums.

Though Mr. Kapasi had been to the temple countless times, it occurred to him, as he, too, gazed at the topless women, that he had never seen his own wife fully naked. Even when they had made love she kept the panels of her blouse hooked together, the string of her petticoat knotted around her waist. He had never admired the backs of his wife's legs the way he now admired those of Mrs. Das, walking as if for his benefit alone. He had, of course, seen plenty of bare limbs before, belonging to the American and European ladies who took his tours. But Mrs. Das was different. Unlike the other women, who had an interest only in the temple, and kept their noses buried in a guidebook, or their eyes behind the lens of a camera, Mrs. Das had taken an interest in him.

Mr. Kapasi was anxious to be alone with her, to continue their private conversation, yet he felt nervous to walk at her side. She was lost behind her sunglasses, ignoring her husband's requests that she pose for another picture, walking past her children as if they were strangers. Worried that he might disturb her, Mr. Kapasi walked ahead, to admire, as he always did, the three life-sized bronze avatars of Surya, the sun god, each emerging from its own niche on the temple facade to greet the sun at dawn, noon, and evening. They wore elaborate headdresses, their languid, elongated eyes closed, their bare chests draped with carved chains and amulets. Hibiscus petals, offerings from previous visitors, were strewn at their gray-green feet. The last statue, on the northern wall of the temple, was Mr. Kapasi's favorite. This Surya had a tired expression, weary after a hard day of work, sitting astride a horse with folded legs. Even his horse's eyes were drowsy. Around his body were smaller sculptures of women in pairs, their hips thrust to one side.

"Who's that?" Mrs. Das asked. He was startled to see that she was standing beside him.

"He is the Astachala-Surya," Mr. Kapasi said. "The setting sun."

"So in a couple of hours the sun will set right here?" She slipped a foot out of one of her square-heeled shoes, rubbed her toes on the back of her other leg.

"That is correct."

She raised her sunglasses for a moment, then put them back on again. "Neat."

Mr. Kapasi was not certain exactly what the word suggested, but he had a feeling it was a favorable response. He hoped that Mrs. Das had understood Surya's beauty, his power. Perhaps they would discuss it further in their letters. He would explain things to her, things about India, and she would explain things to him about America. In its own way this correspondence would fulfill his dream, of serving as an interpreter between nations. He looked at her straw bag, delighted that his address lay nestled among its contents. When he pictured her so many thousands of miles away he plummeted, so much so that he had an overwhelming urge to wrap his arms around her, to freeze with her, even for an instant, in an embrace witnessed by his favorite Surya. But Mrs. Das had already started walking.

"When do you return to America?" he asked, trying to sound placid.

"In ten days."

He calculated. A week to settle in, a week to develop the pictures, a few days to compose her letter, two weeks to get to India by air. According to his schedule, allowing room for delays, he would hear from Mrs. Das in approximately six weeks' time.

The family was silent as Mr. Kapasi drove them back, a little past four-thirty, to Hotel Sandy Villa. The children had bought miniature granite versions of the chariot's wheels at a souvenir stand, and they turned them round in their hands. Mr. Das continued to read his book. Mrs. Das untangled Tina's hair with her brush and divided it into two little ponytails.

Mr. Kapasi was beginning to dread the thought of dropping them off. He was not prepared to begin his six-week wait to hear from Mrs. Das. As he stole glances at her in the rear-view mirror, wrapping elastic bands around Tina's hair, he wondered how he might make the tour last a little longer. Ordinarily he sped back to Puri using a shortcut, eager to return home, scrub his feet and hands with sandalwood soap, and enjoy the evening newspaper and a cup of tea that his wife would serve him in silence. The thought of that silence, something to which he'd long been resigned, now oppressed him. It was then that he suggested visiting the hills at Udayagiri and Khandagiri, where a number of monastic dwellings were hewn out of the ground, facing one another across a defile. It was some miles away, but well worth seeing, Mr. Kapasi told them.

"Oh yeah, there's something mentioned about it in this book," Mr. Das said. "Built by a Jain king or something."

"Shall we go then?" Mr. Kapasi asked. He paused at a turn in the road. "It's to the left."

Mr. Das turned to look at Mrs. Das. Both of them shrugged. "Left, left," the children chanted.

Mr. Kapasi turned the wheel, almost delirious with relief. He did not know what he would do or say to Mrs. Das once they arrived at the hills. Perhaps he would tell her what a pleasing smile she had. Perhaps he would compliment her strawberry shirt, which he found irresistibly becoming. Perhaps, when Mr. Das was busy taking a picture, he would take her hand.

He did not have to worry. When they got to the hills, divided by a steep path thick with trees, Mrs. Das refused to get out of the car. All along the path, dozens of monkeys were seated on stones, as well as on the branches of the trees. Their hind legs were stretched out in front and raised to shoulder level, their arms resting on their knees.

"My legs are tired," she said, sinking low in her seat. "I'll stay here."

"Why did you have to wear those stupid shoes?" Mr. Das said. "You won't be in the pictures."

"Pretend I'm there."

"But we could use one of these pictures for our Christmas card this year. We didn't get one of all five of us at the Sun Temple. Mr. Kapasi could take it."

"I'm not coming. Anyway, those monkeys give me the creeps."

"But they're harmless," Mr. Das said. He turned to Mr. Kapasi. "Aren't they?"

"They are more hungry than dangerous," Mr. Kapasi said. "Do not provoke them with food, and they will not bother you."

Mr. Das headed up the defile with the children, the boys at his side, the little girl on his shoulders. Mr. Kapasi watched as they crossed paths with a Japanese man and woman, the only other tourists there, who paused for a final photograph, then stepped into a nearby car and drove away. As the car disappeared out of view some of the monkeys called out, emitting soft whooping sounds, and then walked on their flat black hands and feet up the path. At one point a group of them formed a little ring around Mr. Das and the children. Tina screamed in delight. Ronny ran in circles around his father. Bobby bent down and picked up a fat stick on the ground.

When he extended it, one of the monkeys approached him and snatched it, then briefly beat the ground.

"I'll join them," Mr. Kapasi said, unlocking the door on his side. "There is much to explain about the caves."

"No. Stay a minute," Mrs. Das said. She got out of the back seat and slipped in beside Mr. Kapasi. "Raj has his dumb book anyway." Together, through the windshield, Mrs. Das and Mr. Kapasi watched as Bobby and the monkey passed the stick back and forth between them.

"A brave little boy," Mr. Kapasi commented.

"It's not so surprising," Mrs. Das said.

"No?"

"He's not his."

"I beg your pardon?"

"Raj's. He's not Raj's son."

Mr. Kapasi felt a prickle on his skin. He reached into his shirt pocket for the small tin of lotus-oil balm he carried with him at all times, and applied it to three spots on his forehead. He knew that Mrs. Das was watching him, but he did not turn to face her. Instead he watched as the figures of Mr. Das and the children grew smaller, climbing up the steep path, pausing every now and then for a picture, surrounded by a growing number of monkeys.

"Are you surprised?" The way she put it made him choose his words with care.

"It's not the type of thing one assumes," Mr. Kapasi replied slowly. He put the tin of lotus-oil balm back in his pocket.

"No, of course not. And no one knows, of course. No one at all. I've kept it a secret for eight whole years." She looked at Mr. Kapasi, tilting her chin as if to gain a fresh perspective. "But now I've told you."

Mr. Kapasi nodded. He felt suddenly parched, and his forehead was warm and slightly numb from the balm. He considered asking Mrs. Das for a sip of water, then decided against it.

"We met when we were very young," she said. She reached into her straw bag in search of something, then pulled out a packet of puffed rice. "Want some?"

"No, thank you."

She put a fistful in her mouth, sank into the seat a little, and looked away from Mr. Kapasi, out the window on her side of the car. "We married when we were still in college. We were in high school when he proposed. We went to the same college, of course. Back then we couldn't stand the thought of being separated, not for a day, not for a minute. Our parents were best friends who lived in the same town. My entire life I saw him every weekend, either at our house or theirs. We were sent upstairs to play together while our parents joked about our marriage. Imagine! They never caught us at anything, though in a way I think it was all more or less a setup. The things we did those Friday and Saturday nights, while our parents sat downstairs drinking tea . . . I could tell you stories, Mr. Kapasi."

As a result of spending all her time in college with Raj, she continued, she did not make many close friends. There was no one to confide in about him at the end of a difficult day, or to share a passing thought or a worry. Her parents now lived on the other side of the world, but she had never been very close to them, anyway. After marrying so young she was overwhelmed by it all, having a child so quickly, and nursing, and warming up bottles of milk and testing their temperature against her wrist while Raj was at work, dressed in sweaters and corduroy pants, teaching his students about rocks and dinosaurs. Raj never looked cross or harried, or plump as she had become after the first baby.

Always tired, she declined invitations from her one or two college girlfriends, to have lunch or shop in Manhattan. Eventually the friends stopped calling her, so that she was left at home all day with the baby, surrounded by toys that made her trip when she walked or wince when she sat, always cross and tired. Only occasionally did they go out after Ronny was born, and even more rarely did they entertain. Raj didn't mind; he looked forward to coming home from teaching and watching television and bouncing Ronny on his knee. She had been outraged when Raj told her that a Punjabi friend, someone whom she had once met but did not remember, would be staying with them for a week for some job interviews in the New Brunswick area.

Bobby was conceived in the afternoon, on a sofa littered with rubber teething toys, after the friend learned that a London pharmaceutical company had hired him, while Ronny cried to be freed from his playpen. She made no protest when the friend touched the small of her back as she was about to make a pot of coffee, then pulled her against his crisp navy suit. He made love to her swiftly, in silence, with an expertise she had never known, without the meaningful expressions and smiles Raj always insisted on afterward. The next day Raj drove the friend to JFK. He was married now, to a Punjabi girl, and they lived in London still, and every year they exchanged Christmas cards with Raj and Mina, each couple tucking photos of their families into the envelopes. He did not know that he was Bobby's father. He never would.

"I beg your pardon, Mrs. Das, but why have you told me this information?" Mr. Kapasi asked when she had finally finished speaking, and had turned to face him once again.

"For God's sake, stop calling me Mrs. Das. I'm twenty-eight. You probably have children my age."

"Not quite." It disturbed Mr. Kapasi to learn that she thought of him as a parent. The feeling he had had toward her, that had made him check his reflection in the rearview mirror as they drove, evaporated a little.

"I told you because of your talents." She put the packet of puffed rice back into her bag without folding over the top.

"I don't understand," Mr. Kapasi said.

"Don't you see? For eight years I haven't been able to express this to anybody, not to friends, certainly not to Raj. He doesn't even suspect it. He thinks I'm still in love with him Well, don't you have anything to say?"

"About what?"

"About what I've just told you. About my secret, and about how terrible it makes me feel. I feel terrible looking at my children, and at Raj, always terrible. I have terrible urges, Mr. Kapasi, to throw things away. One day I had the urge to throw everything I own out the window, the television, the children, everything. Don't you think it's unhealthy?"

He was silent.

"Mr. Kapasi, don't you have anything to say? I thought that was your job."

"My job is to give tours, Mrs. Das."

"Not that. Your other job. As an interpreter."

"But we do not face a language barrier. What need is there for an interpreter?"

"That's not what I mean. I would never have told you otherwise. Don't you realize what it means for me to tell you?"

"What does it mean?"

"It means that I'm tired of feeling so terrible all the time. Eight years, Mr. Kapasi, I've been in pain eight years. I was hoping you could help me feel better, say the right thing. Suggest some kind of remedy."

He looked at her, in her red plaid skirt and strawberry T-shirt, a woman not yet thirty, who loved neither her husband nor her children, who had already fallen out of love with life. Her confession depressed him, depressed him all the more when he thought of Mr. Das at the top of the path, Tina clinging to his shoulders, taking pictures of ancient monastic cells cut into the hills to show his students in America, unsuspecting and unaware that one of his sons was not his own. Mr. Kapasi felt insulted that Mrs. Das should ask him to interpret her common, trivial little secret. She did not resemble the patients in the doctor's office, those who came glassy-eyed and desperate, unable to sleep or breathe or urinate with ease, unable, above all, to give words to their pains. Still, Mr. Kapasi believed it was his duty to assist Mrs. Das. Perhaps he ought to tell her to confess the truth to Mr. Das. He would explain that honesty was the best policy. Honesty, surely, would help her feel better, as she'd put it. Perhaps he would offer to preside over the discussion, as a mediator. He decided to begin with the most obvious question, to get to the heart of the matter, and so he asked, "Is it really pain you feel, Mrs. Das, or is it guilt?"

She turned to him and glared, mustard oil thick on her frosty pink lips. She opened her mouth to say something, but as she glared at Mr. Kapasi some certain knowledge seemed to pass before her eyes, and she stopped. It crushed him; he knew at that moment that he was not even important enough to be properly insulted. She opened the car door and began walking up the path, wobbling a little on her square wooden heels, reaching into her straw bag to eat handfuls of puffed rice. It fell through her fingers, leaving a zigzagging trail, causing a monkey to leap down from a tree and devour the little white grains. In search of more, the monkey began to follow Mrs. Das. Others joined him, so that she was soon being followed by about half a dozen of them, their velvety tails dragging behind.

Mr. Kapasi stepped out of the car. He wanted to holler, to alert her in some way, but he worried that if she knew they were behind her, she would grow nervous. Perhaps she would lose her balance. Perhaps they would pull at her bag or her hair. He began to jog up the path, taking a fallen branch in his hand to scare away the monkeys. Mrs. Das continued walking, oblivious, trailing grains of puffed rice. Near the top of the incline, before a group of cells fronted by a row of squat stone pillars, Mr. Das was kneeling on the ground, focusing the lens of his camera. The children stood under the arcade, now hiding, now emerging from view.

"Wait for me," Mrs. Das called out. "I'm coming."

Tina jumped up and down. "Here comes Mommy!"

"Great," Mr. Das said without looking up. "Just in time. We'll get Mr. Kapasi to take a picture of the five of us."

Mr. Kapasi quickened his pace, waving his branch so that the monkeys scampered away, distracted, in another direction.

"Where's Bobby?" Mrs. Das asked when she stopped.

Mr. Das looked up from the camera. "I don't know. Ronny, where's Bobby?"

Ronny shrugged. "I thought he was right here."

"Where is he?" Mrs. Das repeated sharply. "What's wrong with all of you?"

They began calling his name, wandering up and down the path a bit. Because they were calling, they did not initially hear the boy's screams. When they found him, a little farther down the path under a tree, he was surrounded by a group of monkeys, over a dozen of them, pulling at his T-shirt with their long black fingers. The puffed rice Mrs. Das had spilled was scattered at his feet, raked over by the monkeys' hands. The boy was silent, his body frozen, swift tears running down his startled face. His bare legs were dusty and red with welts from where one of the monkeys struck him repeatedly with the stick he had given to it earlier.

"Daddy, the monkey's hurting Bobby," Tina said.

Mr. Das wiped his palms on the front of his shorts. In his nervousness he accidentally pressed the shutter on his camera; the whirring noise of the advancing film excited the monkeys, and the one with the stick began to beat Bobby more intently. "What are we supposed to do? What if they start attacking?"

"Mr. Kapasi," Mrs. Das shrieked, noticing him standing to one side. "Do something, for God's sake, do something!"

Mr. Kapasi took his branch and shooed them away, hissing at the ones that remained, stomping his feet to scare them. The animals retreated slowly, with a measured gait, obedient but unintimidated. Mr. Kapasi gathered Bobby in his arms and brought him back to where his parents and siblings were standing. As he carried him he was tempted to whisper a secret into the boy's ear. But Bobby was stunned, and shivering with fright, his legs bleeding slightly where the stick had broken the skin. When Mr. Kapasi delivered him to his parents, Mr. Das brushed some dirt off the boy's T-shirt and put the visor on him the right way. Mrs. Das reached into her straw bag to find a bandage which she taped over the cut on his knee. Ronny offered his brother a fresh piece of gum. "He's fine. Just a little scared, right, Bobby?" Mr. Das said, patting the top of his head.

"God, let's get out of here," Mrs. Das said. She folded her arms across the strawberry on her chest. "This place gives me the creeps."

"Yeah. Back to the hotel, definitely," Mr. Das agreed.

"Poor Bobby," Mrs. Das said. "Come here a second. Let Mommy fix your hair." Again she reached into her straw bag, this time for her hairbrush, and began to run it around the edges of the translucent visor. When she whipped out the hairbrush, the slip of paper with Mr. Kapasi's address on it fluttered away in the wind. No one but Mr. Kapasi noticed. He watched as it rose, carried higher and higher by the breeze, into the trees where the monkeys now sat, solemnly observing the scene below. Mr. Kapasi observed it too, knowing that this was the picture of the Das family he would preserve forever in his mind.

Thomas McGuane

COWBOY

The old feller made me go into the big house in my stocking feet. The old lady's in a big chair next to the window. In fact, the whole room's full of big chairs, but she's only in one of them, though as big as she is she could of filled up several. The old man said, "I found this one in the loose-horse pen at the sale yard."

She says, "What's he supposed to be?"

He says, "Supposed to be a cowboy."

"What's he doin in the loose horses?"

I says, "I was lookin for one that would ride."

"You was in the wrong pen, son," says the old man. "Them's canners. They're goin to France in cardboard boxes."

"Once they get a steel bolt in the head." The big old gal in the chair laughed.

Now I'm sore. "There's five in there broke to death. I rode em with nothin but binder twine."

"It don't make a shit," says the old man. "Ever one of them is goin to France."

The old lady didn't believe me. "How'd you get near them loose horses to ride?"

"I went in there at night."

The old lady says, "You one crazy cowboy go in there in the dark. Them broncs kick your teeth down your throat. I suppose you tried bareback."

"Naw, I drug the saddle I usually ride at the Rose Bowl Parade."

"You got a horse for that?"

"I got Trigger. We unstuffed him."

She turns to the old man. "He's got a mouth on him. This much we know."

"Maybe he can tell us what good he is."

I says, "I'm a cowboy."

"You're a outta work cowboy."

"It's a dyin way of life."

"She's about like me. She's wondering if this ranch supposed to be some welfare agency for cowboys."

I've had enough. "You're the dumb honyocker drove me out here."

I thought that was the end, but the old lady said, "Don't get huffy. You got the job. You against conversation or somethin?"

We get outside and the old sumbitch says, "You drawed lucky there, son. That last deal could of pissed her off."

"It didn't make me no never mind if it did or didn't."

"Anymore, she hasn't been well. Used to she was sweet as pudding."

"I'm sorry for that. We don't have health, we don't have nothin."

·   ·   ·

She must of been afflicted something terrible, because she was ugly mornin, noon, and night for as long as she lasted, pick a fight over nothin, and the old sumbitch bound to got the worst of it. I felt sorry for him, little slack as he ever cut me.

Had a hundred seventy-five sweet-tempered horned Herefords and fifteen sleepy bulls. Shipped the calves all over for hybrid vigor, mostly to the south. Had some go clear to Florida. A Hereford still had its horns was a walkin miracle and the old sumbitch had him a smart little deal goin. I soon learned to give him credit for such things, and the old lady barking commands off the sofa weren't no slouch neither. Anybody else seen their books might say they could be winterin in Phoenix.

They didn't have no bunkhouse, just a LeisureLife mobile home that had lost its wheels about thirty years ago, and they had it positioned by the door of the barn so it'd be convenient for the hired man to stagger out at all hours and fight breech birth and scours and any other disorder sent down by the cow gods. We had some doozies. One heifer had got pregnant and her calf was near as big as she was. Had to reach in and take it out in pieces. When we threw the head out on the ground she turned to it and lowed like it was her baby. Everything a cow does is to make itself into meat as fast as it can so somebody can eat it. It's a terrible life, and a cowboy is its little helper.

The old sumbitch and I got along good. We got through calvin and got to see them pairs and bulls run out onto the new grass. Nothin like seeing all that meat feel a little temporary joy. Then we bladed out the corrals and watched em dry under the spring sun at long last. Only mishap was the manure spreader threw a rock and knocked me senseless and I drove the rig into an irrigation ditch.

The old sumbitch never said a word but chained up and pulled us out with his Ford.

We led his cavvy out of the hills afoot with two buckets of sweet feed. Had a little of everything, including a blue roan I fancied, but he said it was a Hancock and bucked like the National Finals in Las Vegas, kicking out behind and squalling, and was just a man-killer. "Stick to the bays," he said. "The West was won on a bay horse."

He picked out three bays, had a keg of shoes, all ones and aughts, and I shod them best I could, three geldings with nice manners, stood good to shoe. About all you could say about the others was they had four legs each; a couple, all white-marked from saddle galls and years of hard work, looked like maybe no more summers after this. They'd been rode many a long mile. We chased em back into the hills and the three that was shod whinnied and fretted. "Back to work," the old sumbitch tells em.

We shod three cause one was going to pack a ton of fencing supplies—barb wire, smooth wire, steel T posts and staples, old wore-out Sunflower fence stretchers that could barely grab on to the wire—and we was at it a good little while where the elk had knocked miles of it down or the cedar finally give out and had to be replaced by steel. But that was how I found out the old sumbitch's last good time was in Korea, where the officers would yell, "Come on up here and die!" Said they was comin in waves. Tells me all this while the stretcher pulls that wire squealin through the staples. He was a tough old bastard.

"They killed a pile of us and we killed a pile of them." *Squeak!*

We hauled the mineral horseback too, in panniers, white salt and iodine salt. He didn't have no use for blocks, so we hauled it in sacks and poured it into the troughs he had on all these bald hilltops where the wind would blow away the flies. Most of his so-called troughs was truck tires nailed onto anything flat—plywood, old doors, and suchlike—but they worked alright. A cow can put her tongue anywhere in a tire and get what she needs, and you can drag one of them flat things with your horse if you need to move em. Most places we salted had old buffalo wallers where them buffalo wallered. They done wallered their last, had to get out of the way for the cow and the man on the bay horse.

I'd been rustlin my own grub in the LeisureLife for a good little while when the old lady said it was time for me to eat with the white folks. This wasn't necessarily a good thing. The old lady's knee replacements had begun to fail, and both me and the old sumbitch was half-afraid of her. She cooked good as ever but she was a bomb waitin to go off, standin bowlegged at the stove and talkin ugly about how much she did for us. When she talked, the old sumbitch would move his mouth like he was saying the same words. If the old lady'd caught him at that they'd a been hell to pay.

Both of them was heavy smokers, to where a oxygen bottle was in sight. So they joined a Smoke-Enders deal the Lutherans had, and this required em to put all their butts in a jar and wear the jar around their neck on a string. The old sumbitch liked this okay because he could just tap his ash right under his chin and not get it on the truck seat, but the more that thing filled up and hung around her neck the meaner the old lady got. She had no idea the old sumbitch was cheatin and settin his jar on the woodpile when we was workin outside. She was just honester than him, and in the end she give up smokin and he smoked away, except he wasn't allowed to in the house no more nor buy readymades, cause the new tax made them too expensive and she wouldn't let him take it out of the cows, which come first. She said it was just a vice, and if he was half the man she thought he was he'd give it up for a bad deal. "You could have a long and happy old age," she told him, real sarcastic-like.

One day me and the old sumbitch is in the house hauling soot out of the fireplace on account of they had a chimney fire last winter. Over the mantel is a picture of a beautiful woman in a red dress with her hair piled on top of her head. The old sumbitch tells me that's the old lady before she joined the motorcycle gang.

"Oh?"

"Them motorcycle gangs," he says, "all they do is eat and work on their motorcycles. They taught her to smoke too, but she's shut of that. Probably outlive us all."

"Oh?"

"And if she ever wants to box you tell her no. She'll knock you on your ass, I guarantee it. Throw you a damn haymaker, son."

I couldn't understand how he could be so casual about the old lady being in a motorcycle gang. When we was smokin in the Lei- sureLife, I asked him about it. That's when I found out him and the old lady was brother and sister. I guess that explained it. If your sister joins some motorcycle gang, that's her business. He said she even had a tattoo—*Hounds from Hell*—a dog shootin flames out of his nos- trils and riding a Harley.

That picture on the mantel kind of stayed in my mind, and I asked the old sumbitch if his sisier'd ever had a boyfriend. Well yes, he said, several, quite a few, quite a damn few. "Our folks run em off. They was only after the land."

By now we was in the barn and he was goin all around the baler, hittin the zerks with his grease gun. "I had a lady friend myself. Do anything. Cook. Gangbusters with a snorty horse and not too damn hard on the eyes. Sis run her off. Said she was just after the land. If she was, I never could see it. Anyway, went on down the road a long time ago."

Fall come around and when we brought the cavvy down, two of them old-timers who'd worked so hard was lame One was stifled, the other sweenied, and both had cripplin quarter cracks. I thought they needed to be at the loose-horse sale, but the old sumbitch says, "No mounts of mine is gonna feed no Frenchmen," and that was that. So we made a hole, led the old-timers to the edge, and shot them with a elk rifle. First one didn't know what hit him. Second one heard the shot and saw his buddy fall, and the old sumbitch had to chase him all around to kill him. Then he sent me down the hole to get the halters back. Liftin them big heads was some chore.

I enjoyed eatin in the big house that whole summer until the sister started givin me come hither looks. They was fairly limited except those days when the old sumbitch was in town after supplies. Then she dialed it up and kind of brushed me every time she went past the table. There was always something special on town days, a pie maybe. I tried to think about the picture on the mantel but it was impossible, even though I knew it might get me out of the Leisure-Life once and for all. She was gettin more and more wound up while I was pretendin to enjoy the food, or goin crazy over the pie. But she didn't buy it—called me a queer, and sent me back to the trailer to make my own meals. By callin me a queer, she more or less admitted to what she'd been up to, and I think that embarrassed her, because she covered up by roaring at everyone and everything, including the poor old sumbitch, who had no idea what had gone sideways while he was away. It was two years before she made another pie, and then it was once a year on my birthday. She made me five birthday pies in all, sand cherry, every one of them.

I broke the catch colt, which I didn't know was no colt as he was the biggest snide in the cavvy. He was four, and it was time. I just got around him for a couple days, then saddled him gentle as I could. The offside stirrup scared him and he looked over at it, but that was all it was to saddlin. I must of had a burst of courage, cause next minute I was on him. That was okay too. I told the old sumbitch to open the corral gate, and we sailed away. The wind blew his tail up under him, and he thought about buckin but rejected the idea, and that was about all they was to breakin Olly, for that was his name. Once I'd rode him two weeks, he was safe for the old sumbitch, and he plumb loved this new horse and complimented me generously for the job I'd did.

We had three hard winters in a row, then lost so many calves to scours we changed our calving grounds. The old sumbitch just come out one day and looked at where he'd calved out for fifty years and said, "The ground's no good. We're movin." So we spent the summer buildin a new corral way off down the creek. When we's finished, he says, "I meant to do this when I got back from overseas, and now it's finished and I'm practically done for too. Whoever gets the place next will be glad his calves don't shit themselves into the next world like mine done."

Neither one of us had a back that was worth a damn, and if we'd had any money we'd of had the surgery. The least we could do was get rid of the square baler and quit heftin them man-killin five-wire bales. We got a round baler and a DewEze machine that let us pick up a bale from the truck without layin a finger on it. We'd smoke in the cab on those cold winter days and roll out a thousand pounds of hay while them old-time horned Herefords followed the truck sayin nice things about me and the old sumbitch while we told stories. That's when I let him find out I'd done some time.

"I figured you musta been in the crowbar hotel."

"How's that?"

"Well, you're a pretty good hand. What's a pretty good hand doin tryin loose horses in the middle of the night at some Podunk sale yard? Folks hang on to a pretty good hand, and nobody was hangin on to you. You want to tell me what you done?"

I'd been with the old sumbitch for three years and out of jail the same amount of time. I wasn't afraid to tell him what I done, for I was starting to trust him, but I sure didn't want him tellin nothin to his sister. I trusted him enough to tell him I did the time, but that was about all I was up to. I told him I rustled some yearlins, and he chuckled like everybody understood that. Unfortunately, it was a lie. I rustled some yearlings, all right, but that's not what I went up for.

The old man paid me in cash, or rather the old lady did, as she handled anything like that. They never paid into workmen's comp, so there was no reason to go to the records. They didn't even have the name right. You tell people around here your name is Shane, and they'll always believe you. The important thing is I was workin my tail off for that old sumbitch, and he knew it. Nothin else mattered, even the fact we'd come to like each other. After all, this was a god-dam ranch.

The old feller had several peculiarities to him, most of which I've forgot. He was one of the few fellers I ever seen who would actually jump up and down on his hat if he got mad enough. You can imagine what his hat looked like. One time he did it cause I let the swather get away from me on a hill and bent it all to hell. Another time a Mormon tried to run down his breeding program to get a better deal on some replacement heifers, and I'll be damned if the old sumbitch didn't throw that hat down and jump on it, until the Mormon got back into his Buick and eased on down the road without another word. One time when we was drivin ring shanks into corral poles I hit my thumb and tried jumpin on my hat, but the old sumbitch gave me such a odd look I never tried it again.

The old lady died sittin down, went in there and there she was, sittin down, and she was dead. After the first wave of grief, the old sumbitch and me fretted about rigor mortis and not being able to move her in that seated position, which would almost require rollin her. So we stretched her onto the couch and called the mortician, and he called the coroner and for some reason the coroner called the ambulance, which caused the old sumbitch to state, "It don't do you no never mind to tell nobody nothin." Course, he was right.

Once the funeral was behind us, I moved out of the LeisureLife once and for all, partly for comfort and partly cause the old sumbitch falled apart after his sister passed, which I never suspected during the actual event. But once she's gone, he says he's all that's left of his family and he's alone in life, and about then he notices me and tells me to get my stuff out of the LeisureLife and move in with him.

We rode through the cattle pretty near ever day, year-round, and he come to trust me enough to show how his breedin program went, with culls and breedbacks and outcrosses and replacements, and he took me to bull sales and showed me what to expect in a bull and which ones was correct and which was sorry. One day we's looking at a pen of yearlin bulls on this outfit near Luther, and he can't make up his mind and says he wishes his sister was with him and starts snufflin and says she had an eye on her wouldn't quit. So I stepped up and picked three bulls out of that pen and he quit snufflin and said damn if I didn't have an eye on me too. That was the beginnin of our partnership.

One whole year I was the cook, and one whole year he was the cook, and back and forth like that but never at the same time. Whoever was cook would change when the other feller got sick of his recipes, and ever once in a while a new recipe would come in the *AgriNews*, like that corn chowder with the sliced hot dogs. I even tried a pie one time, but it just made him lonesome for days gone by, so we forgot about desserts, which was probably good for our health as most sweets call for gobbin in the white sugar.

The sister had never let him have a dog cause she had a cat, and she thought a dog would get the cat and, as she said, if the dog got the cat she'd get the dog. It wasn't much of a cat, anyhow, but it lasted a long time, outlived the old lady by several moons. After it passed on, we took it out to the burn barrel, and the first thing the old sumbitch said was, "We're gettin a dog." It took him that long to realize his sister was gone.

Tony was a border collie we got as a pup from a couple in Miles City that raised them, and they was seven generation of cow dogs just wanted to eat and work stock. You could cup your hands and hold Tony when we got him, but he grew up in one summer and went to work and we taught him *down, here, come by, way to me,* and *hold em,* all in one year or less, cause Tony'd just stay on his belly and study you with his eyes until he knew exactly what you wanted.

Tony helped us gather, mother up pairs, and separate bulls, and he lived in the house for many a good year and kept us entertained with all his tricks.

Finally, Tony got old and died. We didn't take it so good, especially the old sumbitch, who said he couldn't foresee enough summers for another dog. Plus that was the year he couldn't get on a horse no more and he wasn't about to work no stock dog afoot. There was still plenty to do, and most of it fell to me. After all, this was a goddam ranch.

The time come to tell him what I done to go to jail, which was rob that little store at Absarokee and shoot the proprietor, though he didn't die. I had no idea why I did such a thing, then or now. I led the crew on the prison ranch for a number of years and turned out many a good hand. They wasn't nearabout to let me loose till there was a replacement good as me who'd stay awhile. So I trained up a murderer from Columbia Falls; could rope, break horses, keep vaccine records, fence, and irrigate. Once the warden seen how good he was, they paroled me out and turned it all over to the new man, who they said was never getting out. Said he was heinous. The old sumbitch could give a shit less when I told him my story. I could of told him all the years before, when he first hired me, for all he cared. He was a big believer in what he saw with his own eyes.

I don't think I ever had the touch with customers the old sumbitch did. They'd come from all over lookin for horned Herefords and talkin hybrid vigor, which I may or may not have believed. They'd ask what we had and I'd point to the corrals and say, "Go look for yourself." Some would insist on seein the old sumbitch and I'd tell them he was in bed, which was nearly the only place you could find him, once he'd begun to fail. Then the state got wind of his condition and took him to town. I went to see him there right regular, but it just upset him. He couldn't figure out who I was and got frustrated because he knew I was somebody he was supposed to know. And then he failed even worse. They said it was just better if I didn't come around.

The neighbors claimed I'd let the weeds grow and was personally responsible for the spread of spurge, Dalmatian toadflax, and knapweed. They got the authorities involved, and it was pretty clear I was the weed they had in mind. If they could get the court to appoint one of their relatives ranch custodian they'd have all that grass for free till the old sumbitch was in a pine box. The authorities came in all sizes and shapes, but when they got through they let me take one saddle horse, one saddle, the clothes on my back, my hat, and my slicker. I rode that horse clear to the sale yard, where they tried to put him in the loose horses—cause of his age, not cause he was a bronc. I told em I was too set in my ways to start feedin Frenchmen and rode off toward Idaho. There's always an opening for a cowboy, even a old sumbitch like me, if he can halfway make a hand.

James Alan McPherson

A SOLO SONG: FOR DOC

So you want to know this business, youngblood? So you want to be a Waiter's Waiter? The Commissary gives you a book with all the rules and tells you to learn them. And you do, and think that is all there is to it. A big, thick black book. Poor youngblood.

Look at me. *I* am a Waiter's Waiter. I know all the moves, all the pretty, fine moves that big book will never teach you. *I* built this railroad with my moves; and so did Sheik Beasley and Uncle T. Boone and Danny Jackson, and so did Doc Craft. That book they made you learn came from our moves and from our heads. There was a time when six of us, big men, danced at the same time in that little Pantry without touching and shouted orders to the sweating paddies in the kitchen. There was a time when they *had* to respect us because our sweat and our moves supported them. We knew the service and the paddies, even the green dishwashers, knew that we did and didn't give us the crap they pull on you.

Do you know how to sneak a Blackplate to a nasty cracker? Do you know how to rub asses with five other men in the Pantry getting their orders together and still know that you are a man, just like them? Do you know how to bullshit while you work and keep the paddies in their places with your bullshit? Do you know how to breathe down the back of an old lady's dress to hustle a bigger tip?

No. You are summer stuff, youngblood. I am old, my moves are not so good any more, but I know this business. The Commissary hires you for the summer because they don't want to let anyone get as old as me on them. I'm sixty-three, but they can't fire me: I'm in the Union. They can't lay me off for fucking up: I know this business too well. And so they hire you, youngblood, for the summer when the tourists come, and in September you go away with some tips in your pocket to buy pussy and they wait all winter for me to die. I *am* dying, youngblood, and so is this business. Both of us will die together. There'll always be summer stuff like you, but the big men, the big trains, are dying every day and everybody can see it. And nobody but us who are dying with them gives a damn.

Look at the big picture at the end of the car, youngblood. That's the man who built this road. He's in your history books. He's probably in that big black bible you read. He was a great man. He hated people. He didn't want to feed them but the government said he had to. He didn't want to hire me, but he needed me to feed the people. I know this, youngblood, and that is why that book is written for you and that is why I have never read it. That is why you get nervous and jump up to polish the pepper and salt shakers when the word comes down the line that an inspector is getting on at the next stop. That is why you warm the toast covers for every cheap old lady who wants to get coffee and toast and good service for sixty-five cents and a dime tip. You know that he needs you only for the summer and that hundreds of youngbloods like you want to work this summer to buy that pussy in Chicago and Portland and Seattle. The man uses you, but he doesn't need you. But me he needs for the winter, when you are gone, and to teach you something in the summer about this business you can't get from that big black book. He needs me and he knows it and I know it. That is why I am sitting here when there are tables to be cleaned and linen to be changed and silver to be washed and polished. He needs me to die. That is why I am taking my time. I know it. And I will take his service with me when I die, just like the Sheik did and like Percy Fields did, and like Doc.

Who are they? Why do I keep talking about them? Let me think about it. I guess it is because they were the last of the Old School, like me. We made this road. We got a million miles of walking up and down these cars under our feet. Doc Craft was the Old School, like me. He was a Waiter's Waiter. He danced down these aisles with us and swung his tray with the roll of the train, never spilling in all his trips a single cup of coffee. He could carry his tray on two fingers, or on one and a half if he wanted, and he knew all the tricks about hustling tips there are to know. He could work anybody. The girls at the Northland in Chicago knew Doc, and the girls at the Haverville in Seattle, and the girls at the Step-Inn in Portland and all the girls in Winnipeg knew Doc Craft.

But wait. It is just 1:30 and the first call for dinner is not until 5:00. You want to kill some time; you want to hear about the Old School and how it was in my day. If you look in that black book you would see that you should be polishing silver now. Look out the window; this is North Dakota, this is Jerry's territory. Jerry, the Unexpected Inspector. Shouldn't you polish the shakers or clean out the Pantry or squeeze oranges, or maybe change the linen on the tables? Jerry Ewald is sly. The train may stop in the middle of this wheatfield and Jerry may get on. He lives by that book. He knows where to look for dirt and mistakes. Jerry Ewald, the Unexpected Inspector. He knows where to look; he knows how to get you. He got Doc.

Now you want to know about him, about the Old School. You have even put aside your book of rules. But see how you keep your finger in the pages as if the book was more important than what I tell you. That's a bad move, and it tells on you. You will be a waiter. But you will never be a Waiter's Waiter. The Old School died with Doc, and the very last of it is dying with me. What happened to Doc? Take your finger out of the pages, youngblood, and I will tell you about a kind of life these rails will never carry again.

When your father was a boy playing with himself behind the barn, Doc was already a man and knew what the thing was for. But he got tired of using it when he wasn't much older than you, and he set his mind on making money. He had no skills. He was black. He got hungry. On Christmas Day in 1916, the story goes, he wandered into the Chicago stockyards and over to a dining car waiting to be connected up to the main train for the Chicago-to-San Francisco run. He looked up through the kitchen door at the chef storing supplies for the kitchen and said: "I'm hungry."

"What do you want me to do about it?" the Swede chef said.

"I'll work," said Doc.

That Swede was Chips Magnusson, fresh off the boat and lucky to be working himself. He did not know yet that he should save all extra work for other Swedes fresh off the boat. He later learned this by living. But at that time he considered a moment, bit into one of the fresh apples stocked for apple pie, chewed considerably, spit out the seeds and then waved the black on board the big train. "You can eat all you want," he told Doc. "But you work all I tell you."

He put Doc to rolling dough for the apple pies and the train began rolling for Doc. It never stopped. He fell in love with the feel of the wheels under his feet clicking against the track and he got the rhythm of the wheels in him and learned, like all of us, how to roll with them and move with them. After that first trip Doc was never at home on the ground. He worked everything in the kitchen from putting out dough to second cook, in six years. And then, when the Commissary saw that he was good and would soon be going for one of the chef's spots they saved for the Swedes, they put him out of the kitchen and told him to learn this waiter business; and told him to learn how to bullshit on the other side of the Pantry. He was almost thirty, youngblood, when he crossed over to the black side of the Pantry. I wasn't there when he made his first trip as a waiter, but from what they tell me of that trip I know that he was broke in by good men. Pantryman was Sheik Beasley, who stayed high all the time and let the waiters steal anything they wanted as long as they didn't bother his reefers. Danny Jackson, who was black and knew Shakespeare before the world said he could work with it, was second man. Len Dickey was third. Reverend Hendricks was fourth, and Uncle T. Boone, who even in those early days could not straighten his back, ran fifth. Doc started in as sixth waiter, the "mule." They pulled some shit on him at first because they didn't want somebody fresh out of a paddy kitchen on the crew. They messed with his orders, stole his plates, picked up his tips on the sly, and made him do all the dirty work. But when they saw that he could take the shit without getting hot and when they saw that he was set on being a waiter, even though he was older than most of them, they settled down and began to teach him this business and all the words and moves and slickness that made it a good business.

His real name was Leroy Johnson, I think, but when Danny Jackson saw how cool and neat he was in his moves, and how he handled the plates, he began to call him "the Doctor." Then the Sheik, coming down from his high one day after missing the lunch and dinner service, saw how Doc had taken over his station and collected fat tips from his tables by telling the passengers that the Sheik had had to get off back along the line because of a heart attack. The Sheik liked that because he saw that Doc understood crackers and how they liked nothing better than knowing that a nigger had died on the job, giving them service. The Sheik was impressed. And he was not an easy man to impress because he knew too much about life and had to stay high most of the time. And when Doc would not split the tips with him, the Sheik got mad at first and called Doc a barrel of motherfuckers and some other words you would not recognize. But he was impressed. And later that night, in the crew car when the others were gambling and drinking and bullshitting about the women they had working the corners for them, the Sheik came over to Doc's bunk and said: "You're a crafty motherfucker."

"Yeah?" says Doc.

"Yeah," says the Sheik, who did not say much. "You're a crafty motherfucker but I like you." Then he got into the first waiter's bunk and lit up again. But Reverend Hendricks, who always read his Bible before going to sleep and who always listened to anything the Sheik said because he knew the Sheik only said something when it was important, heard what was said and remembered it. After he put his Bible back in his locker, he walked over to Doc's bunk and looked down at him. "Mister Doctor Craft," the Reverend said. "Youngblood Doctor Craft."

"Yeah?" says Doc.

"Yeah," says Reverend Hendricks. "That's who you are."

And that's who he was from then on.

II

I came to the road away from the war. This was after '41, when people at home were looking for Japs under their beds every night. I did not want to fight because there was no money in it and I didn't want to go overseas to work in a kitchen. The big war was on and a lot of soldiers crossed the country to get to it, and as long as a black man fed them on trains he did not have to go to that war. I could have got a job in a Chicago factory, but there was more money on the road and it was safer. And after a while it got into your blood so that you couldn't leave it for anything. The road got into my blood the way it got into everybody's; the way going to the war got in the blood of redneck farm boys and the crazy Polacks from Chicago. It was all right for them to go to the war. They were young and stupid. And they died that way. I played it smart. I was almost thirty-five and I didn't want to go. But I took *them* and fed them and gave them good times on their way to the war, and for that I did not have to go. The soldiers had plenty of money and were afraid not to spend it all before they got to the ships on the Coast. And we gave them ways to spend it on the trains.

Now in those days there was plenty of money going around and everybody stole from everybody. The kitchen stole food from the company and the company knew it and wouldn't pay good wages. There were no rules in those days, there was no black book to go by and nobody said what you couldn't eat or steal. The paddy cooks used to toss boxes of steaks off the train in the Chicago yards for people at the restaurants there who paid them, cash. These were the days when ordinary people had to have red stamps or blue stamps to get powdered eggs and white lard to mix with red powder to make their own butter.

The stewards stole from the company and from the waiters; the waiters stole from the stewards and the company and from each other. I stole. Doc stole. Even Reverend Hendricks put his Bible far back in his locker and stole with us. You didn't want a man on your crew who didn't steal. He made it bad for everybody. And if the steward saw that he was a dummy and would never get to stealing, he wrote him up for something and got him off the crew so as not to slow down the rest of us. We had a red-neck cracker steward from Alabama by the name of Casper who used to say: *"Jesus Christ!* I ain't got time to hate you niggers, I'm making so much money."* He used to keep all his cash at home under his bed in a cardboard box because he was afraid to put it in the bank.

Doc and Sheik Beasley and me were on the same crew together all during the war. Even in those days, as young as we were, we knew how to be Old Heads. We organized for the soldiers. We had to wear skullcaps all the time because the crackers said our hair was poison and didn't want any of it to fall in their food. The Sheik didn't mind wearing one. He kept reefers in his and used to sell them to the soldiers for double what he paid for them in Chicago and three times what he paid the Chinamen in Seattle. That's why we called him the Sheik. After every meal the Sheik would get in the linen closet and light up. Sometimes he wouldn't come out for days. Nobody gave a damn, though; we were all too busy stealing and working. And there was more for us to get as long as he didn't come out.

Doc used to sell bootlegged booze to the soldiers; that was his speciality. He had redcaps in the Chicago stations telling the soldiers who to ask for on the train. He was an open operator and had to give the steward a cut, but he still made a pile of money. That's why that old cracker always kept us together on his crew. We were the three best moneymakers he ever had. That's something you should learn, youngblood. They can't love you for being you. They only love you if you make money for them. All that talk these days about integration and brotherhood, that's a lot of bullshit. The man will love you as long as he can make money with you. I made money. And old Casper had to love me in the open although I knew he called me a nigger at home when he had put that money in his big cardboard box. I know he loved me on the road in the wartime because I used to bring in the biggest moneymakers. I used to handle the girls.

Look out that window. See all that grass and wheat? Look at that big farm boy cutting it. Look at that burnt cracker on that tractor. He probably has a wife who married him because she didn't know what else to do. Back during wartime the girls in this part of the country knew what to do. They got on the trains at night.

You can look out that window all day and run around all the stations when we stop, but you'll never see a black man in any of these towns. You know why, youngblood? These farmers hate you. They still remember when their girls came out of these towns and got on the trains at night. They've been running black men and dark Indians out of these towns for years. They hate anything dark that's not that way because of the sun. Right now there are big farm girls with hair under their arms on the corners in San Francisco, Chicago, Seattle and Minneapolis who got started on these cars back during wartime. The farmers still remember that and they hate you and me for it. But it wasn't for me they got on. Nobody wants a stiff, smelly farm girl when there are sporting women to be got for a dollar in the cities. It was for the soldiers they got on. It was just business to me. But they hate you and me anyway.

I got off in one of these towns once, a long time after the war, just to get a drink while the train changed engines. Everybody looked at me and by the time I got to a bar there were ten people on my trail. I was drinking a fast one when the sheriff came in the bar.

"What are you doing here?" he asks me.

"Just getting a shot," I say.

He spit on the floor. "How long you plan to be here?"

"I don't know," I say, just to be nasty.

"There ain't no jobs here," he says.

"I wasn't looking," I say.

"We don't want you here."

"I don't give a good goddamn," I say.

He pulled his gun on me. "All right, coon, back on the train," he says.

"Wait a minute," I tell him. "Let me finish my drink."

He knocked my glass over with his gun. "You're finished *now*," he says. "Pull your ass out of here *now*!"

I didn't argue.

I was the night man. After dinner it was my job to pull the cloths off the tables and put paddings on. Then I cut out the lights and locked both doors. There was a big farm girl from Minot named Hilda who could take on eight or ten soldiers in one night, white soldiers. These white boys don't know how to last. I would stand by the door and when the soldiers came back from the club car they would pay me and I would let them in. Some of the girls could make as much as one hundred dollars in one night. And I always made twice as much. Soldiers don't care what they do with their money. They just have to spend it.

We never bothered with the girls ourselves. It was just business as far as we were concerned. But there was one dummy we had with us once, a boy from the South named Willie Joe something who handled the dice. He was really hot for one of these farm girls. He used to buy her good whiskey and he hated to see her go in the car at night to wait for the soldiers. He was a real dummy. One time I heard her tell him: "It's all right. They can have my body. I know I'm black inside. *Jesus*, I'm so black inside I wisht I was black all over!"

And this dummy Willie Joe said: *"Baby, don't you ever change!"*

I knew we had to get rid of him before he started trouble. So we had the steward bump him off the crew as soon as we could find a good man to handle the gambling. That old redneck Casper was glad to do it. He saw what was going on.

But you want to hear about Doc, you say, so you can get back to your reading. What can I tell you? The road got into his blood? He liked being a waiter? You won't understand this, but he did. There were no Civil Rights or marches or riots for something better in those days. In those days a man found something he liked to do and liked it from then on because he couldn't help himself. What did he like about the road? He liked what I liked: the money, owning the car, running it, telling the soldiers what to do, hustling a bigger tip from some old maid by looking under her dress and laughing at her, having all the girls at the Haverville Hotel waiting for us to come in for stopover, the power we had to beat them up or lay them if we wanted. He liked running free and not being married to some bitch who would spend his money when he was out of town or give it to some stud. He liked getting drunk with the boys up at Andy's, setting up the house and then passing out from drinking too much, knowing that the boys would get him home.

I ran with that one crew all during wartime and they, Doc, the Sheik and Reverend Hendricks, had taken me under their wings. *I* was still a youngblood then, and Doc liked me a lot. But he never said that much to me; he was not a talker. The Sheik had taught him the value of silence in things that really matter. We roomed together in Chicago at Mrs. Wright's place in those days. Mrs. Wright didn't allow women in the rooms and Doc liked that, because after being out for a week and after stopping over in those hotels along the way, you get tired of women and bullshit and need your privacy. We weren't like you. We didn't need a woman every time we got hard. We knew when we had to have it and when we didn't. And we didn't spend all our money on it, either. You youngbloods think the way to get a woman is to let her see how you handle your money. That's stupid. The way to get a woman is to let her see how you handle other women. But you'll never believe that until it's too late to do you any good.

Doc knew how to handle women. I can remember a time in a Winnipeg hotel how he ran a bitch out of his room because he had had enough of it and did not need her any more. I was in the next room and heard everything.

"Come on, Doc," the bitch said. "Come on honey, let's do it one more time."

"Hell no," Doc said. "I'm tired and I don't want to any more."

"How can you say you're tired?" the bitch said. "How can you say you're tired when you didn't go but two times?"

"I'm tired of it," Doc said, "because I'm tired of you. And I'm tired of you because I'm tired of it and bitches like you in all the towns I been in. You drain a man. And I know if I beat you, you'll still come back when I hit you again. *That's* why I'm tired. I'm tired of having things around I don't care about."

"What do you care about, Doc?" the bitch said.

"I don't know," Doc said. "I guess I care about moving and being somewhere else when I want to be. I guess I care about going out, and coming in to wait for the time to go out again."

"You crazy, Doc," the bitch said.

"Yeah?" Doc said. "I guess I'm crazy all right."

Later that bitch knocked on my door and I did it for her because she was just a bitch and I knew Doc wouldn't want her again. I don't think he ever wanted a bitch again. I never saw him with one after that time. He was just a little over fifty then and could have still done whatever he wanted with women.

The war ended. The farm boys who got back from the war did not spend money on their way home. They did not want to spend any more money on women, and the girls did not get on at night any more. Some of them went into the cities and turned pro. Some of them stayed in the towns and married the farm boys who got back from the war. Things changed on the road. The Commissary started putting that book of rules together and told us to stop stealing. They were losing money on passengers now because of the airplanes and they began to really tighten up and started sending inspectors down along the line to check on us. They started sending in spotters, too. One of them caught that redneck Casper writing out a check for two dollars less than he had charged the spotter. The Commissary got him in on the rug for it. I wasn't there, but they told me he said to the General Superintendent: "Why are you getting on me, a white man, for a lousy son-of-a-bitching two bucks? There's niggers out there been stealing for *years!*"

"Who?" the General Superintendent asked.

And Casper couldn't say anything because he had that cardboard box full of money still under his bed and knew he would have to tell how he got it if any of us was brought in. So he said nothing.

"Who?" the General Superintendent asked him again.

"Why, all them nigger waiters steal, *everybody knows that!*"

"And the cooks, what about them?" the Superintendent said.

"They're white," said Casper.

They never got the story out of him and he was fired. He used the money to open a restaurant someplace in Indiana and I heard later that he started a branch of the Klan in his town. One day he showed up at the station and told Doc, Reverend Hendricks and me: "I'll see you boys get *yours*. Damn if I'm takin' the rap for you niggers."

We just laughed in his face because we knew he could do nothing to us through the Commissary. But just to be safe we stopped steal-ing so much. But they did get the Sheik, though. One day an inspec-tor got on in the mountains just outside of Whitefish and grabbed him right out of that linen closet. The Sheik had been smoking in there all day and he was high and laughing when they pulled him off the train.

That was the year we got in the Union. The crackers and Swedes finally let us in after we paid off. We really stopped stealing and got organized and there wasn't a damn thing the company could do about it, although it tried like hell to buy us out. And to get back at us, they put their heads together and began to make up that big book of rules you keep your finger in. Still, *we* knew the service and they had to write the book the way we gave the service and at first there was nothing for the Old School men to learn. We got seniority through the Union, and as long as we gave the service and didn't steal, they couldn't touch us. So they began changing the rules, and sending us notes about the service. Little changes at first, like how the initials on the doily should always face the customer, and how the silver should be taken off the tables between meals. But we were getting old and set in our old service, and it got harder and harder learning all those little changes. And we had to learn new stuff all the time because there was no telling when an inspector would get on and catch us giving bad service. It was hard as hell. It was hard because we knew that the company was out to break up the Old School. The Sheik was gone, and we knew that Reverend Hendricks or Uncle T. or Danny Jackson would go soon because they stood for the Old School, just like the Sheik. But what bothered us most was knowing that they would go for Doc first, before any-one else, because he loved the road so much.

Doc was over sixty-five then and had taken to drinking hard when we were off. But he never touched a drop when we were on the road. I used to wonder whether he drank because being a Waiter's Waiter was getting hard or because he had to do something until his next trip. I could never figure it. When we had our layovers he would spend all his time in Andy's, setting up the house. He had no wife, no relatives, not even a hobby. He just drank. Pretty soon the slicksters at Andy's got to using him for a good thing. They commenced putting the touch on him because they saw he was getting old and knew he didn't have far to go, and they would never have to pay him back. Those of us who were close to him tried to pull his coat, but it didn't help. He didn't talk about himself much, he didn't talk much about anything that wasn't related to the road; but when I tried to hip him once about the hustlers and how they were closing in on him, he just took another shot and said:

"I don't need no money. Nobody's jiving me. I'm jiving them. You know I can still pull in a hundred in tips in one trip. I *know* this business."

"Yeah, I know, Doc," I said. "But how many more trips can you make before you have to stop?"

"I ain't never gonna stop. Trips are all I know and I'll be making them as long as these trains haul people."

"That's just it," I said. "They don't *want* to haul people any more. The planes do that. The big roads want freight now. Look how they hire youngbloods just for the busy seasons just so they won't get any seniority in the winter. Look how all the Old School waiters are dropping out. They got the Sheik, Percy Fields just lucked up and died before they got to him, they almost got Reverend Hendricks. Even *Uncle T.* is going to retire! And they'll get us too."

"Not me," said Doc. "I know my moves. This old fox can still dance with a tray and handle four tables at the same time. I can still bait a queer and make the old ladies tip big. There's no waiter better than me and I know it."

"Sure, Doc," I said. "I know it too. But please save your money. Don't be a dummy. There'll come a day when you just can't get up to go out and they'll put you on the ground for good."

Doc looked at me like he had been shot. "Who taught you the moves when you were just a raggedy-ass waiter?"

"You did, Doc," I said.

"Who's always the first man down in the yard at train-time?" He threw down another shot. "Who's there sitting in the car every tenth morning while you other old heads are still at home pulling on your longjohns?"

I couldn't say anything. He was right and we both knew it.

"I have to go out," he told me. "Going out is my whole life. I wait for that tenth morning. I ain't never missed a trip and I don't mean to."

What could I say to him, youngblood? What can I say to you? He had to go out, not for the money; it was in his blood. You have to go out too, but it's for the money you go. You hate going out and you love coming in. He loved going out and he hated coming in. Would *you* listen if I told you to stop spending your money on pussy in Chicago? Would he listen if I told him to save *his* money? To stop setting up the bar at Andy's? No. Old men are just as bad as young men when it comes to money. They can't think. They always try to buy what they should have for free. And what they buy, after they have it, is nothing.

They called Doc into the Commissary and the doctors told him he had lumbago and a bad heart and was weak from drinking too much, and they wanted him to get down for his own good. He wouldn't do it. Tesdale, the General Superintendent, called him in and told him that he had enough years in the service to pull down a big pension and that the company would pay for a retirement party for him, since he was the oldest waiter working, and invite all the Old School waiters to see him off, if he would come down. Doc said no. He knew that the Union had to back him. He knew that he could ride as long as he made the trains on time and as long as he knew the service. And he knew that he could not leave the road.

The company called in its lawyers to go over the Union contract. I wasn't there, but Len Dickey was in on the meeting because of his office in the Union. He told me about it later. Those fat company lawyers took the contract apart and went through all their books. They took the seniority clause apart word by word, trying to figure a way to get at Doc. But they had written it airtight back in the days when the company *needed* waiters, and there was nothing in it about compulsory retirement. Not a word. The paddies in the Union must have figured that waiters didn't *need* a new contract when they let us in, and they had let us come in under the old one thinking that all waiters would die on the job, or drink themselves to death when they were still young, or die from buying too much pussy, or just quit when they had put in enough time to draw a pension. But *nothing* in the whole contract could help them get rid of Doc Craft. They were sweating, they were working so hard. And all the time Tesdale, the General Superintendent, was calling them sons-of-bitches for not earning their money. But there was nothing the company lawyers could do but turn the pages of their big books and sweat and promise Tesdale that they would find some way if he gave them more time.

The word went out from the Commissary: "Get Doc." The stewards got it from the assistant superintendents: "Get Doc." Since they could not get him to retire, they were determined to catch him giving bad service. He had more seniority than most other waiters, so they couldn't bump him off our crew. In fact, all the waiters with more seniority than Doc were on the crew with him. There were four of us from the Old School: me, Doc, Uncle T. Boone, and Danny Jackson. Reverend Hendricks wasn't running regular any more; he was spending all his Sundays preaching in his Church on the South Side because he knew what was coming and wanted to have something steady going for him in Chicago when his time came. Fifth and sixth men on that crew were two hardheads who had read the book. The steward was Crouse, and he really didn't want to put the screws to Doc but he couldn't help himself. Everybody wants to work. So Crouse started in to riding Doc, sometimes about moving too fast, sometimes about not moving fast enough. I was on the crew, I saw it all. Crouse would seat four singles at the same table, on Doc's station, and Doc had to take care of all four different orders at the same time. He was seventy-three, but that didn't stop him, knowing this business the way he did. It just slowed him down some. But Crouse got on him even for that and would chew him out in front of the passengers, hoping that he'd start cursing and bother the passengers so that they would complain to the company. It never worked, though. Doc just played it cool. He'd look into Crouse's eyes and know what was going on. And then he'd lay on his good service, the only service he knew, and the passengers would see how good he was with all that age on his back and they would get mad at the steward, and leave Doc a bigger tip when they left.

The Commissary sent out spotters to catch him giving bad service. These were pale-white little men in glasses who never looked you in the eye, but who always felt the plate to see if it was warm. And there were the old maids, who like that kind of work, who would order shrimp or crabmeat cocktails or celery and olive plates because they knew how the rules said these things had to be made. And when they came, when Doc brought them out, they would look to see if the oyster fork was stuck into the thing, and look out the window a long time.

"Ain't no use trying to fight it," Uncle T. Boone told Doc in the crew car one night, "the black waiter is *doomed*. Look at all the good restaurants, the class restaurants in Chicago. *You* can't work in them. Them white waiters got those jobs sewed up fine."

"I can be a waiter anywhere," says Doc. "I know the business and I like it and I can do it anywhere."

"The black waiter is doomed," Uncle T. says again. "The whites is taking over the service in the good places. And when they run you off of here, you won't have no place to go."

"They won't run me off of here," says Doc. "As long as I give the right service they can't touch me."

"You're a goddamn *fool!*" says Uncle T. "You're a nigger and you ain't got no rights except what the Union says you have. And that ain't worth a damn because when the Commissary finally gets you, those niggers won't lift a finger to help you."

"Leave off him," I say to Boone. "If anybody ought to be put off it's you. You ain't had your back straight for thirty years. You even make the crackers sick the way you keep bowing and folding your hands and saying, 'Thank you, Mr. Boss.' Fifty years ago that would of got you a bigger tip," I say, "but now it ain't worth a shit. And every time you do it the crackers hate you. And every time I see you serving with that skullcap on I hate you. The Union said we didn't have to wear them *eighteen years ago*! Why can't you take it off?"

Boone just sat on his bunk with his skullcap in his lap, leaning against his big belly. He knew I was telling the truth and he knew he wouldn't change. But he said: "That's the trouble with the Negro waiter today. He ain't got no humility. And as long as he don't have humility, he keeps losing the good jobs."

Doc had climbed into the first waiter's bunk in his longjohns and I got in the second waiter's bunk under him and lay there. I could hear him breathing. It had a hard sound. He wasn't well and all of us knew it.

"Doc?" I said in the dark.

"Yeah?"

"Don't mind Boone, Doc. He's a dead man. He just don't know it."

"We all are," Doc said.

"Not you," I said.

"What's the use? He's right. They'll get me in the end."

"But they ain't done it yet."

"They'll get me. And they know it and I know it. I can even see it in old Crouse's eyes. He knows they're gonna get me."

"Why don't you get a woman?"

He was quiet. "What can I do with a woman now, that I ain't already done too much?"

I thought for a while. "If you're on the ground, being with one might not make it so bad."

"I hate women," he said.

"You ever try fishing?"

"No."

"You want to?"

"No," he said.

"You can't keep *drinking.*"

He did not answer.

"Maybe you could work in town. In the Commissary."

I could hear the big wheels rolling and clicking along the tracks and I knew by the smooth way we were moving that we were almost out of the Dakota flatlands. Doc wasn't talking. "Would you like that?" I thought he was asleep. "Doc, would you like that?"

"Hell no," he said.

"You have to try something!"

He was quiet again. "I know," he finally said.

III

Jerry Ewald, the Unexpected Inspector, got on in Winachee that next day after lunch and we knew that he had the word from the Commissary. He was cool about it: he laughed with the steward and the waiters about the old days and his hard gray eyes and shining glasses kept looking over our faces as if to see if we knew why he had got on. The two hardheads were in the crew car stealing a nap on company time. Jerry noticed this and could have caught them, but he was after bigger game. We all knew that, and we kept talking to him about the days of the big trains and looking at his white hair and not into the eyes behind his glasses because we knew what was there. Jerry sat down on the first waiter's station and said to Crouse: "Now I'll have some lunch. Steward, let the headwaiter bring me a menu."

Crouse stood next to the table where Jerry sat, and looked at Doc, who had been waiting between the tables with his tray under his arm. The way the rules say. Crouse looked sad because he knew what was coming. Then Jerry looked directly at Doc and said: "Headwaiter Doctor Craft, bring me a menu."

Doc said nothing and he did not smile. He brought the menu. Danny Jackson and I moved back into the hall to watch. There was nothing we could do to help Doc and we knew it. He was the Waiter's Waiter, out there by himself, hustling the biggest tip he would ever get in his life. Or losing it.

"Goddamn," Danny said to me. "Now let's sit on the ground and talk about how *kings* are gonna get fucked."

"Maybe not," I said. But I did not believe it myself because Jerry is the kind of man who lies in bed all night, scheming. I knew he had a plan.

Doc passed us on his way to the kitchen for water and I wanted to say something to him. But what was the use? He brought the water to Jerry. Jerry looked him in the eye. "Now, Headwaiter," he said. "I'll have a bowl of onion soup, a cold roast beef sandwich on white, rare, and a glass of iced tea."

"Write it down," said Doc. He was playing it right. He knew that the new rules had stopped waiters from taking verbal orders.

"Don't be so professional, Doc," Jerry said. "It's me, one of the *boys*."

"You have to write it out," said Doc, "it's in the black book."

Jerry clicked his pen and wrote the order out on the check. And handed it to Doc. Uncle T. followed Doc back into the Pantry.

"He's gonna get you, Doc," Uncle T. said. "I knew it all along. You know why? The Negro waiter ain't got no more humility."

"Shut the fuck up, Boone!" I told him.

"You'll see," Boone went on. "You'll see I'm right. There ain't a thing Doc can do about it, either. We're gonna lose all the good jobs."

We watched Jerry at the table. He saw us watching and smiled with his gray eyes. Then he poured some of the water from the glass on the linen cloth and picked up the silver sugar bowl and placed it right on the wet spot. Doc was still in the Pantry. Jerry turned the silver sugar bowl around and around on the linen. He pressed down on it some as he turned. But when he picked it up again, there was no dark ring on the wet cloth. We had polished the silver early that morning, according to the book, and there was not a dirty piece of silver to be found in the whole car. Jerry was drinking the rest of the water when Doc brought out the polished silver soup tureen, underlined with a doily and a breakfast plate, with a shining soup bowl underlined with a doily and a breakfast plate, and a bread-and-butter plate with six crackers; not four or five or seven, but six, the number the Commissary had written in the black book. He swung down the aisle of the car between the two rows of white tables and you could not help but be proud of the way he moved with the roll of the train and the way that tray was like a part of his arm. It was good service. He placed everything neat, with all company initials showing, right where things should go.

"Shall I serve up the soup?" he asked Jerry.

"Please," said Jerry.

Doc handled that silver soup ladle like one of those Chicago Jew tailors handles a needle. He ladled up three good-sized spoonfuls from the tureen and then laid the wet spoon on an extra bread-and-butter plate on the side of the table, so he would not stain the cloth. Then he put a napkin over the wet spot Jerry had made and changed the ashtray for a prayer-card because every good waiter knows that nobody wants to eat a good meal looking at an ashtray.

"You know about the spoon plate, I see," Jerry said to Doc.

"I'm a waiter," said Doc. "I know."

"You're a damn good waiter," said Jerry.

Doc looked Jerry square in the eye. "I know," he said slowly.

Jerry ate a little of the soup and opened all six of the cracker packages. Then he stopped eating and began to look out the window. We were passing through his territory, Washington State, the country he loved because he was the only company inspector in the state and knew that once we got through Montana he would be the only man the waiters feared. He smiled and then waved for Doc to bring out the roast beef sandwich.

But Doc was into his service now and cleared the table completely. Then he got the silver crumb knife from the Pantry and gathered all the cracker crumbs, even the ones Jerry had managed to get in between the salt and pepper shakers.

"You want the tea with your sandwich, or later?" he asked Jerry.

"Now is fine," said Jerry, smiling.

"You're going good," I said to Doc when he passed us on his way to the Pantry. "He can't touch you or nothing."

He did not say anything.

Uncle T. Boone looked at Doc like he wanted to say something too, but he just frowned and shuffled out to stand next to Jerry. You could see that Jerry hated him. But Jerry knew how to smile at everybody, and so he smiled at Uncle T. while Uncle T. bent over the table with his hands together like he was praying, and moved his head up and bowed it down.

Doc brought out the roast beef, proper service. The crock of mustard was on a breakfast plate, underlined with a doily, initials facing Jerry. The lid was on the mustard and it was clean, like it says in the book, and the little silver service spoon was clean and polished on a bread-and-butter plate. He set it down. And then he served the tea. You think you know the service, youngblood, all of you do. But you don't. Anybody can serve, but not everybody can become a part of the service. When Doc poured that pot of hot tea into that glass of crushed ice, it was like he was pouring it through his own fingers: it was like he and the tray and the pot and the glass and all of it was the same body. It was a beautiful move. It was fine service. The iced tea glass sat in a shell dish, and the iced tea spoon lay straight in front of Jerry. The lemon wedge Doc put in a shell dish half-full of crushed ice with an oyster fork stuck into its skin. Not in the meat, mind you, but squarely under the skin of that lemon, and the whole thing lay in a pretty curve on top of that crushed ice.

Doc stood back and waited. Jerry had been watching his service and was impressed. He mixed the sugar in his glass and sipped. Danny Jackson and I were down the aisle in the hall. Uncle T. stood behind Jerry, bending over, his arms folded, waiting. And Doc stood next to the table, his tray under his arm looking straight ahead and calm because he had given good service and knew it. Jerry sipped again.

"Good tea," he said. "Very good tea."

Doc was silent.

Jerry took the lemon wedge off the oyster fork and squeezed it into the glass, and stirred, and sipped again. "Very good," he said. Then he drained the glass. Doc reached over to pick it up for more ice but Jerry kept his hand on the glass. "Very good service, Doc," he said. "But you served the lemon wrong."

Everybody was quiet. Uncle T. folded his hands in the praying position.

"How's that?" said Doc.

"The service was wrong," Jerry said. He was not smiling now.

"How could it be? I been giving that same service for years, right down to the crushed ice for the lemon wedge."

"That's just it, Doc," Jerry said. "The lemon wedge. You served it wrong."

"Yeah?" said Doc.

"Yes," said Jerry, his jaws tight. "Haven't you seen the new rule?"

Doc's face went loose. He knew now that they had got him.

"Haven't you *seen* it?" Jerry asked again.

Doc shook his head.

Jerry smiled that hard, gray smile of his, the kind of smile that says: "I have always been the boss and I am smiling this way because I know it and can afford to give you something." "Steward Crouse," he said. "Steward Crouse, go get the black bible for the headwaiter."

Crouse looked beaten too. He was sixty-three and waiting for his pension. He got the bible.

Jerry took it and turned directly to the very last page. He knew where to look. "Now, Headwaiter," he said, "listen to this." And he read aloud: "Memorandum Number 22416. From: Douglass A. Tesdale, General Superintendent of Dining Cars. To: Waiters, Stewards, Chefs of Dining Cars. Attention: As of 7/9/65 the proper service for iced tea will be (a) Fresh brewed tea in teapot, poured over crushed ice at table; iced tea glass set in shell dish (b) Additional ice to be immediately available upon request after first glass of tea (c) Fresh lemon wedge will be served on bread-and-butter plate, no doily, with tines of oyster fork stuck into *meat* of lemon." Jerry paused.

"Now you know, Headwaiter," he said.

"Yeah," said Doc.

"But why didn't you know before?"

No answer.

"This notice came out last week."

"I didn't check the book yet," said Doc.

"But that's a rule. Always check the book before each trip. *You* know that, Headwaiter."

"Yeah," said Doc.

"Then that's *two* rules you missed."

Doc was quiet.

"Two rules you didn't read," Jerry said. "You're slowing down, Doc."

"I know," Doc mumbled.

"You want some time off to rest?"

Again Doc said nothing.

"I think you need some time on the ground to rest up, don't you?"

Doc put his tray on the table and sat down in the seat across from Jerry. This was the first time we had ever seen a waiter sit down with a customer, even an inspector. Uncle T., behind Jerry's back, began waving his hands, trying to tell Doc to get up. Doc did not look at him.

"You *are* tired, aren't you?" said Jerry.

"I'm just resting my feet," Doc said.

"Get up, Headwaiter," Jerry said. "You'll have plenty of time to do that. I'm writing you up."

But Doc did not move and just continued to sit there. And all Danny and I could do was watch him from the back of the car. For the first time I saw that his hair was almost gone and his legs were skinny in the baggy white uniform. I don't think Jerry expected Doc to move. I don't think he really cared. But then Uncle T. moved around the table and stood next to Doc, trying to apologize for him to Jerry with his eyes and bowed head. Doc looked at Uncle T. and then got up and went back to the crew car. He left his tray on the table. It stayed there all that evening because none of us, not even Crouse or Jerry or Uncle T., would touch it. And Jerry didn't try to make any of us take it back to the Pantry. He understood at least that much. The steward closed down Doc's tables during dinner service, all three settings of it. And Jerry got off the train someplace along the way, quiet, like he had got on.

After closing down the car we went back to the crew quarters and Doc was lying on his bunk with his hands behind his head and his eyes open. He looked old. No one knew what to say until Boone went over to his bunk and said: "I feel bad for you, Doc, but all of us are gonna get it in the end. The railroad waiter is *doomed*."

Doc did not even notice Boone.

"I could of told you about the lemon but he would of got you on something else. It wasn't no use. Any of it."

"Shut the fuck up, Boone!" Danny said. "The one thing that really hurts is that a crawling son-of-a-bitch like you will be riding when all the good men are gone. Dummies like you and these two hardheads will be working your asses off reading that damn bible and never know a goddamn thing about being a waiter. *That* hurts like a *motherfucker*!"

"It ain't my fault if the colored waiter is doomed," said Boone. "It's your fault for letting go your humility and letting the whites take over the good jobs."

Danny grabbed the skullcap off Boone's head and took it into the bathroom and flushed it down the toilet. In a minute it was half a mile away and soaked in old piss on the tracks. Boone did not try to fight, he just sat on his bunk and mumbled. He had other skullcaps. No one said anything to Doc, because that's the way real men show that they care. You don't talk. Talking makes it worse.

IV

What else is there to tell you, youngblood? They made him retire. He didn't try to fight it. He was beaten and he knew it; not by the service, but by a book. *That book*, that *bible* you keep your finger stuck in. That's not a good way for a man to go. He should die in service. He should die doing the things he likes. But not by a book.

All of us Old School men will be beaten by it. Danny Jackson is gone now, and Reverend Hendricks put in for his pension and took up preaching, full-time. But Uncle T. Boone is still riding. They'll get *me* soon enough, with that book. But it will never get you because you'll never be a waiter, or at least a Waiter's Waiter. You read too much.

Doc got a good pension and he took it directly to Andy's. And none of the boys who knew about it knew how to refuse a drink on Doc. But none of us knew how to drink with him knowing that we would be going out again in a few days, and he was on the ground. So a lot of us, even the drunks and hustlers who usually hang around Andy's, avoided him whenever we could. There was nothing to talk about any more.

He died five months after he was put on the ground. He was seventy-three and it was winter. He froze to death wandering around the Chicago yards early one morning. He had been drunk, and was still steaming when the yard crew found him. Only the few of us left in the Old School know what he was doing there.

I am sixty-three now. And I haven't decided if I should take my pension when they ask me to go or continue to ride. I *want* to keep riding, but I know that if I do, Jerry Ewald or Harry Silk or Jack Tate will get me one of these days. I could get down if I wanted: I have a hobby and I am too old to get drunk by myself. I couldn't drink with you, youngblood. We have nothing to talk about. And after a while you would get mad at me for talking anyway, and keeping you from your pussy. You are tired already. I can see it in your eyes and in the way you play with the pages of your rule book.

I know it. And I wonder why I should keep talking to you when you could never see what I see or understand what I understand or know the real difference between my school and yours. I wonder why I have kept talking this long when all the time I have seen that you can hardly wait to hit the city to get off this thing and spend your money. You have a good story. But you will never remember it. Because all this time you have had pussy in your mind, and your fingers in the pages of that black bible.

Alice Munro

SOME WOMEN

I am amazed sometimes to think how old I am. I can remember when the streets of the town I lived in were sprinkled with water to lay the dust in summer, and when girls wore waist cinchers and crinolines that could stand up by themselves, and when there was nothing much to be done about things like polio and leukemia. Some people who got polio got better, crippled or not, but people with leukemia went to bed, and, after some weeks' or months' decline in a tragic atmosphere, they died.

It was because of such a case that I got my first job, in the summer holidays, when I was thirteen.

Old Mrs. Crozier lived on the other side of town. Her stepson, Bruce, who was usually called Young Mr. Crozier, had come safely home from the war, where he had been a fighter pilot, had gone to college and studied history, and got married, and now he had leukemia. He and his wife were staying with Old Mrs. Crozier. The wife, Sylvia, taught summer school two afternoons a week at the college where they had met, some forty miles away. I was hired to look after Young Mr. Crozier while she wasn't there. He was in bed in the front-corner bedroom upstairs, and he could still get to the bathroom by himself. All I had to do was bring him fresh water and pull the shades up or down and see what he wanted when he rang the little bell on his bedside table.

Usually what he wanted was to have the fan moved. He liked the breeze it created but was disturbed by the noise. So he'd want the fan in the room for a while and then he'd want it out in the hall, but close to his open door.

When my mother heard about this, she wondered why they hadn't put him in a bed downstairs, where they surely had high ceilings and he would have been cooler.

I told her that they did not have any bedrooms downstairs.

"Well, my heavens, couldn't they fix one up? Temporarily?"

That showed how little she knew about the Crozier household and the rule of Old Mrs. Crozier. Old Mrs. Crozier walked with a cane. She made one ominous-sounding journey up the stairs to see her stepson on the afternoons that I was there, and I suppose no more than that on the afternoons when I was not. But the idea of a bedroom downstairs would have outraged her as much as the notion of a toilet in the parlor. Fortunately, there was already a toilet downstairs, behind the kitchen, but I was sure that, if the upstairs one had been the only one, she would have made the laborious climb as often as necessary, rather than pursue a change so radical and unnerving.

My mother was thinking of going into the antique business, so she was very interested in the inside of the Crozier house, which was old and far grander than ours. She did get in, once, my very first afternoon there. I was in the kitchen, and I stood petrified, hearing her yoo-hoo and my own merrily called name. Then her perfunctory knock, her steps on the kitchen stairs. And Old Mrs. Crozier stumping out from the sunroom.

My mother said that she had just dropped by to see how her daughter was getting along. "She's all right," Old Mrs. Crozier said, standing in the hall doorway, blocking the view of antiques. My mother made a few more mortifying remarks and took herself off. That night, she said that Old Mrs. Crozier had no manners, because she was only a second wife, picked up on a business trip to Detroit, which was why she smoked and dyed her hair black as tar and put on lipstick like a smear of jam. She was not even the mother of the invalid upstairs. She did not have the brains to be. (We were having one of our fights then, this one relating to her visit, but that is neither here nor there.)

The way Old Mrs. Crozier saw it, I must have seemed just as intrusive as my mother, just as cheerily self-regarding. Shortly after I began working there, I went into the back parlor and opened the bookcase and took stock of the Harvard Classics set out in a perfect row. Most of them discouraged me, but I took out one that looked like it might be fiction, despite its foreign title, "I Promessi Sposi." It was fiction all right, and it was in English.

I must have had the idea then that all books were free, wherever you found them. Like water from a public tap.

When Old Mrs. Crozier saw me with the book, she asked where I had got it and what I was doing with it. From the bookcase, I said, and I had brought it upstairs to read. The thing that most perplexed her seemed to be that I had got it downstairs but brought it upstairs. The reading part she appeared to let go, as if such an activity were too alien for her to contemplate. Finally, she said that if I wanted a book I should bring one from home.

Of course, there were books in the sickroom. Reading seemed to be acceptable there. But they were mostly open and face down, as if Mr. Crozier just read a little here and there, then put them aside. And their titles did not tempt me. "Civilization on Trial." "The Great Conspiracy Against Russia."

My grandmother had warned me that if I could help it I should not touch anything that the patient had touched, because of germs, and I should always keep a cloth between my fingers and his water glass.

My mother said that leukemia did not come from germs.

"So what does it come from?" my grandmother said.

"The medical men don't know."

"Hunh."

It was Young Mrs. Crozier who picked me up and drove me home, though the distance across town was not far. She was a tall, thin, fair-haired woman with a variable complexion. Sometimes there were patches of red on her cheeks as if she had scratched them. Word had been passed that she was older than her husband, that he had been her student at college. My mother said that nobody seemed to have got around to figuring out that, since he was a war veteran, he could easily have been her student without that making her older. People were just down on her because she had got an education.

Another thing they said was that she should have stayed home and looked after him, as she had promised in the marriage ceremony, instead of going out to teach. My mother again defended her, saying that it was only two afternoons a week and she had to keep up her profession, seeing as how she would be on her own soon enough. And if she didn't get out of the old lady's way once in a while wouldn't you think she'd go crazy? My mother always defended women who worked, and my grandmother always got after her for it.

One day I tried a conversation with Young Mrs. Crozier, Sylvia. She was the only college graduate I knew. Except for her husband, of course, and he had stopped counting.

"Did Toynbee write history books?"

"Beg pardon? Oh. Yes."

None of us mattered to her—not me, or her critics or her defenders. We were no more than bugs on a lampshade.

As for Old Mrs. Crozier, all she really cared about was her flower garden. She had a man who came and helped her; he was about her age, but more limber than she was. His name was Hervey. He lived on our street, and, in fact, it was through him that she had heard about me as a possible employee. At home, he only gossiped and grew weeds, but here he plucked and mulched and fussed, while she followed him around, leaning on her stick and shaded by her big straw hat. Sometimes she sat on a bench, still commenting and giving orders, and smoking a cigarette. Early on, I dared to go between the perfect hedges to ask if she or her helper would like a glass of water, and she cried out, "Mind my borders!" before saying no.

Flowers were never brought into the house. Some poppies had escaped and were growing wild beyond the hedge, almost on the road, so I asked if I could pick a bouquet to brighten the sickroom.

"They'd only die," Mrs. Crozier said, not seeming to realize that this remark had a double edge to it, under the circumstances.

Certain suggestions or notions would make the muscles of her lean spotty face quiver, her eyes go sharp and black, and her mouth work as if there were a despicable taste in it. She could stop you in your tracks then, like a savage thornbush.

The two days a week that I worked were not consecutive. Let us say they were Tuesdays and Thursdays. The first day, I was alone with the sick man and Old Mrs. Crozier. The second day, somebody arrived whom I had not been told about. I was sitting upstairs when I heard a car in the driveway, and someone running briskly up the back steps and entering the kitchen without knocking. Then the person called "Dorothy," which I had not known was Old Mrs. Crozier's name. The voice was a woman's or a girl's, and it was bold and teasing all at once.

I ran down the back stairs, saying, "I think she's in the sunroom."

"Holy Toledo! Who are you?"

I told her who I was and what I was doing there, and the young woman said that her name was Roxanne.

"I'm the masseuse."

I didn't like being caught by a word I didn't know. I didn't say anything, but she saw how things were.

"Got you stumped, eh? I give massages. You ever heard of that?"

Now she was unpacking the bag she had with her. Various pads and cloths and flat velour-covered brushes appeared.

"I'll need some hot water to warm these up," she said. "You can heat me some in the kettle." (The Crozier house was grand, but there was still only cold water on tap, as in my house at home.)

Roxanne had sized me up, apparently, as somebody who was willing to take orders—especially, perhaps, orders given in such a coaxing voice. And she was right, though she may not have guessed that my willingness had more to do with my own curiosity than with her charm.

She was tanned, although it was still early in the summer, and her pageboy hair had a copper sheen—something that you could get easily from a bottle nowadays but that was unusual and enviable then. Brown eyes, a dimple in one cheek—she did so much smiling and joking that you never got a good enough look at her to say whether she was really pretty, or how old she was.

I was impressed by the way her rump curved out handsomely to the back, instead of spreading to the sides.

I learned quickly that she was new in town, married to the mechanic at the Esso station, and that she had two little boys, one four years old and one three. ("It took me a while to figure out what was causing them," she said, with one of her conspiratorial twinkles.)

In Hamilton, where they used to live, she had trained to be a masseuse and it had turned out to be just the sort of thing she'd always had a knack for.

"*Dor*-thee?"

"She's in the sunroom," I told her again.

"I know, I'm just kidding her. Now, maybe you don't know about getting a massage, but when you get one you got to take off all your clothes. Not such a problem when you're young, but when you're older, you know, you can get all embarrassed."

She was wrong about one thing, at least as far as I was concerned. About its not being a problem to take off all your clothes when you're young.

"So maybe you should skedaddle. You're supposed to be upstairs anyway, aren't you?"

This time I took the front staircase, while she was busy with the hot water. That way I got a glance in through the open door of the sunroom—which was not much of a sunroom at all, having its windows on three sides all filled up with the fat leaves of catalpa trees. There I saw Old Mrs. Crozier stretched out on a daybed, on her stomach, her face turned away from me, absolutely naked. A skinny streak of pale flesh. The usually covered length of her body didn't look as old as the parts of her that were daily exposed—her freckled, dark-veined hands and forearms, her brown-blotched cheeks. The skin of her back and legs was yellow-white, like wood freshly stripped of its bark.

I sat on the top step and listened to the sounds of the massage. Thumps and grunts. Roxanne's voice bossy now, cheerful but full of exhortation.

"Stiff knot here. Oh, brother. I'm going to have to whack you one. Just kidding. Aw, come on, just loosen up for me. You know, you got nice skin here. Small of your back—what do they say? It's like a baby's bum. Now I gotta bear down a bit—you're going to feel it here. Take away the tension. Good girl."

Old Mrs. Crozier was making little yelps. Sounds of complaint and gratitude. It went on for quite a while, and I got bored. I went back to reading some old *Canadian Home Journals* that I had found in a cabinet. I read recipes and checked on old-time fashions till I heard Roxanne say, "Now I'll just clean this stuff up and we'll go on upstairs, like you said."

Upstairs. I slid the magazines back into their place in the cabinet that my mother would have coveted, and went into Mr. Crozier's room. He was asleep, or at least he had his eyes closed. I moved the fan a few inches and smoothed his cover and went and stood by the window, twiddling with the blind.

Sure enough, there came a noise on the back stairs, Old Mrs. Crozier with her slow and threatening cane steps, Roxanne running ahead and calling, "Look out, look out, wherever you are. We're coming to get you, wherever you are."

Mr. Crozier had his eyes open now. Behind his usual weariness was a faint expression of alarm. But before he could pretend to be asleep again Roxanne burst into the room.

"So here's where you're hiding. I just told your stepmom I thought it was about time I got introduced to you."

Mr. Crozier said, "How do you do, Roxanne?"

"How did you know my name?"

"Word gets around."

"Fresh fellow you got here," Roxanne said to Old Mrs. Crozier, who now came stumping into the room.

"Stop fooling around with that blind," Old Mrs. Crozier said to me. "Go and fetch me a drink of cool water, if you want something to do. Not cold, just cool."

"You're a mess," Roxanne said to Mr. Crozier. "Who gave you that shave and when was it?"

"A few days ago," he said. "I handle it myself as well as I can."

"That's what I thought," Roxanne said. And to me, "When you're getting her water, how'd you like to heat some more up for me and I'll undertake to give him a decent shave?"

Shaving him became a regular thing, once a week, following the massage. Roxanne told Mr. Crozier that first day not to worry. "I'm not going to pound on you like you must have heard me doing to Dorothy-doodle downstairs. Before I got my massage training I used to be a nurse. Well, a nurse's aide. One of the ones who do all the work and then the nurses come around and boss you. Anyway, I learned how to make people comfortable."

Dorothy-doodle? Mr. Crozier grinned. But the odd thing was that Old Mrs. Crozier grinned, too.

Roxanne shaved him deftly. She sponged his face and neck and torso and arms and hands. She pulled his sheets around, somehow managing not to disturb him, and she punched and rearranged his pillows. Talking all the while, pure nonsense.

"Dorothy, you're a liar. You said you had a sick man upstairs, and I walk in here and I think, Where's the sick man? I don't see a sick man around here. Do I?"

Mr. Crozier said, "What would you say I am, then?"

"Recovering. That's what I would say. I don't mean you should be up and running around, I'm not so stupid as all that. I know you need your bed rest. But I say recovering. Nobody who was sick like you're supposed to be ever looked as good as what you do."

I thought this flirtatious prattle insulting. Mr. Crozier looked terrible. A tall man whose ribs showed like those of a famine survivor when she sponged him, whose head was partly bald, and whose skin looked as if it had the texture of a plucked chicken's, his neck corded like an old man's. Whenever I had waited on him in any way I had avoided looking at him. Though this was not really because he was sick and ugly. It was because he was dying. I would have felt a similar reticence even if he had been angelically handsome. I was aware of an atmosphere of death in the house, which grew thicker as you approached his room, and he was at the center of it, like the Host the Catholics kept in the box so powerfully called the tabernacle. He was the one stricken, marked out from everybody else, and here was Roxanne trespassing on his ground with her jokes and her swagger and her notions of entertainment.

On her second visit, she asked him what he did all day.

"Read sometimes. Sleep."

And how did he sleep at night?

"If I can't sleep I lie awake. Think. Sometimes read."

"Doesn't that disturb your wife?"

"She sleeps in the back bedroom."

"Uh-huh. You need some entertainment."

"Are you going to sing and dance for me?"

I saw Old Mrs. Crozier look aside with her odd involuntary grin.

"Don't you get cheeky," Roxanne said. "Are you up to cards?"

"I hate cards."

"Well, have you got Chinese checkers in the house?"

Roxanne directed this question at Old Mrs. Crozier, who first said she had no idea, then wondered if there might be a board in a drawer of the dining-room buffet.

So I was sent down to look and came back with the board and a jar of marbles.

Roxanne set the game up over Mr. Crozier's legs, and she and I and Mr. Crozier played, Old Mrs. Crozier saying that she had never understood the game or been able to keep her marbles straight. (To my surprise, she seemed to offer this as a joke.) Roxanne might squeal when she made a move or groan whenever somebody jumped over one of her marbles, but she was careful never to disturb the patient. She held her body still and set her marbles down like feathers. I tried to do the same, because she would widen her eyes warningly at me if I didn't. All without losing her dimple.

I remembered Young Mrs. Crozier, Sylvia, saying to me in the car that her husband did not welcome conversation. It tired him out, she told me, and when he was tired he could become irritable. So I thought, If ever there was a time for him to become irritable, it's now. Being forced to play a silly game on his death-bed, when you could feel his fever in the sheets.

But Sylvia must have been wrong. He had developed greater patience and courtesy than she was perhaps aware of. With inferior people—Roxanne was surely an inferior person—he made himself tolerant, gentle. When likely all he wanted to do was lie there and meditate on the pathways of his life and gear up for his future.

Roxanne patted the sweat off his forehead, saying, "Don't get excited. You haven't won yet!"

"Roxanne," he said. "Roxanne. Do you know whose name that was, Roxanne?"

"Hmm?" she said, and I broke in. I couldn't help it.

"It was Alexander the Great's wife's name." My head was a magpie's nest lined with such bright scraps of information.

"Is that so?" Roxanne said. "And who is that supposed to be? Great Alexander?"

I realized something when I looked at Mr. Crozier at that moment. Something shocking, saddening.

He *liked* her not knowing. Her ignorance was a pleasure that melted on his tongue, like a lick of toffee.

On the first day, she had worn shorts, as I did, but the next time and always after that Roxanne wore a dress of some stiff and shiny light-green material. You could hear it rustle as she ran up the stairs. She brought a fleecy pad for Mr. Crozier, so that he would not develop bedsores. She was dissatisfied with the arrangement of his bed-clothes, always had to put them to rights. But however she scolded her movements never irritated him, and she made him admit to feeling more comfortable afterward.

She was never at a loss. Sometimes she came equipped with riddles. Or jokes. Some of the jokes were what my mother would have called smutty and would not have allowed around our house, except when they came from certain of my father's relatives, who had practically no other kind of conversation.

These jokes usually started off with serious-sounding but absurd questions.

Did you hear about the nun who went shopping for a meat grinder?

Did you hear what the bride and groom went and ordered for dessert on their wedding night?

The answers always came with a double meaning, so that whoever told the joke could pretend to be shocked and accuse the listener of having a dirty mind.

And after she had got everybody used to her telling these jokes Roxanne went on to the sort of joke I didn't believe my mother knew existed, often involving sex with sheep or hens or porcupines.

"Isn't that awful?" she always said at the finish. She said she wouldn't know this stuff if her husband didn't bring it home from the garage.

The fact that Old Mrs. Crozier snickered disturbed me as much as the jokes themselves. I wondered if she didn't actually get the jokes but simply enjoyed listening to whatever Roxanne said. She sat there with that chewed-in yet absentminded smile on her face, as if she'd been given a present that she knew she'd like, even though she hadn't got the wrapping off it yet.

Mr. Crozier didn't laugh, but he never laughed, really. He raised his eyebrows, pretending to disapprove, as if he found Roxanne outrageous but endearing all the same. I tried to tell myself that this was just good manners, or gratitude for her efforts, whatever they might be.

I myself made sure to laugh so that Roxanne would not put me down as an innocent prig.

The other thing she did to keep things lively was tell us about her life—how she had come down from some lost little town in northern Ontario to Toronto to visit her older sister, when she was only fourteen, then got a job at Eaton's, first cleaning up in the cafeteria, then being noticed by one of the managers, because she worked fast and was always cheerful, and suddenly finding herself a salesgirl in the glove department. (She made this sound like being discovered by Warner Bros.) And who should have come in one day but Barbara Ann Scott, the skating star, who bought a pair of elbow-length white kid gloves.

Meanwhile, Roxanne's sister had so many boyfriends that she'd flip a coin to see whom she'd go out with almost every night, and she employed Roxanne to meet the rejects regretfully at the front door of the rooming house where they lived, while she herself and her pick of the night sneaked out the back. Roxanne said that maybe that was how she had developed such a gift of gab. And pretty soon some of the boys she had met this way were taking her out, instead of her sister. They did not know her real age.

"I had me a ball," she said.

I began to understand that there were certain talkers—certain girls—whom people liked to listen to, not because of what they, the girls, had to say but because of the delight they took in saying it. A delight in themselves, a shine on their faces, a conviction that whatever they were telling was remarkable and that they themselves could not help but give pleasure. There might be other people—

people like me—who didn't concede this, but that was their loss. And people like me would never be the audience these girls were after, anyway.

Mr. Crozier sat propped up on his pillows and looked for all the world as if he were happy. Happy just to close his eyes and let her talk, then open his eyes and find her still there, like a chocolate bunny on Easter morning. And then with his eyes open follow every twitch of her candy lips and sway of her sumptuous bottom.

The time Roxanne spent upstairs was as long as the time she spent downstairs, giving the massage. I wondered if she was being paid. If she wasn't, how could she afford to stay so long? And who could be paying her but Old Mrs. Crozier?

Why?

To keep her stepson happy and comfortable? To keep herself entertained in a curious way?

One afternoon, when Roxanne had gone downstairs, Mr. Crozier said that he felt thirstier than usual. I went to get him some more water from the pitcher that was always in the refrigerator. Roxanne was packing up to go home.

"I never meant to stay so late," she said. "I wouldn't want to run into that schoolteacher."

I didn't understand for a moment.

"You know. *Syl-vi-a*. She's not crazy about me, either, is she? She ever mention me when she drives you home?"

I said that Sylvia had never mentioned Roxanne to me during any of our drives.

"Dorothy says she doesn't know how to handle him. She says I make him a lot happier than what she does. Dorothy says that. I wouldn't be surprised if she even told her that to her face."

I thought of how Sylvia ran upstairs to her husband's room every afternoon when she got home, before even speaking to me or her mother-in-law, her face flushed with eagerness and desperation. I wanted to say something about that—I wanted to defend her—but I didn't know how. And people as confident as Roxanne often seemed to get the better of me.

"You sure she never says anything about me?"

I said again that she didn't. "She's tired when she gets home."

"Yeah. Everybody's tired. Some just learn to act like they aren't."

I did say something then, to balk her. "I quite like her."

"You *qwat* like her?" Roxanne mocked.

Playfully, sharply, she jerked at a strand of the bangs I had recently cut for myself.

"You ought to do something decent with your hair."

Dorothy says.

If Roxanne wanted admiration, which was her nature, what was it that Old Mrs. Crozier wanted? I had a feeling that there was mischief stirring, but I could not pin it down. Maybe it was just a desire to have Roxanne, her liveliness, in the house, double time?

Midsummer passed. Water was low in the wells. The sprinkler truck stopped coming and some stores put up sheets of what looked like yellow cellophane in their windows to keep their goods from fading. Leaves were spotty, the grass dry.

Old Mrs. Crozier kept her garden man hoeing, day after day. That's what you do in dry weather, hoe and hoe to bring up any moisture that you can find in the ground underneath.

Summer school at the college would end after the second week of August, and then Sylvia Crozier would be home every day.

Mr. Crozier still seemed glad to see Roxanne, but he often fell asleep. He could drift off without letting his head fall back, during one of her jokes or anecdotes. Then after a moment he would wake up again and ask where he was.

"Right here, you sleepy noodle. You're supposed to be paying attention to me. I should bat you one. Or how about I try tickling you instead?"

Anybody could see how he was failing. There were hollows in his cheeks like an old man's, and the light shone through the tops of his ears, as if they were not flesh but plastic. (Though we didn't say plastic then; we said celluloid.)

My last day of work, Sylvia's last day of teaching, was a massage day. Sylvia had to leave for the college early, because of some ceremony, so I walked across town, arriving when Roxanne was already there. She and Old Mrs. Crozier were in the kitchen, and they both looked at me as if they had forgotten I was coming, as if I had interrupted them.

"I ordered them specially," Old Mrs. Crozier said.

She must have been talking about the macaroons sitting in the baker's box on the table.

"Yeah, but I told you," Roxanne said. "I can't eat that stuff. Not no way no how."

"I sent Hervey down to the bakeshop to get them."

"O.K., let Hervey eat them. I'm not kidding—I break out something awful."

"I thought we'd have a treat," Old Mrs. Crozier said. "Seeing it's the last day we've got before—"

"Last day before she parks her butt here permanently? Yeah, I know. Doesn't help to have me breaking out like a spotted hyena."

Who was it whose butt was parked permanently?

Sylvia's. Sylvia.

Old Mrs. Crozier was wearing a beautiful black silk wrapper, with water lilies and geese on it. She said, "No chance of having anything special with her around. You'll see. You won't be able to even get to see him with her around."

"So let's get going and get some time today. Don't bother about this stuff. It's not your fault. I know you got it to be nice."

"'I know you got it to be nice,'" Old Mrs. Crozier imitated in a mean, mincing voice, and then they both looked at me, and Roxanne said, "Pitcher's where it always is."

I took Mr. Crozier's water out of the fridge. It occurred to me that they could offer me one of the golden macaroons sitting in the box, but apparently it did not occur to them.

I'd expected Mr. Crozier to be lying back on the pillows with his eyes closed, but he was wide awake.

"I've been waiting," he said, and took a breath. "For you to get here," he said. "I want to ask you—do something for me. Will you?"

I said sure.

"Keep it a secret?"

I had been worried that he might ask me to help him to the commode that had recently appeared in his room, but surely that would not have to be a secret.

He told me to go to the bureau across from his bed and open the left-hand drawer, and see if I could find a key there.

I did so. I found a large, heavy, old-fashioned key.

He wanted me to go out of his room and shut the door and lock it. Then hide the key in a safe place, perhaps in the pocket of my shorts.

I was not to tell anybody what I had done.

I was not to let anybody know I had the key until his wife came home, and then I was to give it to her privately. Did I understand?

O.K.

He thanked me.

O.K.

All the time he was talking to me there was a film of sweat on his face and his eyes were as bright as if Roxanne were in the room.

"Nobody is to get in."

"Nobody is to get in," I repeated.

"Not my stepmother or—Roxanne. Just my wife."

I locked the door from the outside and put the key in my pocket. But then I was afraid that it could be seen through the light cotton material, so I went downstairs and into the back parlor and hid it between the pages of "I Promessi Sposi." I knew that Roxanne and Old Mrs. Crozier would not hear me, because the massage was going on, and Roxanne was using her professional voice.

"I got my work cut out for me getting these knots out of you today."

And I heard Old Mrs. Crozier's voice, full of her new displeasure.

". . . punching harder than you normally do."

"Well, I gotta."

I was headed upstairs when a further thought came to me.

If he had locked the door himself—which was evidently what he wanted the others to think—and I had been sitting on the top step as usual, I would certainly have heard him and called out and roused the others in the house. So I went back down and sat on the bottom step of the front stairs, a position from which I could conceivably not have heard a thing.

The massage seemed to be brisk and businesslike today; Roxanne was evidently not making jokes. Pretty soon I could hear her running up the back stairs.

She stopped. She said, "Hey, Bruce."

Bruce.

She rattled the knob of the door.

"Bruce."

Then she must have put her mouth to the keyhole, so that he would hear but nobody else would. I could not make out exactly what she was saying, but I could tell that she was pleading. First teasing, then pleading. After a while she sounded as if she were saying her prayers.

When she gave that up, she started pounding on the door with her fists, not too hard but urgently.

Eventually, she stopped that, too.

"Come on," she said in a firmer voice. "If you got to the door to lock it, you can get there to open it up."

Nothing happened. She came and looked over the bannister and saw me.

"Did you take Mr. Crozier's water into his room?"

I said yes.

"So his door wasn't locked or anything then?"

No.

"Did he say anything to you?"

"He just said thanks."

"Well, he's got his door locked and I can't get him to answer."

I heard Old Mrs. Crozier's stick reaching the top of the back stairs.

"What's the commotion up here?"

"He's locked hisself in and I can't get him to answer me."

"What do you mean, locked himself in? Likely the door's stuck. Wind blew it shut and it stuck."

There was no wind that day.

"Try it yourself," Roxanne said. "It's locked."

"I wasn't aware there was a key to this door," Old Mrs. Crozier said, as if her not being aware could negate the fact. Then, perfunctorily, she tried the knob and said, "Well. It'd appear to be locked."

He had counted on this, I thought. That they would not suspect me, that they would assume that he was in charge. And in fact he was.

"We have to get in," Roxanne said. She gave the door a kick.

"Stop that," Old Mrs. Crozier said. "Do you want to wreck the door? You couldn't get through it, anyway—it's solid oak. Every door in this house is solid oak."

"Then we have to call the police."

There was a pause.

"They could get up to the window," Roxanne said.

Old Mrs. Crozier drew in her breath and spoke decisively. "You don't know what you are saying. I won't have the police in this house. I won't have them climbing all over my walls like caterpillars."

"We don't know what he could be doing in there."

"Well, then, that's up to him. Isn't it?"

Another pause.

Now steps—Roxanne's—retreating to the back staircase.

"Yes. You'd better just take yourself away before you forget whose house this is."

Roxanne was going down the stairs. A couple of stomps of the stick went after her, then stopped.

"And don't get the idea you'll go to the constable behind my back. He's not going to take his orders from you. Who gives the orders around here, anyway? It's certainly not you. You understand me?"

Very soon I heard the kitchen door slam shut. And then Roxanne's car start.

I was no more worried about the police than Old Mrs. Crozier was. The police in our town meant Constable McClarty, who came to the school to warn us about sledding on the streets in winter and swimming in the millrace in summer, both of which we continued to do. It was ridiculous to think of him climbing up a ladder or lecturing Mr. Crozier through a locked door.

He would tell Roxanne to mind her own business and let the Croziers mind theirs.

It was not ridiculous, however, to think of Old Mrs. Crozier giving orders, and I thought she might do so now that Roxanne—whom she apparently did not like anymore—was gone. But although I heard her go back to Mr. Crozier's door and stand there, she did not even rattle the knob. She just said one thing.

"Stronger than you'd think," she muttered. Then made her way downstairs. The usual punishing noises with her steady stick.

I waited awhile and then I went out to the kitchen. Old Mrs. Crozier wasn't there. She wasn't in either parlor or in the dining room or the sunroom. I got up my nerve and knocked on the toilet door, then opened it, and she was not there, either. Then I looked out the window over the kitchen sink and I saw her straw hat moving slowly along the cedar hedge. She was out in the garden in the heat, stumping along between her flower beds.

I was not worried by the thought that seemed to have troubled Roxanne. I did not even stop to consider it, because I believed that it would be quite absurd for a person with only a short time to live to commit suicide.

All the same, I was nervous. I ate two of the macaroons that were still sitting on the kitchen table. I ate them hoping that pleasure would bring back normalcy, but I barely tasted them. Then I shoved the box into the refrigerator so that I would not hope to turn the trick by eating more.

Old Mrs. Crozier was still outside when Sylvia got home.

I retrieved the key from between the pages of the book as soon as I heard the car and I told Sylvia quickly what had happened, leaving out most of the fuss. She would not have waited to listen to it, anyway. She went running upstairs.

I stood at the bottom of the stairs to hear what I could hear.

Nothing. Nothing.

Then Sylvia's voice, surprised but in no way desperate, and too low for me to make out what she was saying. Within about five minutes she was downstairs, saying that it was time to get me home. She was flushed, as if the spots on her cheeks had spread all over her face, and she looked shocked, but unable to resist her happiness.

Then, "Oh. Where is Mother Crozier?"

"In the flower garden, I think."

"Well, I suppose I'd better speak to her, just for a moment."

After she had done that, she no longer looked quite so happy.

"I suppose you know," she said as she backed out the car. "I suppose you can imagine Mother Crozier is upset. Not that I am blaming you. It was very good and loyal of you. Doing what Mr. Crozier asked you to do. You weren't scared of anything happening, were you?"

I said no. Then I said, "I think Roxanne was."

"Mrs. Hoy? Yes. That's too bad."

As we were driving down what was known as Crozier's Hill, she said, "I don't think he wanted to frighten them. You know, when you're sick, sick for a long time, you can get not to appreciate other people's feelings. You can get turned against people even when they're doing what they can to help you. Mrs. Crozier and Mrs. Hoy were certainly trying their best. But Mr. Crozier just didn't feel that he wanted them around anymore today. He'd just had enough of them. You understand?"

She did not seem to know that she was smiling when she said this.

Mrs. Hoy.

Had I ever heard that name before?

And spoken so gently and respectfully, yet with light-years of condescension.

Did I believe what Sylvia had said?

I believed that it was what he had told her.

I did see Roxanne again that day. I saw her just as Sylvia was introducing me to this new name. Mrs. Hoy.

She—Roxanne—was in her car and she had stopped at the first cross street at the bottom of Crozier's Hill to watch us drive by. I didn't turn to look at her, because it was all too confusing, with Sylvia talking to me.

Of course, Sylvia would not have known whose car that was. She wouldn't have known that Roxanne must have been waiting to see what was going on, driving around the block all the time since she had left the Croziers' house.

Roxanne would have recognized Sylvia's car, though. She would have noticed me. She would have known that things were all right, from the kindly serious faintly smiling way that Sylvia was talking to me.

She didn't turn the corner and drive back up the hill to the Croziers' house. Oh, no. She drove across the street—I watched in the sideview mirror—toward the east part of town, where the wartime houses had been put up. That was where she lived.

"Feel the breeze," Sylvia said. "Maybe those clouds are going to bring us rain."

The clouds were high and white, glaring. They looked nothing like rain clouds, and there was a breeze only because we were in a moving car with the windows rolled down.

I understood pretty well the winning and losing that had taken place between Sylvia and Roxanne, but it was strange to think of the almost obliterated prize, Mr. Crozier—and to think that he could have had the will to make a decision, even to deprive himself, so late in his life. The carnality at death's door—or the true love, for that matter—was something I wanted to shake off back then, just as I would shake caterpillars off my sleeve.

Sylvia took Mr. Crozier away to a rented cottage on the lake, where he died sometime before the leaves were off.

The Hoy family moved on, as mechanics' families often did.

My mother struggled with a crippling disease, which put an end to all her money-making dreams.

Dorothy Crozier had a stroke, but recovered, and famously bought Halloween candy for the children whose older brothers and sisters she had ordered from her door.

I grew up, and old.

Joyce Carol Oates

HIGH LONESOME

The only people I still love are the ones I've hurt. I wonder if it's the same with you?

Only people I'm lonely for. These nights I can't sleep.

See, my heartbeat is fast. It's the damn medication makes me sweat. Run my fingers over my stub-forefinger—lost most of it in a chain saw accident a long time ago.

Weird how the finger feels like it's all there, in my head. Hurts, too.

Who I think of a lot, we're the same age now, I mean I'm the age Pop was when he died, is my mother's step-daddy who wasn't my actual grandfather. Pop had accidents, too. Farm accidents. Chain saw got away from Pop, too. Would've sliced his foot off at the ankle, except Pop was wearing work boots. Bad enough how Pop's leg was sliced. Dragged himself bleeding like a stuck pig to where somebody could hear him yelling for help.

I wasn't there. Not that day. Maybe I was in school. Never heard Pop yelling from out behind the big barn.

Pop Olafsson was this fattish bald guy with a face like a wrinkled dish rag left in the sun to dry. Palest blue eyes and a kind of slow suspicious snaggletooth smile like he was worried people might be laughing at him. Pulling his leg. He'd say, You kids ain't pullin' my leg, are yah? When we were young we'd stare at Pop's leg, both Pop's legs, ham-sized in these old overalls he wore.

Wondering what the hell Pop Olafsson meant. In this weird singsong voice like his nose is stopped up.

We never called him Grandpa, he wasn't our Grandpa. Mom called him Pop. He was a Pop kind of guy. Until the thing in the newspaper, I don't think I knew his first name which was Hendrick. He was a dairy farmer, he smelled of barns. A dairy farm produces milk and manure. What a barn is, is hay, flies, feed, milk (if it's a dairy barn), and manure. It's a mix where you don't get one ingredient without the rest. Hay flies feed manure. You can smell it coming off a farmer at fifty yards. Why I left that place, moved into town and never looked back.

Except for not sleeping at night, and my stub-finger bothering me. I wouldn't be looking back now.

Pop Olafsson spent his days in the dairy barn. He had between fifteen and twenty Guernseys that are the larger ones, their milk is yellowish and rich and the smell of it, the smell of any milk, the smell of any dairy product, doesn't have to be rancid, turns my stomach. Pop loved the cows, he'd sleep out in the barn when the cows were calving. Sometimes they needed help. Pop would cry when a calf was born dead.

Weird to see a man cry. You lose your respect.

Pop wore bib-overalls over a sweat-stained undershirt with long grimy sleeves. Summers, he'd leave off the undershirt. He wasn't a man to spend time washing. He never smelled himself at fifty yards. There was a joke in the family, a cloud of flies followed Pop Olafsson wherever he went. Mom was ashamed of him, when she was in school. Why her mother married the old man, old enough to be her grandfather not her father, nobody knew. Mom said if her mother had waited, hadn't been desperate after her husband died of lung cancer young at thirty-nine, they'd have done a whole lot better.

Mom made her own mistakes with men. That's another story.

Pop didn't care for firearms. Pop wasn't into hunting like his neighbors. He had an old Springfield .22 rifle like everybody had and a double-barrelled Remington 12-gauge shotgun with a cracked wooden stock, heavy and ugly as a shovel. From one year to the next these guns weren't cleaned. When my cousin Drake came to live with us, Drake cleaned the guns. Drake was five years older than me. He had a natural love for guns. Pop was so clumsy with a gun, he'd be breathing through his mouth hard and jerk the trigger so he'd never hit where the hell he was aiming. Always think the damn thing's gonna blow up in my hands, Pop said.

Pop told us he'd seen a gun accident when he was a boy. He'd seen a man blasted in the chest with a 12-gauge. These were duck hunters. This was in Drummond County in the southern edge of the state. It's a sight you don't forget, Pop said.

Still, Pop taught me to shoot the rifle when I was eleven. When I was a little older, how to shoot the shotgun. It's something that has to be learned, you live on a farm. You need to kill vermin—rats, voles, woodchucks. Pop never actually killed any vermin that I witnessed but we gave them a scare. We never went hunting. Once, I went with Drake and some of his friends deer hunting. Drake was all the time telling me get back! get down!

Must've fucked up. I remember crying. It hurt me, my cousin turning on me in front of his friends. I was thirteen, I looked up to Drake like a big brother.

On the veranda, summer nights, Pop sat with his banjo. People laughed at him saying Pop thinks he's Johnny Cash, well Pop wasn't anywhere near trying to sound like Johnny Cash. I don't know who in hell Pop sounded like—nobody, maybe. His own weird self. He's picking at the banjo, he's making this high old lonesome sound like a ghost tramping the hills. It wasn't singing, more like talking, the kind of whiney rambling a man does who's alone a lot, talks to animals in the barn, and to himself. Pop had big-knuckled hands, splayed fingers and cracked dirt-edged nails. Like he said he was accident-prone and his fingers showed it. Pop kept a crock of hard cider at his feet all the hours he'd sit out there on the porch so it didn't matter how alone he was.

We never paid much attention to Pop. My grandma who'd been his wife died when I was little. That was Mom's mother. Mom still missed her. Pop was just Mom's stepfather she made no secret of the fact. It was just that Pop owned the property, why we moved in there when my dad left us. When Mom was drinking and got unhappy she'd tell Pop that. Pop right away said, Oh I know. I know. I appreciate that, honey.

The songs Pop sang, I wish I'd listened to. They had women's names in them, sometimes. One of them was about a cuckoo-bird. One was about a train wreck. These were songs Pop picked up from growing up in Drummond County. He'd got the banjo in a pawn-shop. He never had any music lessons. Most of the songs, he didn't know all the words to so he'd hum in his high-pitched way rocking from side to side and a dreamy light coming into his face. A banjo isn't like a guitar, looks like it's made of a tin pie plate. A guy from school came by to pick me up one night, there's the old man out on the veranda with that damn plunky banjo singing some weird whiny song like a sick tomcat so Rory makes some crack about my grandpa and my face goes hot. Fuck you Pop ain't no grandpa of mine, he's what you call *in-law.*

Didn't hardly care if Pop heard me, I was feeling so pissed.

WHY'RE YOU SO ANGRY, *Daryl* girls would ask sort of shivery and wide-eyed. *Skin's so hot it's like fever.* Like this is a way to worm into my soul. *You ain't going to hurt me, Daryl, are you?* Hell no it ain't in Daryl McCracken's nature to hurt any girl.

No more than I would wish to hurt my mother. Nor anyone in my family that's my blood kin.

By age seventeen I'd shot up tall as my cousin Drake who's six feet three though I would never get so heavy-muscled as Drake you'd turn your head to observe, seeing him pass by. And in his Beechum County sheriff-deputy uniform that's a kind of gray-olive, and dark glasses, and hair shaved military style, and that way of carrying himself like anybody in his way better get out of his way, Drake looks good.

I was never jealous of Drake. I was proud of my cousin who's a McCracken like me. Went away to the police academy at Port Oriskany and graduated near the top of his class. Came back to Beechum County that's right next to Herkimer so he'd keep his friends and family. A long time Drake would visit us like every week or so, if Mom made supper he'd stay if he hadn't night shift patrolling the highways. Mom teased Drake saying it's God's will Drake turned out a law enforcement officer not one to break the law. Drake would laugh at any remark of Mom's but he'd be pissed at anybody else hinting his cop integrity isn't authentic. You wouldn't want to roil Drake McCracken that way. In school, saluting the American flag felt good to him. Reciting the Pledge of Allegiance. Wearing the Beechum County Sheriff's Department uniform. Keeping his weapon clean. It's a .38-caliber Colt revolver weighing firm and solid in the hand, dismantling the gun and oiling it is some kind of sacred ritual to him Drake says know why? *Your gun is your close friend when you are in desperate need of a friend.*

I have held that gun. Drake allowed me to hold that gun. It was the first handgun I had ever seen close up. Rifles and shotguns everybody has, not little guns you can conceal on your person.

Hey man, I'd like one of these!

Drake scowls at me like this ain't a subject to joke about. You'd have to have a permit, Daryl. Any kind of concealed weapon.

Do you have a permit?

Drake looks at me like old Pop Olafsson, not catching the joke.

Ain't pulling my leg, Daryl, are yah?—I'm a cop.

Yah yah asshole, I get it: you're a *cop*. (For sure, I don't say this aloud.)

Drake's .38-caliber Colt pistol didn't help him, though. Drake was killed off-duty at age twenty-nine, in September 1972.

That long ago! Weird to think my big-brother cousin would be young enough to be my son, now.

Sure I miss him. My wife says I am a hard man but there's an ache in me, that's never been eased since Drake passed away.

We did not part on good terms. Nobody knew this.

There was always rumors in Beechum County and in Herkimer, who killed Drake McCracken. It was believed he'd been ambushed by someone seeking revenge. Friends or relatives of someone he'd arrested and helped send to prison. There were plenty of these. By age twenty-nine, Drake had been a deputy for four years. He'd accumulated enemies.

He'd testified as arresting officer in court. Some guys, the sight of a uniform cop makes them sick. Makes them want to inflict injury. Drake was beat to death with a hammer, it was determined. Skull cracked and crushed and his badge and gun taken from him.

That was the cruel thing. That was hurtful to his survivors. Knowing how Drake wouldn't have wished that. Even in death, to know his badge he was so proud of, his gun he took such care of, were taken from him.

They questioned a whole lot of individuals including some at the time incarcerated. No one was ever arrested for my cousin's murder. No weapon was ever found. Nor Drake's badge or gun. The Beechum County sheriff took it pretty hard, one of his own deputies killed. You'd think from TV the sheriff had known Drake McCracken personally but that wasn't really so. It was a hard time then. Drake's photo in the papers in his dress uniform. Looking good. At the funeral everybody was broke up. Guys he'd gone to school with. Girls he'd gone out with. Relatives who'd known him from when he was born. Mom was the most broke up as anybody, cried and cried so I had to hold her and later we got drunk together, Mom and me.

Saying, It's good Pop isn't here for this. It would kill him.

Back in July, this happens.

On Route 33 north of Herkimer, about six miles from Pop Olafsson's farm, over the county line in Beechum, there's come to be what locals call the Strip—gas stations and fast-food restaurants and discount stores, adult books & videos, Topless Go-Go and Roscoe's Happy Hour Lounge, E-Z Inn Motor Court, etcetera. A few years ago this stretch was farmland and open fields all the fifteen miles to Sparta. Weird how the look of the countryside has changed. There's biker gangs hanging out on the highway, drug dealers, hookers cruising the parking lots, getting cigarettes at the 7-Eleven, using the toilets at McDonald's, standing out on the highway like they're hitch-hiking. Just up the road from King Discount Furniture and Rug Remnant City, that acre-size parking lot between the Sunoco station and the old Sears, you see females in like bikini tops, mini-skirts to the crotch, "hot pants," high-heeled boots to the knee. It's like a freak show, Route 33. High school kids are cruising the scene, racing one another and causing trouble. Mostly this is weekends after dark but sometimes during actual daylight so locals are complaining like hell. Unless a hooker is actually caught soliciting a john, cops can't arrest them. Cops patrol the Strip and make the hookers move on but next night they're back. A few hours later they're back. Got to be junkies, strung out on heroin and what all else. Got to be diseased. Why a man would wish to have sex with a pig! My cousin Drake who's on night shift highway patrol says it's like running off any kind of vermin, they come right back. Kill them, next day it's new vermin taking their place.

None of the sheriff deputies care for this assignment. The Strip is the pus wound of Beechum County. Sparta's the only city, population 15,000. Herkimer ain't hardly any city but it's got more people. Rookies are sent out on the Strip. Older cops, still assigned to highway patrol, you know they fucked up somewhere. There's this undercover team, Drake gets assigned to. He's just backup, in an unmarked van. Five male cops, three females. Sometimes the male cops pretend to be johns, picking up hookers and busting them. Sometimes it's the females are hooker decoys. The female deputies are close in age, looks, behavior to the actual hookers. Sometimes a hooker has darkish skin like she's mixed race but usually they're white females like anybody else. Slutty girls you went to school with, dropped out pregnant and got married and divorced and turned up in Sparta, Chautauqua Falls, Port Oriskany living with some guy or guys, and have another kid maybe mixed-race this time, and turn up back home, and get kicked out from home, and move in somewhere else, and pick up a drug habit, hang out at the E-Z Inn or the Go-Go, Roscoe's, hang out on the Strip, get busted, serve thirty days in Beechum Women's Detention, get out and get back on the Strip, got to be pathetic but you can't feel sorry for them, pigs as they are. The female deputies hate undercover. No dignity in undercover. You wear slut clothes, not your uniform. You wear a wire, not your badge. No weapon, if a john is some sicko wants to hurt you, you got to rely on backup.

Or maybe, undercover is kind of fun. Like Halloween.

Sable Drago, a Beechum County second-year deputy (turns out she is an older cousin of Bobbie Lee Drago, the girl I will marry in 1975) is one of the undercover team who defends the operation. Sable was a high school athlete, belonged to the Young Christian League. Sable believes this is work that has to be done, enforcing the prostitution, loitering, public drunkenness and "public nuisance" statutes. The Beechum County sheriff got elected on a clean-up platform. Sable has a missionary fever about undercover also it can be scary, it's a challenge you're not in your uniform almost you are naked, like any civilian. But when things go right it can feel damn good.

On the Strip Sable is a look-alike hooker. One of those fleshy girls
looking like grown women when they're fifteen, now at thirty-one
Sable is busty and wide-hipped with beet-colored hair frizzed and
sprayed to three times its normal size. Her hard-muscled legs thick
as a man's she hides in tight black toreador pants. Hot-pink satin
froufrou top tied below her breasts to display her fleshy midriff.
Peach-colored makeup thick on her face to hide her freckles. Eye
makeup to hide the steely cop-look in Sable's eyes and crimson lip-
stick shiny as grease. Hey mister wanna party?—wanna date? Hey
mistah? Sable's cruising the parking lot by the old Sears, calling to
guys in slow-moving cars, pickups, vans passing through like they
are intending to turn into the Sunoco station to just get gas, or
drive on. Sable can't wear high heels, has to wear flip-flops on her
size-ten feet but she has polished her toenails, her kid sister gave
her some dime store sexy tattoos to press on exposed parts of her
body. Sable can't drift too near the other hookers, they'd make her
as a cop. Sable's mumbling and laughing into the wire she's wear-
ing down between her sweaty breasts, the guys in the van are her
best buddies, hiding around the corner of the empty Sears. It's a
hot-humid day. It's dusk. It's a time of quickening pulses, anticipa-
tion. If you're a hunter, you know the feeling. Our country cops
are into the kind of arrests where a suspect (drunk, stoned, plain
stupid) has put up some resistance so you rush to knock them on
their ass, flop them over so their face hits the ground, if they don't
turn their face fast enough their nose is broke. You are required to
place your knee in the small of their back. You push, to restrain.
All this while you are yelling, Hands behind your back! Hands
behind your back! Required to bring the suspect under immediate
control. If you lose control, you may be blown away. First thing

you learn at the academy, Drake says, a police officer never loses control of the situation. An officer can lose his gun, he's killed by his own gun, it happens and it's a shameful thing nobody wishes even to speak of, and disgraceful to the family. Better blow away the suspect than get your own brains blown out, Drake says. For sure.

About 9 P.M. Sable is out at the highway thumbing for a ride. Trailer trucks rush past throwing up dirt in her face. There's a smell of diesel fuel, exhaust. Some vehicles, the drivers swerve like they're going to hit her, surprised to see her, or jeering leaning on their horn. Then this mud-splattered pickup comes along at about twenty miles an hour, and slows. Some kind of farm equipment rattling in the rear. Old bald guy at the wheel. The pickup brakes to a clumsy stop on the shoulder of the road and Sable strolls forward calling in a sexy TV voice, Hi there mister! I'm hoping for a ride! And this old guy bald-headed and sweating in dirty bib-overalls, he's peering into the rearview mirror but doesn't say a word. Sable repeats she's hoping for a ride, mistah. Sable perceives this john is old enough to be somebody's granddaddy which is pitiful if it wasn't so disgusting. It takes like three minutes to get the old guy to tell her climb into the cab, he's tongue-tied and stammering and maybe has something wrong with him (speech impediment, hard-of-hearing, drunk), it's going to require Sable's undercover-hooker skill to get his ass busted. (Right! It's Pop Olafsson. But Drake, in the unmarked van, doesn't know this yet.)

Where're yah goin', the old guy asks. He's mumbling, shy of looking at Sable full in the face. Sable says, Where we can party, mister, you'd like that? Huh? There's such smells lifting off this guy, Sable has to fight the impulse to hold her nose. Almost, she's going to have to do this and make a joke of it, manure-smell, barn-feed smell, whiskey-smell, body odor and tobacco and something sweetish like maybe licorice? Oh man! Wishing she could report to the team back in the van, what this scene is.

The old guy has the pickup in gear, doesn't seem to know what to do: drive on? Move onto the shoulder, and off the highway? Sable keeps asking him wanna party mister, wanna date me, hey mistah? but he's too confused. Or maybe just excited and scared, aroused. Not your typical john for sure. Flushed all over including his bumpy bald scalp, you can surmise sex is not too frequent with him. Looks to be late fifties, or older. His wife is old and fat and sick or maybe the wife has died, a long time ago the wife has died, some kind of tumor, she'd started off fat then ended weighing like sixty pounds, his memories of that woman, her last months, years, are not what you'd call romantic. You have to figure, maybe the wife was pretty once, maybe this old man was a sexy young guy once, not a paunchy old snaggletooth grandpa reeking of barn odors, and maybe he's trying to remember that, lonesome for something he hasn't even been getting for thirty years. So Sable is fanning herself with her hand cooing. Ohhh man am I hot, I bet you are hot too, I know a real cool place, up the road here's the E-Z Inn you know where that is mister? in this husky singsong voice like Dolly Parton beating her eyelashes at him so the old guy is smiling, trying to hide his stained teeth but smiling, squirming a little like he's being tickled, happy suddenly this is an actual flirtation, this is an innocent conversation with a woman who seems attracted to him, seems to like him, he isn't thinking exactly where he is, why he's here, what his purpose must have been driving here, north of Herkimer out to Route 33 and the Strip across in the next county a twelve-mile detour on his way back to the farm from picking up the repaired sump pump, no more than he's thinking right now of his blood pressure he can feel pounding in a band around his head, makes the inside of his head feel like a balloon blown up close to bursting, heart racing and lurching in his chest like a pounding fist, almost he feels dreamy, he isn't drunk but dreamy, a pint of Four Roses in the glove compartment he's wondering should he ask the beet-hair woman would she like a drink? thinking maybe he will, he's wanting to grab the woman's hand and kiss it, kiss the fingers, a freckled forearm glowing with sweat, some kind of sexy red heart-tattoo crawling up the arm, it's surprising to him, so wonderful, the woman is smiling at him, nobody smiles at Pop Olafsson especially no female smiles at him in this way, mostly he remembers Agnes scowling at him, staring at him like she was angry with him, crinkling her nose and turning her eyes from him not acknowledging him at all. He isn't thinking this is Beechum County, this is the Strip, sure he's heard about the Strip, been summoning up his courage to drive out here for months but now he's here, damn if he hasn't forgotten why. HEY MISTAH says the beet-hair woman like waking him from a doze, know what you look like a real sweet guy, I'm into older men, see? leaning forward so he can see the tops of her heavy breasts straining against a black lace brassiere like you'd see in a girly magazine, sweat-drops on her freckled chest he'd like to lick off with his tongue that's so swollen and thirsty. All this while the beet-hair woman is speaking to him in her husky voice trying not to sound impatient, the way his daughter is impatient having to scold him for dirtying the kitchen floor or leaving dishes in the sink not soaking, coming to the table smelling of the barn like he can't help no matter how he washes, actually Glenda (his honey-haired daughter, divorced and with a grown son) isn't his daughter but stepdaughter, all he has in the world having had no daughter or son of his own, he'd like to explain this to the beet-hair woman, maybe after they have a few drinks from the pint of Four Roses, the beet-hair woman is asking in a louder voice does he want to go somewhere with her? somewhere private? cozy? air-conditioned E-Z Inn? get acquainted? want to date? want to party mistah? what's ya lookin' at like that mistah? cat got your tongue mistah? or do you like maybe have to get home mistah, wifey's wait-ing for you is that it? and the old guy is stricken suddenly fumbling a smile trying to hide the stained snaggle teeth saying fast and hoarse, Ma'am I buried my wife Agnes Barnstead back in '54, and Sable gives a little cry of hurt and disapproval, Ohhh mister that's not a thing to tell me, if we're gonna party and the old guy looks like he's going to cry, can't seem to think what to say, maybe he's drunker than she thought, so Sable says scornfully placing her hand on the car door handle, Damn mister maybe you don't want to party, huh? maybe I'm wasting my time in this crap rust-buckle smells like a barn? and he's fumbling quick to say no, no don't leave ma'am, stammering, I guess—you would want—money? and Sable says sharp and quick, why'd I want money, mister? and he says, blurting the words out, Ma'am if—if—if we could—be together—and Sable says, Have sex, mister? that's what you're trying to say? and the old guy says, winded like he's been climbing a steep stairs, yes ma'am, and Sable says it's thirty for oral, fifty for straight, it's a deal, mister? and the old guy is blinking and staring at her like he can't comprehend her words so she repeats them, deal, mister? is it? and he says, almost inaudible on the tape being recorded in the unmarked van, yes ma'am.

Okay, you're busted.

.   .   .

Like that it happens. Happens faster than you can figure it out.
You're busted, mister. Step out of the truck, mister. Hey mister
out of the truck keep your hands in sight mister, we are Beechum
County sheriff deputies.

In that instant Sable is vanished. The woman is vanished, it's
loud-talking men, men shouting commands, strangers in T-shirts
yelling at him, impatient when he doesn't step out of the pickup
quick enough, he's dazed, fumbling, confused looking for the
beet-hair woman who was smiling at him, saying you ain't kiddin'
me are yah? pullin' my leg are yah? blinking at flashlight beams
shining into his face confused he's being shown shiny badges. Bee-
chum County sheriff he's hearing, informed he is under arrest for
soliciting an act of sex in violation of New York State law, under
arrest he's on tape, keep your hands where we can see them mister,
spread your legs Pops, y'hear you are UNDER ARREST, you been
operatin' that vehicle while drinkin' Pops? He's confused think-
ing his picture is being taken. Flash going off in his face. Hey yah
pullin' my leg are yah? he's more confused than frightened, more
stunned than smitten with shame, like somebody out of nowhere
has rushed up to him to shove him hard in the chest, spit in his
face, knock him on his ass, these young T-shirt guys he's thinking
might be bikers, doesn't know who in hell they are though they
keep telling him he's under arrest there's this weird smile contort-
ing the lower part of Pop's face like this has got to be a joke, nah
this ain't real, ain't happening, he's clumsy resisting the officers,
gonna have to cuff you Pops, hands behind your back Pops, under
arrest Pops, blinking like a blind man staring at a sight he can't
take in, tall burly young scruff-jaw guy in a black T-shirt—Drake

McCracken?—he'd wanted to think was some nephew of his? in that instant Pop and Drake recognize each other. Drake is stunned like the old guy, sick stunned look in his face his sergeant sees the situation, understands the two are related, tells Drake back off, shift's over he can report back to the station. One of the deputies has cuffed the old man, poor old bastard is pouring sweat moving his head side to side like a panicked cow, his wallet has been taken from his back pocket, driver's license, I.D., name Hendrick Olafsson that's you? Sable is walking away shaking her beet-frizz hair, laughing and shaking her head, the smell in that truck! smell coming off the old man! Sable's undercover-hooker partner is cracking up over the old john, oldest john they've arrested on the Strip, poor bastard. Sable is saying some johns, the guys are psychos you can see. This old guy, he's more like disgusting. There's guys with strangler eyes. Guys with cocks like rubber mallets. Guys into biting. You can tell, there's johns any female would be crazy to climb into any vehicle with, drive off with, shows how desperate they are, junkie-hookers, asking to be murdered and dumped in a ditch and their kids confiscated by the state, Jesus it's hard to be sympathetic you mostly feel disgust.

Well, this old guy! Old-timey farmer. Not a biter for sure, you see those teeth?

Pop is taken into custody, cuffed. Pop is transported in a van to the sheriff's headquarters on Route 29, Beechum County. Pop is booked. Pop's picture is taken. Pop is fingerprinted. Pop is one of seven "johns" arrested by Beechum County deputies on the Strip, night of July 19, 1972. Pop is fifty-seven. Pop is identified as Hendrick Olafsson, R.D.3, Herkimer, New York. Pop is confused and dazed and (maybe) has a minor stroke in the holding cell crowded with strangers. Pop calls my mother on the phone, it's 11:48 P.M. and she can't make sense of what he's saying. Where? Arrested? Pop? Drunk driving, is it? Accident? Pop? Pop is wheezing and whimpering begging Mom to come get him, he don't feel too good. (It will turn out, Pop couldn't remember his own telephone number at the farm, he'd had for thirty years. A female officer on duty looked it up for him.) It's a twelve-mile drive to the sheriff's headquarters over in Sparta. Mom calls me (where I'm living in town, now I work at the stone quarry west of Herkimer Falls) but I'm out. So Mom drives alone. Arrives around 1 A.M. Mom is disbelieving when the charge is read to her, soliciting sex, plus a charge of resisting arrest, Mom insists her stepfather is not a man to solicit prostitutes, he must have thought the officer was hitch-hiking, Pop is the kind of man would give a hitch-hiker a ride, Mom is so agitated she repeats this until the desk sergeant cuts her off saying, Ma'am it's on tape, it's recorded. In the meantime Pop has been taken from the holding cell to rest on a cot. The cuffs are off, his wrists are raw and chafed and he's disoriented but he's okay, Mom is assured he's okay, doesn't want to be taken to a hospital. Mom will be allowed to speak with him and secure a lawyer for him if wished but she can't take him home just yet, bail hasn't been set, bail won't be set until after 9 A.M. next morning when a judge will set bail at the county courthouse and Mom can return then to take her stepfather home. All this, Mom can't take in. Mom is looking for her nephew Drake McCracken who's a Beechum County deputy but she's told Drake is off duty, nowhere on the premises. Mom is beginning to cry like Pop Olafsson is her own father not her stepfather. Mom is wiping tears from her eyes pleading Pop isn't a well man, Pop has high blood pressure,

Pop takes heart pills, this will kill him Mom says, there has got to
be some mistake let me talk to the arresting officers, my stepfather
is not a man who solicits prostitutes! and the desk sergeant says,
Ma'am, none of 'em ever are.

Ever after this, Pop Olafsson's life is run down like an old truck can't
make it uphill.

Nineteen days from the arrest, sixteen days from the front-page
story HERKIMER FARMER, 57, ARRESTED IN "VICE" SWEEP
ON RT. 33 STRIP and photo of Hendrick Olafsson in the *Herkimer
Journal*, Pop's life runs down.

He's so ashamed, he won't show his face. Any vehicle drives up the
lane, Pop skulks away like a kicked dog. He's dizzy, limping. Some
blackouts he can't remember where in hell he is, wakes up in a mess
of hay and manure and the cows bawling to be milked. He's drink-
ing hard cider, whiskey in the morning. Heart pounds so he can't lie
flat in bed, has to sit up through the night. Mom is disgusted with
him she hardly speaks to him, leaves his meals on the back porch like
he's one of the dogs. Other relatives who come around avoid Pop,
too. I drove out to the farm, felt sorry for my mother but for the old
man also he's so fucking pathetic. He's an embarrassment to me, too.
God damn lucky my name is McCracken not Olafsson. At work the
guys are ribbing me bad enough. Quarry workers, they're known for
this. To a point, I can take it. Then I'll break somebody's face. My fist,
somebody's face. Eye socket, cheekbone, nose, teeth. There's a feel
when you break the bone, nothing can come near. Out back of the
high school I punched out more than one guy's front teeth. Got me
expelled, never graduated but it's one good thing I did, I feel good
about remembering. Every scar in my face is worth it. At the house I

asked Mom how it's going and Mom says see for yourself, he's out in the barn drinking. Mom's the one had to deal with Pop Olafsson at the court hearing over in Sparta, signed a check to the court for $350 fine, the old man pleaded guilty to the sex charge, "resisting arrest" was dropped, now he's on twelve-month probation a man of fifty-seven! Mom is feeling bad we haven't heard from Drake, you'd think Drake would come see us, at least call, say how sorry he is what happened to Pop. Like Drake stabbed us in the back, Mom says. His own family.

My feeling about Drake is so charged, I can't talk about it.

Located Pop out back of the silo looking like some broke-back old sick man trying to hide what he's drinking when he sees me like I don't know Pop drinks? this is news to me, Daryl? Why I'd come was to tell Pop how sorry I am what happened, what a lousy trick the fucking cops played on him, but somehow seeing the old man, that look in his face like somebody who's shit his pants. I hear myself say Hey Pop: don't take it too hard in this sarcastic voice like I'm fifteen not going on twenty-five. A few days later Pop blows off the top of his head with the clumsy old 12-gauge, came near to missing but got enough of his brain matter to kill him. It was like Pop to take himself out in a back pasture not in any inside space that would have to be cleaned afterward, and not near any stream that drained into the cows' drinking pond.

Pop left the dairy farm to my mother who never loved him. She felt real bad about it. I never loved the old guy either I guess but I missed him. For a long time I felt guilty how I'd spoken to him when he'd been in pain.

Soon as she could, Mom sold the property and moved to town.

Drake showed up at Pop's funeral, at least. The church part. At the back of the church where he wouldn't have to meet anybody's eye. He was wearing civilian clothes not the deputy uniform. Soon as the ceremony was ended, Drake was gone.

A week after the funeral I'm at the Water Wheel with some guys from the quarry and there's my cousin Drake at the bar with some off-duty deputies. It's Friday night, crowded. But not so crowded we don't see each other. Two hours I'm waiting for my cousin to come over to say something to me, and he doesn't. And he's going to walk out not acknowledging me. And I'm waiting, it's like my heart is grinding slow and hard in waiting, like a fist getting tighter and tighter. It comes over me, Drake killed Pop Olafsson. Like he lifted the 12-gauge himself, aimed the barrels at Pop's head and fired. Drake and his rotten cop friends they'd sell their blood kin for a fucking paycheck. I'm thinking *He is a guilty man. He deserves some hurt.*

Even then, if Drake had come over to me, lay a hand on my shoulder and called me Daryl, I'd forgive him. For sure.

It's a few weeks later, I make my move. All this while I've been waiting. Past 11 P.M. when I drive to this place my cousin is renting in Sparta. For a while Drake had a girlfriend living there but looks like the girlfriend is moved out, this is what I've heard. Knock on the side door and Drake comes to see who it is, in just boxer shorts and T-shirt, and barefoot. Drake sees it's me, and lets me in. His eyes are wary. Right away he says, I know what you want, Daryl, and I say, Right: a cold beer. And Drake says, You want me to say I'm sorry for Pop, well I am. But nobody made Pop drive out to the Strip, see. I tell Drake, Fuck Pop. I'm thirsty, man. So Drake laughs and goes to the refrigerator and his back's turned and the claw hammer is in my hand, been carrying it in my jacket pocket for five, six days. I come up behind Drake and bring the hammer down hard on his head, must be the damn thing kind of

slips my hand is so sweaty, it's just the side of Drake's head the ham-
mer catches, and he's hurt, he's hurt bad, his knees are buckling but he
isn't out, he's dangerous grabbing at me, and I'm shoving at him, and
it's like we're two kids trying to get wrestling holds, and some damn
way Drake is biting me, he's got my left forefinger between his teeth
biting down hard as a pit bull. I'm yelling, this pain is so bad. I'm trying
to get leverage to swing the hammer again but the pain in my finger
is so bad, almost I'm fainting. Drake is bleeding from a deep cut in his
head, a stream of bright blood running into his eye, he's panting his hot
breath into my face, groaning, whimpering, a big hard-muscle bastard
stinking of sweat from the shock of being hit, outweighs me by fifteen
pounds, and desperate to save his life but I've got the hammer free to
swing again, I manage to hit Drake on the back of his neck, another
wide swing and the hammer gets him high on the skull, this time I feel
bone crack. Drake's bulldog jaws open, Drake is on the floor and I'm
swinging the hammer wild and hard as I can, hitting his face, forehead
that's slippery in blood, his cheekbones, eye sockets, I'm walloping him
for the evil in him fucking deputy sheriff betraying his own kind *Like
this! like this! like this!* so at last his hard skull is broke like a melon, I can
feel the hammer sink in to where there's something soft. Such a relief in
this, the hammer goes wild swinging and swinging and when I come
to, the linoleum floor is slippery in blood. There's blood on me, work
trousers, work shoes, both hands wet with it, blood splattered high as
the ceiling, and dripping. I'm stumbling over Drake on the floor twitch-
ing like there's electric current jolting him but feebler and feebler. Mak-
ing this high keening sound like Pop Olafsson singing, so weird Drake
has got to be about dead but making this high sharp lonesome sound it
finally comes to me, is me, myself. Not Drake but me, Daryl, is making
this sound.

Then I see, oh man my finger's about bit in two. One half hanging to the other by some gristle. I'm so pumped up I don't hardly feel the pain, what I need to do is yank the damn thing off, shove it in my pocket with the hammer, see I don't want to leave my fucking finger behind. I'm pumped up but I'm thinking, too. Then I want Drake's deputy badge, and his gun. Fucking brass badge my cousin sold his soul for and fucking .38-caliber Colt revolver in its holster, what I'm doing is confiscating the entire belt heavy as a leather harness.

Last thing I tell Drake is, you did this to yourself, man. Not me.

Ain't pullin' my leg are yah?

These nights it's Pop Olafsson I'm missing. Weird how I hear Pop's voice like his nose is stopped up, thinking I am stone cold sober and awake but must've dozed off. Pop would blink them pale-blue pop-eyes at me seeing the age I am, the face I have now.

My left forefinger, ugly stub-finger, it's a reminder. People ask what happened and I tell them chain saw and they never ask further even my wife, she'd used to kiss the damn thing like it's some kind of test to her, can she accept it. A female will do the damnest things for you as long as they love you.

It's a fact there's "phantom pain." Weird but a kind of comfort like your finger is a whole finger, somewhere. Nothing of you is lost.

These nights I can't sleep. I need to prowl the house downstairs getting a beer from the refrigerator, hanging out the back door staring at the sky. There's a moon, you think it's staring back at you. Some nights I can't hold back, like a magnet pulling me over to the garage. And in the garage I'm shining a flashlight into a toolbox under my workbench, rusted old tools and paint rags and at the bottom Drake McCracken's brass badge and .38-caliber Colt pistol that's a comfort, too. The claw hammer (that was Pop's hammer) covered in blood and brains sticking like fish guts I disposed of in the Chautauqua River with the holster belt, driving home that night. My bloody clothes, I buried deep in the marshy pasture where Pop killed himself.

Pop's banjo that came to me, I kept for twenty years then gave to my son Clayton, damn kid rightaway broke like he's broke about every fucking thing in his life.

All this is so long ago now, you'd think it would be forgotten. But people in Herkimer remember, of a certain age. I need to switch off the flashlight and get back to the house, such a mood comes over me here. This lonesome feeling I'd make a song of, if I knew how.

ZZ Packer

GEESE

When people back home asked her why she was leaving Balti-more for Tokyo, Dina told them she was going to Japan in the hopes of making a pile of money, socking it away, then living somewhere cheap and tropical for a year. Back home, money was the only excuse for leaving, and it was barely excuse enough to fly thousands of miles to where people spoke no English.

"Ja*pan!*" Miss Gloria had said. Miss Gloria was her neighbor: a week before Dina left she sat out on the stoop and shared a pack of cigarettes with Miss Gloria. "Japan," Miss Gloria repeated, looking off into the distance, as though she might be able to see Honshu if she looked hard enough. Across the street sat the boarded-up row houses the city had promised to renovate. Dina tried to look past them, and harbored the vague hope that if she came back to the neighborhood they'd get renovated, as the city had promised. "Well, you go 'head on," Miss Gloria said, trying to sound encouraging. "You go 'head on and *learn* that language.

Find out what they saying about us over at Chong's." Chong's was the local take-out with the best moo goo gai pan around, but if someone attempted to clarify an order, or changed it, or even hesitated, the Chinese family got all huffed, yelling as fast and violent as kung fu itself.

"Chong's is Chinese, Miss Gloria."

"Same difference."

The plan was not well thought-out, she admitted that much. Or rather, it wasn't really a plan at all, but a feeling, a nebulous fluffy thing that had started in her chest, spread over her heart like a fog. It was sparked by movies in which she'd seen Japanese people bowing ceremoniously, torsos seesawing; her first Japanese meal, when she'd turned twenty, and how she'd marveled at the sashimi resting on its bed of rice, rice that lay on a lacquered dish the color of green tea. She grew enamored of the pen strokes of kanji, their black sabers clashing and warring with one another, occasionally settling peacefully into what looked like the outlines of a Buddhist temple, the cross sections of a cozy house. She did not want to say it, because it made no practical sense, but in the end she went to Japan for the delicate sake cups, resting in her hand like a blossom; she went to Japan for loveliness.

After searching for weeks for work in Tokyo, she finally landed a job at an amusement park. It was called Summerland, because, in Japan, anything vaguely amusing had an English name. It was in Akigawa, miles away from the real Tokyo, but each of her previous days of job hunting had sent her farther and farther away from the city. "Economic downturn," one Office Lady told her. The girl, with her exchange-student English and quick appraisal of Dina's frustration, seemed cut out for something better than a receptionist's job, but Dina understood that this, too, was part of the culture. A girl—woman—would work in an office as a glorified photocopier, and when she became Christmasu-keeki, meaning twenty-five years old, she was expected to resign quietly and start a family with a husband. With no reference to her race, only to her Americanness in general, the Office Lady had said, sadly, "Downturn means people want to hire Japanese. It's like, obligation." So when the people at Summerland offered her a job, she immediately accepted.

Her specific job was operator of the Dizzy Teacups ride, where, nestled in gigantic replicas of Victorian teacups, Japanese kids spun and arced and dipped before they were whisked back to cram school. Summerland, she discovered, was the great *gaijin* dumping ground, the one place where a non-Japanese foreigner was sure to land a job. It was at Summerland that she met Arillano Justinio Arroyo, with his perfectly round smiley-face head, his luxurious black hair, always parted in the middle, that fell on either side of his temples like an open book. Ari was her co-worker, which meant they would exchange mop duty whenever a kid vomited.

By summer's end, both she and Ari found themselves unamused and jobless. She decided that what she needed, before resuming her search for another job, was a vacation. At the time, it made a lot of sense. So she sold the return part of her round-trip ticket and spent her days on subways in search of all of Tokyo's corners: she visited Asakusa and gazed at the lit red lanterns of Sensoji Temple; she ate an outrageously expensive bento lunch under the Asahi brewery's giant sperm-shaped modernist sculpture. She even visited Akihabara, a section of Tokyo where whole blocks of stores sold nothing but electronics she couldn't afford. She spent an afternoon in the waterfront township of Odaiji, where women sunned themselves in bikinis during the lunch hour. But she loved Shinjuku the most, that garish part of Tokyo where pachinko parlors pushed against ugly gray earthquake-resistant buildings; where friendly, toothless vendors sold roasted *unagi*, even in rainy weather. Here, the twelve-floor department stores scintillated with slivers of primary colors, all the products shiny as toys. The subcity of Shinjuku always swooned, brighter than Vegas, lurid with sword-clashing kanji in neon. Skinny prostitutes in mini-skirts swished by in pairs like schoolgirls, though their pouty red lips and permed hair betrayed them as they darted into doorways without signs and, seemingly, without actual doors.

At the end of each day, she took the subway, reboarding the Hibiya-sen *tokkyuu*, which would take her back to the *gaijin* hostel in Roppongi. She rented her room month to month, like the Australians, Germans, and Canadians and the occasional American. The only other blacks who lived in Japan were Africans: the Senegalese, with their blankets laid out in front of Masashi-Itsukaiichi station, selling bootleg Beatles albums and Tupperware; the Kenyans in Harajuku selling fierce tribal masks and tarry perfumed oils alongside Hello Kitty notebooks. The Japanese did not trust these black *gaijin*, these men who smiled with every tooth in their mouths and wore their cologne turned on high. And though the Japanese women stared at Dina with the same distrust, the business-suited *sararimen* who passed her in the subway stations would proposition her with English phrases they'd had *gaijin* teach them—"Verrry sexy," they'd say, looking around to make sure women and children hadn't overheard them. And even on the *tokkyuu* itself, where every passenger took a seat and immediately fell asleep, the emboldened men would raise their eyebrows in brushstrokes of innu-endo and loudly whisper, "Verry chah-ming daaark-ku skin."

Ari found another job. Dina didn't. Her three-month visa had expired and the Japanese were too timid and suspicious to hire anyone on the sly. There were usually only two lines of work for American *gaijin*—teaching or modeling. Modeling was out—she was not the right race, much less the right blondness or legginess, and with an expired visa she got turned down for teaching and tutoring jobs. The men conducting the interviews knew her visa had expired, and that put a spin on things, the spin being that they expected her to sleep with them.

Dina had called Ari, wanting leads on jobs the English-language newspapers might not advertise. Ari agreed to meet her at Swensen's, where he bought her a scoop of chocolate mint ice cream.

"I got offered a job at a pachinko parlor," he said. "I can't do it, but you should. They only offered me the job because they like to see other Asians clean their floors."

She didn't tell him that she didn't want to sweep floors, that too many Japanese had already seen American movies in which blacks were either criminals or custodians. So when they met again at Swensen's, Dina still had no job and couldn't make the rent at the foreign hostel. Nevertheless, she bought him a scoop of red bean ice cream with the last of her airplane money. She didn't have a job and he took pity on her, inviting her to live with him in his one-room flat. So she did.

And so did Petra and Zoltan. Petra was five-foot-eleven and had once been a model. That ended when she fell down an escalator, dislocating a shoulder and wrecking her face. She'd had to pay for the reconstructive surgery out of her once sizable bank account and now had no money. And Petra did not want to go back to Moldova, *could* not go back to Moldova, it seemed, though Ari hadn't explained any of this when he brought Petra home. He introduced her to Dina as though they were neighbors who hadn't met, then hauled her belongings up the stairs. While Ari strained and grunted under the weight of her clothes trunks, Petra plopped down in a chair, the only place to sit besides the floor. Dina made tea for her, and though she and Ari had been running low on food, courtesy dictated that she bring out the box of cookies she'd been saving to share with Ari.

"I have threads in my face," Petra said through crunches of cookie. "Threads from the doctors. One whole year"—she held up a single aggressive finger—"I have threads. I am thinking that when threads bust out, va voom, I am having old face back. These doctors here"—Petra shook her head and narrowed her topaz eyes—"they can build a whole car, but cannot again build face? I go to America next. Say, 'Fix my face. Fix face *for actual.*' And they will *fix.*" She nodded once, like a genie, as though a single nod were enough to make it so. Afterward she made her way to the bathroom and sobbed.

Of course, Petra could no longer model; her face had been ripped into unequal quadrants like the sections of a TV dinner, and the stitches had been in long enough to leave fleshy, zipper-like scars in their place. The Japanese would not hire her either; they did not like to view affliction so front and center. In turn, Petra refused to work for them. Whenever Dina went to look for a job, Petra made it known that she did not plan on working for the Japanese: "*I* not work for them even if they *pay* me!"

Her boyfriend Zoltan came with the package. He arrived in toto a week after Petra, and though he tried to project the air of someone just visiting, he'd already tacked pictures from his bodybuilding days above the corner where they slept across from Ari and Dina.

Petra and Zoltan loved each other in that dangerous Eastern European way of hard, sobbing sex and furniture-pounding fights. Dina had been living with Ari for a month and Petra and Zoltan for only two weeks when the couple had their third major fight. Zoltan had become so enraged that he'd stuck his hand on the orange-hot burner of the electric range. Dina had been adding *edamame* to the *udon* Ari was reheating from his employee lunch when Zoltan pushed between the two, throwing the bubbling pot aside and pressing his hand onto the lit burner as easily and noiselessly as if it were a Bible on which he was taking an oath.

"Zoltan!" Dina screamed. Ari muttered a few baffled words of Tagalog. The seared flesh smelled surprisingly familiar, like dumplings, forgotten and burning at the bottom of a pot. The burner left a bull's-eye imprint on Zoltan's palm, each concentric circle sprouting blisters that pussed and bled. Petra wailed when she saw; it took her two weeping hours to scour his melted fingerprints from the burner.

And still, they loved. That same night they shook the bamboo shades with their passion. When they settled down, they baby-talked to each other in Moldovan and Hungarian, though the first time Dina heard them speak this way it sounded to her as if they were reciting different brands of vodka.

After the hand-on-the-range incident, Zoltan maundered about with the look of a beast in his lair. The pictures from his bodybuilding days that he tacked on the walls showed him brown, oiled, and bulging, each muscle delineated as though he were constructed of hundreds of bags of hard-packed sugar. Though he was still a big man, he was no longer glorious, and since they'd all been subsisting on crackers and ramen, Zoltan looked even more deflated. For some reason he had given up bodybuilding once he stepped off the plane at Narita, though he maintained that he was winning prizes right up until then. If he was pressed further than that about his past, Petra, invariably orbiting Zoltan like a satellite, would begin to cry.

Petra cried a lot. If Dina asked Petra about life in Moldova or about modeling in Ginza, she cried. If Dina so much as offered her a carrot, this, too, was cause for sorrow. Dina had given up trying to understand Petra. Or any of them, for that matter. Even Ari. Once she'd asked him why he did it, why he let them stay. Ari held out his hand and said, "See this? Five fingers. One hand." He then made a fist, signifying—she supposed—strength. She didn't exactly understand what he was driving at: none of them helped out in any real way, though she, unlike Petra and Zoltan, had at least attempted to find a job. He looked to her, fist still clenched; she nodded as though she understood, though she felt she never would. Things simply made all of them cry and sigh. Things dredged from the bottoms of their souls brought them pain at the strangest moments.

Then Sayeed came to live with them. He had a smile like a sealed envelope, had a way of eating as though he were horny. She didn't know how Ari knew him, but one day, when Dina was practicing writing kanji characters and Petra was knitting an afghan with Zoltan at her feet, Ari came home from work, Sayeed following on his heels.

"We don't have much," Ari apologized to Sayeed after the introductions. Then he glared at the mess of blankets on the floor, "and as you can see, we are many people, sleeping in a tiny, six-tatami room."

Sayeed didn't seem to mind. They all shared two cans of a Japanese soft drink, Pocari Sweat, taking tiny sips from their sake cups. They shared a box of white chocolate Pokki, and a sandwich from Ari's employee lunch. Sayeed stayed after the meal and passed around cigarettes that looked handmade, though they came from a box. He asked, occasionally gargling his words, what each of them did. Having no jobs, they told stories of their past: Petra told of Milan and the runways and dressing up for the opera at La Scala. But mostly she recalled what she ate: pan-seared foie gras with pickled apricot gribiche sauce; swordfish tangine served with stuffed cherries; gnocchi and lobster, swimming in brown butter.

"Of course," she said, pertly ashing her cigarette, "we had to throw it all up."

"Yes yes yes," Sayeed said, as though this news delighted him.

Zoltan talked of Hungary, and how he was a close relation of Nagy, the folk hero of the '56 revolution. He detailed his bodybuilding regime: how much he could bench-press, how much he could jerk, and what he would eat. Mainly they were heavy foods: soups with carp heads, bones, and fins; doughy breads cooked in rendered bacon fat; salads made of meat rather than lettuce. Some sounded downright inedible, but Zoltan recalled them as lovingly and wistfully as if they were dear departed relations.

Dina did not want to talk about food but found herself describing the salmon croquettes her mother made the week before she died. Vats of collards and kale, the small islands of grease floating atop the pot liquor, cornbread spotted with dashes of hot sauce. It was not the food she ate all the time, or even the kind she preferred, but it was the kind she wanted whenever she was sick or lonely; the kind of food that—when she got it—she stuffed in her mouth like a pacifier.

Even recollecting food from the corner stores made her stomach constrict with pleasure and yearning: barbecue, Chong's take-out, peach cobbler. All of it delicious in a lardy, fatty, condiment-heavy way. Miasmas of it so strong that they pushed through the styrofoam boxes bagged in brown paper.

"Well," Ari said, when Dina finished speaking.

Since they had nothing else to eat, they smoked.

They waited to see what Sayeed would do, and as the hours passed, waited for him to leave. He never did. That night Ari gave him a blanket and Sayeed stretched out on a tatami, in the very middle of the room. Instead of pushing aside the low tea table, he simply arranged his blanket under it, and as he lay down, head under the tea table, he looked as though he had been trying to retrieve something from under it and had gotten stuck.

Over the next few days they found out that Sayeed had married a non-Moroccan woman instead of the woman he was arranged to marry. His family, her family, the whole country of Morocco, it seemed, disowned him. Then his wife left him. He had moved to Tokyo in the hope of opening a business, but the money that was supposed to have been sent to him was not sent.

"They know! They know!" he'd mutter while smoking or praying or boiling an egg. Dina assumed he meant that whoever was supposed to send Sayeed money knew about his non-Moroccan ex-wife, but she could never be sure. Whenever Sayeed mused over how life had gone wrong, how his wife had left him, how his family had refused to speak to him, he glared at Dina, as though she were responsible.

One night she awoke to find Sayeed panting over her, holding a knife at her throat. His chest was bare; his pajama bottoms glowed from the streetlights outside the window. Dina screamed, waking

Petra, who turned on a light and promptly began to cry. Ari and Zoltan gradually turtled out of their sleep, saw Sayeed holding the knife at her throat, saw that she was still alive, and looked at her hopelessly, as though she were an actress failing to play her part and die on cue. When Zoltan saw that it had nothing to do with him, he went back to sleep. Sayeed rattled off accusingly at Dina in Arabic until Ari led him into the hallway.

She sat straight up in the one pair of jeans she hadn't sold and a nearly threadbare green bra. Ari came back, exhausted. She didn't know where Sayeed was, but she could hear Japanese voices in the hallway, their anger and complaints couched in vague, seemingly innocuous phrases. *They have a lot of people living there, don't they?* meant, *Those foreigners! Can't they be quiet and leave us in peace!* And *I wonder if Roppongi would offer them more opportunities* meant, *They should go to Roppongi where their own kind live!* Ari tried to slam the door shut, as if to defy the neighbors, as if to add a dramatic coda to the evening, but Zoltan had broken the door in one of his rages, and it barely closed at all.

"He probably won't do it again," he said.

"What! What do you mean by 'probably won't'?"

Zoltan sleepily yelled for her to shut up. Petra sat in her corner with a stray tear running in a rivulet along one of her scars.

Then Ari was suddenly beside Dina, talking to her in broken English she hadn't the energy to try to understand. He turned the light out, his arm around her neck. Soon they heard Petra and Zoltan going at it, panting and pounding at each other till it seemed as though they'd destroy the tatami under them.

Dina and Ari usually slept side by side, not touching, but that night he'd settled right beside her and put his arm around her neck.

Ari smelled like fresh bread, and as she inhaled his scent it occurred to her that his arm around her neck was meant to calm her, to shut her up—nothing romantic. Nevertheless, she nudged him, ran her palm against his arm, the smoothest she ever remembered touching, the hairs like extensions of liquid skin. He politely rolled away. "You should wear more clothes."

She tugged the sheet away from him and said. "I can't take this."

She hated how they all had to sleep in the tiny, six-tatami room, how they slept so close to one another that in the dark Dina could tell who was who by smell alone. She hated how they never had enough to eat, and how Ari just kept inviting more people to stay. It should have been just he and she, but now there were three others, one of whom had just tried to kill her, and she swore she could not—would not—take it anymore.

"Can't take?" he asked, managing to yell without actually yelling. "Can't take, can't take!" he tried to mimic. He turned on the light as if to get a better look at her, as if he'd have to check to make sure it was the same woman he'd let sleep under his roof. "But you must!"

She had nowhere else to go. So she and Sayeed worked out a schedule—not a schedule exactly, but a way of doing things. If he returned from a day of looking for work, he might ask everyone how the day had gone. In that case, she would not answer, because she was to understand that he was not speaking to her. If she was in one corner of the room, he would go to another.

Sometimes she would take a crate and sit outside the stoopless apartment building and try to re-create the neighborhood feeling she'd had at home with Miss Gloria. The sun would shine hotly on the pavement, and the movement of people everywhere, busy and self-absorbed, would have to stand in for the human music of Baltimore. The corner grocery stores back home were comforting in their dinginess, packed high with candies in their rainbow-colored wrappings, menthols, tallboys and magnums, racks of chips and sodas, but best of all, homemade barbecue sandwiches, the triangled white bread sopping up the orange-red sauce like a sponge. Oh, how she missed it. The men who loitered outside playing their lottery numbers and giving advice to people too young to take it, the mothers who yelled viciously at their children one minute, only to hug and kiss them the next. How primping young boys played loud music to say the things they couldn't say. How they followed the unspoken rules of the neighborhood: Never advertise your poverty. Dress immaculately. Always smell good, not just clean.

For a few minutes, the daydream would work, even in Japan.

Once, when looking for a job in Shibuya, she eyed a cellophane Popsicle wrapper nestled up against a ginkgo. It was gaudily beautiful with its stripes of orange ooze from where a kid had licked it. Just when she felt a rush of homesickness, a Japanese streetworker, humbly brown from daily hours in the sun, conscientiously swept the little wrapper into his flip-top box, and it was gone.

The day after Sayeed tried to kill her, she took the train to Roppongi, and though she had no money for train fare, she pounded on the window of the information booth, speaking wildly in English, peppering her rant with a few words of Japanese. She said the machine hadn't issued her a ticket. The Japanese girl at the information counter looked dumbly at the Plexiglas, repeating that the machine had *never* broken. They would not outwit her: Dina knew that the

Japanese did not like to cause scenes, nor be recipients of them. She pitched her voice loudly, until everyone in the station turned around. Finally, the information girl pressed a hidden button and let her through.

She did not want to go back to Roppongi, where she'd first lived, where she had unsuccessfully searched for jobs before, but Sayeed's knife convinced her to redouble her efforts. She hoped to get a job from Australians or Canadians who might overlook her lack of visa. She wished she'd taken the job at the pachinko parlor, but now it was gone; she hoped for a job doing anything—dishwasher, street cleaner, glass polisher, leaflet passer—but she did not get one.

They could not go starving, so they began to steal. While Ari was away at work, Zoltan swiped packaged steaks, Sayeed swiped fruit and bread and one time even couscous, opening the package and pouring every single grain into two pants pockets. Even though she never would have stolen anything in America, stealing in Japan gave Dina the same giddy, weightlessness that cursing in another language did. You did it because it was unimportant and foreign. She stole spaghetti, rice, fruit, Keebler cookies all the way from America. But Petra outdid them all. She went in with a sack rigged across her stomach, then stuffed a sweater in it to look as though she was pregnant, and began shopping. When the sack got full, she'd go to the bathroom, put on her sweater, and pay for a loaf of bread.

But Petra's trick didn't last long. She went to get Zoltan a watermelon for his birthday and the sack gave way. She gave birth to the watermelon, which split open wide and red, right in front of her. The store manager, a nervous Japanese man in his forties, brought her to Zoltan, telling him, in smiling, broken English, to keep her at home.

Since then, the stores in the area became suspicious of foreigners, pregnant or otherwise. They'd all been caught. They'd all made mad dashes down the street, losing themselves in crowds and alleys. And they didn't even have the money to get on the train to steal food elsewhere. It was impossible to jump the turnstiles—they were all electronic. Eventually they got to a point where they never left their one-room flat, knowing that they would see people selling food, stores selling food, people eating food, people whose faces reminded them of food.

And then they simply gave up. Some alloy of disgust and indifference checked the most human instinct, propelling them into a stagnant one-room dementia. It was a secret they shared: there were two types of hunger—one in which you would do anything for food, the other in which you could not bring yourself to complete the smallest task for it.

Ari came home from work and declared that they must all go to the park. They looked at him uncomprehendingly. Sayeed went to his corner of the room and said, under his breath, "They know." Zoltan stood there, looking as though he had somewhere to go but had forgotten where. Petra bit her fingernails, her sunset-blond hair in unwashed clumps, framing her scars.

"Why the park?" Dina asked.

"Look," he said, reaching into his back pack to show them a block of cheese that was hardened on the ends, some paprika, a box of crackers, a plum. Dina remembered that all that was left in the refrigerator were two grapefruits. She salivated when her gaze settled on the bunch of bananas on the countertop. These he did not take.

"Let's go," he said.

Sayeed rose from where he'd been sitting on the tatami; Zoltan grabbed Petra's arm and led her toward the door. Once they'd gathered at the doorway, they looked at one another in silence, as if they had nothing further to say. Ari did not bother to lock the door.

They sat in Shakuji-koen Park, dazed with the sunlight, surrounded by an autumn of yellow ginkgo trees. For the most part, the sky was gray, shot through with fibrous clouds. The Japanese families sat like cookies arranged on a plate. The son of the family closest to them was as bronzed as Dina, a holdover tan from the summer. He bit into the kind of neat, crustless sandwiches Dina had seen mothers unwrap at Summerland. The girl was singing while her mother was talking to another mother, who agreed, *"Ne, ne, ne!"* as she bounced a swaddled baby on her hip. The father dozed off on a blanket of red and white squares.

The boy nibbled at his sandwich as the five of them watched. When the boy saw the foreigners staring at him, at his sandwich, he ran to his sister and pointed. Five *gaijin*, all together, sitting Buddha-like. The boy looked as though he wanted to come right up and ask them questions in the monosyllabic English he had learned from older boys who had spoken to *gaijin* before. Do you have tails? If so, would you kindly show them to me and my sister? Do you come out at night and suck blood? He would look at Dina and ask if the color rubbed off. He wanted to ask them these questions and more, if his limited English permitted, but the girl had enough shyness for the both of them, and held him back, a frightened smile on her face.

Ari took out the crackers, the cheese with the hard ends, the paprika, the salt, and the plum.

"I lost my job," he said.

Quietly, shamefully, they mustered out their *Sorrys*. She'd expected him to lash out, tell all of them to leave, but he didn't.

"I'll pay you back," Dina said, "every penny."

"You mean yen," Ari said.

They ate the crackers with sliced plum and cheese on top. Then Petra spoke.

"I do not like cheese," she said. Everyone looked at her, her pouting lips and unblinking eyes. Zoltan clenched her arm. Petra had taken her slices of cheese off her sandwiches and Zoltan grabbed the slices with one fist and thrust them at her. They fell humbly into the folds of her shirt.

"You don't have to eat them," Ari said. But Petra knew she had to eat the cheese, that the cheese mattered. She ate it and looked as if she might cry, but didn't. They sat for a while. The food melted in Dina's stomach just as the sunset melted, their synchronized fading seeming to make the whole world go dimmer and volumeless. Then she felt a sharp pain, as though the corners of the crackers had gone down her throat unchewed. None of them spoke, and that seemed to make the pain in her stomach worse. They watched the people and the lake and the sun, now only a thread of light.

"Look," Sayeed said.

Geese. Stretching their necks, paying no mind to humans. Zoltan bolted upright from where he lay and ran after them. For a few moments, the geese flew hysterically, but then landed yards away from him, waddling toward escape, all the while snapping up bits of crackers the Japanese had thrown just for them. When Zoltan started the chase anew, Dina realized he was not after the crackers but the geese themselves. She imagined Zoltan grabbing one of the thin, long necks, breaking it with a deft turn of wrist. And what would all the Japanese, quietly sitting in the park, make of it all? She skipped over that scene, speeding ahead to the apartment, everyone happily defeathering the bird, feathers lifting and floating then descending on their futons and blankets, the down like snow, the underfeathers like ash. They'd land on Petra's trunks, empty now that all her clothes had been sold, and they'd land on the tea table at which they used to eat. They would make a game of adjusting the oven dials, then wait out the hours as the roasted gamy smell of the goose made them stagger and salivate. And there would be a wishbone, but it wouldn't matter, because they'd all have the same wish.

Zoltan ran as haphazard as a child chasing after them, and when he seemed within grasp of a few tailfeathers, the geese flew off for good. When he returned, he dusted off the blanket before sitting down, as though nothing had happened.

All Japanese eyes were on them, and it was the first time Dina thought she had actually felt embarrassment in the true Japanese sense. Everyone was looking at them, and she'd never felt more foreign, more *gaijin*. Someone laughed. At first she thought it was Sayeed, his high-pitched laughter that made you happy. Then Dina saw that it was one of the Japanese picnickers. Families clapped, one after the other, cautious, tentative, like the first heavy rains on a rooftop, then suddenly everyone was clapping. Applause and even whistles, all for Zoltan, as though he had meant to entertain them. Ari made a motion for them to stop, but they continued for what seemed like minutes, as if demanding an encore. They did not stop, even when Zoltan nuzzled his head into Petra's gray corduroy shirt so no one could see him weep.

·   ·   ·

It was a week after they saw the geese that Ari sliced up the grapefruit and banana into six pieces each. Dina watched them eat. Sayeed, his face dim as a brown fist, took his banana slice and put it underneath his tongue. He would transfer the warm disk of banana from side to side in his mouth until, it seemed, it had grown so soft that he swallowed it like liquid. He nibbled away at half a wedge of the grapefruit, tearing the fibers from fruit to skin with his bitten-down lips. He popped what was left of his grapefruit into his mouth like a piece of chewing gum.

Petra let her slices sit for a while and finally chewed the banana, looking off from the side of her eye as if someone had a gun pointed to her head. She wrapped up her grapefruit slice in a bit of leftover Saran Wrap and went to her corner to lie down.

Zoltan rubbed his eyes, put the banana slice on the flat side of the grapefruit and swallowed them both whole, grapefruit peel and all.

Ari ate his slices with delicate motions, and after he'd finished, smiled like a Buddha.

Dina ate her fruit the way she thought any straightforward, normal American would. She bit into it. One more piece sat on the plate.

"Anybody want that?" Dina asked. No one said anything. She looked around to make sure. No one had changed. She ate the last piece, wiped the grapefruit juice from around the corners of her mouth, looked at the semicircle of foreign faces around her, and knew she had done the wrong thing.

She needed to go to Shinjuku. Once again, she claimed the turnstile wouldn't issue her a ticket, and although the girl at the counter didn't look convinced, she gave Dina a ticket. When she got to Shinjuku, it was going on noon. *Sararimen* hurled by, smiling with their colleagues, bowing for their bosses to enter doors first. Mothers shopped, factory workers sighed, shopworkers chattered with other shopworkers. The secretaries and receptionists—the "Office Ladies"—all freshened their lipstick and straightened their hairbows. The women in the miniskirts rushed past as though late.

She stood in the Shinjuku station, though she hadn't ridden the train to get there. She read an old magazine she'd brought along. Finally, a *sarariman* approached her.

"Verrrry sexy."

He paid for the love motel with a wad of yen. "CAN RENT ROOM BY OUR!" screamed a red-lettered sign on the counter. Dina ascended the dark winding staircase, the *sarariman* following. The room had only a bed and a nightstand, though these simple furnishings now seemed like luxuries. He watched her undress and felt her skin only after she'd taken everything off. He rubbed it as if he were trying to find something underneath.

The inside of her closed eyelids were orange from a slit of sunlight that had strayed into the room. The *sarariman* shook her. She opened her eyes. He raised his eyebrows, looking from Dina to the nightstand. The nightstand had a coin-operated machine attached.

"Sex toy?" he asked, in English.

"No," she said, in Japanese.

The motel room sheets were perfect and crisp, reminding her of sheets from home. She touched the *sarariman*'s freshly cut Asian hair, each shaft sheathed in a sheer liquid of subway sweat. The ends of the shortest hairs felt like the tips of lit, hissing firecrackers.

He was apologetic about the short length of time. "No problem," she told him in Japanese.

. . .

She left with a wad of yen. While riding the *tokkyuu* she watched life pass, alert employees returning to work, uniformed school children on a field trip. It all passed by—buildings, signs, throngs of people everywhere. When the train ran alongside a park, yellow ginkgo leaves waved excited farewells as the train blazed past them. Fall had set in, and no one was picnicking, but there were geese. At first they honked and waddled as she'd seen them a week ago when Zoltan had chased them, but then, as the train passed, agitating them, they rose, as though connected to a single string. Soon the geese were flying in formation, like planes she had once seen in a schoolbook about Japan.

The book told of kamikaze pilots, flying off to their suicide missions. How each scrap-metal plane and each rickety engine could barely stand the pressures of altitude, how each plane was allotted just enough fuel for its one-way trip. The pilots had made a pledge to the emperor, and they'd kept their promises. She remembered how she'd marveled when she'd read it, amazed that anyone would do such a thing; how—in the all-knowing arrogance of youth—she'd been certain that given the same circumstances, she would have done something different.

J. F. Powers

THE VALIANT WOMAN

They had come to the dessert in a dinner that was a shambles. "Well, John," Father Nulty said, turning away from Mrs. Stoner and to Father Firman, long gone silent at his own table. "You've got the bishop coming for confirmations next week."

"Yes," Mrs. Stoner cut in, "and for dinner. And if he don't eat any more than he did last year—"

Father Firman, in a rare moment, faced it. "Mrs. Stoner, the bishop is not well. You know that."

"And after I fixed that fine dinner and all." Mrs. Stoner pouted in Father Nulty's direction.

"I wouldn't feel bad about it, Mrs. Stoner," Father Nulty said. "He never eats much anywhere."

"It's funny. And that new Mrs. Allers said he ate just fine when he was there," Mrs. Stoner argued, and then spit out, "but she's a damned liar!"

Father Nulty, unsettled but trying not to show it, said, "Who's Mrs. Allers?"

"She's at Holy Cross," Mrs. Stoner said.

"She's the housekeeper," Father Firman added, thinking Mrs. Stoner made it sound as though Mrs. Allers were the pastor there.

"I swear I don't know what to do about the dinner this year," Mrs. Stoner said.

Father Firman moaned. "Just do as you've always done, Mrs. Stoner."

"Huh! And have it all to throw out! Is that any way to do?"

"Is there any dessert?" Father Firman asked coldly.

Mrs. Stoner leaped up from the table and bolted into the kitchen, mumbling. She came back with a birthday cake. She plunged it in the center of the table. She found a big wooden match in her apron pocket and thrust it at Father Firman.

"I don't like this bishop," she said. "I never did. And the way he went and cut poor Ellen Kennedy out of Father Doolin's will!"

She went back into the kitchen.

"Didn't they talk a lot of filth about Doolin and the housekeeper?" Father Nulty asked.

"I should think they did," Father Firman said. "All because he took her to the movies on Sunday night. After he died and the bishop cut her out of the will, though I hear he gives her a pension privately, they talked about the bishop."

"I don't like this bishop at all," Mrs. Stoner said, appearing with a cake knife. "Bishop Doran—there was the man!"

"We know," Father Firman said. "All man and all priest."

"He did know real estate," Father Nulty said.

Father Firman struck the match.

"Not on the chair!" Mrs. Stoner cried, too late.

Father Firman set the candle burning—it was suspiciously large and yellow, like a blessed one, but he could not be sure. They watched the fluttering flame.

"I'm forgetting the lights!" Mrs. Stoner said, and got up to turn them off. She went into the kitchen again.

The priests had a moment of silence in the candlelight.

"Happy birthday, John," Father Nulty said softly. "Is it fifty-nine you are?"

"As if you didn't know, Frank," Father Firman said, "and you the same but one."

Father Nulty smiled, the old gold of his incisors shining in the flickering light, his collar whiter in the dark, and raised his glass of water, which would have been wine or better in the bygone days, and toasted Father Firman.

"Many of 'em, John."

"Blow it out," Mrs. Stoner said, returning to the room. She waited by the light switch for Father Firman to blow out the candle.

Mrs. Stoner, who ate no desserts, began to clear the dishes into the kitchen, and the priests, finishing their cake and coffee in a hurry, went to sit in the study.

Father Nulty offered a cigar.

"John?"

"My ulcers, Frank."

"Ah, well, you're better off." Father Nulty lit the cigar and crossed his long black legs. "Fish Frawley has got him a Filipino, John. Did you hear?"

Father Firman leaned forward, interested. "He got rid of the woman he had?"

"He did. It seems she snooped."

"Snooped, eh?"

"She did. And gossiped. Fish introduced two town boys to her, said, 'Would you think these boys were my nephews?' That's all, and the next week the paper had it that his two nephews were visiting him from Erie. After that, he let her believe he was going East to see his parents, though both are dead. The paper carried the story. Fish returned and made a sermon out of it. Then he got the Filipino."

Father Firman squirmed with pleasure in his chair. "That's like Fish, Frank. He can do that." He stared at the tips of his fingers bleakly. "You could never get a Filipino to come to a place like this."

"Probably not," Father Nulty said. "Fish is pretty close to Minneapolis. Ah, say, do you remember the trick he played on us all in Marmion Hall!"

"That I'll not forget!" Father Firman's eyes remembered. "Getting up New Year's morning and finding the toilet seats all painted!"

"*Happy Circumcision!* Hah!" Father Nulty had a coughing fit.

When he had got himself together again, a mosquito came and sat on his wrist. He watched it a moment before bringing his heavy hand down. He raised his hand slowly, viewed the dead mosquito, and sent it spinning with a plunk of his middle finger.

"Only the female bites," he said.

"I didn't know that," Father Firman said.

"Ah, yes . . ."

Mrs. Stoner entered the study and sat down with some sewing—Father Firman's black socks.

She smiled pleasantly at Father Nulty. "And what do you think of the atom bomb, Father?"

"Not much," Father Nulty said.

Mrs. Stoner had stopped smiling. Father Firman yawned.

Mrs. Stoner served up another: "Did you read about this communist convert, Father?"

"He's been in the Church before," Father Nulty said, "and so it's not a conversion, Mrs. Stoner."

"No? Well, I already got him down on my list of Monsignor's converts."

"It's better than a conversion, Mrs. Stoner, for there is more rejoicing in heaven over the return of . . . uh, he that was lost, Mrs. Stoner, is found."

"And that congresswoman, Father?"

"Yes. A convert—she."

"And Henry Ford's grandson, Father. I got him down."

"Yes, to be sure."

Father Firman yawned, this time audibly, and held his jaw.

"But he's one only by marriage, Father," Mrs. Stoner said. "I always say you got to watch those kind."

"Indeed you do, but a convert nonetheless, Mrs. Stoner. Remember, Cardinal Newman himself was one."

Mrs. Stoner was unimpressed. "I see where Henry Ford's making steering wheels out of soybeans, Father."

"I didn't see that."

"I read it in the *Reader's Digest* or some place."

"Yes, well . . ." Father Nulty rose and held his hand out to Father Firman. "John," he said. "It's been good."

"I heard Hirohito's next," Mrs. Stoner said, returning to converts.

"Let's wait and see, Mrs. Stoner," Father Nulty said.

The priests walked to the door.

"You know where I live, John."

"Yes. Come again, Frank. Good night."

Father Firman watched Father Nulty go down the walk to his car at the curb. He hooked the screen door and turned off the porch light. He hesitated at the foot of the stairs, suddenly moved to go to bed. But he went back into the study.

"Phew!" Mrs. Stoner said. "I thought he'd never go. Here it is after eight o'clock."

Father Firman sat down in his rocking chair. "I don't see him often," he said.

"I give up!" Mrs. Stoner exclaimed, flinging the holey socks upon the horsehair sofa. "I'd swear you had a nail in your shoe."

"I told you I looked."

"Well, you ought to look again. And cut your toenails, why don't you? Haven't I got enough to do?"

Father Firman scratched in his coat pocket for a pill, found one, swallowed it. He let his head sink back against the chair and closed his eyes. He could hear her moving about the room, making the preparations: and how he knew them—the fumbling in the drawer for a pencil with a point, the rip of the page from his daily calendar, and finally the leg of the card table sliding up against his leg.

He opened his eyes. She yanked the floor lamp alongside the table, setting the bead fringe tinkling on the shade, and pulled up her chair on the other side. She sat down and smiled at him for the first time that day. Now she was happy.

She swept up the cards and began to shuffle with the abandoned virtuosity of an old river-boat gambler, standing them on end, fanning them out, whirling them through her fingers, dancing them halfway up her arms, cracking the whip over them. At last they lay before him tamed into a neat deck.

"Cut?"

"Go ahead," he said. She liked to go first.

She gave him her faint, avenging smile and drew a card, cast it aside for another which he thought must be an ace from the way she clutched it face down.

She was getting all the cards, as usual, and would have been invincible if she had possessed his restraint and if her cunning had been of a higher order. He knew a few things about leading and lying back that she would never learn. Her strategy was attack, forever attack, with one baffling departure: she might sacrifice certain tricks as expendable if only she could have the last ones, the heartbreaking ones, if she could slap them down one after another, shatteringly.

She played for blood, no bones about it, but for her there was no other way; it was her nature, as it was the lion's, and for this reason he found her ferocity pardonable, more a defect of the flesh, venial, while his own trouble was all in the will, mortal. He did not sweat and pray over each card as she must, but he did keep an eye out for reneging and demanded a cut now and then just to aggravate her, and he was always secretly hoping for aces.

With one card left in her hand, the telltale trick coming next, she delayed playing it, showing him first the smile, the preview of defeat. She laid it on the table—so! She held one more trump than he had reasoned possible. Had she palmed it from somewhere? No, she would not go that far; that would not be fair, was worse than reneging, which so easily and often happened accidentally, and she believed in being fair. Besides he had been watching her.

God smote the vines with hail, the sycamore trees with frost, and offered up the flocks to the lightning—but Mrs. Stoner! What a cross Father Firman had from God in Mrs. Stoner! There were other housekeepers as bad, no doubt, walking the rectories of the world, yes, but . . . yes. He could name one and maybe two priests who were worse off. One, maybe two. Cronin. His scraggly blonde of sixty—take her, with her everlasting banging on the grand piano, the gift of the pastor: her proud talk about the goiter operation at the Mayo Brothers', also a gift: her honking the parish Buick at passing strange priests because they were all in the game together. She was worse. She was something to keep the home fires burning. Yes sir. And Cronin said she was not a bad person really, but what was he? He was quite a freak himself.

For that matter, could anyone say that Mrs. Stoner was a bad person? No. He could not say it himself, and he was no freak. She had her points, Mrs. Stoner. She was clean. And though she cooked poorly, could not play the organ, would not take up the collection in an emergency, and went to card parties, and told all—even so, she was clean. She washed everything. Sometimes her underwear hung down beneath her dress like a paratrooper's pants, but it and everything she touched was clean. She washed constantly. She was clean.

She had her other points, to be sure—her faults, you might say. She snooped—no mistake about it—but it was not snooping for snooping's sake; she had a reason. She did other things, always with a reason. She overcharged on rosaries and prayer books, but that was for the sake of the poor. She censored the pamphlet rack, but that was to prevent scandal. She pried into the baptismal and matrimonial records, but there was no other way if Father was out, and in this way she had once uncovered a bastard and flushed him out of the rectory, but that was the perverted decency of the times. She held her nose over bad marriages in the presence of the victims, but that was her sorrow and came from having her husband buried in a mine. And he had caught her telling a bewildered young couple that there was only one good reason for their wanting to enter into a mixed marriage—the child had to have a name, and that—that was what?

She hid his books, kept him from smoking, picked his friends (usually the pastors of her colleagues), bawled out people for calling after dark, had no humor, except at cards, and then it was grim, very grim, and she sat hatchet-faced every morning at Mass. But she went to Mass, which was all that kept the church from being empty some mornings. She did annoying things all day long. She said annoying things into the night. She said she had given him the best years of her life. Had she? Perhaps—for the miner had her only a year. It was too bad, sinfully bad, when he thought of it like that. But all talk of best years and life was nonsense. He had to consider the heart of the matter, the essence. The essence was that housekeepers were hard to get, harder to get than ushers, than willing workers, than organists, than secretaries—yes, harder to get than assistants or vocations.

And she was a *saver*—saved money, saved electricity, saved string, bags, sugar, saved—him. That's what she did. That's what she said she did, and she was right, in a way. In a way, she was usually right. In fact, she was always right—in a way. And you could never get a Filipino to come way out here and live. Not a young one anyway, and he had never seen an old one. Not a Filipino. They liked to dress up and live.

Should he let it drop about Fish having one, just to throw a scare into her, let her know he was doing some thinking? No. It would be a perfect cue for the one about a man needing a woman to look after him. He was not up to that again, not tonight.

Now she was doing what she liked most of all. She was making a grand slam, playing it out card for card, though it was in the bag, prolonging what would have been cut short out of mercy in gentle company. Father Firman knew the agony of losing.

She slashed down the last card, a miserable deuce trump, and did in the hapless king of hearts he had been saving.

"Skunked you!"

She was awful in victory. Here was the bitter end of their long day together, the final murderous hour in which all they wanted to say—all he wouldn't and all she couldn't—came out in the cards. Whoever won at honeymoon won the day, slept on the other's scalp, and God alone had to help the loser.

"We've been at it long enough, Mrs. Stoner," he said, seeing her assembling the cards for another round.

"Had enough, huh!"

Father Firman grumbled something.

"No?"

"Yes."

She pulled the table away and left it against the wall for the next time. She went out of the study carrying the socks, content and clucking. He closed his eyes after her and began to get under way in the rocking chair, the nightly trip to nowhere. He could hear her brewing a cup of tea in the kitchen and conversing with the cat. She made her way up the stairs, carrying the tea, followed by the cat, purring.

He waited, rocking out to sea, until she would be sure to be through in the bathroom. Then he got up and locked the front door (she looked after the back door) and loosened his collar going upstairs.

In the bathroom he mixed a glass of antiseptic, always afraid of pyorrhea, and gargled to ward off pharyngitis.

When he turned on the light in his room, the moths and beetles began to batter against the screens, the lighter insects humming. . . .

Yes, and she had the guest room. How did she come to get that? Why wasn't she in the back room, in her proper place? He knew, if he cared to remember. The screen in the back room—it let in mosquitoes, and if it didn't do that she'd love to sleep back there, Father, looking out at the steeple and the blessed cross on top. Father, if it just weren't for the screen, Father. Very well, Mrs. Stoner, I'll get it fixed or fix it myself. Oh, could you now, Father? I could, Mrs. Stoner, and I will. In the meantime you take the guest room. Yes, Father, and thank you, Father, the house ringing with amenities then. Years ago, all that. She was a pie-faced girl then, not really a girl perhaps, but not too old to marry again. But she never had. In fact, he could not remember that she had even tried for a husband since coming to the rectory, but, of course, he could be wrong, not knowing how they went about it. God! God save us! Had she got her wires crossed and mistaken him all these years for *that*? *That!* Him! Suffering God! No. That was going too far. That was getting morbid. No. He must not think of that again, ever. No.

But just the same she had got the guest room and she had it yet. Well, did it matter? Nobody ever came to see him any more, nobody to stay overnight anyway, nobody to stay very long . . . not any more. He knew how they laughed at him. He had heard Frank humming all right—before he saw how serious and sad the situation was and took pity—humming, "Wedding Bells Are Breaking Up That Old Gang of Mine." But then they'd always laughed at him for something—for not being an athlete, for wearing glasses, for having kidney trouble . . . and mail coming addressed to Rev. and Mrs. Stoner.

Removing his shirt, he bent over the table to read the volume left open from last night. He read, translating easily, "Eisdem licet cum illis . . . Clerics are allowed to reside only with women about whom there can be no suspicion, either because of a natural bond (as mother, sister, aunt) or of *advanced age*, combined in both cases with good repute."

Last night he had read it, and many nights before, each time as though this time to find what was missing, to find what obviously was not in the paragraph, his problem considered, a way out. She was not mother, not sister, not aunt, and *advanced age* was a relative term (why, she was younger than he was) and so, eureka, she did not meet the letter of the law—but, alas, how she fulfilled the spirit! And besides it would be a slimy way of handling it after all her years of service. He could not afford to pension her off, either.

He slammed the book shut. He slapped himself fiercely on the back, missing the wily mosquito, and whirled to find it. He took a magazine and folded it into a swatter. Then he saw it—oh, the pre-ternatural cunning of it!—poised in the beard of St. Joseph on the bookcase. He could not hit it there. He teased it away, wanting it to light on the wall, but it knew his thoughts and flew high away. He swung wildly, hoping to stun it, missed, swung back, catching St. Joseph across the neck. The statue fell to the floor and broke.

Mrs. Stoner was panting in the hall outside his door.

"What is it!"

"Mosquitoes!"

"What is it, Father? Are you hurt?"

"Mosquitoes—damn it! And only the female bites!"

Mrs. Stoner, after a moment, said, "Shame on you, Father. She needs the blood for her eggs."

He dropped the magazine and lunged at the mosquito with his bare hand.

She went back to her room, saying, "Pshaw, I thought it was bur-glars murdering you in your bed."

He lunged again.

Annie Proulx

JOB HISTORY

Leeland Lee is born at home in Cora, Wyoming, November 17, 1947, the youngest of six. In the 1950s his parents move to Unique when his mother inherits a small dog-bone ranch. The ranch lies a few miles outside town. They raise sheep, a few chickens and some hogs. The father is irascible and, as soon as they can, the older children disperse. Leeland can sing "That Doggie in the Window" all the way through. His father strikes him with a flyswatter and tells him to shut up. There is no news on the radio. A blizzard has knocked out the power.

Leeland's face shows heavy bone from his mother's side. His neck is thick and his red-gold hair plastered down in bangs. Even as a child his eyes are as pouchy as those of a middle-aged alcoholic, the brows rod-straight above wandering, out-of-line eyes. His nose lies broad and close to his face, his mouth seems to have been cut with a single chisel blow into easy flesh. In the fifth grade, horsing around with friends, he falls off the school's fire escape and breaks his pelvis. He is in a body cast for three months. On the news an announcer says that the average American eats 8.6 pounds of margarine a year but only 8.3 pounds of butter. He never forgets this statistic.

When Leeland is seventeen he marries Lori Bovee. They quit school. Lori is pregnant and Leeland is proud of this. His pelvis gives him no trouble. She is a year younger than he, with an undistinguished, oval face, hair of medium length. She is a little stout but looks a confection in pastel sweater sets. Leeland and his mother fight over this marriage and Leeland leaves the ranch. He takes a job pumping gas at Egge Service Station. Ed Egge says, "You may fire when ready, Gridley," and laughs. The station stands at the junction of highway 16 and a county road. Highway 16 is the main tourist road to Yellowstone. Leeland buys Lori's father's old truck for fifty dollars and Ed rebuilds the engine. Vietnam and Selma, Alabama, are on the news.

The federal highway program puts through the new four-lane interstate forty miles south of highway 16 and parallel with it. Overnight the tourist business in Unique falls flat. One day a hundred cars stop for gas and oil, hamburgers, cold soda. The next day only two cars pull in, both driven by locals asking how business is. In a few months there is a FOR SALE sign on the inside window of the service station. Ed Egge gets drunk and, driving at speed, hits two steers on the county road.

Leeland joins the army, puts in for the motor pool. He is stationed in Germany for six years and never learns a word of the language. He comes back to Wyoming heavier, moodier. He works with a snow-fence crew during spring and summer, then moves Lori and the children—the boy and a new baby girl—to Casper where he drives oil trucks. They live in a house trailer on Poison Spider Road, jammed between two rioting neighbors. On the news they hear that an enormous diamond has been discovered somewhere. The second girl is born. Leeland can't seem to get along with the oil company dispatcher. After a year they move back to Unique. Leeland and his mother make up their differences.

Lori is good at saving money and she has put aside a small nest egg. They set up in business for themselves. Leeland believes people will be glad to trade at a local ranch supply store that saves a long drive into town. He rents the service station from Mrs. Egge who has not been able to sell it after Ed's death. They spruce it up, Leeland doing all the carpenter work, Lori painting the interior and exterior. On the side Leeland raises hogs with his father. His father was born and raised in Iowa and knows hogs.

It becomes clear that people relish the long drive to a bigger town where they can see something different, buy fancy groceries, clothing, bakery goods as well as ranch supplies. One intensely cold winter when everything freezes from God to gizzard, Leeland and his father lose 112 hogs. They sell out. Eighteen months later the ranch supply business goes under. The new color television set goes back to the store.

After the bankruptcy proceedings Leeland finds work on a road construction crew. He is always out of town, it seems, but back often enough for what he calls "a good ride" and so makes Lori pregnant again. Before the baby is born he quits the road crew. He can't seem to get along with the foreman. No one can, and turnover is high. On his truck radio he hears that hundreds of religious cult members have swallowed Kool-Aid and cyanide.

Leeland takes a job at Tongue River Meat Locker and Processing. Old Man Brose owns the business. Leeland is the only employee. He has an aptitude for sizing up and cutting large animals. He likes wrapping the tidy packages, the smell of damp bone and chill. He can throw his cleaver unerringly and when mice run along the wall they do not run far if Leeland is there. After months of discussion with Old Man Brose, Leeland and Lori sign a ten-year lease on the meat locker operation. Their oldest boy graduates from high school, the first in the family to do so, and joins the army. He signs up for six years. There is something on the news about school lunches and ketchup is classed as a vegetable. Old Man Brose moves to Albuquerque.

The economy takes a dive. The news is full of talk about recession and unemployment. Thrifty owners of small ranches go back to doing their own butchering, cutting and freezing. The meat locker lease payments are high and electricity jumps up. Leeland and Lori have to give up the business. Old Man Brose returns from Albuquerque. There are bad feelings. It didn't work out, Leeland says, and that's the truth of it.

It seems like a good time to try another place. The family moves to Thermopolis where Leeland finds a temporary job at a local meat locker during hunting season. A hunter from Des Moines, not far from where Leeland's father was born, tips him $100 when he loads packages of frozen elk and the elk's head onto the man's single-engine plane. The man has been drinking. The plane goes down in the Medicine Bow range to the southeast.

During this long winter Leeland is out of work and stays home with the baby. Lori works in the school cafeteria. The baby is a real crier and Leeland quiets him down with spoonsful of beer.

In the spring they move back to Unique and Leeland tries truck driving again, this time in long-distance rigs on coast-to-coast journeys that take him away two and three months at a time. He travels all over the continent, to Texas, Alaska, Montreal and Corpus Christi. He says every place is the same. Lori works now in the kitchen of the Hi-Lo Café in Unique. The ownership of the café changes three times in two years. West Klinker, an elderly rancher, eats three meals a day at the Hi-Lo. He is sweet on Lori. He reads her an article from the newspaper—a strange hole has appeared in the ozone layer. He confuses ozone with oxygen.

One night while Leeland is somewhere on the east coast the baby goes into convulsions following a week's illness of fever and cough. Lori makes a frightening drive over icy roads to the distant hospital. The baby survives but he is slow. Lori starts a medical emergency response group in Unique. Three women and two men sign up to take the first aid course. They drive a hundred miles to the first aid classes. Only two of them pass the test on the first try. Lori is one of the two. The other is Stuttering Bob, an old bachelor. One of the failed students says Stuttering Bob has nothing to do but study the first aid manual as he enjoys the leisured life that goes with a monthly social security check.

Leeland quits driving trucks and again tries raising hogs with his father on the old ranch. He becomes a volunteer fireman and is at the bad February fire that kills two children. It takes the fire truck three hours to get in to the ranch through the wind-drifted snow. The family is related to Lori. When something inside explodes, Leeland tells, an object flies out of the house and strikes the fire engine hood. It is a Nintendo player and not even charred.

Stuttering Bob has cousins in Muncie, Indiana. One of the cousins works at the Muncie Medical Center. The cousin arranges for the Medical Center to donate an old ambulance to the Unique Rescue Squad although they had intended to give it to a group in Mississippi. Bob's cousin, who has been to Unique, persuades them. Bob is afraid to drive through congested cities so Leeland and Lori take a series of buses to Muncie to pick up the vehicle. It is their first vacation. They take the youngest boy with them. On the return trip Lori leaves her purse on a chair in a restaurant. The gas money for the return trip is in the purse. They go back to the restaurant, wild with anxiety. The purse has been turned in and nothing is missing. Lori and Leeland talk about the goodness of people, even strangers. In their absence Stuttering Bob is elected president of the rescue squad.

A husband and wife from California move to Unique and open a taxidermy business. They say they are artists and arrange the animals in unusual poses. Lori gets work cleaning their workshop. The locals make jokes about the coyote in their window, posed lifting a leg against sagebrush where a trap is set. The taxidermists hold out for almost two years, then move to Oregon. Leeland's and Lori's oldest son telephones from overseas. He is making a career of the service.

Leeland's father dies and they discover the hog business is deeply in debt, the ranch twice-mortgaged. The ranch is sold to pay off debts. Leeland's mother moves in with them. Leeland continues long-distance truck driving. His mother watches television all day. Sometimes she sits in Lori's kitchen, saying almost nothing, picking small stones from dried beans.

The youngest daughter baby-sits. One night, on the way home, her employer feels her small breasts and asks her to squeeze his penis, because, he says, she ate the piece of chocolate cake he was saving. She does it but runs crying into the house and tells Lori who advises her to keep quiet and stay home from now on. The man is Leeland's friend; they hunt elk and antelope together.

Leeland quits truck driving. Lori has saved a little money. Once more they decide to go into business for themselves. They lease the old gas station where Leeland had his first job and where they tried the ranch supply store. Now it is a gas station again, but also a convenience store. They try surefire gimmicks: plastic come-on banners that pop and tear in the wind, free ice cream cones with every fill-up, prize drawings. Leeland has been thinking of the glory days when a hundred cars stopped. Now highway 16 seems the emptiest road in the country. They hold on for a year, then Leeland admits that it hasn't worked out and he is right. He is depressed for days when San Francisco beats Denver in the Super Bowl.

Their oldest boy is discharged from the service and will not say why but Leeland knows it is chemical substances, drugs. Leeland is driving long-distance trucks again despite his back pain. The oldest son is home, working as a ranch hand in Pie. Leeland studies him, looking for signs of addiction. The son's eyes are always red and streaming.

The worst year comes. Leeland's mother dies. Leeland hurts his back, and, in the same week, Lori learns that she has breast cancer and is pregnant again. She is forty-six. Lori's doctor advises an abortion. Lori refuses.

The oldest son is discovered to have an allergy to horses and quits the ranch job. He tells Leeland he wants to try raising hogs. Pork prices are high. For a few days Leeland is excited. He can see it clearly: Leeland Lee & Son, Livestock. But the son changes his mind when a friend he knew in the service comes by on a motorcycle. The next morning both of them leave for Phoenix.

Lori spontaneously aborts in the fifth month of the pregnancy and then the cancer burns her up. Leeland is at the hospital with her every day. Lori dies. The daughters, both married now, curse Leeland. No one knows how to reach the oldest son and he misses the funeral. The youngest boy cries inconsolably. They decide he will live in Billings, Montana, with the oldest sister who is expecting her first child.

Two springs after Lori's death a middle-aged woman from Ohio buys the café, paints it orange, renames it Unique Eats and hires Leeland to cook. He is good with meat, knows how to choose the best cuts and grill or do them chicken-fried style to perfection. He has never cooked anything at home and everyone is surprised at this long-hidden skill. The oldest son comes back and next year they plan to lease the old gas station and convert it to a motorcycle repair shop and steak house. Nobody has time to listen to the news.

Lewis Robinson

OFFICER FRIENDLY

Ziegler was into cheap thrills, like me, and cared only about not getting caught. We had this routine which involved going to the J.M. Biggies parking lot and sending bottle rockets over the road. Cars often stopped but we hid behind J.M. Biggies' dumpsters so people couldn't find us. One night a cop came into the parking lot at full speed without his lights on. This startled us. We started running. On the rink in skates I was quicker than Ziegler but on foot he had me. The cop spun to a stop in the snow and hopped out, like a pro. He hoofed it after us. Ziegler hit the snowbank just as the cop yelled "Freeze!"

I couldn't believe it. He actually yelled "Freeze!" as though he was in charge of the situation. We knew all the cops in Point Allison. They were subpar. This one yells "Freeze!" just as Ziegler is getting over the snowbank. I'm still running, and I'm thinking, This chump's going to shoot me. Shoot me dead for sending up bottle rockets. Sixteen years alive and I was going to get shot in the back by a Point Allison cop. The local force was generally incompetent but capable of occasional displays of accidental heroism. So I stopped, and the cop kept running, and just as I turned around he tackled me in the snowbank.

I'll hand it to the guy: it was a great takedown, executed cleanly, powerfully. In fact, the enthusiasm of the tackle sent his fur hat to the top of the snowbank. He held me and caught his breath. He was wheezing and his warm stomach was pressed against my chest.

"Don't . . ." he said, but then he had to catch his breath and start again. "Don't . . . ever . . . run . . . from . . . an officer . . . of . . . the law."

His nose was inches from my forehead. It was Officer Friendly, the cop who in fifth grade had visited our classroom to write the word DRUGS on the chalkboard. Later in his speech, he crossed the word out, and later still, he erased it. This routine was mimicked by many of us in the years that followed.

When he put his hands on the snow on either side of me to push himself up, his arms sunk in and he was pinning me again. I was pressed deeper into the snowbank.

"Just a minute," he said.

"No problem," I said.

In his squad car, we sat in silence near the sidewalk on Main Street. He idled the engine and set the heat at full blast, the blowers on our faces, and I wondered if he was trying to compose what he was going to say, or if his strategy was more fine-tuned, if in fact the silence was his way of trying to scare me, trying to get me to realize the gravity of the situation, the detriment of firecrackers. His breath was loud because he pushed it through his teeth. Aside from his gig as Officer Friendly, he patrolled the hockey games; I'd seen him standing by the entrance before the puck dropped, and once the action started he'd go up into the bleachers. His name tag said Belliveau. He looked my dad's age.

"You know what running does?" he asked.

I chose not to answer. It was obviously a trap. I almost said, Well, running got my buddy up and over the snowbank so he didn't have to get pinned by you in the snow, but I resisted.

"What running does, my friend, is that it makes you look like a real criminal," he said. "My guess is that you're not a real criminal. Why would you want me to think you're a real criminal?"

I suppose I didn't want to look like a criminal but I was annoyed that my jean jacket, black wool hat, and steel-toed boots didn't speak danger. Belliveau obviously didn't know the half of it.

"There are a lot of things you could have been doing back there," he said. "For all I know, you could have been using a controlled substance. I could go right down the list. Assault, vandalism, kidnapping, arson. The people who run away are the people who are doing the worst things. That makes sense to you, doesn't it, son?"

"Of course, sir," I said. But I was thinking: Right, Officer Friendly, okay, you're an idiot. That guy who got over the snowbank? I was kidnapping him, and now he's gotten away.

"What's your name, son?" he asked. There were dark stains under his arms and down the middle of his chest. He switched the heat to defrost. He'd done his share of good cop, now he'd go to bad cop. I knew the whole shtick.

"Charlie . . . Pinkie," I said.

"Pinkie. Huh. Haven't heard that name. Maybe you have some identification, Mr. Pinkie? Curious how you spell 'Pinkie.' If it's with a *y* or an *i-e* or *e-y*. Or is it double *e*?

Officer Friendly was getting cute on me. I didn't like that. It was common, though, among Point Allison cops. Ziegler and I would walk across the snowpack in front of the high school late at night and the cops would roll by slowly, then turn around even slower, so you could hear the squeal of the power steering and ice snapping under their tires. We loved it when they used the cruiser's loudspeaker. "HEY, YOU, UP BY THE SCHOOL."

This always made me shiver, in the good way—like when I saw myself on TV for the first time, Channel Six sports highlights, the Lewiston game. I was skating up the boards, and I was only on for a flash, but it was definitely me, in the blue helmet, right there on Channel Six.

"COME OVER HERE," they'd say into the loudspeaker, or better yet, "DROP TO THE GROUND."

They lowered their windows electronically; they clicked on their mag lights and shined them in our eyes. And all of them, every one, used that cute tone. Even Officer Friendly: full-guns cute.

"I don't have my wallet with me," I said.

"Mr. Pinkie doesn't have his wallet," he said, staring straight ahead. He adjusted himself. "What do you say I recognize you? That I know you play hockey with my son? I can make one quick call to dispatch. I find out exactly who you are. Find out exactly who your folks are. How about if I call them up? Tell them where you're at, that you're sitting here with me?"

So Belliveau had some moves. But I could call his bluff. There was no Belliveau on my hockey team. "Edward McFrance," I said. "My friends call me Eddie."

He picked up his police radio and said, "Joyce, patch me through to home, will you? Thanks."

The sound of a phone ringing came over the radio, and then someone picked up.

"Hello?" said the voice.

"Johnny, who's that kid on your team with the bad attitude, the one who scored the second goal on Sunday—he was in the crease but the ref didn't see it—you know, he put up his arms like he had just won the gold medal?"

"Jake Ritchie," the voice said.

"And who's his buddy?"

"Travis Ziegler."

"Okay, thanks, Johnny."

Johnny fucking Anderson. Damn. His mom marries a cop, and just like that he's an informant. Coach had a drill and Johnny fucking Anderson always had it in for me. Coach called the drill "battle chops." He'd select one of us to be the "war dog" and another to be the "gunner." Then he'd pick up a puck and throw it to the far corner of the ice, where it would slap and bounce its way to the boards. With a nod, Coach would send out the war dog, wait a few beats, and with a second nod, send in the gunner. Johnny Anderson always seemed to be my gunner. He'd catch me with his stick right under the shoulder blades, and when I bent over from the hit, he'd spear me in the gut. But Ziegler was Johnny's gunner once, and he dropped Johnny to the ice with a knee to the kidneys. I thought it was great. In fact, I laughed my ass off.

Belliveau took a small notepad from his chest pocket and clicked his pen against it. "Mr. Jake Ritchie, now I've got your name. And your friend Travis. You guys are on my list. You know about my list?"

I looked over and saw that he had spelled my name wrong and butchered Ziegler's. We were the only two names on the page. Then he wrote, in parentheses: Charlie Pinkie, Eddie McFrance.

"No, sir, I don't, sir," I said.

"Mr. Ritchie, don't be smart with me. Fleeing the scene, false imper-sonation. You deserve more than being on my list, not that being on my list is any small shake. This list goes to all the other cops, and if they catch you doing anything stupid—which is a long shot, right?—you'll be talking to me again, and it won't be anything like this."

Then he gave me more silence. There were no cars on the street. Where there wasn't snow, there was sand and ice. I looked down the street, toward Stegger's package store—Stegger had closed up hours ago, but he kept his fluorescents on. I looked back up the other way and saw an old man, stooped over, in a full-length trench coat. His move-ment down the sidewalk was so slow that it was barely noticeable.

Belliveau watched the old man as he neared the cruiser's head-lights. I'll agree that the guy was something worth staring at. Every step he took was hesitant, like a robot, and he was hunched so far over and had his hat pulled so far down that you couldn't see his face. He was shaking everywhere. He looked about a hundred years old. He must have really needed to get to Stegger's, and he must not have known that Stegger's was closed. It was 1 A.M. and well below freezing.

We were parked close enough to the sidewalk so that when the old man got in the beam of the headlights—and these were amped-up cop headlights—he moved like he was in strobe. He stopped in the lights and shook there, and when he took his next step, his feet went out from under him and he landed with a thud on his back.

"Wait here," said Belliveau. He got out of the cruiser and went to the old man, who was crumpled in a ball on his side.

It was obvious Belliveau didn't quite know how to approach the situation. He seemed the kind of cop comfortable breaking up pot parties or patrolling the ice rink during hockey games, drinking hot chocolate and nodding and smirking at the moms who had been in his high school class. He crouched down next to the old man and rested a hand on his crumpled trench coat. The old man was still shaking, but then he turned and with great force the old man yelled "FREEZE!" and I saw that it was not an old man at all; it was Ziegler.

Belliveau leapt back, but only seemed startled for a second: then I saw his face blazing in the headlights. His eyes were wide and his mouth was open and he went after Ziegler with his hands up like a linebacker. Ziegler sprung up and raced across the lot. Belliveau was after him. This was not much of a contest. Ziegler was a streak to the dumpsters, leaving Belliveau alone in the orange fluorescent lights, galloping, black uniform cast against the snowpack. I'll give it to Officer Friendly: he had a long stride and put in an admirable effort. He was just fat and slow.

At the dumpsters, again Belliveau was outmatched. We knew those dumpsters well. There was a crawl space underneath the middle one, and that's where Ziegler was hiding. I could see his breath coming out from below. Ziegler could have just sprinted over the snowbank again, but he wanted to mess with Belliveau, so just as Belliveau went looking behind the dumpsters, Ziegler shot out from the crawl space and was sprinting back across the lot. He was coming toward me, yelling, "Fuckface! Get out of the car!" Belliveau was still kicking like hell, and just as he sputtered a breathless "Freeze!" he belly-flopped on the snowpack.

Ziegler got to the cruiser and screamed, "Let's go!"

I pointed back in the direction of Belliveau. He was facedown, arms spread, legs spread, as though he had been dropped from the sky.

I got out of the cruiser and stood next to Ziegler and we stared back at Belliveau. He started moving his arms awkwardly, like he was trying to make a snow angel, but only in a lazy kind of way.

The first steps we took toward Belliveau felt wrong. Then we ran, and when we got to him, we could hear him moaning. Steam rose from his back. We struggled to flip him over. He had a scratch on his forehead, spit pooling on his chin, and two slugs of snot coming from his nostrils. He said, "My pocket." We just crouched there as he fumbled his hands around his belly. His eyes were wide and his face was red. He almost looked like a baby, jerking his arms without any real control. I put my hand in the rough pocket of his patrol pants but didn't find anything. Ziegler had his hand in the other pocket and he took out a small tin. He handed it to Belliveau, but Belliveau dropped it in the snow. Ziegler picked it up and handed it back to Belliveau and Belliveau dropped it again. Then Ziegler opened up the lid and took a tiny white pill from the tin and placed it under Belliveau's raised tongue. Belliveau closed his mouth, moaned again, held his chest, and rolled on his side.

"Let's get the fuck out of here," said Ziegler.

"Let's put him in the car," I said.

He could walk when the two of us flanked him, his arms around our shoulders. He was still wheezing but seemed better. He didn't look at us. We laid him in the back of the cruiser. Then Ziegler got in the driver's seat and picked up the part of the radio you talk into, stretching the curled cord. "Officer Friendly's hurt. He's at J.M. Biggies. We didn't do it."

He dropped the radio and we ran across the parking lot, past the dumpsters, over the snowbank, and across the soccer field behind the high school. The snow was over our knees so we had to high-step. I thought Ziegler knew where he was going and he probably thought

I knew where I was going. There were several fields linked up to the soccer field, most of them overgrown with crinkled milkweeds sticking up through the snow. We ran through a bunch of fields, too winded to talk. It was actually a pretty nice night, cold with lots of moonlight and no wind. I suspected we might he taking the fields in a round-about loop to Ziegler's brother's house. That was Wedge; he was a pothead who worked at Radio Shack and lived on his own. As we walked through the last field, I trudged in Ziegler's tracks, and when we got to Hanover Street we sat on a snowbank to catch our breath. All the nearby houses were dark.

"Johnny fucking Anderson," I said.

"What about him?" said Ziegler.

"His mom married Officer Friendly."

"Shitty luck."

Ziegler kicked an ice ball into the street and watched breath steam from his mouth. Then he got up and I followed; we walked the two blocks to Wedge's house. We could see from the light in the windows that his TV was on. We bounded up the stairs and through the front door. His living room was aglow with the show he was watching and Wedge was stretched out in his La-Z-Boy with a canister of potato chips. We jumped on his couch.

"What's up, boys," said Wedge. It was his usual greeting.

We were still winded, and my face burned from the heat of the room. My feet were numb. Wedge ate his chips and laughed at the TV.

"Hey, Wedge," said Ziegler. "We're fucking heroes."

James Salter

FOREIGN SHORES

Mrs. Pence and her white shoes were gone. She had left two days before, and the room at the top of the stairs was empty, cosmetics no longer littering the dresser, the ironing board finally taken down. Only a few scattered hairpins and a dusting of talcum remained. The next day Truus came with two suitcases and splotched cheeks. It was March and cold. Christopher met her in the kitchen as if by accident. "Do you shoot people?" he asked.

She was Dutch and had no work permit, it turned out. The house was a mess. "I can pay you $135 a week," Gloria told her.

Christopher didn't like her at first, but soon the dishes piled on the counter were washed and put away, the floor was swept, and things were more or less returned to order—the cleaning girl came only once a week. Truus was slow but diligent. She did the laundry, which Mrs. Pence who was a registered nurse had always refused to do, shopped, cooked meals, and took care of Christopher. She was a

hard worker, nineteen, and in sulky bloom. Gloria sent her to Eliza-
beth Arden's in Southampton to get her complexion cleared up and
gave her Mondays and one night a week off.

Gradually Truus learned about things. The house, which was a
large, converted carriage house, was rented. Gloria, who was twenty-
nine, liked to sleep late, and burned spots sometimes appeared in
the living room rug. Christopher's father lived in California, and
Gloria had a boyfriend named Ned. "That son of a bitch," she often
said, "might as well forget about seeing Christopher again until he
pays me what he owes me."

"Absoutely," Ned said.

When the weather became warmer Truus could be seen in the
village in one shop or another or walking along the street with
Christopher in tow. She was somewhat drab. She had met another
girl by then, a French girl, also an *au pair*, with whom she went to the
movies. Beneath the trees with their new leaves the expensive cars
glided along, more of them every week. Truus began taking Chris-
topher to the beach. Gloria watched them go off. She was often still
in her bathrobe. She waved and drank coffee. She was very lucky.
All her friends told her and she knew it herself: Truus was a prize.
She had made herself part of the family.

"Truus knows where to get pet mices," Christopher said.

"To get what?"

"Little mices."

"Mice," Gloria said.

He was watching her apply makeup, which fascinated him.
Face nearly touching the mirror, intent, she stroked her long lashes
upward. She had a great mass of blonde hair, a mole on her upper

lip with a few untouched hairs growing from it, a small blemish on her forehead, but otherwise a beautiful face. Her first entrance was always stunning. Later you might notice the thin legs, aristocratic legs she called them, her mother had them, too. As the evening wore on her perfection diminished. The gloss disappeared from her lips, she misplaced earrings. The highway patrol all knew her. A few weeks before she had driven into a ditch on the way home from a party and walked down Georgica Road at three in the morning, breaking two panes of glass to get in the kitchen door.

"Her friend knows where to get them," Christopher said.

"Which friend?"

"Oh, just a friend," Truus said.

"We met him."

Gloria's eyes shifted from their own reflection to rest for a moment on that of Truus who was watching no less absorbed.

"Can I have some mices?" Christopher pleaded.

"Hmm?"

"Please."

"No, darling."

"Please!"

"No, we have enough of our own as it is."

"Where?"

"All over the house."

"Please!"

"No. Now stop it." To Truus she remarked casually, "Is it a boy-friend?"

"It's no one," Truus said. "Just someone I met."

"Well, just remember you have to watch yourself. You never know who you're meeting, you have to be careful." She drew back slightly and examined her eyes, large and black-rimmed. "Just thank God you're not in Italy," she said.

"Italy?"

"You can't even walk out on the street there. You can't even buy a pair of shoes, they're all over you, touching and pawing."

It happened outside Dean and Deluca's when Christopher insisted on carrying the bag and just past the door had dropped it.

"Oh, look at that," Truus said in irritation. "I told you not to drop it."

"I didn't drop it. It slipped."

"Don't touch it," she warned. "There's broken glass."

Christopher stared at the ground. He had a sturdy body, bobbed hair, and a cleft in his chin like his banished father's. People were walking past them. Truus was annoyed. It was hot, the store was crowded, she would have to go back inside.

"Looks like you had a little accident," a voice said. "Here, what'd you break? That's all right, they'll exchange it. I know the cashier."

When he came out again a few moments later he said to Christopher, "Think you can hold it this time?"

Christopher was silent.

"What's your name?"

"Well, tell him," Truus said. Then after a moment, "His name is Christopher."

"Too bad you weren't with me this morning, Christopher. I went to a place where they had a lot of tame mice. Ever seen any?"

"Where?" Christopher said.

"They sit right in your hand."

"Where is it?"

"You can't have a mouse," Truus said.

"Yes, I can." He continued to repeat it as they walked along. "I can have anything I want," he said.

"Be quiet." They were talking above his head. Near the corner they stopped for a while. Christopher was silent as they went on talking. He felt his hair being tugged but did not look up.

"Say good-bye, Christopher."

He said nothing. He refused to lift his head.

In midafternoon the sun was like a furnace. Everything was dark against it, the horizon lost in haze. Far down the beach in front of one of the prominent houses a large flag was waving. With Christopher following her, Truus trudged through the sand. Finally she saw what she had been looking for. Up in the dunes a figure was sitting.

"Where are we going?" Christopher asked.

"Just up here."

Christopher soon saw where they were headed.

"I have mices" was the first thing he said.

"Is that right?"

"Do you want to know their names?" In fact they were two desperate gerbils in a tank of wood shavings. "Catman and Batty," he said.

"Catman?"

"He's the big one." Truus was spreading a towel, he noticed. "Do we have to stay here?"

"Yes."

"Why?" he asked. He wanted to go down near the water. Finally Truus agreed.

"But only if you stay where I can see you," she said.

The shovel fell out of his bucket as he ran off. She had to call him to make him come back. He went off again and she pretended to watch him.

"I'm really glad you came. You know, I don't know your name. I know his, but I don't know yours."

"Truus."

"I've never heard that name before. What is it, French?"

"It's Dutch."

"Oh, yeah?"

His name was Robbie Werner, "not half as nice," he said. He had an easy smile and pale blue eyes. There was something spoiled about him, like a student who has been expelled and is undisturbed by it. The sun was roaring down and striking Truus' shoulders beneath her shirt. She was wearing a blue, one-piece bathing suit underneath. She was aware of being too heavy, of the heat, and of the thick, masculine legs stretched out near her.

"Do you live here?" she said.

"I'm just here on vacation."

"From where?"

"Try and guess."

"I don't know," she said. She wasn't good at that kind of thing.

"Saudi Arabia," he said. "It's about three times this hot."

He worked there, he explained. He had an apartment of his own and a free telephone. At first she did not believe him. She glanced at him as he talked and realized he was telling the truth. He got two months of vacation a year, he said, usually in Europe. She imagined it as sleeping in hotels and getting up late and going out to lunch. She did not want him to stop talking. She could not think of anything to say.

"How about you?" he said. "What do you do?"

"Oh, I'm just taking care of Christopher."

"Where's his mother?"

"She lives here. She's divorced," Truus said.

"It's terrible the way people get divorced," he said.

"I agree with you."

"I mean, why get married?" he said. "Are your parents still married?"

"Yes," she said, although they did not seem to be a good example. They had been married for nearly twenty-five years. They were worn out from marriage, her mother especially.

Suddenly Robbie raised himself slightly. "Uh-oh," he said.

"What is it?"

"Your kid. I don't see him."

Truus jumped up quickly, looked around, and began to run toward the water. There was a kind of shelf the tide had made which hid the ocean's edge. As she ran she finally saw, beyond it, the little blond head. She was calling his name.

"I told you to stay up where I could see you," she cried, out of breath, when she reached him. "I had to run all the way. Do you know how much you frightened me?"

Christopher slapped aimlessly at the sand with his shovel. He looked up and saw Robbie. "Do you want to build a castle?" he asked innocently.

"Sure," Robbie said after a moment. "Come on, let's go down a little further, closer to the water. Then we can have a moat. "Do you want to help us build a castle?" he said to Truus.

"No," Christopher said, "she can't."

"Sure, she can. She's going to do a very important part of it for us."

"What?"

"You'll see." They were walking down the velvety slope dampened by the tide.

"What's your name?" Christopher asked.

"Robbie. Here's a good place." He kneeled and began scooping out large handfuls of sand.

"Do you have a penis?"

"Sure."

"I do, too," Christopher said.

She was preparing his dinner while he played outside on the terrace, banging on the slate with his shovel. It was hot. Her clothes were sticking to her and there was moisture on her upper lip, but afterward she would go up and shower. She had a room on the second floor—not the one Mrs. Pence had—a small guest room painted white with a crude patch on the door where the original lock had been removed. Just outside the window were trees and the thick hedge of the neighboring house. The room faced south and caught the breeze. Often in the morning Christopher would crawl into her bed, his legs cool and hair a little sour-smelling. The room was filled with molten light. She could feel sand in the sheets, the merest trace of it. She turned her head sleepily to look at her watch on the night table. Not yet six. The first birds were singing. Beside her, eyes closed, mouth parted to reveal a row of small teeth, lay this perfect boy.

He had begun digging in the border of flowers. He was piling dirt on the edge of the terrace.

"Don't, you'll hurt them," Truus said. "If you don't stop, I'm going to put you up in the tree, the one by the shed."

The telephone was ringing. Gloria picked it up in the other part of the house. After a moment. "It's for you," she called.

"Hello?" Truus said.

"Hi." It was Robbie.

"Hello," she said. She couldn't tell if Gloria had hung up. Then she heard a click.

"Are you going to be able to meet me tonight?"

"Yes, I can meet you," she said. Her heart felt extraordinarily light.

Christopher had begun to scrape his shovel across the screen. "Excuse me," she said, putting her hand over the mouthpiece. "Stop that," she commanded.

She turned to him after she hung up. He was watching from the door. "Are you hungry?" she asked.

"No."

"Come, let's wash your hands."

"Why are you going out?"

"Just for fun. Come on."

"Where are you going?"

"Oh, stop, will you?"

That night the air was still. The heat spread over one immediately, like a flush. In the thunderous cool of the Laundry, past the darkened station, they sat near the bar which was lined with men. It was noisy and crowded. Every so often someone passing by would say hello.

"Some zoo, huh?" Robbie said.

Gloria came there often, she knew.

"What do you want to drink?"

"Beer," she said.

There were at least twenty men at the bar. She was aware of occasional glances.

"You know, you don't look bad in a bathing suit," Robbie said.

The opposite, she felt, was true.

"Have you ever thought of taking off a few pounds?" he said. He had a calm, unhurried way of speaking. "It could really help you."

"Yes, I know," she said.

"Have you ever thought of modeling?"

She would not look at him.

"I'm serious," he said. "You have a nice face."

"I'm not quite a model," she murmured.

"That's not the only thing. You also have a very nice ass, you don't mind me saying that?"

She shook her head.

Later they drove past large, dark houses and down a road which unexpectedly opened at the end like the vista she knew was somehow opening to her. There were gently rolling fields and distant lights. A street sign saying Egypt Lane—she was too dizzy to read it—floated for an instant in the headlights.

"Do you know where we are?"

"No," she said.

"That's the Maidstone Club."

They crossed a small bridge and went on. Finally they turned into a driveway. She could hear the ocean when he shut off the ignition. There were two other cars parked nearby.

"Is someone here?"

"No, they're all asleep," he whispered.

They walked on the grass to the other side of the house. His room was in a kind of annex. There was a smell of dampness. The dresser was strewn with clothes, shaving gear, magazines. She saw all this vaguely when he struck a match to light a candle.

"Are you sure no one's here?" she said.

"Don't worry."

It was all a little clumsy. Afterward they showered together.

There was almost nothing on the menu Gloria was interested in eating.

"What are you going to have?" she said.

"Crab salad," Ned said.

"I think I'll have the avocado," she decided.

The waiter took the menus.

"A pharmaceutical company, you say?"

"I think he works for some big one," she said.

"Which one?"

"I don't know. It's in Saudi Arabia."

"Saudi Arabia?" he said doubtfully.

"That's where all the money is, isn't it?" she said. "It certainly isn't here."

"How'd she meet this fellow?"

"Picked him up, I think."

"Typical," he said. He pushed his rimless glasses higher on his nose with one finger. He was wearing a string sweater with the sleeves pulled up. His hair was faded by the sun. He looked very boyish and handsome. He was thirty-three and had never been married. There were only two things wrong with him: his mother had all the money in a trust, and his back. Something was wrong with it. He had terrible spasms and sometimes had to lie for hours on the floor.

"Well, I'm sure he knows she's just a baby-sitter. He's here on vacation. I hope he doesn't break her heart," Gloria said. "Actually, I'm glad he showed up. It's better for Christopher. She's less likely to return the erotic feelings he has for her."

"The what?"

"Believe me. I'm not imagining it."

"Oh, come on, Gloria."

"There's something going on. Maybe she doesn't know it. He's in her bed all the time."

"He's only five."

"They can have erections at five," Gloria said.

"Oh, really."

"Darling, I've seen him with them."

"At five?"

"You'd be surprised," she said. "They're born with them. You just don't remember, that's all."

She did not become lovesick, she did not brood. She was more silent in the weeks that followed but also more settled, not particularly sad. In the flat-heeled shoes which gave her a slightly dumpy appearance she went shopping as usual. The thought even crossed Gloria's mind that she might be pregnant.

"Is everything all right?" she asked.

"Pardon?"

"Darling, do you feel all right? You know what I mean."

There were times when the two of them came back from the beach and Truus patiently brushed the sand from Christopher's feet that Gloria felt great sympathy for her and understood why she was quiet. How much of fate lay in one's appearance! Truus' face seemed empty, without expression, except when she was playing with Christopher and then it brightened. She was so like a child anyway, a bulky child, an unimaginative playmate who in the course of things would be forgotten. And the foolishness of her dreams! She wanted to become a fashion designer, she said one day. She was interested in designing clothes.

What she actually felt after her boyfriend left, no one knew. She came in carrying the groceries, the screen door banged behind her. She answered the phone, took messages. In the evening she sat on the worn couch with Christopher watching television upstairs. Sometimes they both laughed. The shelves were piled with games, plastic toys, children's books. Once in a while Christopher was told to bring one down so his mother could read him a story. It was very important that he like books, Gloria said.

It was a pale blue envelope with Arabic printing in the corner. Truus opened it standing at the kitchen counter and began to read the letter. The handwriting was childish and small. *Dear Truus,* it said. *Thank you for your letter. I was glad to receive it. You don't have to put so many stamps on letters to Saudi Arabia though. One U.S. airmail is enough. I'm glad to hear you miss me.* She looked up. Christopher was banging on something in the doorway.

"This won't work," he said.

He was dragging a toy car that had to be pumped with air to run.

"Here, let me see," she said. He seemed on the verge of tears. "This fits here, doesn't it?" She attached the small plastic hose. "There, now it will work."

"No, it won't," he said.

"No, it won't," she mimicked.

He watched gloomily as she pumped. When the handle grew stiff she put the car on the floor, pointed it, and let it go. It leapt across the room and crashed into the opposite wall. He went over and nudged it with his foot.

"Do you want to play with it?"

"No."

"Then pick it up and put it away."

He didn't move.

"Put . . . it . . . away . . ." she said, in a deep voice, coming toward him one step at a time. He watched from the corner of his eye. Another tottering step. "Or I eat you," she growled.

He ran for the stairs shrieking. She continued to chant, shuffling slowly toward the stairs. The dog was barking. Gloria came in the door, reaching down to pull off her shoes and kick them to one side. "Hi any calls?" she asked.

Truus abandoned her performance. "No. No one."

Gloria had been visiting her mother, which was always tiresome. She looked around. Something was going on, she realized. "Where's Christopher?"

A glint of blond hair appeared above the landing.

"Hello, darling," she said. There was a pause. "Mummy said hello. What's wrong? What's happening?"

"We're just playing a game," Truus explained.

"Well, stop playing for a moment and come and kiss me."

She took him into the living room. Truus went upstairs. Sometime later she heard her name being called. She folded the letter which she had read for the fifth or sixth time and went to the head of the stairs. "Yes?"

"Can you come down?" Gloria called. "He's driving me crazy.

"He's impossible," she said, when Truus arrived. "He spilled his milk, he's kicked over the dog water. Look at this mess!"

"Let's go outside and play a game," Truus said to him. reaching for his hand which he pulled away. "Come. Or do you want to go on the pony?"

He stared at the floor. As if she were alone in the room she got down on her hands and knees. She shook her hair loose and made a curious sound, a faint neigh, pure as the tinkle of glass. She turned to gaze indifferently at him over her shoulder. He was watching.

"Come," she said calmly. "Your pony is waiting."

After that when the letters arrived, Truus would fold them and slip them into her pocket while Gloria went through the mail: bills, gallery openings, urgent requests for payment, occasionally a letter. She wrote very few herself but always complained when she did not receive them. Comments on the logic of this only served to annoy her.

The fall was coming. Everything seemed to deny it. The days were still warm, the great, terminal sun poured down. The leaves, more luxuriant than ever, covered the trees. Behind the hedges, lawn mowers made a final racket. On the warm slate of the terrace, left behind, a grasshopper, a veteran in dark green and yellow, limped along. The birds had torn off one of his legs.

One morning Gloria was upstairs when something happened to catch her eye. The door to the little guest room was open and on the night table, folded, was a letter. It lay there in the silence, half of it raised like a wing in the air. The house was empty. Truus had gone to shop and pick up Christopher at nursery school. With the curios-

ity of a schoolgirl, Gloria sat down on the bed. She unfolded the
envelope and took out the pages. The first thing her eye fell upon
was a line just above the middle. It stunned her. For a moment she
was dazed. She read the letter through nervously. She opened the
drawer. There were others. She read them as well. Like love letters
they were repetitions, but they were not love letters. He did more
than work in an office, this man, much more. He went through
Europe, city after city, looking for young people who in hotel rooms
and cheap apartments—she was horrified by her images of it—
stripped and were immersed in a river of sordid acts. The letters
were like those of a high school boy, that was the most terrible part.
They were letters of recruitment, so simple they might have been
copied out by an illiterate.

Sitting there framed in the doorway, her hand nearly trem-
bling, she could not think of what to do. She felt deeply upset,
frightened, betrayed. She glanced out the window. She wondered
if she should go immediately to the nursery school—she could
be there in minutes—and take Christopher somewhere where he
would be safe. No, that would he foolish. She hurried downstairs
to the telephone.

"Ned," she said when she reached him—her voice was shak-
ing. She was looking at one of the letters which asked a number of
matter-of-fact questions.

"What is it? Is anything wrong?"

"Come right away. I need you. Something's happened."

For a while then she stood there with the letters in her hand.
Looking around hurriedly, she put them in a drawer where garden
seeds were kept. She began to calculate how long it would he before
he would be there, driving out from the city.

She heard them come in. She was in her bedroom. She had regained her composure, but as she entered the kitchen she could feel her heart beating wildly. Truus was preparing lunch.

"Mummy, look at this," Christopher said. He held up a sheet of paper. "Do you see what this is?"

"Yes. It's very nice."

"This is the engine," he said. "These are the wings. These are the guns."

She tried to focus her attention on the scrawled outline with its garish colors, but she was conscious only of the girl at work behind the counter. As Truus brought the plates to the table, Gloria tried to look calmly at her face, a face she realized she had not seen before. In it she recognized for the first time depravity, and in Truus' limbs, their smoothness, their volume, she saw brutality and vice. Outside, in the ordinary daylight, were the trees along the side of the property, the roof of a house, the lawn, some scattered toys. It was a landscape that seemed ominous, too idyllic, too still.

"Don't use your fingers. Christopher," Truus said, sitting down with him. "Use your fork."

"It won't reach," he said.

She pushed the plate an inch or two toward him.

"Here, try now," she said.

Later, watching them play outside on the grass, Gloria could not help noticing a wild, almost a bestial aspect in her son's excitement, as if a crudeness were somehow becoming part of him. soiling him. A line from the many that lay writhing in her head came forth. *I hope you will be ready to take my big cock when I see you again. P.S. Have you had any big cocks lately? I miss you and think of you and it makes me very hard.*

"Have you ever read anything like that?" Gloria asked.

"Not exactly."

"It's the most disgusting thing. I can't believe it."

"Of course, she didn't write them," Ned said.

"She kept them, that's worse."

He had them all in his hand. *If you came to Europe it would be great,* one said. *We would travel and you could help me. We could work together. I know you would be very good at it. The girls we would be looking for are between 13 and 18 years old. Also guys, a little older.*

"You have to go in there and tell her to leave," Gloria said. "Tell her she has to be out of the house."

He looked at the letters again. *Some of them are very well developed, you would be surprised. I think you know the type we are looking for.*

"I don't know . . . Maybe these are just a silly kind of love letter."

"Ned, I'm not kidding, she said.

Of course, there would be a lot of fucking, too.

"I'm going to call the FBI."

"No," he said, "that's all right. Here, take these. I'll go and tell her."

Truus was in the kitchen. As he spoke to her he tried to see in her grey eyes the boldness he had overlooked. There was only confusion. She did not seem to understand him. She went in to Gloria. She was nearly in tears. "But why?" she wanted to know.

"I found the letters" was all Gloria would say.

"What letters?"

They were lying on the desk. Gloria picked them up.

"They're mine," Truus protested. "They belong to me."

"I've called the FBI," Gloria said.

"Please, give them to me."

"I'm not giving them to you. I'm burning them."

"Please let me have them," Truus insisted.

She was confused and weeping. She passed Ned on her way upstairs. He thought he could see the attributes praised in the letters, the Saudi letters, as he later called them.

In her room Truus sat on the bed. She did not know what she would do or where she would go. She began to pack her clothes, hoping that somehow things might change if she took long enough. She moved very slowly.

"Where are you going?" Christopher said from the door.

She did not answer him. He asked again, coming into the room.

"I'm going to see my mother," she said.

"She's downstairs."

Truus shook her head.

"Yes, she is," he insisted.

"Go away. Don't bother me right now," she said in a flat voice.

He began kicking at the door with his foot. After a while he sat on the couch. Then he disappeared.

When the taxi came for her, he was hiding behind some trees out near the driveway. She had been looking for him at the end.

"Oh, there you are," she said. She put down her suitcases and kneeled to say good-bye. He stood with his head bent. From a distance it seemed a kind of submission.

"Look at that," Gloria said. She was in the house. Ned was standing behind her. "They always love sluts," she said.

Christopher stood beside the road after the taxi had gone.

That night he came down to his mother's room. He was crying and she turned on the light.

"What is it?" she said. She tried to comfort him. "Don't cry, darling. Did something frighten you? Here, Mummy will take you upstairs. Don't worry. Everything will be all right."

"Good night, Christopher," Ned said.

"Say good night, darling."

She went up, climbed into bed with him, and finally got him to sleep, but he kicked so much she came back down, holding her robe closed with her hand. Ned had left her a note: his back was giving him trouble, he had gone home.

Truus' place was taken by a Colombian woman who was very religious and did not drink or smoke. Then by a black girl named Mattie who did both but stayed for a long time.

One night in bed, reading *Town and Country*, Gloria came across something that stunned her. It was a photograph of a garden party in Brussels, only a small photograph but she recognized a face, she was absolutely certain of it, and with a terrible sinking feeling she moved the page closer to the light. She was without makeup and at her most vulnerable. She examined the picture closely. She was no longer talking to Ned, she hadn't seen him for over a year, but she was tempted to call him anyway. Then, reading the caption and looking at the picture again she decided she was mistaken. It wasn't Truus, just someone who resembled her, and anyway what did it matter? It all seemed long ago. Christopher had forgotten about her. He was in school now, doing very well, on the soccer team already, playing with eight- and nine-year-olds, bigger than them and bright. He would be six three. He would have girlfriends hanging all over him, girls whose families had houses in the Bahamas. He would devastate them.

Still, lying there with the magazine on her knees she could not help thinking of it. What had actually become of Truus? She looked at the photograph again. Had she found her way to Amsterdam or

Paris and, making dirty movies or whatever, met someone? It was unbearable to think of her being invited to places, slimmer now, sitting in the brilliance of crowded restaurants with her complexion still bad beneath the makeup and the morals of a housefly. The idea that there is an unearned happiness, that certain people find their way to it, nearly made her sick. Like the girl Ned was marrying who used to work in the catering shop just off the highway near Bridgehampton. That had been a blow, that had been more than a blow. But then nothing, almost nothing, really made sense anymore.

Jim Shepard

MINOTAUR

Kenny I hadn't seen in, what, three, four years. Kenny started with me way back when, the two of us standing there with our hands in our pants right outside the wormhole. Kenny wanders into the Windsock last night like the Keith Richards version of himself with this girl who looks like some movie star's daughter. "Is that you?" he says when he spots me in a booth. "This is the guy you're always talking about?" Carly asks once we're a few minutes into the conversation. The girl's name turns out to be Celestine. Talking to me, every so often he gets distracted and we have to wait until he takes his mouth away from hers.

"So my husband brings you up all the time and then, when I ask what you did together, he always goes, 'I can't help you there,'" Carly tells him. "Which of course he knows I know. But he likes to say it anyway."

With her fingers Celestine brings his cheek over toward her, like nobody's talking, and once they're kissing she works on gently opening his mouth with hers. After a while he makes a sound that's apparently the one she wanted to hear, and she disengages and returns her attention to us.

"How's your wife?" Carly asks him.

Kenny says they're separated and that she's settled down with a project manager from Lockheed.

"Nice to meet you," Carly tells Celestine.

"Mmm-*hmm*," Celestine says.

The wormhole for Kenny and me was what people in the industry call the black world, which is all about projects so far off the books that you're not even allowed to put CLASSIFIED in the gap in your résumé afterwards. You're told during recruitment that people in the know will know, and that when it comes to everybody else you shouldn't give a shit.

If you want to know how big the black world is, go click on *COMPTROLLER* and then *RESEARCH AND DEVELOPMENT* on the DOD's Web site and make a list of the line items with names like Cerulean Blue and budgets listed as "No Number." Then compare the number of budget items you *can* add up, and subtract that from the DOD's printed budget. Now *there's* an eye-opener for you home actuaries: you're looking at a difference of forty billion dollars.

The black world's everywhere: regular air bases have restricted compounds; defense industries have permanently segregated sites. And anywhere that no one in his right mind would ever go to in the Southwest, there's a black base. Drive along a wash in the back of nowhere in Nevada and you'll suddenly hit a newish fence that goes on forever. Follow the fence and you'll encounter some bland-looking guys in an unmarked pickup. Refuse to do what they say and they'll shoot the tires out from under you and give you a lift to the county lockup.

All of this was *before* 9/11. You can imagine what it's like now.

For a while Kenny helped out at Groom Lake as an engineering troubleshooter for a C-5 airlift squadron that flew only late-night operations, ferrying classified aircraft from the aerospace plants to the test sites. They had a patch that featured a crescent moon over *NOYFB*. "None Of Your Fucking Business," he explained when I first saw it. He said that during the down time he hung with the stealth-bomber guys with their *Huge Deposit–No Return* jackets, and he told his wife when she asked that he worked in the Nellis Range, which was a little like telling someone that you worked in the Alps.

I'd met him a few years earlier when Minotaur was hatched out at Lockheed's Skunk Works. He'd been brought in for the sister program, Minion. We were developing an ATOP—an Advanced Technology Observation Platform—and even over the crapper it read: *Furtim Vigilans: Vigilance Through Stealth.*

It wasn't the secrecy as much as the slogans and patches and badges that drove Carly nuts. "Only you guys would have *patches* for secret programs," she said. "Like what're we supposed to do, be *intrigued? Guess* what's going on?"

In the old days Kenny's unit had as its symbol the mushroom, and under it, in Latin: *Always in the Dark.* The black world's big on patches and Latin. I had one for Minotaur that read *Doing God's Work with Other People's Money.* I'd heard there was a unit out at Point Mugu that had the ultimate patch: just a black-on-black circle.

"'*Gustatus Similis Pullus,*'" Carly said. She was tilting her head to read an oval yellow patch on Kenny's shoulder.

"You know Latin?" he asked.

"Do you know how long I've been tired of this?" she told him.

"*I* don't know Latin," Celestine volunteered.

"'Tastes Like Chicken,'" he translated.

"Nice," Carly told him.

"I don't get it," Celestine said.

"Neither does she," he told her.

"Oooh. Snap," Carly said.

"People're supposed to taste like chicken," I finally told them.

"Oh, right," Carly said. "So what're you guys doing, eating people?"

"That's what we do: we eat people," Kenny agreed. He made teeth with his forefingers and thumbs and had them bite up and down.

Carly gave him a head shake and turned to the bar. "Are we gonna order?" she asked.

It's all infowar now. Delivering or screwing up content. We can convince a surface-to-air missile that it's a Maytag dryer. Tell an over-the-horizon radar array that it's through for the day, or that it wants to play music. And we've got lookdown capabilities that can tell you from space whether your aunt's having a Diet Coke or a regular.

What Carly's forgetting is that it's not just about teasing. There's something to be said for esprit de corps. There's all that home-team stuff.

I heard from various sources that Kenny's been all over: Kirtland, Hanscom, White Sands, Groom Lake, Tonopah. "What's my motto?" he said, in front of his wife, the last time I saw him. "'A Lifetime of Silence,'" she answered back, as though he'd told her in the nicest possible way to go fuck herself.

What's it like? Carly asked me once. Not being able to tell the people you're *closest* to anything about what you care about most? She was talking about how upset I was at Kenny's having dropped right off the face of the earth. He'd gone off to his new assignment without a backwards glance some two weeks before, with not even a *Have a good one, bucko* left behind on a Post-it. She was talking about having just come home from a good vacation with her husband and watching him throw his drink onto the roof because of an e-mail in response to some inquiries that read *No can do, in terms of a back tell. Your Hansel stipulated no bread crumbs.*

The glass had rolled back off the shingles into the azaleas. By way of explaining the duration of my upset, I'd let her in on a little of what I'd risked by that little fishing expedition. I asked if she had any idea how long it took to get the kind of security clearance her breadwinner toted around or how many federales with pocket protectors had fine-tooth-combed my every last Visa bill.

"I almost said hello to you two Christmases ago," Kenny told me now. "Out at SWC in Schriever."

"You were at SWC in Schriever?" I asked.

"Oh, for Christ's sake," Carly said. "Don't talk like this if you're not going to tell us what it means."

"The Space Warfare Center in Colorado," Kenny said, shrugging when he saw my face. "Let's give the bad guys a fighting chance."

"I didn't know we *had* a Space Warfare Center," Celestine said.

"A Space Warfare Center?" Kenny asked her.

At our rehearsal dinner, now three years back in the rearview mirror, during a lull at our table Carly's college roommate said, "I never had a black eye, but I always kinda wished I did." Carly looked surprised and said, "Well, I licked one all over once." And everybody looked at her. "You licked a black eye?" I finally asked. And Carly went, "Oh, I thought she said 'black *guy*.'"

"You licked a black guy all over?" I asked her later that night. She couldn't see my face in the dark but she knew what I was getting at.

"I did. And it was *so* good," she said. Then she put a hand on the inside of each of my knees and spread my legs as wide as she could.

"What's the biggest secret you think I ever kept from you?" she asked during our most recent relocation, which was last Memorial Day. We had a parakeet in the backseat and were bouncing a U-Haul over a road that you would have said hadn't seen vehicular traffic in twenty-five years. I'd been lent out to Northrup and couldn't even tell her for how long.

"I don't know," I told her. "I figured you had nothing but secrets." Then she dropped the subject, so for two weeks I went through her e-mails.

"I don't know anything about this Kenny guy," she told me the day I threw the drink. "Except that you can't get over that he disappeared."

"You know, sometimes you just register a connection," I told her later that night in bed. "And not talking about it doesn't have to be some big deal."

"So it was kind of a romantic thing," she said.

"Yeah, it was totally physical," I told her. "Like you and your mom."

Carly had gotten this far by telling herself that compartmentalizing wasn't *all* bad: that some doors may have been shut off but that the really important ones were wide open. And in terms of intimacy, she was far and away as good as things were going to get for me. We had this look we gave each other in public that said, *I know. I already thought that.* We'd each been engaged when we met and we'd stuck with each other through a lot of other people's crap. Late at night we lay nose to nose in the dark and told each other stuff nobody else had ever heard us say. I told her about some of the times

I'd been a dick and she told me about a kid she'd miscarried, and about another she'd put up for adoption when she was seventeen. She had no idea where he was now, but not a day went by that she didn't think about it. We called them both Little Jimmy. And for a while there was all this magical thinking, and not asking each other all that much because we thought we already knew.

That not-being-on-the-same-page thing had become a bigger issue for me lately, though that's something she didn't know. Which is perfect, she would've said.

What I'd been working on at that point had gone south a little. Another way of putting it would be to say that what I was doing was wrong. The ATOP we'd developed for Minotaur had been an unarmed drone that could hover above one spot like a satellite couldn't, providing instant lookdown for as long as a battlefield commander wanted it. But how long had it taken for us to retrofit them with air-to-surface missiles? And how many Fiats and Citroëns have those drones taken out because somebody back in Langley thought the right target was in the car?

There was an army of us out there up to the same sorts of hijinks and not able to talk about it. Where I worked, everything was black: not only the test flights, but also the resupply, the maintenance, the search-and-rescue. And the security scrutiny never went away. The guy who led my last project team, at home when he went to bed, after he hit the lights, waved to the surveillance guys. His wife never understood why even in August they had to do everything under the sheets.

On black-world patches you see a lot of sigmas because that's the engineering symbol for the unknown value.

"The Minotaur's the one in the labyrinth, right?" the materials guy in my project team asked the first day. When I told him it was, he wanted to know if the Minotaur was supposed to know where it was going, or if it was lost, too. That'd be funny, I told him. And we joked about the monster and the hero just wandering around through all these dark corridors, nobody finding anybody.

And now here I was and here Kenny was, with poor Carly trying to get a fix on either one of us.

"So what brings you to this neck of the woods?" I finally asked him once we were well into our second drinks.

"You know how *sad* he was," Carly asked, "when he couldn't get in touch with you anymore?"

"How sad?" Kenny asked. Celestine seemed curious, too.

"I thought we were gonna have to get him some counseling," Carly said.

"It's hard to adjust to not being with me anymore," Kenny told her.

"So did he ever talk to you about me?" she asked.

"You came up," Kenny answered, and even Celestine picked up on the unpleasantness.

"I'm listening," Carly said.

"Oh, he was all hot to trot whenever he talked about you," Kenny said.

"Sang my praises, did he?" Carly's face had the expression she gets when somebody's tracked something into the house.

"When he wasn't shooting himself in the foot about you, he was pretty happy," Kenny said. "I called it his good-woman face."

"As in, I had one," I explained.

"Whenever he tied himself in knots about something, I called it his Little Jimmy face," he said. When Carly swung around toward him, he said, "Sorry, chief."

"That was a comic thing for you?" Carly asked me. "The kind of thing you'd tell like a funny story?"

"I never thought it was a funny story," I told her.

"There's his Little Jimmy face now," Kenny noted. When she looked at him again, he used his index fingers to pull down on his lower eyelids and made an Emmett Kelly frown.

"We started calling potential targets Little Jimmies," he said, "whenever we were going to bring the hammer down and maximize collateral damage."

Carly was looking at something in front of her the way you try not to move even your eyes to keep from throwing up. "What is that supposed to mean?" she finally said in a low voice.

"You know," Kenny told her. "'I don't wike the *wooks* of this . . .'"

"Is that Elmer *Fudd* you're doing?" Celestine wanted to know.

And how could you not laugh, watching him do his poor-sap-in-the-crosshairs shtick?

"This is just the fucking House of Mirth, isn't it?" Carly said. Because she saw on my face just how many doors she'd been dealing with all along, both open and shut, and she also saw the We're-in-the-boat-and-you're-in-the-water expression that guys cut from our project teams always got when they asked if there was anything *we* could do to keep them onboard.

"Jesus Fucking Christ," she said to herself, because her paradigm had suddenly shifted beyond what even she could have imagined. She thought she'd put up with however many years of stonewalling for a good reason, and she'd just figured out that as far as Castle Hubby went, she hadn't even crossed the moat yet.

Because here's the thing we hadn't talked about, nose to nose on our pillows in the dark: how *I've never been closer to anyone* isn't the

same as *We're so close*. That night I threw the drink, she asked why *I*
was so perfect for the black world, and I wanted to tell her, How am
I *not* perfect for it? It's a sinkhole for resources. Everyone involved
with it obsesses about it all the time. Even what the *insiders* know
about it is incomplete. Whatever stories you do get arrive without
context. What's not inconclusive is enigmatic, what's not enigmatic
is unreliable, and what's not unreliable is quixotic.

She hasn't left yet, which surprises *me*, let me tell you. The wait-
ress is showing some alarm at Carly's distress and I've got a hand on
her back. She accepts a little rubbing and then has to pull away. "I
gotta get out of here," she goes.

"That girl is not happy," Celestine says after she's gone.

"Does she even know about *your* kid?" Kenny asks.

The waitress asks if there's going to be a third round.

"What'd you do that for?" I ask him.

"What'd *I* do that for?" Kenny asks.

Celestine leans into him. "Can we *go*?" she asks. "Will you take
me back to the *room*?"

"So are you going after her?" Kenny asks.

"Yeah," I tell him.

"Just not right now?" Kenny goes.

I'd told Carly about the first time I noticed him. I'd heard about
this guy in design in a sister program who'd raised a stink about
housing the designers next to the production floor so there'd be
on-the-spot back-and-forth about problems as they developed. He
was twenty-seven at that point. I'd heard that he was so good at
aerodynamics that his co-workers claimed he could *see* air. As he
moved up we had more dealings with him at Minotaur. He had zero
patience for the corporate side, and when the programs rolled out

their annual reports on performance and everyone did their song-and-dance with charts and graphs, when his turn came he'd walk to the blackboard and write two numbers. He'd point to the first and go "That's how many we presold," and point to the second and go "That's how much we made," and then toss the chalk on the ledge and announce he was going back to work. He wanted to pick my brain about how I hid budgetary items on Minotaur and invited me over to his house and served hard liquor and martini olives. His wife hadn't come out of the bedroom. After an hour I asked if they had any crackers and he said no.

That last time I saw him, it was like he'd had me over just to watch him fight with his wife. When I got there, he handed me a Jose Cuervo and went after her. "What put a bug in *your* ass?" she finally shouted. And after he'd gone to pour us some more Cuervo, she said, "Would you please get outta here? Because you're not help-ing at all." So I followed him into the kitchen to tell him I was hitting the road, but it was like he'd disappeared in his own house.

On the drive home I'd pieced together, in my groping-in-the-dark way, that he was better at this whole lockdown-on-everybody-near-you deal than I was. And worse at it. He fell into it easier, and was more wrecked by it than I would ever be.

I told Carly as much when I got home, and she said, "Anyone's more wrecked by *everything* than you'll ever be."

And she'd asked me right then if I thought I was worth the work that was going to be involved in my renovation. By which she meant, she explained, that she needed to know if *I* was going to put in the work. Because she didn't intend to be in this alone. I was definitely willing to put in the work, I told her. And because of that she said that so was she.

She couldn't have done anything more for me than that. Meaning she's that amazing, and I'm that far gone. Because there's one thing I could tell her that I haven't told anybody else, including Kenny. At Penn my old classics professor had been a big-time pacifist—he always went on about having been in Chicago in '68—and on the last day of Dike, Eros, and Arete he announced to the class that one of our number had signed up with the military. I thought to myself: *Fuck you. I can do whatever I want.* I was already the odd man out in that class, the one whose comments made everyone look away and then move on. A pretty girl who I'd asked out shot me a look and then gave herself a pursed-lips little smile and checked her daily planner.

"So wish him luck," my old prof said, "as he commends himself over to the god of chaos." I remember somebody called out, "Good luck!" And I remember being enraged that I might be turning colors. "About whom," the prof went on, "Homer wrote, 'Whose wrath is relentless. Who, tiny at first, grows until her head plows through heaven as she strides the Earth. Who hurls down bitterness. Who breeds suspicion and divides. And who, everywhere she goes, makes our pain proliferate.'"

Elizabeth Strout

PHARMACY

For many years Henry Kitteridge was a pharmacist in the next town over, driving every morning on snowy roads, or rainy roads, or summertime roads, when the wild raspberries shot their new growth in brambles along the last section of town before he turned off to where the wider road led to the pharmacy. Retired now, he still wakes early and remembers how mornings used to be his favorite, as though the world were his secret, tires rumbling softly beneath him and the light emerging through the early fog, the brief sight of the bay off to his right, then the pines, tall and slender, and almost always he rode with the window partly open because he loved the smell of the pines and the heavy salt air, and in the winter he loved the smell of the cold.

The pharmacy was a small two-story building attached to another building that housed separately a hardware store and a small grocery. Each morning Henry parked in the back by the large metal bins, and then entered the pharmacy's back door, and went about switching on the lights, turning up the thermostat, or, if it was summer, getting the fans going. He would open the safe, put money in the register, unlock the front door, wash his hands, put on his white lab coat. The ritual was pleasing, as though the old store— with its shelves of toothpaste, vitamins, cosmetics, hair adornments, even sewing needles and greeting cards, as well as red rubber hot water bottles, enema pumps—was a person altogether steady and steadfast. And any unpleasantness that may have occurred back in his home, any uneasiness at the way his wife often left their bed to wander through their home in the night's dark hours—all this receded like a shoreline as he walked through the safety of his pharmacy. Standing in the back, with the drawers and rows of pills, Henry was cheerful when the phone began to ring, cheerful when Mrs. Merriman came for her blood pressure medicine, or old Cliff Mott arrived for his digitalis, cheerful when he prepared the Valium for Rachel Jones, whose husband ran off the night their baby was born. It was Henry's nature to listen, and many times during the week he would say, "Gosh, I'm awful sorry to hear that," or "Say, isn't that something?"

Inwardly, he suffered the quiet trepidations of a man who had witnessed twice in childhood the nervous breakdowns of a mother who had otherwise cared for him with stridency. And so if, as rarely happened, a customer was distressed over a price, or irritated by the quality of an Ace bandage or ice pack, Henry did what he could to rectify things quickly. For many years Mrs. Granger worked for him; her husband was a lobster fisherman, and she seemed to carry with her the cold breeze of the open water, not so eager to please a wary customer. He had to listen with half an ear as he filled prescriptions, to make sure she was not at the cash register dismissing a complaint. More than once he was reminded of that same sensation in watching to see that his wife, Olive, did not bear down too hard on Christopher over a homework assignment or a chore left undone; that sense of his attention hovering—the need to keep everyone content. When he heard a briskness in Mrs. Granger's voice, he would step down from his back post, moving toward the center of the store to talk with the customer himself. Otherwise, Mrs. Granger did her job well. He appreciated that she was not chatty, kept perfect inventory, and almost never called in sick. That she died in her sleep one night astonished him, and left him with some feeling of responsibility, as though he had missed, working alongside her for years, whatever symptom might have shown itself that he, handling his pills and syrups and syringes, could have fixed.

"Mousy," his wife said, when he hired the new girl. "Looks just like a mouse."

Denise Thibodeau had round cheeks, and small eyes that peeped through her brown-framed glasses. "But a nice mouse," Henry said. "A cute one."

"No one's cute who can't stand up straight," Olive said. It was true that Denise's narrow shoulders sloped forward, as though apologizing for something. She was twenty-two, just out of the state university of Vermont. Her husband was also named Henry, and Henry Kitteridge, meeting Henry Thibodeau for the first time, was taken with what he saw as an unself-conscious excellence. The young man was vigorous and sturdy-featured with a light in his eye that seemed to lend a flickering resplendence to his decent, ordinary face. He was a plumber, working in a business owned by his uncle. He and Denise had been married one year.

"Not keen on it," Olive said, when he suggested they have the young couple to dinner. Henry let it drop. This was a time when his son—not yet showing the physical signs of adolescence—had become suddenly and strenuously sullen, his mood like a poison shot through the air, and Olive seemed as changed and changeable as Christopher, the two having fast and furious fights that became just as suddenly some blanket of silent intimacy where Henry, clueless, stupefied, would find himself to be the odd man out.

But standing in the back parking lot at the end of a late summer day, while he spoke with Denise and Henry Thibodeau, and the sun tucked itself behind the spruce trees, Henry Kitteridge felt such a longing to be in the presence of this young couple, their faces turned to him with a diffident but eager interest as he recalled his own days at the university many years ago, that he said, "Now, say. Olive and I would like you to come for supper soon."

He drove home, past the tall pines, past the glimpse of the bay, and thought of the Thibodeaus driving the other way, to their trailer on the outskirts of town. He pictured the trailer, cozy and picked up—for Denise was neat in her habits—and imagined them sharing the news of their day. Denise might say, "He's an easy boss." And Henry might say, "Oh, I like the guy a lot."

He pulled into his driveway, which was not a driveway so much as a patch of lawn on top of the hill, and saw Olive in the garden. "Hello, Olive," he said, walking to her. He wanted to put his arms around her, but she had a darkness that seemed to stand beside her like an acquaintance that would not go away. He told her the Thibodeaus were coming for supper. "It's only right," he said.

Olive wiped sweat from her upper lip, turned to rip up a clump of onion grass. "Then that's that, Mr. President," she said. "Give your order to the cook."

On Friday night the couple followed him home, and the young Henry shook Olive's hand. "Nice place here," he said. "With that view of the water. Mr. Kitteridge says you two built this yourselves."

"Indeed, we did."

Christopher sat sideways at the table, slumped in adolescent gracelessness, and did not respond when Henry Thibodeau asked him if he played any sports at school. Henry Kitteridge felt an unexpected fury sprout inside him; he wanted to shout at the boy, whose poor manners, he felt, revealed something unpleasant not expected to be found in the Kitteridge home.

"When you work in a pharmacy," Olive told Denise, setting before her a plate of baked beans, "you learn the secrets of everyone in town." Olive sat down across from her, pushed forward a bottle of ketchup. "Have to know to keep your mouth shut. But seems like you know how to do that."

"Denise understands," Henry Kitteridge said.

Denise's husband said, "Oh, sure. You couldn't find someone more trustworthy than Denise."

"I believe you," Henry said, passing the man a basket of rolls. "And please. Call me Henry. One of my favorite names," he added. Denise laughed quietly; she liked him, he could see this.

Christopher slumped farther into his seat.

Henry Thibodeau's parents lived on a farm inland, and so the two Henrys discussed crops, and pole beans, and the corn not being as sweet this summer from the lack of rain, and how to get a good asparagus bed.

"Oh, for God's sake," said Olive, when, in passing the ketchup to the young man, Henry Kitteridge knocked it over, and ketchup lurched out like thickened blood across the oak table. Trying to pick up the bottle, he caused it to roll unsteadily, and ketchup ended up on his fingertips, then on his white shirt.

"Leave it," Olive commanded, standing up. "Just leave it alone, Henry. For God's sake." And Henry Thibodeau, perhaps at the sound of his own name being spoken sharply, sat back, looking stricken.

"Gosh, what a mess I've made," Henry Kitteridge said.

For dessert they were each handed a blue bowl with a scoop of vanilla ice cream sliding in its center. "Vanilla's my favorite," Denise said.

"Is it," said Olive.

"Mine, too," Henry Kitteridge said.

As autumn came, the mornings darker, and the pharmacy getting only a short sliver of the direct sun before it passed over the building and left the store lit by its own overhead lights, Henry stood in the back filling the small plastic bottles, answering the telephone, while Denise stayed up front near the cash register. At lunchtime, she unwrapped a sandwich she brought from home, and ate it in the back where the storage was, and then he would eat his lunch, and sometimes when there was no one in the store, they would linger with a cup of coffee bought from the grocer next door. Denise seemed a naturally quiet girl, but she was given to spurts of sudden talkativeness "My mother's had MS for years, you know, so starting way back we all learned to help out. All three of my brothers are different. Don't you think it's funny when it happens that way?" The oldest brother, Denise said, straightening a bottle of shampoo, had been her father's favorite until he'd married a girl her father didn't like. Her own in-laws were wonderful, she said. She'd had a boyfriend before Henry, a Protestant, and his parents had not been so kind to her. "It wouldn't have worked out," she said, tucking a strand of hair behind her ear.

"Well, Henry's a terrific young man," Henry answered.

She nodded, smiling through her glasses like a thirteen-year-old girl. Again, he pictured her trailer, the two of them like overgrown puppies tumbling together; he could not have said why this gave him the particular kind of happiness it did, like liquid gold being poured through him.

She was as efficient as Mrs. Granger had been, but more relaxed. "Right beneath the vitamins in the second aisle," she would tell a customer. "Here, I'll show you." Once, she told Henry she sometimes let a person wander around the store before asking if she could help them. "That way, see, they might find something they didn't know they needed. And your sales will go up." A block of winter sun was splayed across the glass of the cosmetics shelf, a strip of wooden floor shone like honey.

He raised his eyebrows appreciatively. "Lucky for me, Denise, when you came through that door." She pushed up her glasses with the back of her hand, then ran the duster over the ointment jars.

Jerry McCarthy, the boy who delivered the pharmaceuticals once a week from Portland—or more often if needed—would sometimes have his lunch in the back room. He was eighteen, right out of high school; a big, fat kid with a smooth face, who perspired so much that splotches of his shirt would be wet, at times even down over his breasts, so the poor fellow looked to be lactating. Seated on a crate, his big knees practically to his ears, he'd eat a sandwich that had spilling from it mayonnaisey clumps of egg salad or tuna fish, landing on his shirt.

More than once Henry saw Denise hand him a paper towel. "That happens to me," Henry heard her say one day. "Whenever I eat a sandwich that isn't just cold cuts, I end up a mess." It couldn't have been true. The girl was neat as a pin, if plain as a plate.

"Good afternoon," she'd say when the telephone rang. "This is the Village Pharmacy. How can I help you today?" Like a girl playing grown-up.

And then: On a Monday morning when the air in the pharmacy held a sharp chill, he went about opening up the store, saying, "How was your weekend, Denise?" Olive had refused to go to church the day before, and Henry, uncharacteristically, had spoken to her sharply. "Is it too much to ask," he had found himself saying, as he stood in the kitchen in his undershorts, ironing his trousers. "A man's wife accompanying him to church?" Going without her seemed a public exposure of familial failure.

"Yes, it most certainly is too goddamn much to ask!" Olive had almost spit, her fury's door flung open. "You have no idea how tired I am, teaching all day, going to foolish meetings where the goddamn principal is a moron! Shopping. Cooking. Ironing. Laundry. Doing Christopher's homework with him! And *you*—" She had grabbed on to the back of a dining room chair, and her dark hair, still uncombed from its night's disarrangement, had fallen across her eyes. "*You*, Mr. Head Deacon Claptrap Nice Guy, expect me to give up my Sunday mornings and go sit among a bunch of snot-wots!" Very suddenly she had sat down in the chair. "Well, I'm sick and tired of it," she'd said, calmly. "Sick to death."

A darkness had rumbled through him; his soul was suffocating in tar. The next morning, Olive spoke to him conversationally. "Jim's car smelled like upchuck last week. Hope he's cleaned it out."

Jim O'Casey taught with Olive, and for years took both Christopher and Olive to school.

"Hope so," said Henry, and in that way their fight was done.

"Oh, I had a wonderful weekend," said Denise, her small eyes behind her glasses looking at him with an eagerness that was so childlike it could have cracked his heart in two. "We went to Henry's folks and dug potatoes at night. Henry put the headlights on from the car and we dug potatoes. Finding the potatoes in that cold soil—like an Easter egg hunt!"

He stopped unpacking a shipment of penicillin, and stepped down to talk to her. There were no customers yet, and below the front window the radiator hissed. He said, "Isn't that lovely, Denise."

She nodded, touching the top of the vitamin shelf beside her. A small motion of fear seemed to pass over her face. "I got cold and went and sat in the car and watched Henry digging potatoes, and I thought: It's too good to be true."

He wondered what in her young life had made her not trust happiness, perhaps her mother's illness. He said, "You enjoy it, Denise. You have many years of happiness ahead." Or maybe, he thought, returning to the boxes, it was part of being Catholic—you were made to feel guilty about everything.

The year that followed—was it the happiest year of his own life? He often thought so, even knowing that such a thing was foolish to claim about any year of one's life, but in his memory, that particular year held the sweetness of a time that contained no thoughts of a beginning and no thoughts of an end, and when he drove to the pharmacy in the early morning darkness of winter, then later in the breaking light of spring, the full-throated summer opening before him, it was the small pleasures of his work that seemed in their simplicities to fill him to the brim. When Henry Thibodeau drove into the gravelly lot, Henry Kitteridge often went to hold the door open for Denise, calling out, "Hello there, Henry," and Henry Thibodeau would stick his head through the open car window and call back, "Hello there, Henry," with a big grin on a face lit with decency and humor. Sometimes there was just a salute. "Henry!" And the other Henry would return, "Henry!" They got a kick out of this, and Denise, like a football tossed gently between them, would duck into the store.

When she took off her mittens, her hands were as thin as a child's, yet when she touched the buttons on the cash register, or slid something into a white bag, they assumed the various shapes of a graceful grown woman's hands, hands—thought Henry—that would touch her husband lovingly, that would, with the quiet authority of a woman, someday pin a baby's diaper, smooth a fevered forehead, tuck a gift from the tooth fairy under a pillow.

Watching her, as she poked her glasses back up onto her nose while reading over the list of inventory, Henry thought she was the stuff of America, for this was back when the hippie business was beginning, and reading in *Newsweek* about the marijuana and "free love" could cause an unease in Henry that one look at Denise dispelled. "We're going to hell like the Romans," Olive said triumphantly. "America's a big cheese gone rotten." But Henry would not stop believing that the temperate prevailed, and in his pharmacy, every day he worked beside a girl whose only dream was to someday make a family with her husband. "I don't care about Women's Lib," she told Henry. "I want to have a house and make beds." Still, if he'd had a daughter (he would have loved a daughter), he would have cautioned her against it. He would have said: Fine, make beds, but find a way to keep using your head. But Denise was not his daughter, and he told her it was noble to be a homemaker—vaguely aware of the freedom that accompanied caring for someone with whom you shared no blood.

He loved her guilelessness, he loved the purity of her dreams, but this did not mean of course that he was in love with her. The natural reticence of her in fact caused him to desire Olive with a new wave of power. Olive's sharp opinions, her full breasts, her stormy moods and sudden, deep laughter unfolded within him a new level of aching eroticism, and sometimes when he was heaving in the dark of night, it was not Denise who came to mind but, oddly, her strong, young husband—the fierceness of the young man as he gave way to the animalism of possession—and there would be for Henry Kitteridge a flash of incredible frenzy as though in the act of loving his wife he was joined with all men in loving the world of women, who contained the dark, mossy secret of the earth deep within them.

"Goodness," Olive said, when he moved off her.

In college, Henry Thibodeau had played football, just as Henry Kitteridge had. "Wasn't it great?" the young Henry asked him one day. He had arrived early to pick Denise up, and had come into the store. "Hearing the people yelling from the stands? Seeing that pass come right at you and knowing you're going to catch it? Oh boy, I loved that." He grinned, his clear face seeming to give off a refracted light. "Loved it."

"I suspect I wasn't nearly as good as you," said Henry Kitteridge. He had been good at the running, the ducking, but he had not been aggressive enough to be a really good player. It shamed him to remember that he had felt fear at every game. He'd been glad enough when his grades slipped and he had to give it up.

"Ah, I wasn't that good," said Henry Thibodeau, rubbing a big hand over his head. "I just liked it."

"He was good," said Denise, getting her coat on. "He was really good. The cheerleaders had a cheer just for him." Shyly, with pride, she said. "Let's go, Thibodeau, let's *go*."

Heading for the door, Henry Thibodeau said, "Say, we're going to have you and Olive for dinner soon."

"Oh, now—you're not to worry."

Denise had written Olive a thank-you note in her neat, small handwriting. Olive had scanned it, flipped it across the table to Henry. "Handwriting's just as cautious as she is," Olive had said. "She is the *plainest* child I have ever seen. With her pale coloring, why does she wear gray and beige?"

"I don't know," he said, agreeably, as though he had wondered himself. He had not wondered.

"A simpleton," Olive said.

But Denise was not a simpleton. She was quick with numbers, and remembered everything she was told by Henry about the pharmaceuticals he sold. She had majored in animal sciences at the university, and was conversant with molecular structures. Sometimes on her break she would sit on a crate in the back room with the Merck Manual on her lap. Her child-face, made serious by her glasses, would be intent on the page, her knees poked up, her shoulders slumped forward.

Cute, would go through his mind as he glanced through the doorway on his way by. He might say, "Okay, then, Denise?"

"Oh, yeah, I'm fine."

His smile would linger as he arranged his bottles, typed up labels. Denise's nature attached itself to his as easily as aspirin attached itself to the enzyme COX-2; Henry moved through his day pain free. The sweet hissing of the radiators, the tinkle of the bell when someone came through the door, the creaking of the wooden floors, the ka-*ching* of the register: He sometimes thought in those days that the pharmacy was like a healthy autonomic nervous system in a workable, quiet state.

Evenings, adrenaline poured through him. "All I do is cook and clean and pick up after people," Olive might shout, slamming a bowl of beef stew before him. "People just waiting for me to serve them, with their faces hanging out." Alarm made his arms tingle.

"Perhaps you need to help out more around the house," he told Christopher.

"How dare you tell him what to do? You don't even pay enough attention to know what he's going through in social studies class!" Olive shouted this at him while Christopher remained silent, a smirk on his face. "Why, Jim O'Casey is more sympathetic to the kid than you are," Olive said. She slapped a napkin down hard against the table.

"Jim teaches at the school, for crying out loud, and sees you and Chris every day. What *is* the matter with social studies class?"

"Only that the goddamn teacher is a moron, which Jim understands instinctively," Olive said. "You see Christopher every day, too. But you don't know anything because you're safe in your little world with Plain Jane."

"She's a good worker," Henry answered. But in the morning the blackness of Olive's mood was often gone, and Henry would be able to drive to work with a renewal of the hope that had seemed evanescent the night before. In the pharmacy there was goodwill toward men.

Denise asked Jerry McCarthy if he planned on going to college. "I dunno. Don't think so." The boy's face colored—perhaps he had a little crush on Denise, or perhaps he felt like a child in her presence, a boy still living at home, with his chubby wrists and belly.

"Take a night course," Denise said, brightly. "You can sign up right after Christmas. Just one course. You should do that." Denise nodded, and looked at Henry, who nodded back.

"It's true, Jerry," Henry said, who had never given a great deal of thought to the boy. "What is it that interests you?"

The boy shrugged his big shoulders.

"Something must interest you."

"This stuff." The boy gestured toward the boxes of packed pills he had recently brought through the back door.

And so, amazingly, he had signed up for a science course, and when he received an A that spring, Denise said, "Stay right there." She returned from the grocery store with a little boxed cake, and said, "Henry, if the phone doesn't ring, we're going to celebrate."

Pushing cake into his mouth, Jerry told Denise he had gone to mass the Sunday before to pray he did well on the exam.

This was the kind of thing that surprised Henry about Catholics. He almost said, God didn't get an A for you, Jerry; you got it for yourself, but Denise was saying, "Do you go every Sunday?"

The boy looked embarrassed, sucked frosting from his finger. "I will now," he said, and Denise laughed, and Jerry did, too, his face pink and glowing.

.   .   .

Autumn now, November, and so many years later that when Henry runs a comb through his hair on this Sunday morning, he has to pluck some strands of gray from the black plastic teeth before slipping the comb back into his pocket. He gets a fire going in the stove for Olive before he goes off to church. "Bring home the gossip," Olive says to him, tugging at her sweater while she peers into a large pot where apples are burbling in a stew. She is making applesauce from the season's last apples, and the smell reaches him briefly—sweet, familiar, it tugs at some ancient longing—before he goes out the door in his tweed jacket and tie.

"Do my best," he says. No one seems to wear a suit to church anymore.

In fact, only a handful of the congregation goes to church regularly anymore. This saddens Henry, and worries him. They have been through two ministers in the last five years, neither one bringing much inspiration to the pulpit. The current fellow, a man with a beard, and who doesn't wear a robe, Henry suspects won't last long. He is young with a growing family, and will have to move on. What worries Henry about the paucity of the congregation is that perhaps others have felt what he increasingly tries to deny—that this weekly gathering provides no real sense of comfort. When they bow their heads or sing a hymn, there is no sense anymore—for Henry—that God's presence is blessing them. Olive herself has become an unapologetic atheist. He does not know when this happened. It was not true when they were first married; they had talked of animal dissections in their college biology class, how the system of respiration alone was miraculous, a *creation* by a splendid power.

He drives over the dirt road, turning onto the paved road that will take him into town. Only a few leaves of deep red remain on the otherwise bare limbs of the maples, the oak leaves are russet and wrinkled; briefly through the trees is the glimpse of the bay, flat and steel-gray today with the overcast November sky.

He passes by where the pharmacy used to be. In its place now is a large chain drugstore with huge glass sliding doors, covering the ground where both the old pharmacy and grocery store stood, large enough so that the back parking lot where Henry would linger with Denise by the dumpster at day's end before getting into their separate cars—all this is now taken over by a store that sells not only drugs, but huge rolls of paper towels and boxes of all sizes of garbage bags. Even plates and mugs can be bought there, spatulas, cat food. The trees off to the side have been cut down to make a parking lot. You get used to things, he thinks, without getting used to things.

It seems a very long time ago that Denise stood shivering in the winter cold before finally getting into her car. How young she was! How painful to remember the bewilderment on her young face; and yet he can still remember how he could make her smile. Now, so far away in Texas—so far away it's a different country—she is the age he was then. She had dropped a red mitten one night; he had bent to get it, held the cuff open and watched while she'd slipped her small hand in.

The white church sits near the bare maple trees. He knows why he is thinking of Denise with this keenness. Her birthday card to him did not arrive last week, as it has, always on time, for the last twenty years. She writes him a note with the card. Sometimes a line or two stands out, as in the one last year when she mentioned that Paul, a freshman in high school, had become obese. Her word. "Paul has developed a full-blown problem now—at three hundred pounds, he is obese." She does not mention what she or her husband will do about this, if in fact they can "do" anything. The twin girls, younger, are both athletic and starting to get phone calls from boys "which horrifies me," Denise wrote. She never signs the card "love," just her name in her small neat hand, "Denise."

In the gravel lot by the church, Daisy Foster has just stepped from her car, and her mouth opens in a mock look of surprise and pleasure, but the pleasure is real, he knows—Daisy is always glad to see him. Daisy's husband died two years ago, a retired policeman who smoked himself to death, twenty-five years older than Daisy; she remains ever lovely, ever gracious with her kind blue eyes. What will become of her, Henry doesn't know. It seems to Henry, as he takes his seat in his usual middle pew, that women are far braver than men. The possibility of Olive's dying and leaving him alone gives him glimpses of horror he can't abide.

And then his mind moves back to the pharmacy that is no longer there.

"Henry's going hunting this weekend," Denise said one morning in November. "Do you hunt, Henry?" She was getting the cash drawer ready and didn't look up at him.

"Used to," Henry answered. "Too old for it now." The one time in his youth when he had shot a doe, he'd been sickened by the way the sweet, startled animal's head had swayed back and forth before its thin legs had folded and it had fallen to the forest floor. "Oh, you're a softie," Olive had said.

"Henry goes with Tony Kuzio." Denise slipped the cash drawer into the register, and stepped around to arrange the breath mints and gum that were neatly laid out by the front counter. "His best friend since he was five."

"And what does Tony do now?"

"Tony's married with two little kids. He works for Midcoast Power, and fights with his wife." Denise looked over at Henry. "Don't say that I said so."

"No."

"She's tense a lot, and yells. Boy, I wouldn't want to live like that."

"No, it'd be no way to live."

The telephone rang and Denise, turning on her toe playfully, went to answer it. "The Village Pharmacy. Good morning. How may I help you?" A pause. "Oh, yes, we have multivitamins with no iron. . . . You're very welcome."

On lunch break, Denise told the hefty, baby-faced Jerry, "My husband talked about Tony the whole time we were going out. The scrapes they'd get into when they were kids. Once, they went off and didn't get back till way after dark, and Tony's mother said to him, 'I was so worried, Tony. I could kill you.'" Denise picked lint off the sleeve of her gray sweater. "I always thought that was funny. Worrying that your child might be dead and then saying you'll kill him."

"You wait," Henry Kitteridge said, stepping around the boxes Jerry had brought into the back room. "From their very first fever, you never stop worrying."

"I *can't* wait," Denise said, and for the first time it occurred to Henry that soon she would have children and not work for him anymore.

Unexpectedly Jerry spoke. "Do you like him? Tony? You two get along?"

"I do like him," Denise said. "Thank goodness. I was scared enough to meet him. Do you have a best friend from childhood?"

"I guess," Jerry said, color rising in his fat, smooth cheeks. "But we kind of went our separate ways."

"My best friend," said Denise, "when we got to junior high school, she got kind of fast. Do you want another soda?"

A Saturday at home: Lunch was crabmeat sandwiches, grilled with cheese. Christopher was putting one into his mouth, but the telephone rang, and Olive went to answer it. Christopher, without being asked, waited, the sandwich held in his hand. Henry's mind seemed to take a picture of that moment, his son's instinctive deference at the very same time they heard Olive's voice in the next room. "Oh, you poor child," she said, in a voice Henry would always remember—filled with such dismay that all her outer Olive-ness seemed stripped away. "You poor, poor child."

And then Henry rose and went into the other room, and he didn't remember much, only the tiny voice of Denise, and then speaking for a few moments to her father-in-law.

The funeral was held in the Church of the Holy Mother of Contrition, three hours away in Henry Thibodeau's hometown. The church was large and dark with its huge stained-glass windows, the priest up front in a layered white robe, swinging incense back and forth, Denise already seated in the front near her parents and sisters by the time Olive and Henry arrived. The casket was closed, and had been closed at the wake the evening before. The church was almost full. Henry, seated next to Olive toward the back, recognized no one, until a silent large presence made him look up, and there was Jerry McCarthy. Henry and Olive moved over to make room for him.

Jerry whispered, "I read about it in the paper," and Henry briefly rested a hand on the boy's fat knee.

The service went on and on; there were readings from the Bible, and other readings, and then an elaborate getting ready for Communion. The priest took cloths and unfolded them and draped them over a table, and then people were leaving their seats aisle by aisle to go up and kneel and open their mouths for a wafer, all sipping from the same large silver goblet, while Henry and Olive stayed where they were. In spite of the sense of unreality that had descended over Henry, he was struck with the unhygienic nature of all these people sipping from the same cup, and struck—with cynicism—at how the priest, after everyone else was done, tilted his beaky head back and drank whatever drops were left.

Six young men carried the casket down the center aisle. Olive nudged Henry with her elbow, and Henry nodded. One of the pallbearers—one of the last ones—had a face that was so white and stunned that Henry was afraid he would drop the casket. This was Tony Kuzio, who, thinking Henry Thibodeau was a deer in the early morning darkness just a few days ago, had pulled the trigger of his rifle and killed his best friend.

Who was to help her? Her father lived far upstate in Vermont with a wife who was an invalid, her brothers and their wives lived hours away, her in-laws were immobilized by grief. She stayed with her in-laws for two weeks, and when she came back to work, she told Henry she couldn't stay with them much longer; they were kind, but she could hear her mother-in-law weeping all night, and it gave her the willies; she needed to be alone so she could cry by herself.

"Of course you do, Denise."

"But I can't go back to the trailer."

"No."

That night he sat up in bed, his chin resting on both hands. "Olive," he said, "the girl is utterly helpless. Why, she can't drive a car, and she's never written a check."

"How can it be," said Olive, "that you grow up in Vermont and can't even drive a car?"

"I don't know," Henry acknowledged. "I had no idea she couldn't drive a car."

"Well, I can see why Henry married her. I wasn't sure at first. But when I got a look at his mother at the funeral—ah, poor thing. But she didn't seem to have a bit of oomph to her."

"Well, she's about broken with grief."

"I understand that," Olive said patiently. "I'm simply telling you he married his mother. Men do." After a pause, "Except for you."

"She's going to have to learn to drive," Henry said. "That's the first thing. And she needs a place to live."

"Sign her up for driving school."

Instead, he took her in his car along the back dirt roads. The snow had arrived, but on the roads that led down to the water, the fishermen's trucks had flattened it. "That's right. Slowly up on the clutch." The car bucked like a wild horse, and Henry put his hand against the dashboard.

"Oh, I'm sorry," Denise whispered.

"No, no. You're doing fine."

"I'm just scared. Gosh."

"Because it's brand-new. But, Denise, *nitwits* can drive cars."

She looked at him, a sudden giggle coming from her, and he laughed himself then, without wanting to, while her giggle grew, spilling out so that tears came to her eyes, and she had to stop the car and take the white handkerchief he offered. She took her glasses off and he looked out the window the other way while she used the handkerchief. Snow had made the woods alongside the road seem like a picture in black and white. Even the evergreens seemed dark, spreading their boughs above the black trunks.

"Okay," said Denise. She started the car again, again he was thrown forward. If she burned out the clutch, Olive would be furious.

"That's perfectly all right," he told Denise. "Practice makes perfect, that's all."

In a few weeks, he drove her to Augusta, where she passed the driving test, and then he went with her to buy a car. She had money for this. Henry Thibodeau, it turned out, had had a good life insurance policy, so at least there was that. Now Henry Kitteridge helped her get the car insurance, explained how to make the payments. Earlier, he had taken her to the bank, and for the first time in her life she had a checking account. He had shown her how to write a check.

He was appalled when she mentioned at work one day the amount of money she had sent the Church of the Holy Mother of Contrition, to ensure that candles were lit for Henry every week, a mass said for him each month. He said, "Well, that's nice, Denise." She had lost weight, and when, at the end of the day, he stood in the darkened parking lot, watching from beneath one of the lights on the side of the building, he was struck by the image of her anxious head peering over the steering wheel; and as he got into his own car, a sadness shuddered through him that he could not shake all night.

"What in hell ails you?" Olive said.

"Denise," he answered. "She's helpless."

"People are never as helpless as you think they are," Olive answered. She added, clamping a cover over a pot on the stove, "God, I was afraid of this."

"Afraid of what?"

"Just take the damn dog out," Olive said. "And sit yourself down to supper."

An apartment was found in a small new complex outside of town. Denise's father-in-law and Henry helped her move her few things in. The place was on the ground floor and didn't get much light. "Well, it's clean," Henry said to Denise, watching her open the refrigerator door, the way she stared at the complete emptiness of its new insides. She only nodded, closing the door. Quietly, she said, "I've never lived alone before."

In the pharmacy he saw that she walked around in a state of unreality; he found his own life felt unbearable in a way he would never have expected. The force of this made no sense. But it alarmed him; mistakes could be made. He forgot to tell Cliff Mott to eat a banana for potassium, now that they'd added a diuretic with his digitalis. The Tibbets woman had a bad night with erythromycin; had he not told her to take it with food? He worked slowly, counting pills sometimes two or three times before he slipped them into their bottles, checking carefully the prescriptions he typed. At home, he looked at Olive wide-eyed when she spoke, so she would see she had his attention. But she did not have his attention. Olive was a frightening stranger; his son often seemed to be smirking at him. "Take the garbage out!" Henry shouted one night, after opening the cupboard beneath the kitchen sink, seeing a bag full of eggshells and dog hairs and balled-up waxed paper. "It's the only thing we ask you to do, and you can't even manage that!"

"Stop shouting," Olive told him. "Do you think that makes you a man? How absolutely pathetic."

Spring came. Daylight lengthened, melted the remaining snows so the roads were wet. Forsythias bloomed clouds of yellow into the chilly air, then rhododendrons screeched their red heads at the world. He pictured everything through Denise's eyes, and thought the beauty must be an assault. Passing by the Caldwells' farm, he saw a handwritten sign, FREE KITTENS, and he arrived at the pharmacy the next day with a kitty-litter box, cat food, and a small black kitten, whose feet were white, as though it had walked through a bowl of whipped cream.

"Oh, Henry," Denise cried, taking the kitten from him, tucking it to her chest.

He felt immensely pleased.

Because it was such a young thing, Slippers spent the days at the pharmacy, where Jerry McCarthy was forced to hold it in his fat hand, against his sweat-stained shirt, saying to Denise, "Oh, yuh. Awful cute. That's nice," before Denise freed him of this little furry encumbrance, taking Slippers back, nuzzling her face against his, while Jerry watched, his thick, shiny lips slightly parted. Jerry had taken two more classes at the university, and had once again received A's in both. Henry and Denise congratulated him with the air of distracted parents, no cake this time.

She had spells of manic loquaciousness, followed by days of silence. Sometimes she stepped out the back door of the pharmacy, and returned with swollen eyes. "Go home early, if you need to," he told her. But she looked at him with panic. "No. Oh, gosh, no I want to be right here."

It was a warm summer that year. He remembers her standing by the fan near the window, her thin hair flying behind her in little undulating waves, while she gazed through her glasses at the windowsill. Standing there for minutes at a time. She went, for a week, to see one of her brothers. Took another week to see her parents. "This is where I want to be," she said, when she came back.

"Where's she going to find another husband in this tiny town?" Olive asked.

"I don't know. I've wondered," Henry admitted.

"Someone else would go off and join the Foreign Legion, but she's not the type."

"No. She's not the type."

Autumn arrived, and he dreaded it. On the anniversary of Henry Thibodeau's death, Denise went to mass with her in-laws. He was relieved when that day was over, when a week went by, and another, although the holidays loomed, and he felt trepidation, as though he were carrying something that could not be set down. When the phone rang during supper one night, he went to get it with a sense of foreboding. He heard Denise make small screaming sounds—Slippers had gotten out of the house without her seeing, and planning to drive to the grocery store just now, she had run over the cat.

"Go," Olive said. "For God's sake. Go over and comfort your girlfriend."

"Stop it, Olive," Henry said. "That's unnecessary. She's a young widow who ran over her cat. Where in God's name is your compassion?" He was trembling.

"She wouldn't have run over any goddamn cat if you hadn't given it to her."

He brought with him a Valium. That night he sat on her couch, helpless while she wept. The urge to put his arm around her small shoulders was very strong, but he sat holding his hands together in his lap. A small lamp shone from the kitchen table. She blew her nose on his white handkerchief, and said, "Oh, Henry. Henry." He was not sure which Henry she meant. She looked up at him, her small eyes almost swollen shut; she had taken her glasses off to press the handkerchief to them. "I talk to you in my head all the time," she said. She put her glasses back on. "Sorry," she whispered.

"For what?"

"For talking to you in my head all the time."

"No, no."

He put her to bed like a child. Dutifully she went into the bathroom and changed into her pajamas, then lay in the bed with the quilt to her chin. He sat on the edge of the bed, smoothing her hair until the Valium took over. Her eyelids drooped, and she turned her head to the side, murmuring something he couldn't make out. As he drove home slowly along the narrow roads, the darkness seemed alive and sinister as it pressed against the car windows. He pictured moving far upstate, living in a small house with Denise. He could find work somewhere up north; she could have a child. A little girl who would adore him; girls adored their fathers.

"Well, widow-comforter, how is she?" Olive spoke in the dark from the bed.

"Struggling," he said.

"Who isn't."

The next morning he and Denise worked in an intimate silence. If she was up at the cash register and he was behind his counter, he could still feel the invisible presence of her against him, as though she had become Slippers, or he had—their inner selves brushing up against the other. At the end of the day, he said, "I will take care of you," his voice thick with emotion.

She stood before him, and nodded. He zipped her coat for her.

. . .

To this day he does not know what he was thinking. In fact, much of it he can't seem to remember. That Tony Kuzio paid her some visits. That she told Tony he must stay married, because if he divorced, he would never be able to marry in the church again. The piercing of jealousy and rage he felt to think of Tony sitting in Denise's little place late at night, begging her forgiveness. The feeling that he was drowning in cobwebs whose sticky maze was spinning about him. That he wanted Denise to continue to love him. And she did. He saw it in her eyes when she dropped a red mitten and he picked it up and held it open for her. *I talk to you in my head all the time.* The pain was sharp, exquisite, unbearable.

"Denise," he said one evening as they closed up the store. "You need some friends."

Her face flushed deeply. She put her coat on with a roughness to her gestures. "I have friends," she said, breathlessly.

"Of course you do. But here in town." He waited by the door until she got her purse from out back. "You might go square dancing at the Grange Hall. Olive and I used to go. It's a nice group of people."

She stepped past him, her face moist, the top of her hair passing by his eyes. "Or maybe you think that's square," he said in the parking lot, lamely.

"I am square," she said, quietly.

"Yes," he said, just as quietly. "I am too." As he drove home in the dark, he pictured being the one to take Denise to a Grange Hall dance. "Spin your partner, and promenade . . . ," her face breaking into a smile, her foot tapping, her small hands on her hips. No—it was not bearable, and he was really frightened now by the sudden emergence of anger he had inspired in her. He could do nothing for her. He could not take her in his arms, kiss her damp forehead, sleep beside her while she wore those little-girl flannel pajamas she'd worn the night Slippers died. To leave Olive was as unthinkable as sawing off his leg. In any event, Denise would not want a divorced Protestant; nor would he be able to abide her Catholicism.

They spoke to each other little as the days went by. He felt coming from her now an unrelenting coldness that was accusatory. What had he led her to expect? And yet when she mentioned a visit from Tony Kuzio, or made an elliptical reference to seeing a movie in Portland, an answering coldness arose in him. He had to grit his teeth not to say, "Too square to go square dancing, then?" How he hated that the words *lovers' quarrel* went through his head.

And then just as suddenly she'd say—ostensibly to Jerry McCarthy, who listened those days with a new comportment to his bulky self, but really she was speaking to Henry (he could see this in the way she glanced at him, holding her small hands together nervously)—"My mother, when I was very little, and before she got sick, would make special cookies for Christmas. We'd paint them with frosting and sprinkles. Oh, I think it was the most fun I ever had sometimes"—her voice wavering while her eyes blinked behind her glasses. And he would understand then that the death of her husband had caused her to feel the death of her girlhood as well; she was mourning the loss of the only *herself* she had ever known—gone now, to this new, bewildered young widow. His eyes, catching hers, softened.

Back and forth this cycle went. For the first time in his life as a pharmacist, he allowed himself a sleeping tablet, slipping one each day into the pocket of his trousers. "All set, Denise?" he'd say when

it was time to close. Either she'd silently go get her coat, or she'd
say, looking at him with gentleness, "All set, Henry. One more day."

Daisy Foster, standing now to sing a hymn, turns her head and
smiles at him. He nods back and opens the hymnal. "A mighty for-
tress is our God, a bulwark never failing." The words, the sound
of the few people singing, make him both hopeful and deeply sad.
"You can learn to love someone," he had told Denise, when she'd
come to him in the back of the store that spring day. Now, as he
places the hymnal back in the holder in front of him, sits once more
on the small pew, he thinks of the last time he saw her. They had
come north to visit Jerry's parents, and they stopped by the house
with the baby, Paul. What Henry remembers is this: Jerry saying
something sarcastic about Denise falling asleep each night on the
couch, sometimes staying there the whole night through. Denise
turning away, looking out over the bay, her shoulders slumped, her
small breasts just slightly pushing out against her thin turtleneck
sweater, but she had a belly, as though a basketball had been cut in
half and she'd swallowed it. No longer the girl she had been—no
girl stayed a girl—but a mother, tired, and her round cheeks had
deflated as her belly had expanded, so that already there was a look
of the gravity of life weighing her down. It was at that point Jerry
said sharply, "Denise, stand up straight. Put your shoulders back."
He looked at Henry, shaking his head. "How many times do I keep
telling her that?"

   "Have some chowder," Henry said. "Olive made it last night." But
they had to get going, and when they left, he said nothing about their
visit, and neither did Olive, surprisingly. He would not have thought
Jerry would grow into that sort of man, large, clean-looking—thanks

to the ministrations of Denise—not even so much fat anymore, just a big man earning a big salary, speaking to his wife in a way Olive had sometimes spoken to Henry. He did not see her again, although she must have been in the region. In her birthday notes, she reported the death of her mother, then, a few years later, her father. Of course she would have driven north to go to the funerals. Did she think of him? Did she and Jerry stop and visit the grave of Henry Thibodeau?

"You're looking fresh as a daisy," he tells Daisy Foster in the parking lot outside the church. It is their joke; he has said it to her for years.

"How's Olive?" Daisy's blue eyes are still large and lovely, her smile ever present.

"Olive's fine. Home keeping the fires burning. And what's new with you?"

"I have a beau." She says this quietly, putting a hand to her mouth.

"Do you? Daisy, that's wonderful."

"Sells insurance in Heathwick during the day, and takes me dancing on Friday nights."

"Oh, that's wonderful," Henry says again. "You'll have to bring him around for supper."

"Why do you need everyone married?" Christopher has said to him angrily, when Henry has asked about his son's life. "Why can't you just leave people alone?"

He doesn't want people alone.

At home, Olive nods to the table, where a card from Denise lies next to an African violet. "Came yesterday," Olive says. "I forgot."

Henry sits down heavily and opens it with his pen, finds his glasses, peers at it. Her note is longer than usual. She had a scare late in the summer. Pericardial effusion, which turned out to be nothing. "It changed me," she wrote, "as experiences do. It put all my priorities straight, and I have lived every day since then with the deepest gratitude for my family. Nothing matters except family and friends," she wrote, in her neat, small hand. "And I have been blessed with both."

The card, for the first time ever, was signed, "Love."

"How is she?" asks Olive, running water into the sink. Henry stares out at the bay, at the skinny spruce trees along the edge of the cove, and it seems beautiful to him, God's magnificence there in the quiet stateliness of the coastline and the slightly rocking water.

"She's fine," he answers. Not at the moment, but soon, he will walk over to Olive and put his hand on her arm. Olive, who has lived through her own sorrows. For he understood long ago—after Jim O'Casey's car went off the road, and Olive spent weeks going straight to bed after supper, sobbing harshly into a pillow—Henry understood then that Olive had loved Jim O'Casey, had possibly been loved by him, though Henry never asked her and she never told, just as he did not tell her of the gripping, sickening need he felt for Denise until the day she came to him to report Jerry's proposal, and he said: "Go."

He puts the card on the windowsill. He has wondered what it has felt like for her to write the words *Dear Henry*. Has she known other Henrys since then? He has no way of knowing. Nor does he know what happened to Tony Kuzio, or whether candles are still being lit for Henry Thibodeau in church.

Henry stands up, Daisy Foster fleeting through his mind, her smile as she spoke of going dancing. The relief that he just felt over

Denise's note, that she is glad for the life that unfolded before her, gives way suddenly, queerly, into an odd sense of loss, as if something significant has been taken from him. "Olive," he says.

She must not hear him because of the water running into the sink. She is not as tall as she used to be, and is broader across her back. The water stops. "Olive," he says, and she turns. "You're not going to leave me, are you?"

"Oh, for God's sake, Henry. You could make a woman sick." She wipes her hands quickly on a towel.

He nods. How could he ever tell her—he could not—that all these years of feeling guilty about Denise have carried with them the kernel of still having her? He cannot even bear this thought, and in a moment it will be gone, dismissed as not true. For who could bear to think of himself this way, as a man deflated by the good fortune of others? No, such a thing is ludicrous.

"Daisy has a fellow," he says. "We need to have them over soon."

Eudora Welty

DEATH OF A
TRAVELING SALESMAN

R. J. Bowman, who for fourteen years had traveled for a shoe company through Mississippi, drove his Ford along a rutted dirt path. It was a long day! The time did not seem to clear the noon hurdle and settle into soft afternoon. The sun, keeping its strength here even in winter, stayed at the top of the sky, and every time Bowman stuck his head out of the dusty car to stare up the road, it seemed to reach a long arm down and push against the top of his head, right through his hat—like the practical joke of an old drummer, long on the road. It made him feel all the more angry and helpless. He was feverish, and he was not quite sure of the way.

This was his first day back on the road after a long siege of influenza. He had had very high fever, and dreams, and had become weakened and pale, enough to tell the difference in the mirror, and he could not think clearly. . . . All afternoon, in the midst of his anger, and for no reason, he had thought of his dead grandmother. She had been a comfortable soul. Once more Bowman wished he could fall into the big feather bed that had been in her room. . . . Then he forgot her again.

This desolate hill country! And he seemed to be going the wrong way—it was as if he were going back, far back. There was not a house in sight. . . . There was no use wishing he were back in bed, though. By paying the hotel doctor his bill he had proved his recovery. He had not even been sorry when the pretty trained nurse said good-bye. He did not like illness, he distrusted it, as he distrusted the road without signposts. It angered him. He had given the nurse a really expensive bracelet, just because she was packing up her bag and leaving.

But now—what if in fourteen years on the road he had never been ill before and never had an accident? His record was broken, and he had even begun almost to question it. . . . He had gradually put up at better hotels, in the bigger towns, but weren't they all, eternally, stuffy in summer and drafty in winter? Women? He could only remember if he thought of one woman he saw the worn loneliness that the furniture of that room seemed built of. And he himself—he was a man who always wore rather wide-brimmed black hats, and in the wavy hotel mirrors had looked something like a bullfighter, as he paused for that inevitable instant on the landing, walking downstairs to supper. . . . He leaned out of the car again, and once more the sun pushed at his head.

Bowman had wanted to reach Beulah by dark, to go to bed and sleep off his fatigue. As he remembered, Beulah was fifty miles away from the last town, on a graveled road. This was only a cow trail.

How had he ever come to such a place? One hand wiped the sweat from his face, and he drove on.

He had made the Beulah trip before. But he had never seen this hill or this petering-out path before—or that cloud, he thought shyly, looking up and then down quickly—any more than he had seen this day before. Why did he not admit he was simply lost and had been for miles? . . . He was not in the habit of asking the way of strangers, and these people never knew where the very roads they lived on went to; but then he had not even been close enough to anyone to call out. People standing in the fields now and then, or on top of the haystacks, had been too far away, looking like leaning sticks or weeds, turning a little at the solitary rattle of his car across their countryside, watching the pale sobered winter dust where it chunked out behind like big squashes down the road. The stares of these distant people had followed him solidly like a wall, impenetrable, behind which they turned back after he had passed.

The cloud floated there to one side like the bolster on his grandmother's bed. It went over a cabin on the edge of a hill, where two bare chinaberry trees clutched at the sky. He drove through a heap of dead oak leaves, his wheels stirring their weightless sides to make a silvery melancholy whistle as the car passed through their bed. No car had been along this way ahead of him. Then he saw that he was on the edge of a ravine that fell away, a red erosion, and that this was indeed the road's end.

He pulled the brake. But it did not hold, though he put all his strength into it. The car, tipped toward the edge, rolled a little. Without doubt, it was going over the bank.

He got out quietly, as though some mischief had been done him and he had his dignity to remember. He lifted his bag and sample case out, set them down, and stood back and watched the car roll over the edge. He heard something—not the crash he was listening for, but a slow, unuproarious crackle. Rather distastefully he went to look over, and he saw that his car had fallen into a tangle of immense grapevines as thick as his arm, which caught it and held it, rocked it like a grotesque child in a dark cradle, and then, as he watched, concerned somehow that he was not still inside it, released it gently to the ground.

He sighed.

Where am I? he wondered with a shock. Why didn't I do something? All his anger seemed to have drifted away from him. There was the house, back on the hill. He took a bag in each hand and with almost childlike willingness went toward it. But his breathing came with difficulty, and he had to stop to rest.

It was a shotgun house, two rooms and an open passage between, perched on the hill. The whole cabin slanted a little under the heavy heaped-up vine that covered the roof, light and green, as though forgotten from summer. A woman stood in the passage.

He stopped still. Then all of a sudden his heart began to behave strangely. Like a rocket set off, it began to leap and expand into uneven patterns of beats which showered into his brain, and he could not think. But in scattering and falling it made no noise. It shot up with great power, almost elation, and fell gently, like acrobats into nets. It began to pound profoundly, then waited irresponsibly, hitting in some sort of inward mockery first at his ribs, then against his eyes, then under his shoulder blades, and against the roof of his mouth when he tried to say, "Good afternoon, madam." But he could not hear his heart—it was as quiet as ashes falling. This was rather comforting; still, it was shocking to Bowman to feel his heart beating at all.

Stock-still in his confusion, he dropped his bags, which seemed to drift in slow bulks gracefully through the air and to cushion themselves on the gray prostrate grass near the doorstep.

As for the woman standing there, he saw at once that she was old. Since she could not possibly hear his heart, he ignored the pounding and now looked at her carefully, and yet in his distraction dreamily, with his mouth open.

She had been cleaning the lamp, and held it, half blackened, half clear, in front of her. He saw her with the dark passage behind her. She was a big woman with a weather-beaten but unwrinkled face; her lips were held tightly together, and her eyes looked with a curious dulled brightness into his. He looked at her shoes, which were like bundles. If it were summer she would be barefoot. . . . Bowman, who automatically judged a woman's age on sight, set her age at fifty. She wore a formless garment of some gray coarse material, rough-dried from a washing, from which her arms appeared pink and unexpectedly round. When she never said a word, and sustained her quiet pose of holding the lamp, he was convinced of the strength in her body.

"Good afternoon, madam," he said.

She stared on, whether at him or at the air around him he could not tell, but after a moment she lowered her eyes to show that she would listen to whatever he had to say.

"I wonder if you would be interested—" He tried once more. "An accident—my car . . ."

Her voice emerged low and remote, like a sound across a lake. "Sonny he ain't here."

"Sonny?"

"Sonny ain't here now."

Her son—a fellow able to bring my car up, he decided in blurred relief. He pointed down the hill. "My car's in the bottom of the ditch. I'll need help."

"Sonny ain't here, but he'll be here."

She was becoming clearer to him and her voice stronger, and Bowman saw that she was stupid.

He was hardly surprised at the deepening postponement and tedium of his journey. He took a breath, and heard his voice speaking over the silent blows of his heart. "I was sick. I am not strong yet. . . . May I come in?"

He stooped and laid his big black hat over the handle on his bag. It was a humble motion, almost a bow, that instantly struck him as absurd and betraying of all his weakness. He looked up at the woman, the wind blowing his hair. He might have continued for a long time in this unfamiliar attitude; he had never been a patient man, but when he was sick he had learned to sink submissively into the pillows, to wait for his medicine. He waited on the woman.

Then she, looking at him with blue eyes, turned and held open the door, and after a moment Bowman, as if convinced in his action, stood erect and followed her in.

Inside, the darkness of the house touched him like a professional hand, the doctor's. The woman set the half-cleaned lamp on a table in the center of the room and pointed, also like a professional person, a guide, to a chair with a yellow cowhide seat. She herself crouched on the hearth, drawing her knees up under the shapeless dress.

At first he felt hopefully secure. His heart was quieter. The room was enclosed in the gloom of yellow pine boards. He could see the other room, with the foot of an iron bed showing, across the passage. The bed had been made up with a red-and-yellow pieced quilt that looked like a map or a picture, a little like his grandmother's girlhood painting of Rome burning.

He had ached for coolness, but in this room it was cold. He stared at the hearth with dead coals lying on it and iron pots in the corners. The hearth and smoked chimney were of the stone he had seen ribbing the hills, mostly slate. Why is there no fire? he wondered.

And it was so still. The silence of the fields seemed to enter and move familiarly through the house. The wind used the open hall. He felt that he was in a mysterious, quiet, cool danger. It was necessary to do what? . . . To talk.

"I have a nice line of women's low-priced shoes . . ." he said.

But the woman answered, "Sonny'll be here. He's strong. Sonny'll move your car."

"Where is he now?"

"Farms for Mr. Redmond."

Mr. Redmond. Mr. Redmond. That was someone he would never have to encounter, and he was glad. Somehow the name did not appeal to him. . . . In a flare of touchiness and anxiety, Bowman wished to avoid even mention of unknown men and their unknown farms.

"Do you two live here alone?" He was surprised to hear his old voice, chatty, confidential, inflected for selling shoes, asking a question like that—a thing he did not even want to know.

"Yes. We are alone."

He was surprised at the way she answered. She had taken a long time to say that. She had nodded her head in a deep way too. Had she wished to affect him with some sort of premonition? he wondered unhappily. Or was it only that she would not help him, after all, by talking with him? For he was not strong enough to receive the impact of unfamiliar things without a little talk to break their fall. He had lived a month in which nothing had happened except in his head and his body—an almost inaudible life of heartbeats and dreams that came back, a life of fever and privacy, a delicate life which had left him weak to the point of—what? Of begging. The pulse in his palm leapt like a trout in a brook.

He wondered over and over why the woman did not go ahead with cleaning the lamp. What prompted her to stay there across the room, silently bestowing her presence upon him? He saw that with her it was not a time for doing little tasks. Her face was grave; she was feeling how right she was. Perhaps it was only politeness. In docility he held his eyes stiffly wide; they fixed themselves on the woman's clasped hands as though she held the cord they were strung on.

Then, "Sonny's coming," she said.

He himself had not heard anything, but there came a man passing the window and then plunging in at the door, with two hounds beside him. Sonny was a big enough man, with his belt slung low about his hips. He looked at least thirty. He had a hot, red face that was yet full of silence. He wore muddy blue pants and an old military coat stained and patched. World War? Bowman wondered. Great God, it was a Confederate coat. On the back of his light hair he had a wide filthy black hat which seemed to insult Bowman's own. He pushed down the dogs from his chest. He was strong, with dignity and heaviness in his way of moving. . . . There was the resemblance to his mother.

They stood side by side. . . . He must account again for his presence here.

"Sonny, this man, he had his car to run off over the prec'pice an' wants to know if you will git it out for him," the woman said after a few minutes.

Bowman could not even state his case.

Sonny's eyes lay upon him.

He knew he should offer explanations and show money—at least appear either penitent or authoritative. But all he could do was to shrug slightly.

Sonny brushed by him going to the window, followed by the eager dogs, and looked out. There was effort even in the way he was looking, as if he could throw his sight out like a rope. Without turning Bowman felt that his own eyes could have seen nothing: it was too far.

"Got me a mule out there an' got me a block an' tackle," said Sonny meaningfully. "I *could* catch me my mule an' git me my ropes, an' before long I'd git your car out the ravine."

He looked completely around the room, as if in meditation, his eyes roving in their own distance. Then he pressed his lips firmly and yet shyly together, and with the dogs ahead of him this time, he lowered his head and strode out. The hard earth sounded, cupping to his powerful way of walking—almost a stagger.

Mischievously, at the suggestion of those sounds, Bowman's heart leapt again. It seemed to walk about inside him.

"Sonny's goin' to do it," the woman said. She said it again, singing it almost, like a song. She was sitting in her place by the hearth.

Without looking out, he heard some shouts and the dogs barking and the pounding of hoofs in short runs on the hill. In a few minutes Sonny passed under the window with a rope, and there was a brown mule with quivering, shining, purple-looking ears. The mule actually looked in the window. Under its eyelashes it turned target-like eyes into his. Bowman averted his head and saw the woman looking serenely back at the mule, with only satisfaction in her face.

She sang a little more, under her breath. It occurred to him, and it seemed quite marvelous, that she was not really talking to him, but rather following the thing that came about with words that were unconscious and part of her looking.

So he said nothing, and this time when he did not reply he felt a curious and strong emotion, not fear, rise up in him.

This time, when his heart leapt, something—his soul—seemed to leap too, like a little colt invited out of a pen. He stared at the woman while the frantic nimbleness of his feeling made his head sway. He could not move; there was nothing he could do, unless perhaps he might embrace this woman who sat there growing old and shapeless before him.

But he wanted to leap up, to say to her, I have been sick and I found out then, only then, how lonely I am. Is it too late? My heart puts up a struggle inside me, and you may have heard it, protesting against emptiness. . . . It should be full, he would rush on to tell her, thinking of his heart now as a deep lake, it should be holding love like other hearts. It should be flooded with love. There would be a warm spring day. . . . Come and stand in my heart, whoever you are, and a whole river would cover your feet and rise higher and take your knees in whirlpools, and draw you down to itself, your whole body, your heart too.

But he moved a trembling hand across his eyes, and looked at the placid crouching woman across the room. She was still as a statue. He felt ashamed and exhausted by the thought that he might, in one more moment, have tried by simple words and embraces to com-

municate some strange thing—something which seemed always to
have just escaped him. . . .

Sunlight touched the furthest pot on the hearth. It was late
afternoon. This time tomorrow he would be somewhere on a good
graveled road, driving his car past things that happened to people,
quicker than their happening. Seeing ahead to the next day, he was
glad, and knew that this was no time to embrace an old woman.
He could feel in his pounding temples the readying of his blood for
motion and for hurrying away.

"Sonny's hitched up your car by now," said the woman. "He'll git
it out the ravine right shortly."

"Fine!" he cried with his customary enthusiasm.

Yet it seemed a long time that they waited. It began to get dark.
Bowman was cramped in his chair. Any man should know enough
to get up and walk around while he waited. There was something
like guilt in such stillness and silence.

But instead of getting up, he listened. . . . His breathing
restrained, his eyes powerless in the growing dark, he listened
uneasily for a warning sound, forgetting in wariness what it
would be. Before long he heard something—soft, continuous,
insinuating.

"What's that noise?" he asked, his voice jumping into the dark.
Then wildly he was afraid it would be his heart beating so plainly in
the quiet room, and she would tell him so.

"You might hear the stream," she said grudgingly.

Her voice was closer. She was standing by the table. He won-
dered why she did not light the lamp. She stood there in the dark
and did not light it.

Bowman would never speak to her now, for the time was past. I'll sleep in the dark, he thought, in his bewilderment pitying himself.

Heavily she moved on to the window. Her arm, vaguely white, rose straight from her full side and she pointed out into the darkness.

"That white speck's Sonny," she said, talking to herself.

He turned unwillingly and peered over her shoulder; he hesitated to rise and stand beside her. His eyes searched the dusky air. The white speck floated smoothly toward her finger, like a leaf on a river, growing whiter in the dark. It was as if she had shown him something secret, part of her life, but had offered no explanation. He looked away. He was moved almost to tears, feeling for no reason that she had made a silent declaration equivalent to his own. His hand waited upon his chest.

Then a step shook the house, and Sonny was in the room. Bowman felt how the woman left him there and went to the other man's side.

"I done got your car out, mister," said Sonny's voice in the dark. "She's settin' a-waitin' in the road, turned to go back where she come from."

"Fine!" said Bowman, projecting his own voice to loudness. "I'm surely much obliged—I could never have done it myself—I was sick. . . ."

"I could do it easy," said Sonny.

Bowman could feel them both waiting in the dark, and he could hear the dogs panting out in the yard, waiting to bark when he should go. He felt strangely helpless and resentful. Now that he could go, he longed to stay. Of what was he being deprived? His chest was rudely shaken by the violence of his heart. These people cherished something here that he could not see, they withheld some ancient promise of food and warmth and light. Between them they had a conspiracy. He thought of the way she had moved away from him and gone to Sonny, she had flowed toward him. He was shaking with cold, he was tired, and it was not fair. Humbly and yet angrily he stuck his hand into his pocket.

"Of course I'm going to pay you for everything—"

"We don't take money for such," said Sonny's voice belligerently.

"I want to pay. But do something more. . . . Let me stay— tonight. . . ." He took another step toward them. If only they could see him, they would know his sincerity, his real need! His voice went on, "I'm not very strong yet, I'm not able to walk far, even back to my car, maybe, I don't know—I don't know exactly where I am—"

He stopped. He felt as if he might burst into tears. What would they think of him!

Sonny came over and put his hands on him. Bowman felt them pass (they were professional too) across his chest, over his hips. He could feel Sonny's eyes upon him in the dark.

"You ain't no revenuer come sneakin' here, mister, ain't got no gun?"

To this end of nowhere! And yet he had come. He made a grave answer. "No."

"You can stay."

"Sonny," said the woman, "you'll have to borry some fire."

"I'll go git it from Redmond's," said Sonny.

"What?" Bowman strained to hear their words to each other.

"Our fire, it's out, and Sonny's got to borry some, because it's dark an' cold," she said.

"But matches—I have matches—"

"We don't have no need for 'em," she said proudly. "Sonny's goin'
after his own fire."

"I'm goin' to Redmond's," said Sonny with an air of importance,
and he went out.

After they had waited a while, Bowman looked out the window
and saw a light moving over the hill. It spread itself out like a little
fan. It zigzagged along the field, darting and swift, not like Sonny
at all. . . . Soon enough, Sonny staggered in, holding a burning stick
behind him in tongs, fire flowing in his wake, blazing light into the
corners of the room.

"We'll make a fire now," the woman said, taking the brand.

When that was done she lit the lamp. It showed its dark and light.
The whole room turned golden-yellow like some sort of flower, and the
walls smelled of it and seemed to tremble with the quiet rushing of the
fire and the waving of the burning lampwick in its funnel of light.

The woman moved among the iron pots. With the tongs she
dropped hot coals on top of the iron lids. They made a set of soft
vibrations, like the sound of a bell far away.

She looked up and over at Bowman, but he could not answer. He
was trembling. . . .

"Have a drink, mister?" Sonny asked. He had brought in a chair
from the other room and sat astride it with his folded arms across
the back. Now we are all visible to one another, Bowman thought,
and cried, "Yes sir, you bet, thanks!"

"Come after me and do just what I do," said Sonny.

It was another excursion into the dark. They went through the
hall, out to the back of the house, past a shed and a hooded well.
They came to a wilderness of thicket.

"Down on your knees," said Sonny.

"What?" Sweat broke out on his forehead.

He understood when Sonny began to crawl through a sort of tunnel that the bushes made over the ground. He followed, startled in spite of himself when a twig or a thorn touched him gently without making a sound, clinging to him and finally letting him go.

Sonny stopped crawling and, crouched on his knees, began to dig with both his hands into the dirt. Bowman shyly struck matches and made a light. In a few minutes Sonny pulled up a jug. He poured out some of the whisky into a bottle from his coat pocket, and buried the jug again. "You never know who's liable to knock at your door," he said, and laughed. "Start back," he said, almost formally. "Ain't no need for us to drink outdoors, like hogs."

At the table by the fire, sitting opposite each other in their chairs, Sonny and Bowman took drinks out of the bottle, passing it across. The dogs slept; one of them was having a dream.

"This is good," said Bowman. "This is what I needed." It was just as though he were drinking the fire off the hearth.

"He makes it," said the woman with quiet pride.

She was pushing the coals off the pots, and the smells of corn bread and coffee circled the room. She set everything on the table before the men, with a bone-handled knife stuck into one of the potatoes, splitting out its golden fiber. Then she stood for a minute looking at them, tall and full above them where they sat. She leaned a little toward them.

"You all can eat now," she said, and suddenly smiled.

Bowman had just happened to be looking at her. He set his cup back on the table in unbelieving protest. A pain pressed at his eyes.

He saw that she was not an old woman. She was young, still young. He could think of no number of years for her. She was the same age as Sonny, and she belonged to him. She stood with the deep dark corner of the room behind her, the shifting yellow light scattering over her head and her gray formless dress, trembling over her tall body when it bent over them in its sudden communication. She was young. Her teeth were shining and her eyes glowed. She turned and walked slowly and heavily out of the room, and he heard her sit down on the cot and then lie down. The pattern on the quilt moved.

"She's goin' to have a baby," said Sonny, popping a bite into his mouth.

Bowman could not speak. He was shocked with knowing what was really in this house. A marriage, a fruitful marriage. That simple thing. Anyone could have had that.

Somehow he felt unable to be indignant or protest, although some sort of joke had certainly been played upon him. There was nothing remote or mysterious here—only something private. The only secret was the ancient communication between two people. But the memory of the woman's waiting silently by the cold hearth, of the man's stubborn journey a mile away to get fire, and how they finally brought out their food and drink and filled the room proudly with all they had to show, was suddenly too clear and too enormous within him for response. . . .

"You ain't as hungry as you look," said Sonny.

The woman came out of the bedroom as soon as the men had finished, and ate her supper while her husband stared peacefully into the fire.

Then they put the dogs out, with the food that was left.

"I think I'd better sleep here by the fire, on the floor," said Bowman.

He felt that he had been cheated, and that he could afford now to be generous. Ill though he was, he was not going to ask them for their bed. He was through with asking favors in this house, now that he understood what was there.

"Sure, mister."

But he had not known yet how slowly he understood. They had not meant to give him their bed. After a little interval they both rose and looking at him gravely went into the other room.

He lay stretched by the fire until it grew low and dying. He watched every tongue of blaze lick out and vanish. "There will be special reduced prices on all footwear during the month of January," he found himself repeating quietly, and then he lay with his lips tight shut.

How many noises the night had! He heard the stream running, the fire dying, and he was sure now that he heard his heart beating, too, the sound it made under his ribs. He heard breathing, round and deep, of the man and his wife in the room across the passage. And that was all. But emotion swelled patiently within him, and he wished that the child were his.

He must get back to where he had been before. He stood weakly before the red coals and put on his overcoat. It felt too heavy on his shoulders. As he started out he looked and saw that the woman had never got through with cleaning the lamp. On some impulse he put all the money from his billfold under its fluted glass base, almost ostentatiously.

Ashamed, shrugging a little, and then shivering, he took his bags and went out. The cold of the air seemed to lift him bodily. The moon was in the sky.

On the slope he began to run, he could not help it. Just as he reached the road, where his car seemed to sit in the moonlight like a boat, his heart began to give off tremendous explosions like a rifle, bang bang bang.

He sank in fright onto the road, his bags falling about him. He felt as if all this had happened before. He covered his heart with both hands to keep anyone from hearing the noise it made.

But nobody heard it.

Tobias Wolff

THE DEPOSITION

The witness was playing hard to get. Statements he had made earlier to his girlfriend, another nurse, statements crucial to Burke's case, the witness now declined to repeat under oath. He claimed not to remember just what he'd said, or even to recall clearly the episode in question: an instance of surgical haste and sloppiness amounting to malpractice. As the result of a routine procedure—removal of a ganglion cyst—outrageously, indefensibly botched, Burke's client had lost the fine motor skills of her left hand. She'd worked the reservations desk at a car-rental office: what was to become of a fifty-eight-year-old booking agent who could no longer use a keyboard?

Burke decided to ask for a breather. He'd flown out from San Francisco only the day before to take this deposition in person. He was still ragged from the unpleasant journey: delayed departure from SFO, a run through Dulles to make his puddle jumper to Albany, then the poky drive upriver to New Delft. Long trip,

sleepless night. He'd shown some temper at the witness's forget-
fulness, and the witness had in turn become sullen and grudging,
the last thing Burke wanted. He hoped that a little time off would
cool things down and allow the man's conscience to help out his
memory, if he was still open to such influences. Burke suspected
that he was.

Witness's counsel agreed to the break: forty-five minutes.
Burke turned down the offer of cake and coffee in favor of a brisk
walk. He left the building, a Federalist mansion converted to
law offices, and started down the hill toward the river. It was a
fine October afternoon, warm and golden, trees ablaze, air dense
with the must of fallen leaves. That smell, the honeyed light . . .
Burke faltered in his march, subdued by the memory of days like
this in the Ohio town where he'd grown up. There was that one
Indian summer, his junior year in high school, when day after day,
flooded with desire, shaking with it, he'd hurried to an older girl's
house to glory in her boldness for a mad hour before her mother
got home from work. Julie Rose. The hourglass birthmark on her
throat . . . he could still see it, and the filmy curtains fluttering at
her bedroom window, the brilliance of the leaves stirring in the
warm breeze.

But what crap! Wallowing in nostalgia for a place he'd come to
despise and dreamed only of escaping.

The river was farther than Burke had thought. He was a big bull-
shouldered man who struggled to trim his bulk with diets and exer-
cise, but he'd been putting in long hours lately, eating on the fly and
missing his workouts; even this easy jaunt was making him sweat.
He loosened his tie. When he reached the bottom of the hill he took
off his suit jacket and flung it over his shoulder.

Burke had hoped to find a path beside the river, but the way was barred by a pair of factory buildings that loomed along the bank behind padlocked chain-link fences. The factories were derelict, bricks fallen from the walls, all but the highest windows broken: these glittered gaily in the late sunshine. Splintered pallets lay here and there across the weed-cracked asphalt of the factory yards. He examined this scene with sour recognition before turning away.

Burke followed the fence a few hundred yards and then circled back uphill on what appeared to be a commercial street. A cloying, briny smell poured from the open door of a Chinese takeout, a half-eaten plate of noodles surrounded by soy-sauce packets on the single table inside. The bespectacled woman at the counter looked up from her newspaper to meet his gaze. He looked away and walked on, past an old movie theater with empty poster casings and a blank marquee: a dog-grooming salon, its windows filled with faded snapshots of a man with orange hair grinning over various pooches made ridiculous by his labors: past a five-and-dime converted to a Goodwill, and a tailor shop with a CLOSED sign in the window. On the corner stood an abandoned Mobil station, windows boarded over, the pumps long gone.

Burke stopped and looked up at the winged red horse still rearing over the lot, then took in the block he'd just traveled. A stooped woman in an overcoat was hobbling down the opposite sidewalk—the only person in sight. It might have been a street in his hometown, with its own bankrupt industries and air of stagnation. Burke's widowed mother still lived in the old house. He visited dutifully with his wife, who claimed to find the town charming and soothingly tranquil, but Burke couldn't imagine living there and wasn't sure why anyone else did.

In fact, it seemed to him that for all the talk of family and faith and neighborliness—the heartland virtues held up in rebuke of competitive, materialistic Gomorrahs like San Francisco—there was something not quite wholesome in this placidity, something lazy and sensual Burke felt it when he wandered the streets of his hometown, and he felt it now.

He crossed against the light, quickening his pace; he would have to move smartly to make it back in time. All signs of commerce ended at the gas station. He passed several blocks of small houses squeezed together on puny lots—no doubt the homes of those who'd spent their lives in the factories. Most of them were in bad repair: roofs sagging, paint scaling, screens rusting out. No disposable income around here.

Burke knew the story—he'd bet the farm on it. Unions broken or bought off. Salaries and benefits steadily cut under threat of layoffs that happened anyway as the jobs went to foreign wage slaves, the owners meanwhile conjuring up jolly visions of the corporate "family" and better days to come, before selling out just in time to duck the fines for a century of fouling the river; then the new owners, vultures with MBAs, gliding in to sack the pension fund before declaring bankruptcy. Burke knew the whole story, and it disgusted him—especially the workers who'd let the owners screw them like this while patting them on the head, congratulating them for being the backbone of the country, salt of the earth, the true Americans. Jesus! And still they ate it up, and voted like robbers instead of the robbed. Served them right.

Burke's pounding heart sent a rush of heat to his face and left him strangely light-headed, as if he were floating above the sidewalk. He took the hill in long, thrusting strides. A boy with blond dreadlocks was raking leaves into a garbage bag. As Burke went past, the boy leaned on the rake and gaped at him, a jarring, surflike percussion leaking from his earphones.

The whole country was being hollowed out like this, devoured from the inside, with nobody fighting back. It was embarrassing, and vaguely shameful, to watch people get pushed around without a fight. That's why he'd taken on his little pop-eyed pug of a client with the fucked-up hand—she was a battler. Stonewalled at every turn, bombarded with demands for documents, secretly video-taped, insulted with dinky settlement offers, even threatened with a countersuit, she just lowered her head and kept coming. She'd spent all her savings going after the surgeon who'd messed her up, to the point where she'd had to move to San Francisco to live with her son, a paralegal in Burke's firm. Her lawyer back here in New Delft had suffered a stroke and bowed out. The case was a long shot but Burke had taken it on contingency because he knew she wouldn't back off, that she'd keep pushing right to the end.

And now it seemed she might have a chance after all. They'd got-ten a break the past month, hearing about this nurse's complaints to his now-embittered ex-girlfriend. The account Burke had of these conversations was hearsay, not enough in itself to take to court or even to compel a fair settlement, but it told him that the witness harbored feelings of guilt and anger. That he had some pride and resented being made party to a maiming. He was no doubt under great pressure to stand by the surgeon, but the witness hadn't actu-ally denied seeing what he'd seen or saying what he'd said. He sim-ply claimed not to recall it clearly.

What a man forgets he can remember. It was a question of will. And even in the witness's evasions Burke could detect his reluctance to lie and, beyond that, his desire—not yet decisive but persistent and troubling—to tell the truth.

Burke believed that he had a gift for sensing not only a person's truthfulness on a given question, but also, and more important, his natural inclination toward the truth. It was like a homing instinct in those who had it. No matter what the risk, no matter how carefully they might defend themselves with equivocation and convenient lapses of memory, it was still there, fidgeting to be recognized. Over the years he had brought considerable skill to the work of helping people overcome their earlier shufflings and suppressions, even their self-interest, to say what they really wanted to say. The nurse needed to tell his story; Burke was sure of that, and sure of his own ability to coax the story forth. He would master this coy witness.

And as he considered how he would do this he felt himself moving with ease for the first time that day. He had his rhythm and his wind, a pleasant sense of strength. But for his flimsy, very expensive Italian loafers, he might have broken into a run.

The houses were growing larger as he climbed, the lawns deeper and darker. Great maples arched high above the street. Burke slowed to watch a sudden fall of leaves, how they rocked and dipped and stalled in their descent, eddying in gusts so light and warm he hardly felt them on the back of his neck, like teasing breaths. Then a bus roared past and pulled to the curb just ahead, and the doors hissed open, and the girl stepped out.

Burke held back—though barely aware of holding back, or of the catch in his throat. She was tall, to his eyes magnificently tall. He caught just a glance of lips painted black before her long dark hair swung forward and veiled her face as she looked down to find her

footing on the curb. She stopped on the sidewalk and watched the
bus pull away in a belch of black smoke. Then she set her bag down
and stretched luxuriously, going up on her toes, hands raised high
above her head. Still on tiptoe, she joined her fingers together and
moved her hips from side to side. She was no more than twenty feet
away, but it was clear to Burke that she hadn't noticed him, that she
thought she was alone out here. He felt himself smile. He waited.
She dropped her arms, did a few neck rolls, then hiked her bag back
onto her shoulder and started up the street. He followed, matching
his pace to hers.

She walked slowly, with the deliberate, almost flat-footed tread
of a dancer, toes turned slightly outward. She was humming a song.
Her knee-length plaid skirt swayed a little as she walked, but she
held her back straight and still. The white blouse she wore had two
sweat-spots below her shoulder blades. Burke could picture her lean-
ing back against the plastic seat on the bus, drowsing in the swampy
air as men stole looks at her over their folded papers.

The tone of her humming changed, grew more rhythmic, less
tuneful. Her hips rolled under the skirt, her shoulders shifting in
subtle counterpoint. On the back of her right calf there was a dark
spot the size of a penny—maybe a mole, or a daub of mud.

She fell silent and reached into her bag. It was a large canvas bag,
full to bulging, but she found what she was after without looking
down and brought it out and slipped it over her wrist, a furry red
band. She reached both hands behind her neck and gathered her hair
and lifted it and gave her head a shake and let her hair fall back. She
was moving even more slowly now, languorously, dreamily. Again
she reached back and lifted her hair and began twisting it into a
single strand. In one motion she gave it a last twist and slid the red

band off her wrist and up the thick rope of hair, pulled it forward over her shoulder, and commenced picking at the ends.

Burke stared at the curve of her neck, so white, so bare. It looked damp and tender. She went on in her slow glide and he followed. He had been walking in time with her but such was his absorption that he lost the beat, and at the sound of his footsteps she wheeled around and looked into his face. Burke was right behind her—he had closed the distance without realizing it. Her eyes went wide. He was held by them, fixed. They were a deep, bruised blue, almost violet, and darkly rimmed with liner. He heard her suck in a long ragged breath.

Burke tried to speak, to reassure her, but his throat was tight and dry and not a sound came. He swallowed. He couldn't think what to say.

He stood looking into her face. Blotchy white skin, the pathetic hipness of the black lips. But those eyes, the high and lovely brow—beautiful; more beautiful even than he had imagined. The girl took a step back, her eyes still holding his, then turned and began angling across a lawn toward a large white house. Halfway there she broke into a run.

This somehow released Burke. He continued on his way, deliberately holding himself to a dignified pace, even stopping for a moment to put on his suit jacket—shoot the cuffs, shrug into the shoulders, give a tug at the lapels. He did not allow himself to look back. As the tightness in his throat eased he found himself hungry for air, almost panting, and realized that he'd taken hardly a breath while walking behind the girl. How frightened she seemed! What was that all about, anyway? He put this question to himself with a wonderment he didn't actually feel. He knew; he knew what had been in his face. He let it go.

Burke walked on. He had just reached the top of the hill, some nine or ten long blocks from where he'd left the girl, and was about to turn right toward the law office, already in view at the end of the cross street, when a siren yelped behind him. Only one sharp, imperative cry, nothing more—but he recognized the sound, and stopped and closed his eyes for a moment before turning to watch the cruiser nosing toward the curb.

He waited. A gray-haired woman glared at him from the rear window. The girl was beside her, leaning forward to look at him, nodding to the cop in front. He opened a notebook on the steering wheel, wrote something, then laid the notebook on the seat beside him, set his patrolman's cap on his head, adjusted its angle, and got out of the cruiser. He walked around to the back door and held it open as the woman and the girl slid out. Each of these actions was executed with plodding deliberation, *performed*. Burke understood, as an unnerving show of method and assurance.

He nodded as the cop came toward him. "Officer. What can I do for you?"

"Identification, please."

Burke could have objected to this, but instead he shrugged, fetched his wallet from his jacket pocket, and handed over his driver's license.

The cop examined it, looked up at Burke, lowered his eyes to the license again. He was young, his face bland as a baby's in spite of his wispy blond mustache. "You're not from here," he finally said.

Burke had a business card ready. He held it out, and after eyeing it warily the cop took it. "I'm a lawyer," Burke said. "Here to take a deposition, in, let's see . . ." He held up his watch. "Three minutes ago. Four-thirty. Right down there on Clinton Street." He gestured vaguely. "So what's the problem?"

The gray-haired woman had come up close to Burke and was staring fiercely into his face. The girl lingered by the cruiser, pallid, hands dangling awkwardly at her sides.

"We have a complaint," the officer said. "Stalking," he added uncertainly.

"*Stalking*? Stalking *who*?"

"You know who," the woman said in a gravelly voice, never taking her eyes off him. She was handsome in a square-jawed way and deeply tanned. Ropy brown arms sticking out of her polo shirt, grass stains on the knees of her khakis. Burke could see her on the deck of a boat, coolly reefing sails in a blow.

"The young lady there?" Burke asked.

"Don't play cute with me," the woman said. "I've never seen any-one so terrified. The poor thing could hardly speak when she came to my door."

"Something sure scared her," the cop said.

"And what was my part in this?" Burke looked directly at the girl. She was hugging herself, sucking on her lower lip. She was younger than he'd thought; she was just a kid. He said, gently, "Did I do something to you?"

She glanced at him, then averted her face.

In the same voice, he said, "Did I say anything to you?"

She stared at the ground by her feet.

"Well?" the cop said sharply. "What'd he do?"

The girl didn't answer.

"Aren't you the smooth one," the woman said.

"I do remember passing her a while back," Burke said, address-ing himself to the cop. "Maybe I surprised her—I guess I must have. I was in kind of a hurry." Then, speaking with absolute calm, Burke explained his business in New Delft, and the forty-five-minute break, and the route he'd taken and the necessity of moving right along to get back on time, even if that meant overtaking other people on the sidewalk. All this could be confirmed at the law office—where they'd be already waiting for him—and Burke invited the cop to come along and settle the matter forthwith. "I'm sorry if I surprised you," he said in the girl's direction. "I certainly didn't mean to."

The cop looked at him, then at the girl. "Well?" he repeated.

She turned her back to them, rested her elbows on the roof of the cruiser, and buried her face in her hands.

The cop watched her for a moment. "Ah, jeez," he said. He gave the driver's license another once-over, handed it back with the card, and walked over to the girl. He murmured something, then took her by the elbow and began to help her into the backseat.

The woman didn't move. Burke felt her eyes on him as he replaced the license and card in his wallet. Finally he looked up and met her stare, so green and cold. He held it and did not blink. Then came a flash of bursting pain and his head snapped sideways so hard he felt a crack at the base of his neck. The shock scorched his eyes with hot, blinding tears. His face burned. His tongue felt jammed back in his throat.

"Liar," she said.

Until Burke heard her voice he didn't understand that she'd struck him—he was that stunned. It gave him a kind of relief, as if without knowing it he'd been gripped by fear of something worse.

He heard the doors of the cruiser slam shut, one-two! He bent down with his hands on his knees, steadying himself, then straightened up and rubbed at his eyes. The cruiser was gone. The left side of his face still burned, hot even to the touch. A bearded man in a black suit walked past him down the hill, shooting Burke a glance and then locking his gaze straight ahead. Burke checked his watch. He was seven minutes late.

He took a step, and another, and went on, amazed at how surely he walked, and how lightly. Down the street a squirrel jabbered right into his ear, or so it seemed, but when he glanced up he found it chattering on a limb high above him. Still, its voice was startling— raw, close. The light in the crowns of the trees had the quality of mist.

Burke stopped outside the law office and gave his shoes a quick buff on the back of his pant legs. He mounted the steps and paused at the door. The blow was still warm on his cheek. Did it show? Would they ask about it? No matter—he'd think of something. But he couldn't help touching it again, tenderly, as if to cherish it, as he went inside to nail this witness down.

Richard Yates

A GLUTTON FOR PUNISHMENT

For a little while when Walter Henderson was nine years old he thought falling dead was the very zenith of romance, and so did a number of his friends. Having found that the only truly rewarding part of any cops-and-robbers game was the moment when you pretended to be shot, clutched your heart, dropped your pistol and crumpled to the earth, they soon dispensed with the rest of it—the tiresome business of choosing up sides and sneaking around—and refined the game to its essence. It became a matter of individual performance, almost an art. One of them at a time would run dramatically along the crest of a hill, and at a given point the ambush would occur: a simultaneous jerking of aimed toy pistols and a chorus of those staccato throaty sounds—a kind of hoarse-whispered *"Pk-k-ew! Pk-k-ew!"*—with which little boys simulate the noise of gunfire. Then the performer would stop, turn, stand poised for a moment in graceful agony, pitch over and fall down the hill in a whirl of arms and legs and a splendid cloud of dust, and finally sprawl flat at the bottom, a rumpled corpse. When he got up and brushed off his clothes, the others would criticize his form ("Pretty good," or "Too stiff," or "Didn't look natural"), and then it would be the next player's turn. That was all there was to the game, but Walter Henderson loved it. He was a slight, poorly coordinated boy, and this was the only thing even faintly like a sport at which he excelled. Nobody could match the abandon with which he flung his limp body down the hill, and he reveled in the small acclaim it won him. Eventually the others grew bored with the game, after some older boys had laughed at them; Walter turned reluctantly to more wholesome forms of play, and soon he had forgotten about it.

But he had occasion to remember it, vividly, one May afternoon nearly twenty-five years later in a Lexington Avenue office building, while he sat at his desk pretending to work and waiting to be fired. He had become a sober, keen-looking young man now, with clothes that showed the influence of an Eastern university and neat brown hair that was just beginning to thin out on top. Years of good health had made him less slight, and though he still had trouble with his coordination it showed up mainly in minor things nowadays, like an inability to coordinate his hat, his wallet, his theater tickets and his change without making his wife stop and wait for him, or a tendency to push heavily against doors marked "Pull." He looked, at any rate, the picture of sanity and competence as he sat there in the office. No one could have told that the cool sweat of anxiety was sliding under his shirt, or that the fingers of his left hand, concealed in his pocket, were slowly grinding and tearing a book of matches into a moist cardboard pulp. He had seen it coming for weeks, and this morning, from the minute he got off the elevator, he had sensed that this was the day it would happen. When several of his superiors said, "Morning,

Walt," he had seen the faintest suggestion of concern behind their smiles; then once this afternoon, glancing out over the gate of the cubicle where he worked, he'd happened to catch the eye of George Crowell, the department manager, who was hesitating in the door of his private office with some papers in his hand. Crowell turned away quickly, but Walter knew he had been watching him, troubled but determined. In a matter of minutes, he felt sure, Crowell would call him in and break the news—with difficulty, of course, since Crowell was the kind of boss who took pride in being a regular guy. There was nothing to do now but let the thing happen and try to take it as gracefully as possible.

That was when the childhood memory began to prey on his mind, for it suddenly struck him—and the force of it sent his thumbnail biting deep into the secret matchbook—that letting things happen and taking them gracefully had been, in a way, the pattern of his life. There was certainly no denying that the role of good loser had always held an inordinate appeal for him. All through adolescence he had specialized in it, gamely losing fights with stronger boys, playing football badly in the secret hope of being injured and carried dramatically off the field ("You got to hand it to old Henderson for one thing, anyway," the high-school coach had said with a chuckle, "he's a real little glutton for punishment"). College had offered a wider scope to his talent—there were exams to be flunked and elections to be lost—and later the Air Force had made it possible for him to wash out, honorably, as a flight cadet. And now, inevitably, it seemed, he was running true to form once more. The several jobs he'd held before this had been the beginner's kind at which it isn't easy to fail; when the opportunity for this one first arose it had been, in Crowell's phrase, "a real challenge."

"Good," Walter had said. "That's what I'm looking for." When he related that part of the conversation to his wife she had said, "Oh, wonderful!" and they'd moved to an expensive apartment in the East Sixties on the strength of it. And lately, when he started coming home with a beaten look and announcing darkly that he doubted if he could hold on much longer, she would enjoin the children not to bother him ("Daddy's very tired tonight"), bring him a drink and soothe him with careful, wifely reassurance, doing her best to conceal her fear, never guessing, or at least never showing, that she was dealing with a chronic, compulsive failure, a strange little boy in love with the attitudes of collapse. And the amazing thing, he thought—the really amazing thing— was that he himself had never looked at it that way before.

"Walt?"

The cubicle gate had swung open and George Crowell was standing there, looking uncomfortable. "Will you step into my office a minute?"

"Right, George." And Walter followed him out of the cubicle, out across the office floor, feeling many eyes on his back. Keep it dignified, he told himself. The important thing is to keep it dignified. Then the door closed behind them and the two of them were alone in the carpeted silence of Crowell's private office. Automobile horns blared in the distance, twenty-one stories below; the only other sounds were their breathing, the squeak of Crowell's shoes as he went to his desk and the creak of his swivel chair as he sat down. "Pull up a chair, Walt," he said. "Smoke?"

"No thanks." Walter sat down and laced his fingers tight between his knees.

Crowell shut the cigarette box without taking one for himself, pushed it aside and leaned forward, both hands spread flat on the plate-glass top of the desk. "Walt, I might as well give you this straight from the shoulder," he said, and the last shred of hope slipped away. The funny part was that it came as a shock, even so. "Mr. Harvey and I have felt for some time that you haven't quite caught on to the work here, and we've both very reluctantly come to the conclusion that the best thing to do, in your own best interests as well as ours, is to let you go. Now," he added quickly, "this is no reflection on you personally, Walt. We do a highly specialized kind of work here and we can't expect everybody to stay on top of the job. In your case particularly, we really feel you'd be happier in some organization better suited to your—abilities."

Crowell leaned back, and when he raised his hands their moisture left two gray, perfect prints on the glass, like the hands of a skeleton. Walter stared at them, fascinated, while they shriveled and disappeared.

"Well," he said, and looked up. "You put that very nicely, George. Thanks."

Crowell's lips worked into an apologetic, regular guy's smile. "Awfully sorry," he said. "These things just happen." And he began to fumble with the knobs of his desk drawers, visibly relieved that the worst was over. "Now," he said, "we've made out a check here covering your salary through the end of next month. That'll give you something in the way of—severance pay, so to speak—to tide you over until you find something." He held out a long envelope.

"That's very generous," Walter said. Then there was a silence, and Walter realized it was up to him to break it. He got to his feet. "All right, George. I won't keep you."

Crowell got up quickly and came around the desk with both hands held out—one to shake Walter's hand, the other to put on his

shoulder as they walked to the door. The gesture, at once friendly
and humiliating, brought a quick rush of blood to Walter's throat,
and for a terrible second he thought he might be going to cry. "Well,
boy," Crowell said, "good luck to you."

"Thanks," he said, and he was so relieved to find his voice steady
that he said it again, smiling. "Thanks. So long, George."

There was a distance of some fifty feet to be crossed on the way
back to his cubicle, and Walter Henderson accomplished it with
style. He was aware of how trim and straight his departing shoul-
ders looked to Crowell; he was aware too, as he threaded his way
among desks whose occupants either glanced up shyly at him or
looked as if they'd like to, of every subtle play of well-controlled
emotion in his face. It was as if the whole thing were a scene in
a movie. The camera had opened the action from Crowell's view-
point and dollied back to take in the entire office as a frame for Wal-
ter's figure in lonely, stately passage; now it came in for a long-held
close-up of Walter's face, switched to other brief views of his col-
leagues' turning heads (Joe Collins looking worried, Fred Holmes
trying to keep from looking pleased), and switched again to Walter's
viewpoint as it discovered the plain, unsuspecting face of Mary, his
secretary, who was waiting for him at his desk with a report he had
given her to type.

"I hope this is all right, Mr. Henderson."

Walter took it and dropped it on the desk. "Forget it, Mary," he
said. "Look, you might as well take the rest of the day off, and go see
the personnel manager in the morning. You'll be getting a new job.
I've just been fired."

Her first expression was a faint, suspicious smile—she thought
he was kidding—but then she began to look pale and shaken. She

was very young and not too bright; they had probably never told her in secretarial school that it was possible for your boss to get fired. "Why, that's *terrible*, Mr. Henderson. I—well, but why would they *do* such a thing?"

"Oh, I don't know," he said. "Lot of little reasons, I guess." He was opening and slamming the drawers of his desk, cleaning out his belongings. There wasn't much: a handful of old personal letters, a dry fountain pen, a cigarette lighter with no flint, and half of a wrapped chocolate bar. He was aware of how poignant each of these objects looked to her, as she watched him sort them out and fill his pockets, and he was aware of the dignity with which he straightened up, turned, took his hat from the stand and put it on.

"Doesn't affect you, of course, Mary," he said. "They'll have a new job for you in the morning. Well." He held out his hand. "Good luck."

"Thank you; the same to you. Well, then, g'night"—and here she brought her chewed fingernails up to her lips for an uncertain little giggle—"I mean, g'bye, then, Mr. Henderson."

The next part of the scene was at the water cooler, where Joe Collins's sober eyes became enriched with sympathy as Walter approached him.

"Joe," Walter said. "I'm leaving. Got the ax."

"No!" But Collins's look of shock was plainly an act of kindness; it couldn't have been much of a surprise. "Jesus, Walt, what the hell's the matter with these people?"

Then Fred Holmes chimed in, very grave and sorry, clearly pleased with the news: "Gee, boy, that's a damn shame."

Walter led the two of them away to the elevators, where he pressed the "down" button; and suddenly other men were bearing down on him from all corners of the office, their faces stiff with sorrow, their hands held out.

"Awful sorry, Walt . . ."

"Good luck, boy . . ."

"Keep in touch, okay, Walt? . . ."

Nodding and smiling, shaking hands, Walter said, "Thanks," and "So long," and "I certainly will"; then the red light came on over one of the elevators with its little mechanical "ding!" and in another few seconds the doors slid open and the operator's voice said, "Down!" He backed into the car, still wearing his fixed smile and waving a jaunty salute to their earnest, talking faces, and the scene found its perfect conclusion as the doors slid shut, clamped, and the car dropped in silence through space.

All the way down he stood with the ruddy, bright-eyed look of a man fulfilled by pleasure; it wasn't until he was out on the street, walking rapidly, that he realized how completely he had enjoyed himself.

The heavy shock of this knowledge slowed him down, until he came to a stop and stood against a building front for the better part of a minute. His scalp prickled under his hat, and his fingers began to fumble with the knot of his tie and the button of his coat. He felt as if he had surprised himself in some obscene and shameful act, and he had never felt more helpless, or more frightened.

Then in a burst of action he set off again, squaring his hat and setting his jaw, bringing his heels down hard on the pavement, trying to look hurried and impatient and impelled by business. A man could drive himself crazy trying to psychoanalyze himself in the middle of Lexington Avenue, in the middle of the afternoon. The thing to do was get busy, now, and start looking for a job.

The only trouble, he realized, coming to a stop again and looking around, was that he didn't know where he was going. He was somewhere in the upper Forties, on a corner that was bright with florist shops and taxicabs, alive with well dressed men and women walking in the clear spring air. A telephone was what he needed first. He hurried across the street to a drugstore and made his way through smells of toilet soap and perfume and ketchup and bacon to the rank of phone booths along the rear wall; he got out his address book and found the page showing the several employment agencies where his applications were filed; then he got his dimes ready and shut himself into one of the booths.

But all the agencies told him the same thing: no openings in his field at the moment; no point in his coming in until they called him. When he was finished he dug for the address book again, to check the number of an acquaintance who had told him, a month before, that there might soon be an opening in his office. The book wasn't in his inside pocket; he plunged his hands into the other pockets of his coat and then his pants, cracking an elbow painfully against the wall of the booth, but all he could find were the old letters and the piece of chocolate from his desk. Cursing, he dropped the chocolate on the floor and, as if it were a lighted cigarette, stepped on it. These exertions in the heat of the booth made his breathing rapid and shallow. He was feeling faint by the time he saw the address book right in front of him, on top of the coin box, where he'd left it. His finger trembled in the dial, and when he started to speak, clawing the collar away from his sweating neck with his free hand, his voice was as weak and urgent as a beggar's.

"Jack," he said. "I was just wondering—just wondering if you'd heard anything new on the opening you mentioned a while back."

"On the which?"

"The opening. You know. You said there might be a job in your—"

"Oh, that. No, haven't heard a thing, Walt. I'll be in touch with you if anything breaks."

"Okay, Jack." He pulled open the folding door of the booth and leaned back against the stamped-tin wall, breathing deeply to welcome the rush of cool air. "I just thought it might've slipped your mind or something," he said. His voice was almost normal again. "Sorry to bother you."

"Hell, that's okay," said the hearty voice in the receiver. "What's the matter, boy? Things getting a little sticky where you are?"

"*Oh* no," Walter found himself saying, and he was immediately glad of the lie. He almost never lied, and it always surprised him to discover how easy it could be. His voice gained confidence. "No, I'm all *right* here, Jack, it's just that I didn't want to—*you* know, I thought it might have slipped your mind, is all. How's the family?"

When the conversation was over, he guessed there was nothing more to do but go home. But he continued to sit in the open booth for a long time, with his feet stretched out on the drugstore floor, until a small, canny smile began to play on his face, slowly dissolving and changing into a look of normal strength. The ease of the lie had given him an idea that grew, the more he thought it over, into a profound and revolutionary decision.

He would not tell his wife. With luck he was sure to find some kind of work before the month was out, and in the meantime, for once in his life, he would keep his troubles to himself. Tonight, when she asked how the day had gone, he would say, "Oh, all right," or even "Fine." In the morning he would leave the house at the usual time and stay away all day, and he would go on doing the same thing every day until he had a job.

The phrase "Pull yourself together" occurred to him, and there was more than determination in the way he pulled himself together there in the phone booth, the way he gathered up his coins and straightened his tie and walked out to the street: there was a kind of nobility.

Several hours had to be killed before the normal time of his home-coming, and when he found himself walking west on Forty-second Street he decided to kill them in the Public Library. He mounted the wide stone steps importantly, and soon he was installed in the reading room, examining a bound copy of last year's *Life* magazines and going over and over his plan, enlarging and perfecting it.

He knew, sensibly, that there would be nothing easy about the day-to-day deception. It would call for the constant vigilance and cunning of an outlaw. But wasn't it the very difficulty of the plan that made it worthwhile? And in the end, when it was all over and he could tell her at last, it would be a reward worth every minute of the ordeal. He knew just how she would look at him when he told her—in blank disbelief at first and then, gradually, with the dawning of a kind of respect he hadn't seen in her eyes for years.

"You mean you kept it to yourself all this *time*? But *why*, Walt?"

"Oh well," he would say casually, even shrugging, "I didn't see any point in upsetting you."

When it was time to leave the library he lingered in the main entrance for a minute, taking deep pulls from a cigarette and looking down over the five o'clock traffic and crowds. The scene held a special nostalgia for him, because it was here, on a spring evening five years before, that he had come to meet her for the first time.

"Can you meet me at the top of the library steps?" she had asked over the phone that morning, and it wasn't until many months later, after they were married, that this struck him as a peculiar meeting place. When he asked her about it then, she laughed at him. "Of *course* it was inconvenient—that was the whole point. I wanted to pose up there, like a princess in a castle or something, and make you climb up all those lovely steps to claim me."

And that was exactly how it had seemed. He'd escaped from the office ten minutes early that day and hurried to Grand Central to wash and shave in a gleaming subterranean dressing room; he had waited in a fit of impatience while a very old, stout, slow attendant took his suit away to be pressed. Then, after tipping the attendant more than he could afford, he had raced outside and up Forty-second Street, tense and breathless as he strode past shoe stores and milk bars, as he winnowed his way through swarms of intolerably slow-moving pedestrians who had no idea of how urgent his mission was. He was afraid of being late, even half afraid that it was all some kind of a joke and she wouldn't be there at all. But as soon as he hit Fifth Avenue he saw her up there in the distance, alone, standing at the top of the library steps—a slender, radiant brunette in a fashionable black coat.

He slowed down, then. He crossed the avenue at a stroll, one hand in his pocket, and took the steps with such an easy, athletic nonchalance that nobody could have guessed at the hours of anxiety, the days of strategic and tactical planning this particular moment had cost him.

When he was fairly certain she could see him coming he looked up at her again, and she smiled. It wasn't the first time he had seen her smile that way, but it was the first time he could be sure it was intended wholly for him, and it caused warm tremors of pleasure in his chest. He couldn't remember the words of their greeting, but he remembered being quite sure that they were all right, that it was starting off well—that her wide shining eyes were seeing him exactly as he most wanted to be seen. The things he said, whatever they were, struck her as witty, and the things she said, or the sound of her voice when she said them, made him feel taller and stronger and broader of shoulder than ever before in his life. When they turned and started down the steps together he took hold of her upper arm, claiming her, and felt the light jounce of her breast on the backs of his fingers with each step. And the evening before them, spread out and waiting at their feet, seemed miraculously long and miraculously rich with promise.

Starting down alone, now, he found it strengthening to have one clear triumph to look back on—one time in his life, at least, when he had denied the possibility of failure, and won. Other memories came into focus when he crossed the avenue and started back down the gentle slope of Forty-second Street: they had come this way that evening too, and walked to the Biltmore for a drink, and he remembered how she had looked sitting beside him in the semidarkness of the cocktail lounge, squirming forward from the hips while he helped her out of the sleeves of her coat and then settling back, giving her long hair a toss and looking at him in a provocative sidelong way as she raised the glass to her lips. A little later she had said, "Oh, let's go down to the river—I love the river at this time of day," and they had left the hotel and walked there. He walked there now, down through the clangor of Third Avenue and up toward Tudor City—it seemed a much longer walk alone—until he was standing at the little balustrade, looking down over the swarm of sleek cars on the East River Drive and at the slow, gray water moving beyond it. It was on this very spot, while a tugboat moaned somewhere under the darkening skyline of Queens, that he had drawn her close and kissed her for the first time. Now he turned away, a new man, and set out to walk all the way home.

The first thing that hit him, when he let himself in the apartment door, was the smell of Brussels sprouts. The children were still at their supper in the kitchen: he could hear their high mumbled voices over the clink of dishes, and then his wife's voice, tired and coaxing. When the door slammed he heard her say, "There's Daddy now," and the children began to call, "Daddy! Daddy!"

He put his hat carefully in the hall closet and turned around just as she appeared in the kitchen doorway, drying her hands on her apron and smiling through her tiredness. "Home on time for once," she said. "How lovely. I was afraid you'd be working late again."

"No," he said. "No, I didn't have to work late." His voice had an oddly foreign, amplified sound in his own ears, as if he were speaking in an echo chamber.

"You do look tired, though, Walt. You look worn out."

"Walked home, that's all. Guess I'm not used to it. How's everything?"

"Oh, fine." But she looked worn out herself.

When they went together into the kitchen he felt encircled and entrapped by its humid brightness. His eyes roamed dolefully over the milk cartons, the mayonnaise jars and soup cans and cereal boxes, the peaches lined up to ripen on the windowsill, the remarkable frailty and tenderness of his two children, whose chattering faces were lightly streaked with mashed potato.

Things looked better in the bathroom, where he took longer than necessary over the job of washing up for dinner. At least he could be alone here, braced by splashings of cold water; the only intrusion was the sound of his wife's voice rising in impatience with the older child. "All right, Andrew Henderson. No story for you tonight unless you finish up all that custard *now*." A little later came the scraping of chairs and stacking of dishes that meant their supper was over, and the light scuffle of shoes and the slamming door that meant they had been turned loose in their room for an hour to play before bath time.

Walter carefully dried his hands; then he went out to the living-room sofa and settled himself there with a magazine, taking very slow, deep breaths to show how self-controlled he was. In a minute she came in to join him, her apron removed and her lipstick replenished, bringing the cocktail pitcher full of ice. "Oh," she said with a sigh. "Thank God that's over. Now for a little peace and quiet."

"I'll get the drinks, honey," he said, bolting to his feet. He had hoped his voice might sound normal now, but it still came out with echo-chamber resonance.

"You will not," she commanded. "You sit down. You deserve to sit still and be waited on, when you come home looking so tired. How did the day go, Walt?"

"Oh, all right," he said, sitting down again. "Fine." He watched her measuring out the gin and vermouth, stirring the pitcher in her neat, quick way, arranging the tray and bringing it across the room.

"There," she said, settling herself close beside him. "Will you do the honors, darling?" And when he had tilled the chilled glasses she raised hers and said, "Oh, lovely. Cheers." This bright cocktail mood was a carefully studied effect, he knew. So was her motherly sternness over the children's supper; so was the brisk, no-nonsense efficiency with which, earlier today, she had attacked the supermarket; and so, later tonight, would be the tenderness of her surrender in his arms. The orderly rotation of many careful moods was her life, or rather, was what her life had become. She managed it well, and it was only rarely, looking very closely at her face, that he could see how much the effort was costing her.

But the drink was a great help. The first bitter, ice-cold sip of it seemed to restore his calm, and the glass in his hand looked reassuringly deep. He took another sip or two before daring to look at her again, and when he did it was a heartening sight. Her smile was almost completely free of tension, and soon they were chatting together as comfortably as happy lovers.

"Oh, isn't it nice just to sit down and unwind?" she said, allowing her head to sink back into the upholstery. "And isn't it lovely to think it's Friday night?"

"Sure is," he said, and instantly put his mouth in his drink to hide his shock. Friday night! That meant there would be two days before he could even begin to look for a job—two days of mild imprisonment in the house, or of dealing with tricycles and popsicles in the park, without a hope of escaping the burden of his secret. "Funny," he said. "I'd almost forgotten it was Friday."

"Oh, how can you forget?" She squirmed luxuriously deeper into the sofa. "I look forward to it all week. Pour me just a tiny bit more, darling, and then I must get back to the chores."

He poured a tiny bit more for her and a full glass for himself. His hand was shaking and he spilled a little of it, but she didn't seem to notice. Nor did she seem to notice that his replies grew more and more strained as she kept the conversation going. When she got back to the chores—basting the roast, drawing the children's baths, tidying up their room for the night—Walter sat alone and allowed

his mind to slide into a heavy, gin-fuddled confusion. Only one per-
sistent thought came through, a piece of self-advice that was as clear
and cold as the drink that rose again and again to his lips: Hold on.
No matter what she says, no matter what happens tonight or tomor-
row or the next day, just hold on. Hold on.

But holding on grew less and less easy as the children's splash-
ing bath-noises floated into the room; it was more difficult still by
the time they were brought in to say goodnight, carrying their
teddy bears and dressed in clean pajamas, their faces shining and
smelling of soap. After that, it became impossible to stay seated on
the sofa. He sprang up and began stalking around the floor, light-
ing one cigarette after another, listening to his wife's clear, modu-
lated reading of the bedtime story in the next room ("You may go
into the fields, or down the lane, but don't go into Mr. McGregor's
garden . . .").

When she came out again, closing the children's door behind
her, she found him standing like a tragic statue at the window, look-
ing down into the darkening courtyard. "What's the matter, Walt?"

He turned on her with a false grin. "Nothing's the matter,"
he said in the echo-chamber voice, and the movie camera started
rolling again. It came in for a close-up of his own tense face, then
switched over to observe her movements as she hovered uncertainly
at the coffee table.

"Well," she said. "I'm going to have one more cigarette and then
I must get the dinner on the table." She sat down again—not leaning
back this time, or smiling, for this was her busy, getting-the-dinner-
on-the-table mood. "Have you got a match, Walt?"

"Sure." And he came toward her, probing in his pocket as if to
bring forth something he had been saving to give her all day.

"God," she said. "Look at those matches. What *happened* to them?"

"These?" He stared down at the raddled, twisted matchbook as if it were a piece of incriminating evidence. "Must've been kind of tearing them up or something," he said. "Nervous habit."

"Thanks," she said, accepting the light from his trembling fingers, and then she began to look at him with wide, dead-serious eyes. "Walt, there *is* something wrong, isn't there?"

"Of course not. Why should there be anything wr—"

"Tell me the truth. Is it the job? Is it about—what you were afraid of last week? I mean, did anything happen today to make you think they might—Did Crowell say anything? Tell me." The faint lines on her face seemed to have deepened. She looked severe and competent and suddenly much older, not even very pretty any more—a woman used to dealing with emergencies, ready to take charge.

He began to walk slowly away toward an easy chair across the room, and the shape of his back was an eloquent statement of impending defeat. At the edge of the carpet he stopped and seemed to stiffen, a wounded man holding himself together; then he turned around and faced her with the suggestion of a melancholy smile.

"Well, darling—" he began. His right hand came up and touched the middle button of his shirt, as if to unfasten it, and then with a great deflating sigh he collapsed backward into the chair, one foot sliding out on the carpet and the other curled beneath him. It was the most graceful thing he had done all day. "They got me," he said.

EDITOR'S NOTE

Readers will notice the conspicuous absence, in this volume, of the distinguished work of Raymond Carver. The editor regrets that Raymond Carver's estate declined to allow his story "Elephant" to be included.

ABOUT THE CONTRIBUTORS

MAX APPLE was born in Grand Rapids, Michigan, and received a Ph.D. from the University of Michigan in 1970. He is the author of the story collections *The Oranging of America*, *Free Agents*, and *The Jew of Home Depot and Other Stories*; two novels; two nonfiction books; and several screenplays. He has received grants from the National Endowment for the Arts and the Guggenheim Foundation. He teaches at the University of Pennsylvania.

RUSSELL BANKS, a Massachusetts-born author, has published eleven novels, including *Continental Drift*, *Cloudsplitter*, and *The Reserve*, and five short story collections, including *The New World*, *Success Stories*, and *The Angel on the Roof*. He is the recipient of a John Dos Passos Prize, an Ingram Merrill Award, an American Academy of Arts and Letters Literature Award, and a Guggenheim Fellowship. He lives in upstate New York.

DONALD BARTHELME (1931–1989) was born in Philadelphia but grew up in Houston. Originally a journalist, he moved to New

York in 1961 and began writing fiction for publications such as *The New Yorker*. He published four novels and numerous volumes of short stories, of which *Sixty Stories* won the PEN/Faulkner Award. Barthelme was the recipient of many awards and honors, including a Guggenheim Fellowship. He spent the last decade of his life teaching at the University of Houston, where he helped found its Creative Writing Program.

RICHARD BAUSCH was born in Fort Benning, Georgia, in 1945. He has taught creative writing at several schools, including the University of Virginia, Beloit College, the University of Tennessee, Sewanee, and Bread Loaf, and is presently Moss Chair of Excellence in the Writing Program at the University of Memphis. He is the author of *Peace, Hello to the Cannibals, The Last Good Time, Mr. Field's Daughter, In the Night Season, Wives & Lovers, Something Is Out There*, and many other books. His work has won two National Magazine Awards. Bausch is the recipient of a Guggenheim Fellowship and a PEN/Malamud Award.

ANN BEATTIE has written seven novels and eight short story collections, and her work has appeared in *The New Yorker, Esquire, The Atlantic, McSweeney's*, and *The Best American Short Stories of the Century*. She has received a PEN/Malamud Award, a Rea Award for the Short Story, an American Academy of Arts and Letters Literature Award, four O. Henry Awards, and a Guggenheim Fellowship. Her most recent books include the novella *Walks With Men* and the collection *The New Yorker Stories*. Beattie currently teaches at the University of Virginia, where she is the Edgar Allan Poe Professor of English.

T. CORAGHESSAN BOYLE has published more than twenty books of fiction and short stories, most recently *The Women, When the Killing's Done*, and *Wild Child & Other Stories*. His writing has appeared in *The New Yorker*, *Harper's*, *Esquire*, *The Atlantic*, *Playboy*, and *McSweeney's*, and his many honors include five O. Henry Awards, a PEN/Malamud Award, a PEN/Faulkner Award, and a Guggenheim Fellowship. In 1978 he joined the faculty of the University of Southern California, where he currently serves as a Distinguished Professor of English.

GEORGE CHAMBERS is the author of story collections *The Bonnyclabber*, *The Scourging of W.H.D. Wretched Hutchinson*, *The Last Man Standing*, and *Null Set*, and with Raymond Federman is coauthor of *The Twilight of the Bums*, a collection of short stories that was recently reprinted by Starcherone Press. His writing has appeared in *December* and elsewhere. He is a Professor of English at Bradley University.

JOHN CHEEVER (1912–1982) wrote numerous short stories and four novels. His first novel, *The Wapshot Chronicle*, won a National Book Award, and in 1978 the collection *The Stories of John Cheever* became the only work of fiction to win the Pulitzer Prize, the National Book Award, and the National Book Critics Circle Award. He taught at the Iowa Writers' Workshop and at Boston University. Two collections of his writing were released by the Library of America in 2009.

CHARLES D'AMBROSIO is the author of two short story collections, *The Point* (a Hemingway Foundation/PEN Award finalist) and *The Dead Fish Museum*, and *Orphans*, a collection of essays. In 2006 he received a Whiting Writers' Award and in 2008 he was awarded a Lannan Foundation Fellowship. He has taught creative writing for such renowned programs as the Iowa Writers' Workshop, the Tin House Summer Writers Workshop, and the Warren Wilson MFA Program for Writers. He is an Associate Professor of English at Portland State University.

NICHOLAS DELBANCO is a novelist and a writer of nonfiction whose books include *What Remains*, *The Count of Concord*, and *Anywhere Out of the World*. His twenty-fifth book, *Lastingness: The Art of Old Age*, was published in 2011. Delbanco's writing has earned him a Guggenheim Fellowship and two National Endowment for the Arts Writing Fellowships. He has served as the Chair of the Fiction Panel for the National Book Awards, and has taught at Bennington College, Skidmore College, and the University of Michigan, where he was director of the MFA Program and continues to serve as Director of the Hopwood Awards Program.

JUNOT DÍAZ won the Pulitzer Prize for Fiction in 2008 for his debut novel, *The Brief Wondrous Life of Oscar Wao*. His writing has appeared in *The New Yorker*, *Story*, and *The Paris Review*, as well as in *Best American Short Stories* and *PEN/O. Henry Prize Stories*. He teaches creative writing at the Massachusetts Institute of Technology. He is a founding member of the Voices of Our Nations Arts Writing Workshop, which focuses on writers of color, and serves as the fiction editor for *The Boston Review*. In 2009 Diaz was a Millet Writing Fellow at Wesleyan University.

ANDRE DUBUS (1936–1999) was a short story writer hailing from Lake Charles, Louisiana. His story collections include *Dancing After Hours*, *Adultery and Other Choices*, *The Last Worthless Evening*, and *Finding a Girl in America*. His novella *We Don't Live Here Anymore* was made into a movie in 2004. During his lifetime he was awarded the PEN/Malamud Award, the Jean Stein Award from the American Academy of Arts and Letters, and fellowships from the National Endowment for the Arts, the Guggenheim Foundation, and the MacArthur Foundation.

STUART DYBEK is the acclaimed author of the story collections *Childhood and Other Neighborhoods*, *I Sailed with Magellan*, and *The Coast of Chicago*, and the poetry collections *Brass Knuckles* and *Streets in Their Own Ink*. He received his MFA from the University of Iowa in 1973 and is a Distinguished Writer in Residence at Northwestern University. His many awards include a MacArthur Fellowship, the Rea Award for the Short Story, a PEN/Malamud Prize, a Lannan Award, and a Whiting Writers' Award.

DEBORAH EISENBERG is the author of four story collections: *Transactions in a Foreign Currency*, *Under the 82nd Airborne*, *All Around Atlantis*, and *Twilight of the Superheroes*. She is the recipient of a Whiting Writer's Award, a Rea Award for the Short Story, an American Academy of Arts and Letters Literature Award, five O. Henry Awards, a Lannan Foundation Fellowship, a Guggenheim Fellowship, and a MacArthur Fellowship. She teaches fiction writing at the University of Virginia.

JEFFREY EUGENIDES was born in Detroit and attended Brown University and Stanford University. His first novel, *The Virgin Suicides*, was published in 1993 and later made into a film by Sofia Coppola. His second novel, *Middlesex*, won the Pulitzer Prize for Fiction and the Ambassador Book Award. It was also a finalist for the National Book Critics Circle Award. In 2008, he was editor of *My Mistress's Sparrow Is Dead*, a collection of love stories which helped fund the free youth writing programs at 826 Chicago.

RICHARD FORD is the author of the story collections *Rock Springs*, *Women with Men*, and *A Multitude of Sins*, as well as six novels, among them *The Sportswriter, Wildlife, Independence Day*, which won both the Pulitzer Prize and the PEN/Faulkner Award for Fiction, and, most recently, *The Lay of the Land*, which was a finalist for the National Book Critics Circle Award. Ford is at work on a new novel and a collection of stories. He lives in Maine and New Orleans.

EDWARD P. JONES is a writer from Washington, D.C. His novel, *The Known World*, won the Pulitzer Prize and a National Book Critics Circle Award in 2004 and the International IMPAC Dublin Literary Award in 2005. In 2006 he published his third book, *All Aunt Hagar's Children*, a collection of fourteen stories that are linked thematically to his first collection, *Lost in the City*, from 1992. He teaches creative writing at George Washington University. In 2010 he received the PEN/Malamud award.

JHUMPA LAHIRI is the author of three books: *Interpreter of Maladies*, a story collection and Pulitzer Prize winner; *Unaccustomed Earth*, a story collection; and *The Namesake*, a novel which was made into a movie in 2006. She is a Vice President of the PEN American Center and serves on the President's Committee on the Arts and Humanities. She lives in Brooklyn.

THOMAS McGUANE's body of work includes novels, stories, screenplays, and essays. He finished his first novel, *The Sporting Club*, on a Wallace Stegner Fellowship, and was nominated for the National Book Award for his novel *Ninety-Two in the Shade*. His other books include *The Bushwacked Piano, Nobody's Angel, Nothing but Blue Skies*, and *Gallatin Canyon*, a story collection, while his screenplays include *Rancho Deluxe, The Missouri Breaks*, and *92 in the Shade* (which he also directed). His novel *Driving on the Rim* was released in October 2010.

JAMES ALAN MCPHERSON is a writer of short stories and essays. He won the Pulitzer Prize for his story collection *Elbow Room* in 1978, the first time it was awarded to an African American. He is also the recipient of both a Guggenheim Fellowship and a MacArthur Fellowship, and his writing has been selected for inclusion in *Best American Essays* and *Best American Short Stories of the Century*. McPherson was inducted into the American Academy of Arts and Sciences in 1995. He is a member of the permanent faculty of the Iowa Writers' Workshop.

ALICE MUNRO grew up in Wingham, Ontario, and attended the University of Western Ontario. She has published eleven story collections, including *Dance of the Happy Shades*; *The Moons of Jupiter*; *Hateship, Friendship, Courtship, Loveship, Marriage*; and, most recently, 2009's *Too Much Happiness*. She has also published a volume of selected stories as well as a novel, *Lives of Girls and Women*. She is the recipient of many honors, including a PEN/Malamud Award, an O. Henry Award, and a Man Booker International Prize. Her stories have appeared in *The New Yorker*, *The Atlantic*, *The Paris Review*, and other publications, and her collections have been translated into numerous languages.

JOYCE CAROL OATES is the author of numerous works of fiction, including the recent novels *The Gravedigger's Daughter* and *Little Bird of Heaven*. In 2009 she received the Ivan Sandrof Award for Literature from the National Book Critics Circle and in 2010 the Deauville Literary Prize. Her most recent book is *Sourland: Stories*.

ZZ PACKER is the author of the short story collection *Drinking Coffee Elsewhere*, which was a finalist for the PEN/Faulkner Award. Her short story "Brownies" was selected for publication in *Best American Short Stories 2000*. She is a graduate of the Iowa Writers' Workshop and was a Wallace Stegner Fellow at Stanford University. In 2005, she was awarded a Guggenheim Fellowship. She lives in California.

J. F. POWERS (1917–1999) wrote short stories and novels, often inspired by the calling of priesthood in the Catholic Church. Greatly admired by his peers, he published relatively little in his lifetime: only three books of short fiction and two novels. In 1963, his debut novel, *Morte d'Urban*, won the National Book Award. His stories were collected in 1999 in *The Stories of J. F. Powers*.

ANNIE PROULX is the author of *Postcards*, *The Shipping News*, and several other books, including three volumes of *Wyoming Stories*. Her honors include a Pulitzer Prize for Fiction for *The Shipping News*, a John Dos Passos Prize, a PEN/Faulkner Award, two O. Henry Awards, and a Guggenheim Fellowship. Her short story "Brokeback Mountain" was adapted into an Academy Award–winning major motion picture in 2005. She lives in Wyoming and Newfoundland.

LEWIS ROBINSON's writing has appeared in *Sports Illustrated*, *The Boston Globe*, *Tin House*, *Open City*, and *The Missouri Review*. He has written a novel, *Water Dogs*, and a short story collection, *Officer Friendly and Other Stories*, which won the PEN Oakland/Josephine Miles Literary Award. He lives and teaches in Portland, Maine.

JAMES SALTER has written novels, screenplays, and short fiction. His first novel, *The Hunters*, was based on his service as a fighter pilot in the Korean War. Four of his stories have appeared in the O. Henry

Prize collections, and one was anthologized in *Best American Short Stories* in 1984. *Dusk and Other Stories* won the PEN/Faulkner Award in 1989. His best known novels are *Light Years, A Sport and a Pastime*, and *Solo Faces*.

JIM SHEPARD is the author of six novels and four story collections. His stories are published regularly in such magazines as *The New Yorker, The Atlantic, McSweeney's, Tin House, Zoetrope: All-Story, Playboy*, and *Vice*, among others. "Minotaur" appears in his most recent book, *You Think That's Bad: Stories*. He lives in Williamstown, Massachusetts.

ELIZABETH STROUT is the author of *Olive Kitteridge*, for which she received the Pulitzer Prize in 2009. Her first novel, *Amy and Isabelle*, was also short-listed for the Orange Prize and nominated for the PEN/Faulkner Award. Her stories have appeared in *The New Yorker, Redbook,* and *New Letters*. She teaches at Queens University in Charlotte, North Carolina.

EUDORA WELTY (1909–2001) was a novelist and short story writer from Mississippi. During the 1930s she was employed by the Works Progress Administration, and photographs she took during that period were later collected in two books. She published her first story collection, *A Curtain of Green*, in 1941, and in 1973 the last of her five novels, *The Optimist's Daughter*, won the Pulitzer Prize for Fiction. She was also awarded the Presidential Medal of Freedom, the National Medal of Arts, and the French Legion of Honor. In 2004 the house she lived in for nearly eighty years was declared a National Historic Landmark.

Tobias Wolff has written short stories, novels, and memoirs, and has edited several short fiction anthologies, including *Best American Short Stories* in 1994. Some of his best-known works include *This Boy's Life*, *The Night in Question*, and *Our Story Begins*. His fiction has received the PEN/Faulkner and other awards. He teaches literature and writing at Stanford University.

Richard Yates (1926–1992) was a novelist and short story writer from Yonkers, New York. Before his writing career took off, he worked as a journalist, ghostwriter, publicity writer, and professor. His first novel, *Revolutionary Road*, was nominated for the National Book Award in Fiction, and in 2008 it was adapted for the screen, directed by Sam Mendes. The film was nominated for the BAFTAs, Golden Globes, and Academy Awards. Yates's work includes six more novels—*A Special Providence*, *Disturbing the Peace*, *The Easter Parade*, *A Good School*, *Young Hearts Crying*, and *Cold Spring Harbor*—and two collections of short fiction—*Eleven Kinds of Loneliness* and *Liars in Love*.

PERMISSIONS